T5-BCB-253

1.

GOING BACK was difficult. And making it worse, the weather was changing. The late afternoon sky, overcast and threatening, was a sure sign of a quick change. It was typical of the English Channel. During the morning hours, as the ferry had departed, the water was calm and it appeared to be the beginning of a beautiful day. Now, the wind and the water were working together to form a troublesome duo, and it would soon be treacherous in the water.

I had been in England on leave for two weeks. I had gone there with mixed feelings. Colonel Margolies had suggested a change of scenery for me, and without giving it much thought, I agreed. He had called a few hours after Ariane had been killed, saying it would be best to get away for a while. He knew I had just suffered the worst blow of my life, and he was trying to help.

Going back to Bad Welmsburg and the things that would remind me of Ariane, would be traumatic. Hardly a moment had passed since her death when my mind was not flashing pictures of her. But the Colonel was right, a change of scenery was best.

The ferry from Weymouth to Le Havre had been restored and put to use quickly when the war had come to an end. Oddly enough, the date I was returning from England, June 6, 1945, was one year to the day from the date of the D-Day landings in Normandy. It seemed much longer than a year. The port of Le Havre was still in shambles. It had taken a terrific pounding early in the war and had never been fully restored. After the Allies had made sure it would be of no further use to the Germans, they had moved on to other targets. Temporary buildings were in use, and I saw as I walked down the steps from the ferry, a sign on a building nearby that stated, "U.S. Personnel." I headed in that direction.

There was not much of a delay in Le Havre. In less than two hours after I had arrived on the ferry, transportation had been arranged and I was driven in a jeep by a young GI from the dock to the rail station.

He helped me with the two large bags that contained my clothing, going all the way with me to the seat I found inside one of the passenger cars of the train. After I was settled, he grinned as he turned to leave and said, "Have a good trip, sir."

"Thanks."

In the railcar there was a broad mix of people; U.S. servicemen, both officers and enlisted men, and, military people from various other nations. Most were like me and had been on leave. Eventually a British officer sat beside me, a man perhaps thirty years old with the insignia of a captain on his uniform. He told me his name, Captain Jonathon Brown, and I in turn said, "I'm Major Max Gordon." He was friendly and after small-talk for a while we were comfortable with each other. The train, which would take us to Paris, began moving and he commented on it.

"Well now, we're under way at last. Paris here we come! Is that your destination, sir, or are you going on?"

"I'm going on. Germany. My unit is in a small town there."

"So, you're facing a long ride, then. How long will it take?"

"It's twenty four hours to Frankfurt I believe, and then it will take another three hours to Bad Welmsburg, my final destination."

"What type unit are you with?"

"Military Government."

"Will you be serving there for a while?"

"Most likely."

He turned and grinned at me.

"I'd venture a guess then that you might be looking for some female companionship one of these days."

I smiled in return.

"No, not any more."

"Sounds like you already met someone. Did it go sour?"

He was the type person who listens well, and he had been receptive to my previous comments. I decided to tell him about Ariane. It was an easy decision because I wanted to talk about her anyway. I started at the beginning.

"I met a young German woman the first week of May. She came to the house where I was billeted late one evening. I can remember every detail about her, even yet, as she stood in my doorway. She was brunette with greenish blue eyes that were rounded and set apart perfectly. She had a delicate nose with full lips and beautiful white teeth. Her hair was dark, though when I saw her later, in daylight, I realized it was not as dark as it had appeared at first, and I considered her coloring to be more like that of a medium brunette. Her hair was rather long, shoulder length, and on that particular occasion she had it parted in the middle. With her hair clinging around her face in slight waves, perfectly in place, it was obvious that she most likely had been assisted in her grooming by a person who was well qualified. She appeared to be slender, and rather tall, maybe as much as five-seven or five-eight in height." I paused to give him a chance to comment. He didn't and continued to look at me with anticipation so I continued. "She and her husband were together, though he didn't come up to the door with her. They came to report that they had seen a German man we wanted, a man named Rombach. They had seen him earlier at the rail station boarding the Frankfurt Express. She said they wanted to cooperate with us."

"Did you believe her . . . straight-away?"

"Yeah, I think so. She seemed sincere and I thought there was a chance, too, that they might want some favor from us."

"Was she really a good-looker?"

"She was beautiful. I had never seen a woman like her. She had an unusual way of looking at me. It was pleasant, with a slight smile that seemed to be mixed with a faint sadness. I wanted to reach out for her, hold her, comfort her, and love her, all at the same time."

"Sounds like you were sunk from the moment you first saw her."

"I was. She told me during our initial conversation that she was married, but it didn't matter to me. Nothing mattered. I couldn't let anything keep me from being with her. I had never thrown away good judgment and discipline so completely and quickly."

"And I'm assuming you did see her."

"Yes. I could sense from the beginning that she was interested in me. We met at her home the next day, and even though her husband was there, I was able to arrange a meeting with her for the following day. And we became more involved each day. We met when we could, and where we could. We couldn't stay away from each other. And soon, we were completely, and irreversibly, in love."

He grinned.

"Major, you sound like a real scoundrel."

I returned his smile.

"It's not as bad as it sounds, Captain. I had an unhappy marriage and so did she. In fact, my wife and I had already agreed to a divorce and she was working out the details so that we would not have to go through an unpleasant time when I returned to the States."

"Oh, well then, it was as you said, not so bad after all. How about the German woman?"

"She was unhappy almost from the day she married. She and her husband were opposites. He was rich and powerful, she was beautiful, and he swept her off her feet. And, like a lot of other people during a war, they married too quickly."

"So you were both, in a sense, free, or perhaps in her case, she wanted to be free."

"You're exactly right, Captain."

When I arrived at Bad Welmsburg I was tired. I had slept very little. The seats in the railcar were designed for people to sit upright, of course, and there was no way to find a position that would be comfortable enough to sleep.

At seven in the evening I called Virgil from the station and he was soon there. He seemed glad to see me.

"Hello Major—how are you, sir?"

"Okay, Virgil. How about you?"

"Aw, I'm fine sir. We missed you."

"Thanks, I appreciate that. Everything going okay?"

"Yes, sir, it's going okay. I'm sure the Colonel will bring you up to date on things. And by the way, sir, he asked me to tell you to go home and get a good night of sleep and he will plan to see you in the morning."

"Sounds good to me, Virgil."

The next morning I was well rested and felt much better. I had not realized how tiring the trip had been until I had gone to bed. I was "out like a light" for about twelve hours.

When I reached the office I went in to see Colonel Margolies immediately. He got up and came around his desk to greet me, grinning, and we shook hands.

"Max, it's great to see you! How was London?"

"London was fine. And thanks, Colonel, it's good to see you too."

"Did you see Moira's sister . . . what's her name?"

"Victoria. Yes sir, I saw her. We spent quite a bit of time together. She knew about the divorce, she had heard it from Moira, and she said she understood."

"Good. Have a seat, Max, we've got a lot to talk about."

He walked back to the chair behind his desk and I took a seat nearby. He looked at me in a uncertain way and I knew what his next question would be.

"Ah, Max, did you—were you able to . . ."

He didn't know how to finish the question and paused. I understood what he wanted to say, he wanted to know how I was feeling about Ariane, and I answered.

"It's the same, Colonel. I guess it will take more time."

"I understand. I think you're right, time will help. It was a hell of a thing and I know it hurt. I'm just glad the bastard didn't get away with it." He was talking about Rombach, the man who killed Ariane. I agreed and he continued.

"Max, did you know we had a nest of those bastards here? Officers from Division Headquarters have been here swarming all over the place. Wegner was hiding seven or eight big-shot Nazis on his estate, in that lodge he had on the side of the mountain up behind his home. They had gathered here and were holed up waiting to jump off for a town up north."

"How did you get the details about them?"

"We got a couple of the German enlisted men to talk. Their plan was to use German enlisted men who could speak English to drive them to a town called Flensburg, up near Denmark. They were trying to escape."

"Who were they?"

"Wassermann was here. So were Kranz, Glazer, and Thiele. And there was a doctor who was close to Hitler, Dr. Voss. We don't know what happened to him. Schraeder was here and he's still missing too."

"How were they able to manage it? What did they do about identification papers?"

"Had them faked. They were staying out of circulation anyway. They apparently had planned it for months."

"Have we got all of the others, the rest of them?"

"We don't know. We don't know how many were here. That's one thing we have to talk about. I want you to get started on it as soon as possible."

"Okay, I'll start immediately. It sounds like Wegner was the key to the whole operation. I'll start with him, or I should say, I'll start with anybody who knew him or can tell me about him."

"Yeah, I was going to suggest that. Too bad the poor son-of-a-bitch got killed. We were able to get a confession out of Grebmann. He finally admitted he killed Wegner on orders from General Kranz—I think Kranz wanted to be sure Wegner wouldn't talk later and give away their plans."

"What happened to Kranz?"

"He went to Berchtesgaden. I think he must have been nuts. He was hiding in Hitler's teahouse, you know, the place on top of a mountain peak, and our guys cornered him. When he tried to run one of our enlisted men chased him up a narrow pathway and he fell . . . fell off the top of the mountain, and they never found him. I understand it was about a mile straight down."

"So that means all of them, except Schraeder and Dr. Voss, are accounted for, at least all that we know about."

"Yeah. But, like I said, we're not sure how many were here, and that's what we've got to work on. Use as many people as you need, Max. Oh, by the way, Wegner's wife . . . Ariane . . . knew nothing about it."

"I'm sure that was true, Colonel. She was telling me all that she knew and it was almost nothing. You remember during the inquest she said that she and her husband talked very little, and the only things she ever learned were from conversations she overheard when he was talking to others. I know she would have told me if she had known."

"I'm sure of that, too. Okay, to move on, we'll have a brief staff meeting each morning to review things. I want good communications established. It's an urgent matter, Max, and I want to be damn sure none of them get away. I'm glad you're back to take over—let me know if you need anything."

"Yes sir, I'll do that. Colonel, if you agree I'll start by interviewing all of our civilian employees. Some of them may have information that is going around through the grapevine and maybe if I work it right I can draw it out of them."

"Good idea. I'll tell Sergeant Newton to assist you. When do you want to start?"

"Right now. Tell Newton to send them, one by one, to my office beginning at ten this morning."

"You've got it, Max. See you at dinner tonight and you can tell me all about your trip."

"I'll look forward to it, Colonel."

I went to my office and took out the files on all of our civilian employees. We had screened them carefully in the beginning so I didn't actually suspect any of them. I was hoping to put together pertinent information from a lot of different people that could somehow be coordinated in a way that might tell me something.

Leni Schoenbrun was the first person to be sent in by Sergeant Newton. When she came in she appeared to be nervous and I tried to put her at ease as quickly as possible.

"Hello Leni. How are you?"

"I'm fine, Herr Major Gordon."

She obviously was anxious and she was speaking with an uneasy formality. I wanted to change that and get her to loosen up. I asked her to be seated.

"Leni, as you undoubtedly know, there has been some excitement around here lately. I'm in the process of talking to all of our employees, just in general, to see if I can learn anything that might be helpful to us." I paused and smiled and she returned the smile. I continued. "Do you mind answering a few questions?"

"No, I don't mind, Herr Major. May I say something before we begin?"

"Yes, of course."

"I made a terrible mistake. Hans Grebmann lied to me and that is why I sent the letter to your Division Headquarters. Can you forgive me, sir?"

"I can, and I do. I know you felt you were doing the right thing."

"Thank you, sir. Believe me, I am very sorry about Frau Wegner and what happened. Everyone loved her."

"I know. Don't feel you were responsible, or contributed to her death. It would have happened anyway."

"Yes sir, I believe that is true. It is so unfortunate. She was a wonderful person. Just the opposite, it seems, of her husband."

"Speaking of that, do you know much about her husband?"

"Only what most people have learned in the last month. He was, unjust and unfair, and he was not kind to Ariane . . . and he had no love for her. He only remained with her because of his pride, and I think he must have been seeing many other women. It is easy to understand how she was very unhappy with him."

"Yes, I know."

I paused, reflecting on what she had said, and she spoke again.

"Herr Major Gordon, if I may, I would like to say something that involves you."

"Certainly, Leni, go ahead."

"The people of Bad Welmsburg loved Ariane, and when they learned that she . . . was in love with you . . . they were happy for her. There was no resentment, I mean, because you were an American, it didn't matter. It made me realize, later of course, how foolish I was to be misguided by Hans Grebmann. Let me say again, sir, I deeply regret that I wrote the letter accusing you and Ariane in connection with the death of her husband, Karl Wegner."

"Thanks, Leni. I accept what you have said and I admire you for making these statements. I have no resentment toward you. We will consider it a closed matter."

I smiled, and so did she. I continued.

"Now, you've heard I'm sure about the men who were being hidden by Karl Wegner. Wassermann, Schraeder, General Kranz, and others. Have you heard the names of anyone else who might have been here? Men who might have been in the German Army, or high-ranking Nazi officials, or anyone who would have been a part of the escape plan? We need help from you, or people you may know, who might have information."

She reacted in a way I could not judge well. I think it is possible that she was being drawn in two directions: a loyalty to her homeland, in which case she would say very little even if she knew anything, or, a loyalty toward us that she might be feeling in her efforts to atone for writing the letter and the vague connection it had to the death of Ariane. She was thoughtful for a few moments before speaking.

"There are so many people who have come here since the end of the war it is difficult to know about each person. But, to answer your question, I have no knowledge of anyone who is a part of what Herr Wegner was attempting to do."

"Okay, thanks Leni. Keep thinking about it and if you remember anything please let me know."

"I'll do that, Herr Major."

Leni was an attractive young woman, about twenty, who had seemed grateful to be working in our offices. There were not many jobs available in the city for the civilians, and she, like the others we hired, felt quite fortunate to be earning money from the U.S. Army. We were able to choose people who spoke the English language efficiently, and Leni not only could do that, she could write well, too.

She realized our conversation was over and she stood. She had a question before leaving.

"Herr Major, may I ask, where was Ariane taken to be buried?"

"I don't know, Leni. I intend to find out and I will let you know."

"Did you know that her aunt is here now?"

"No. Where is she?"

"In the Wegner mansion. She came to take care of everything."

"I'm very glad to know about that—I'll go to see her today. Thanks for telling me."

As she turned to leave, she paused, and spoke once again.

"Good luck to you, sir. You . . . have many . . . there are many people here who admire you."

I smiled to acknowledge the compliment and she walked out of the room. What she had said about Ariane's aunt had almost stunned me. Learning that someone so close to Ariane was nearby aroused an unusual feeling, a sensation like a sudden chill. I would go immediately to see her aunt.

I told Sergeant Newton to hold up on the interviews, I would be away for a while to follow up on information just received. Then, I walked out of the office to my jeep.

Driving in the direction of the mountain road, and the location of the Wegner estate, I was reminded of the first time I had gone there. I had met Ariane the night before and I was eager to see her again. And then, when I did see her, I knew I would do whatever was necessary to continue seeing her. She, too, that day, had let me know that she was interested, and I was certain we both felt the same way.

Ariane had never told me much about her aunt, her nearest living relative, and I didn't know what to expect. I parked in front of the huge house and walked to the door. I remembered the two house servants, Else and Karen, and I wondered if they would be there.

The woman who met me at the door was about fifty. She didn't smile and I judged that she would not be too friendly. It didn't matter, I had important questions on my mind and I didn't plan to be deterred. Even so, I tried to be amiable.

"Good morning. My name is Max Gordon. I am looking for the aunt of Ariane Wegner. Are you . . . that person?"

She continued to be reserved, and possibly cautious. She did not speak immediately and it occurred to me that she might not speak English, so I asked her.

"Do you speak English—did you understand what I asked?"

"Yes, I understand, and yes, I am the aunt of Ariane Wegner."

"I would like to talk to you. Is that agreeable?"

"Herr Gordon . . . I believe it is Major Gordon . . . I have already talked to your soldiers. There is nothing more for me to say."

"I believe there is more to say. First, will you tell me your name?"

"Frau Erhlich."

"Thank you. Frau Erhlich, there are many details about Ariane that I do not have, and I must insist that you answer my questions."

"I prefer not to discuss her, Herr Major."

"Can you tell me why?"

"Many people have already been here and I think it must now be finished."

I became a little more forceful.

"As far as I am concerned it is not finished. I am head of security for the American Army in Bad Welmsburg, and there is information I do not have. I will have to insist on your cooperation."

She must have seen something in my face, or noticed a change in my voice tone, because her attitude changed at once.

"Excuse me, sir . . . I . . . you must understand . . . she was in great danger. I have cooperated fully with your other men. But, yes, of course, I will answer your questions. Please come in."

We walked from the doorway into the foyer, and I thought of the remark she had just made, "she was in great danger." Why would she say that at this point? Ariane obviously had been in great danger, and that would have no bearing on a discussion at present.

We sat in the large room, the same room where I was taken when I had gone there the first time. It had not changed and still contained the exquisite furnishings that were there originally. The room, with a ceiling that would be at least twelve feet, was, I would guess, forty feet in length and about the same in width. It reminded me again of the tremendous wealth of Wegner. After we were seated, she spoke.

"And now, sir, what do you wish to know?"

"Many things. I've been away since it happened and there are even small details that I do not know."

"And what are the details?"

"Did she die immediately?"

"Yes."

"Where was she hit, what part of her body?"

"In the middle part."

"But not in the face?"

"No."

"I'm glad about that. And I'm glad, too, that she didn't suffer."

She didn't speak, so I continued.

"I know she was taken away from Bad Welmsburg to be buried. Where was she taken . . . where is she buried?"

"Ah, sir. . . ."

"Yes?"

"Major, she is buried in another city."

"I know that. I want to know the name of the city."

"It is only . . . you see, we have preferred to protect her privacy. There are people who hated her."

"I know that, too, but I am not one of them. I want to know where she is buried."

She had a white handkerchief in her left hand. She used it to wipe each cheek in a motion that clearly indicated nervousness. She remained silent and I spoke again.

"Frau Erhlich, I was not her enemy. In fact, I was a close friend."

"Yes, I know. I know about you, Major. She told me. It is only that I prefer to keep some things secret. Since I have been here in Bad Welmsburg I have learned that there are men who might still be here, terrible men, who might do disgraceful things to her, to try to destroy the peace of her final resting place."

I thought about it, and I didn't believe her. What more could be done to Ariane? Why would anyone carry it further? I had to get more out of Frau Erhlich but pushing her too hard might not work. I wondered how much time I would have, how long she would be in Bad Welmsburg.

"Frau Erhlich, do you plan to be in Bad Welmsburg for a while?"

"Yes, there are many things to be done and it will take a few days."

"I understand. Well, I'll leave you for today, but I will be back tomorrow. What time will be convenient for you?"

"You can come at any time, Herr Major."

"Good. I'll see you at eleven in the morning."

Going down the long driveway in the jeep I had some thoughts that made my heart pick up it's pace. Could it be possible that . . . no, I couldn't let myself even hope, it would be too much . . . Ariane was gone and I would only be opening a wound deeper to allow myself to imagine anything else.

I began going over details in my mind. The day she was shot, she was standing in front of the building where the inquest into the death of her husband, Karl Wegner, had just concluded. Before it happened many of the townspeople had crowded around her to embrace her, and visit with her, and I knew she would be there for a while. Two of our men, Virgil and Jim Santini, had stayed to take her home. I left and had just arrived back in our offices when a telephone call came in from a civilian reporting gun shots in the area where the inquest had been held. I rushed back, and it was too late. Ariane had been taken into the nearby hospital. Virgil told me that Doctor Reuss was there, and he had come out to say that she . . . didn't make it. Virgil wanted to spare me what he thought would be a sickening experience, and he strongly suggested that I not go in to see Ariane. I remember he said, "There's absolutely no question, sir, she's gone."

I accepted what he said, mainly because I was in shock, and I just wanted to get away. I went to the house where I was billeted to be alone. Several hours later Colonel Margolies called and said final arrangements for Ariane had been taken care of by an aunt. At the end of the conversation he suggested that I take a leave, which I did the next day. I could not bring myself to go and view the body of Ariane. I didn't even want to discuss it with anyone. I imagined that she might be disfigured and I did not want to see her that way. In fact, I didn't want to hear a description of it. I was devastated and the only thing I wanted to do was to be some other place. So, without learning any additional details, I left for England the next day. I just simply had to move on for a while.

Now, I would begin to consider the details I had avoided before. I thought of Doctor Reuss and decided to start with him. I drove directly to his office near the hospital.

The outer room in the office of Doctor Reuss was nearly full of people, all most likely his patients, and I knew he was there. There was a young woman moving about through the room assisting him. I told her I would like to see the doctor, and she realized, from my manner, that it was urgent. She said, "Yes, sir, I go at once to tell him," and she disappeared through a door. In less than a minute, she had returned.

"Sir, if you can wait five minutes Herr Doctor will see you."

I nodded. We normally didn't use the power we had as conquerors of the Germans to intimidate them, or make unnecessary requests. Instead we were striving to treat them firmly, but fairly. I think we were all trying to forget the past and do the job that had to be done. But they were accustomed to discipline and they responded well to it. It was a way of life for them, and they expected it from us, and if we did not show a touch of it they would not respect us.

Soon a woman came through the door, obviously a patient, followed by the doctor. He looked at me and spoke.

"Come in, Herr Major."

I walked in and he closed the door. He stood facing me and didn't suggest that we be seated.

"And now, Herr Major, how can I help you?"

"I have some questions to ask about Ariane Wegner."

He appeared to be slightly irritated.

"But, sir, you can see how busy I am today."

"I know. This will only take a few minutes."

"I have given all the details to your soldiers . . . I do not understand."

"I've been away, Doctor. I am now in process of investigating the death of Frau Wegner and I want all of the details."

"There is nothing more I can tell you. It has been fully explained in the past."

It was time to be firm.

"Doctor, I am going to ask you some questions and I want straight forward answers. Do you understand?"

He changed immediately.

"Yes, of course, I understand."

"The day it happened, at the time it happened, where were you?"

"At the moment it happened I was inside the hospital."

"So, you were only a few hundred feet—a hundred meters or so—from the place where she was standing when she was hit?"

"That is correct."

"How soon, or quickly, did you get to her?"

"Oh, it was only a matter of a very few minutes."

"And she was lying on the street?"

"Yes."

"Was she conscious?"

"Ah, possibly, but I think very nearly to being unconscious."

"Did she speak?"

"No."

"What did you do immediately as you reached her?"

"I looked at the wound and . . ."

I interrupted.
"Where was the wound?"
"In the middle of her body."
"Was there more than one part of her body that was affected, or, did more than one bullet strike her?"
"No. Only one. I do not remember if I could determine that at the scene, or later, but it was only one bullet."
"Was the wound in the stomach, or intestinal area?"
"At first I thought both areas might be affected. There was much bleeding."
"Did you . . . what did you learn when you examined her later, in the hospital?"
"Ah . . . the loss of blood . . . and the shock . . . it was the cause of death."
"Had you treated people with wounds of that type before?"
He answered quickly.
"Oh, yes. You see, I served in Russia with the army for a while. There I treated wounds of all types, including the kind that was sustained by Frau Wegner."
"The wound that she had . . . what was your first impression? Did you believe it to be a fatal wound?"
"I do not remember. I knew it was serious and I requested that she be taken inside the hospital at once."
"Where was she taken in the hospital, what room?"
"It was at first, it was the large room for emergency treatment. But soon I removed her to a room nearby where I could treat her without . . . I wanted her to be in a private room . . . I . . ."
"You removed her? Did you have assistance from others?"
"At first, yes, but then at the end I was with her in the room alone."
"Why was that, Doctor? Why didn't you have the assistance of others?"
"Ah . . . we . . . there was a shortage of people . . ."
He was beginning to lose his confidence, and I was beginning to doubt some of his answers. Was he trying to cover up a bungled job? Or was it something else? I questioned him again.
"What time did she die?"
"It was, I believe, twelve, fifteen minutes after she was brought in."
"What did you do when you realized she had died?"
"I walked out of the room to make the notification to others."
"You left her in the room alone?"
"Yes. Oh, I believe I locked the door. Yes, I did that."
"Why did you lock the door?"
"To protect her privacy."
"Who did you notify?"
"Nurse Helgermann. And then I walked quickly to the outside and met one of your men at the entrance. His name, I am certain, is Virgil. He said he would notify all of the other Americans."

"What did you do next?"

"I went to the room that serves as my office in the hospital. There, I made a telephone call."

"To whom?"

"To the aunt of Frau Wegner who lives in Fulda. I knew her, and I knew how to reach her by telephone."

"She told you how to handle the final arrangements?"

"Yes."

"Did you call someone to remove the body?"

"Ah, Major, we do not have the luxuries that we would have had at one time. I agreed to handle the arrangements in the only way it was possible. I told Frau Erhlich that I would bring the body of Frau Wegner to Fulda."

"You? Why would you do that?"

"Because I have, from your Military Government, an allotment of fuel for my car. It is because I am a doctor and your office has given me a generous supply of fuel so that I can administer medical needs in the city."

"And so you drove her to Fulda?"

"Yes."

I had to think about that and I paused. Maybe it was the truth. I knew that we did allow him to have a reliable car and plenty of gasoline. It was because he was responsible for taking care of the medical needs of the civilians in the city. During the pause he used the opportunity to volunteer information.

"May I inform you, Herr Major, about my relationship with Frau Wegner?"

"Yes. I would like to hear about that."

"I knew her quite well. I have been in her home on many occasions. You might say that we were very good friends, and she confided in me. I knew, for example, that she was unhappy with her husband, and some of the reasons. I came to know this because of the relationship that occurs when a doctor sees a patient on a regular basis, or on routine matters, and the patient will speak about things that no one else knows."

"I see. And you admired her, and you were a very good friend in addition to being her doctor?"

"Yes."

"You drove her to Fulda, you transported her body to Fulda, when was that?"

"The day she was killed."

"To the place where her aunt requested, a facility where she could be prepared for burial?"

"Yes."

"You saw her aunt while there?"

"Yes."

"How long did you stay in Fulda?"

"Ah, let's see, it was the next day, I believe, when I returned."

"Why did you stay until the next day?"

"It was late, and I could not travel at night."

"And so you returned to Bad Welmsburg the next morning?"

"I had planned to return in the morning, but, . . . you see . . . ah, the motor car, there was a problem and I could not return at that time."

"When did you return?"

"It was two days . . . let's see . . . maybe it was three days before it could be repaired."

"So you were away three days. Did you stay with Frau Erhlich?"

"Yes."

"And you attended the burial of Frau Wegner in Fulda?"

He looked perplexed and I knew he would struggle with an answer. I continued to stare and after a pause of a few moments, he spoke.

"Major, this is a matter I would prefer not to discuss. It was the wish of Frau Erhlich that the place of burial be kept secret."

"Are you saying that you do not know the place of burial?"

"I do not know the place of burial."

"Why was it important that it be kept secret?"

"Men had come to Bad Welmsburg, some that even you, or the other American soldiers, had not heard about. These men were dangerous, and they had come to destroy Frau Wegner to be sure that she would be humiliated even in death. It was partly because her sister was married to the Jewish man, and also because she was, in the thoughts of these men, not loyal to her homeland."

"Would that be because of her relationship with me? Was she hated because of that?"

"Unfortunately, that was part of it."

I thought of everything he had said and paused. He was quiet this time and waited for me to speak. There was one question I had to settle.

"Doctor, I must know the place of burial. It is important to me. You must know more than you have told me."

He became more agitated and he obviously could not think of an answer immediately. I waited, and after a few moments he spoke.

"Major, please understand my position. The information you seek must come from Frau Wegner's aunt. Can you understand this?"

"All right, Doctor, I will discuss it with Frau Erhlich. Tell me who helped you at the hospital when Frau Wegner was placed in your car."

"Two men who work there. Braun and Hillermann."

"And you left immediately for Fulda?"

"Yes."

His story didn't seem exactly right. Part of what he was saying was understandable, but part was questionable. Why was it so urgent to get Ariane to Fulda? Could it be because of the need for embalming? Possibly. But even if there were men in Bad Welmsburg who hated her, what could they do if she was dead? Then, a thought occurred to me that I had not previously allowed to come into my mind. What if she was not dead? It would be much more likely that she would need protection if she was still alive. I could feel that I was becoming tense and emotional. I had to have an answer, quickly, and my next comment was made more forcefully.

"Doctor, if you lie to me I will have you punished. I do not wish to do that, so, I suggest you consider your next answer carefully. Is Ariane Wegner alive?"

The question disturbed him. He glanced away and quickly turned back to face me. He moved his hands, reaching up and rubbing his arms on opposite sides in an up and down motion. Finally, he fixed a stare on me and seemed to resign himself to the inevitable, and spoke.

"Yes."

It was a tremendous shock to hear what he said. It was difficult to absorb and process into my mind. I began to see her in my thoughts, and I had a vision of her, smiling, and it was as if she knew at that moment, wherever she was, that we would see each other again soon. It was a stunning moment for me, one that was almost completely unexpected, though not entirely without hope.

I was silent for a while, as was the doctor; then, in a soft tone, he spoke.

"Herr Major, I can see that this is a matter that affects you deeply. Please forgive me, sir, because I could not state freely what I have just said."

"It's okay, Doctor, I just need a little time. If you will give me a minute or so, I would like to continue our conversation."

"I will be happy to do that, Major."

I walked to one side of the room, near the window. All of a sudden, with one word, the world had changed for me, and a consuming sadness had been taken away.

I thought of her as she was that last day. I saw her as she was standing in the large room where the inquest into the death of her husband had been conducted. It had just been completed, the inquest was over. She had been erroneously implicated in his death, and she had just been cleared. The inquest had been held in a very large room that was filled to capacity with the townspeople, and as the announcement was made, clearing her, the people surged forward to embrace her, and shake her hand. I knew I couldn't get to her because of the people who were crowded around her, and she knew too, so we only made eye contact briefly, during which time she smiled, beautifully, at me.

2.

AFTER A SHORT INTERLUDE, during which time I became a little more composed, I was ready to continue the discussion with Doctor Reuss. I walked back across the room to a spot near him. I wanted to let him know, first of all, that I appreciated his cooperation.

"Thank you, Doctor. I'm sure you had good reason to withhold the information. We can talk about that later. First, tell me where she is."

"Major, you must try to believe me, I do not know where she is."

"All right, I will accept that for now. Tell me about her condition."

"She is making a very good recovery. When she was brought in, I made an incision and repaired the problems quickly. I believed that if I could get her to a safe place, she could recover. But I also knew that she was in grave danger. You see, the men who wanted to kill her believed that she knew the details of what her husband was doing, helping with the escape plan, and they wanted to be sure she would be killed . . . it was to be done without failure."

"But didn't they believe you? You advised people that she had been killed."

"Everyone believed except one man, and unfortunately, he told the others, the ones who were assigned to kill her."

"Who was the man?"

"Braun. He noticed, as he helped Hillermann put her in my car, that she was still alive. I saw him at the time, and I could see as he placed her on the back seat of my car—he was holding the upper part of her body—and it was obvious that he knew. I also knew he would tell the men who were involved in the escape plan, he was that type, and so, I realized at that moment that Frau Wegner would have to disappear. Only Frau Erhlich and I knew she was alive, and we decided to hide her and let everyone else think that she had been killed."

"And you remained with her in Fulda for three days to treat her?"

"Yes."

"How many people knew you were taking her to Fulda?"

"I told no one. But many people knew about her aunt, and, they were aware that she lived in Fulda. So, I think most people would have believed that Ariane was to be buried there."

"Did anyone attempt to question you later, when you returned to Bad Welmsburg . . . and I mean by that, anyone who would be suspicious?"

"Three men. They were formerly with the SS."

"What are their names?"

"Hueber, Stelling and Augenberg."

"What did they ask you?"

"They wanted to know details about the death of Frau Wegner. They said they were friends, that she had been kind to them. I learned later who they really were. However, at the time I was talking to them, I said that Frau Wegner was dead and I did not know the place of burial."

"Good. We will begin searching for them immediately. But tell me more about Ariane, have you heard anything more about her recently?"

"She is continuing to make a good recovery. When her aunt arrived in Bad Welmsburg just a few days ago we met privately. She told me that Ariane can now take care of herself, and that is the reason Frau Erhlich decided to come here, to make our story about her death appear to be true."

"A good idea. Tell me a little more about the wound. How bad was it?"

"Actually, Major, it turned out not to be as bad as I thought when I first saw her on the street. The bullet passed through her body, and it was like a miracle because a minimum amount of damage had occurred. It was painful, of course, and she was unconscious as I did what had to be done, working as fast as possible, but making sure that it was done with great care."

"What did you have to do?"

"I made a small incision and traced the path of the bullet. No organs were damaged, so I closed her up. I sedated her because it was at that time that I conceived the idea of taking her away, to protect her."

"I'm glad you reacted so quickly, it probably saved her life."

"Well, it was, of course, my hope that I could prevent the death of a wonderful young woman."

"And I appreciate that, very much. Now, I must go. There are many things to be done. I'll go first and see Frau Erhlich."

"Major, I know you must realize that no one is to know that she is alive. Can we agree that only you and I and Frau Erhlich will know until such time that it is safe?"

"Yes, we can agree on that. I will be in touch with you soon."

He nodded, we shook hands, and I walked out of his office.

I drove immediately to the Wegner estate. When Frau Erhlich met me at the door she was surprised. I explained at once why I had returned.

"Frau Erhlich, I have just seen Doctor Reuss, and I know all of the details about Ariane. I know she is alive."

She appeared to be shocked, and she became anxious again, as before. I tried to reassure her.

"Don't worry, I will help you. I believe you and Doctor Reuss have handled things well so far. Is it safe to talk here . . . is anyone in the house?"

"No one is here at present, Major."

"Who is normally here?"

"The two maids, Else and Karen. They are both away at present."

"Good. I would like to come in and talk briefly."

"Yes, of course, come in."

After we were seated, I spoke.

"Doctor Reuss told me that he took Ariane to Fulda, to your home. But he also told me that he does not know where she is at this time. Can you explain that to me?"

"I told Doctor Reuss last evening that she had to be moved. There was danger and my son, Rolfe, called yesterday to let me know."

"He didn't tell you where she was being taken?"

"No. We have to be careful. The men who are searching for her believe that she knows the details of the escape plan—they believe, we are quite sure, that she is the only remaining person who knows, now that her husband has been killed, and they want her to be eliminated, just as he was."

"Your son . . . said nothing to let you know where they would be, or when to expect another call?"

"It would be too dangerous on the telephone, Major. We had prepared for the possibility that it could happen, and if it became necessary for Rolfe to go with Ariane to another location, he was to call and say, "I am going to Marburg for a few days." And that is what he said during our conversation yesterday."

"Do you have any idea where he would take her?"

"We considered three cities where Rolfe has friends. Koln, Aachen, and the small city of Frankenberg."

"I'm familiar with Frankenberg, but before going there I will need more information. When will Rolfe contact you again?"

"I do not know. He will only do what is safe."

I was disappointed. It seemed there was nothing more we could do and we would just have to wait, for a while, at least. I wanted to talk about Ariane again before leaving.

"How is Ariane at present, Frau Erhlich?"

"She is fine. The wound is almost healed and she is very nearly back to normal."

"That's wonderful. As you can imagine, I am very anxious to see her. I'm sure you must know how we felt about each other."

"I do know, Major. She told me everything. We . . . wanted to tell you that she was alive, Ariane wanted us to tell you, and we would have at the right time. We discussed it and decided it would be too dangerous at first, even for you to know. And so, it was our decision to wait, hoping that something would happen, maybe these men would be caught, or go away. I hope you can understand."

"I do, and I think you and Doctor Reuss have handled everything well. We will help you now, at least I can help you. I assure you that I will use all of the resources at my disposal to find these men and put them away."

"And we will be glad when that happens. I know she will be overcome with joy when it will become possible for you to be with her. She told me how happy she was with you. Nothing in her life had happened before that gave her so much pleasure and joy. She told me that she was going to marry you."

"That's true. After her husband was killed, we had made plans—I'm sure she told you that my wife and I were getting a divorce."

"She did tell me. She told me many things, she liked to remember everything about you. She laughed because you were concerned about being a little older . . . she was twenty-eight, you were forty-five . . . and it was nothing to her, she said it amused her when you mentioned it."

"I can remember that occasion very well. Actually, we were in Frankenberg at the time."

"In the hotel."

I smiled.

"Well, I see that she did tell you many things."

She had warmed up and was unlike the woman who met me earlier in the day.

"Major, she was so much in love I sometimes would have to try to get her to speak about something different." And she laughed.

"It was the same with me. When I thought I had lost her, it affected me severely. I couldn't face it and I had to go away for a while. Nothing had ever happened like that before."

"And she knew that. She knew you so well. Once, she said, 'I have to let him know I am alive,' but we warned her, and she agreed to wait until it would be safe."

For the first time in ages I was enjoying myself. But I had to go, I had to work out a plan to find Ariane, and the men who were after her.

"Frau Erhlich, I have many things to do and I have to leave. If you hear anything, day or night, call me at once."

"I will be sure to do that."

Driving through the grounds of the Wegner estate leading down to the road, I planned my next move. I would go to the hospital. I wanted to see the man named Braun. He was the one, according to Doctor Reuss, who told the assassins that Ariane was alive. I had to find out exactly what he told them. Doctor Reuss had said that Braun worked at the hospital, and I anticipated that he would be there, on duty, when I arrived.

I would question Braun with firmness, quickly. There was not enough time to do otherwise. Both Frau Erhlich and Doctor Reuss had emphasized repeatedly the danger facing Ariane. Normally I would approach it with a different plan, using a technique that might stretch out over time. However, I knew the SS men were deadly, and I had to move fast.

Inside the hospital I spoke to the director in his office. He was German, of course, a man who appeared to be in his sixties. We sat alone in his office. I used a firm and formal manner of speech. Knowing how the Germans perceived such an attitude, I knew he would comply quickly with any request. I told him I wanted to use a private office for an interview with one of his employees. He responded at once.

"Of course, Herr Major. This room where we are sitting, is it adequate?"

I looked around and could see only one door and one window. It was probably as sound proof as any room in the building, and I answered, addressing him by title, purposely not using his name.

"This room will be adequate, Herr Director."

I told him I wanted to see Braun, and I asked if he, Braun, could speak English.

He quickly took a file out of a cabinet, and after a brief look, he turned to me.

"Yes, according to his records, he does speak English."

"Very good. All right, you can go now and send Braun to this room. We are to be left alone here."

"I will go immediately, Herr Major."

He walked out of the room. I had impressed him with an urgency so that he would consider it a matter of significant importance. The Germans, after years of living under Nazi authority, were well oriented in performing expediently when it was needed.

In less than five minutes there was a knock on the door. I spoke out rather loudly, saying, "come in." A man who was short and small in size, opened the door. He was about forty, had a full head of hair that seemed to have a slight tint of a reddish color, and he had blue eyes. He had the facial features of many Germans, including a square jaw and thin lips. He took two steps inside the room and stopped, staring at me for instructions. I looked at him without speaking, staring hard into his eyes. I wanted him to believe that he was in a precarious situation. After a few moments I walked past him and closed the door. Then, I walked to a chair behind the desk of the director and sat down, leaving Braun standing. I wanted to establish an atmosphere that would be conducive to the demands I would make, if necessary, in questioning him. A minute or more had passed before I spoke.

"Your name is Braun?"

"Yes."

He did not say "yes sir," as would most Germans in such a situation. It told me he would be defiant, at least in the beginning. I continued.

"Were you in the Wehrmacht?"

"No."

"Why not?"

"I was trained to perform other valuable services."

"What services?"

"I was trained for medical work. It was very important work, duty that only a few could perform with great skill."

He was most likely turned down by the army because of his size, though he would be reluctant to admit it. He obviously had pride and he did not want to be looked upon as someone who had not served his homeland in good fashion. Some of the Germans, in that category, were more bothersome to us than the men who had been soldiers; they were still trying to prove their value to the cause, or, set aside any loss of respect by their fellow countrymen. I spoke again.

"How long have you worked in this hospital?"

"Two years."

"You know most of the people of the city?"

"Yes."

"Did you know General Karl Wegner?"

"I did not know him."

"But you knew who he was?"

"Yes."

"Did you know his wife, or did you recognize her and realize who she was when you saw her?"

"Yes."

"You saw her the day she was shot?"

"Yes."

"Do you know who shot her?"

"Yes, of course. All people in the city know who shot her." He had used a cynical tone to respond, and a smirk was formed on his lips.

I answered with firmness.

"I didn't ask you for additional comments. Only answer the questions I ask. Do you understand?"

"Yes."

"And when I speak to you, you are to answer yes sir, or no sir."

"Yes, sir."

"Did you assist Doctor Reuss as he treated Frau Wegner?"

"No, sir."

"Who assisted him?"

"Nurse Helgermann."

"Where were you?"

"Nearby, assisting others."

"How long was Frau Wegner in the hospital, how many minutes, before Doctor Reuss reported that she was dead?"

“I estimate it was thirty minutes.”

I wanted to know how closely he had been watching the doctor.

“Do you believe Doctor Reuss did all possible to save Frau Wegner?”

“Yes, sir.”

“What took place, what can you say from your observations, when Doctor Reuss reported that Frau Wegner was dead?”

“He . . . I believe he made notification to Nurse Helgermann, and he walked to the outside . . . but quickly returned and went into an office . . . then, in about ten minutes he came out and returned to the room where Frau Wegner had been taken.”

He apparently had been watching closely. It gave me an opportunity to bring him into focus with the next question.

“So, you were nearby. What did Doctor Reuss say to you at that time?”

“He said that he was to take the responsibility of moving the body of Frau Wegner. He asked that I find Hillermann and report back to him.”

“And you did that?”

“Yes, sir.”

“So then, you and Hillermann moved the body of Frau Wegner, took her to the rear of the hospital, to the car of Doctor Reuss?”

“Yes, sir.”

“Was there much blood on her clothing? And could you see from the blood what part of her body had been struck?”

“There was much blood. She had been hit in the stomach.”

“Doctor Reuss was with you . . . what comments did he make?”

“He said that he would remove the body to a place to be prepared for burial.”

“What place?”

“He did not say.”

“What did you believe, where was the body to be taken?”

“I do not know.”

I paused, thinking carefully about the way I would proceed. He was beginning to show the first sign of anxiety, only slightly, and I was encouraged that his attitude had changed. I decided to probe in a different direction.

“Where do you live, Braun?”

He gave me the address. It seemed to bother him. I noticed that he was holding himself rigidly, and he was like a soldier standing at attention. He looked at me continuously, awaiting each new question. I continued.

“Do you live alone?”

“Yes, sir.”

“Do you have relatives in Bad Welmsburg?”

“No sir.”

“Where do you come from, originally?”

“Munchen.”

"Were you ever a member of the Nazi Party?"

He was shaken some by the question, and he hesitated before speaking. "Yes sir."

"How long, how many years?"

"Ah . . . about eight years, sir."

"All right, my next question is very important. Think carefully before you answer . . . and I warn you, if you do not answer truthfully, you may be arrested. Do you know, or have you heard the names of the following men: Stelling, Hueber, and Augenberg?"

"Yes sir."

"Are they members of the SS?"

"I do not know sir."

"Have you talked to these men recently, any one of them?"

"No sir."

"Are you certain about that? If you lie to me, in any way, I will take you away immediately to one of the prison camps we have for war criminals. You will leave this building with me today, now, under arrest."

It had the effect on him I was trying to achieve, and even before he spoke, I knew what his answer would be.

"Ah, I believe sir, I did, on one occasion, speak to Augenberg."

"When was that . . . was it the day Frau Wegner had been shot?"

"Yes sir, I believe it was that day."

"Where did the conversation take place?"

"At the place where I live."

"What time did he come?"

"It was late, maybe twenty-three hundred hours."

"How did he happen to come there? Had he been there before . . . were you friends?"

"No sir, we were not friends. He only came to ask questions about Frau Wegner."

"What did he ask?"

"He . . . wanted to know where she was to be taken . . . he had been told, or he knew, that Doctor Reuss was taking her away in his car."

"What did you say?"

"I told him I did not know where she was to be taken."

"Did you assume, like many other people, that she was to be taken to Fulda?"

"No sir, I did not assume that."

"Was Augenberg very intense, very demanding in what he asked? Did he speak forcefully?"

"He . . . yes sir, he was intense. He made it clear that he was eager to learn all details."

"Why do you think it was important to him? Do you believe he felt that Frau Wegner was not dead, and the Doctor was taking her away to treat her in another location?"

"I do not know, sir."

"I believe you do know. Did he ask you about her, if you knew positively that she was dead?"

"Yes sir, he asked me if she was dead."

"And what did you say?"

"I . . . you see, sir . . . when a person is dead for a few minutes it is difficult to know . . . I . . ."

"Yes?"

"I could not be sure that she was dead."

"And you told Augenberg that you could not be sure?"

"Yes sir."

"And then, what did he want to know?"

"He asked me if the Doctor returned to the hospital later that day."

"What did you say?"

"I told him the Doctor did not return later that day, and . . ."

"Yes?"

"I told him that I heard the Doctor tell Nurse Helgermann that he might be away for a day or so."

"What did Augenberg say?"

"He said . . . he believed, at that time . . . he believed that Frau Wegner was not dead. He said, 'She must have been taken to an American hospital,' and he said, 'The American Major is involved and he must have arranged it,' and then, it was not so long when he went away."

"Describe Augenberg."

"Ah, he is the same, about the same size, as you, sir. And he is with blonde hair and blue eyes. I think he must be forty or forty-five in years."

"Where can I find him?"

"Sir, I do not know. He and the other two are like ghosts. I think it is impossible to find them."

"No, it's not impossible. We will find them. But what is your opinion, Braun, do you feel that Doctor Reuss took Frau Wegner to a place to treat her or have her treated? Do you believe she is alive?"

"I cannot say, Herr Major. As we moved her to the car, the Doctor placed a sheet over her, and I could not see her. I could only feel her. She, didn't move . . . but, she was . . . I saw her for only a moment before the sheet was placed over her. We lifted her on to a mobile stretcher, with wheels, and she was pushed on the stretcher to the car. At the car, the sheet remained over her as she was lifted inside, only, it was out of place for a moment, showing her face as she was placed on the back seat of the car. Then, Herr Doctor quickly covered her again, and he seemed . . ."

"Yes?"

"He did not wish for her face to be seen."

"And it was then that you could not be sure that she was dead?"

"Yes, sir. When I was lifting her, her body felt . . . she could have been dead, she could have been alive. Possibly she was alive."

Finally, he was speaking truthfully. I asked him for a description of the other two SS men who were traveling with Augenberg. He responded with vague descriptions, but it didn't matter, I would call Doctor Reuss and get the information from him. It was time to conclude the discussion with Braun.

"You are free to go now, Braun. Do not tell anyone about this conversation. You lied once during this discussion and I am placing you under a probational watch. If there is trouble, from anything you say or do, you will go to prison. Also, if you see Augenberg, or the other two, you are to report it to me immediately. And if any person should ask you about Frau Wegner, you are to tell me at once. Do you understand?

"Yes, sir."

I nodded in the direction of the door and he wasted no time in leaving.

In my office, later in the day, I asked Sergeant Glenn Newton to come in for a conference. I told him we would issue a confidential communique that would be distributed to all U.S. Army personnel in the area. It would describe the three SS men, emphasizing that they were dangerous, and we would ask for assistance from all U.S. units in our efforts to find them. I told Sergeant Newton that I would begin a search in Bad Welmsburg as soon as possible and he had a suggestion.

"Sir, you know, these men are as dangerous to the civilians as they are to us. I'm wondering if you can find them through contacts with the civilians? Like, if you can locate the right people, and talk to them under the right circumstances, I think you might be able to tap into some good information."

"Yeah, I believe that might work. Do you have any suggestions on how to go about it?"

"Well, Major, if you want to go where a lot of the civilians are hanging out at night, try that place that opened up in the center of town. You know, sir, the place that is a bar? I think the people who operated it before we got here asked for permission to reopen."

"Yes, I know the place. And you might be right about the civilians, Glenn, most of the time they know more than we do . . . even about our own operation."

He laughed. Even though I said it as a joke, there was some truth in the statement. He got up to leave and as he did I made a final comment, and added a couple of questions.

"Maybe it's worth a try, going in the bar. But I'm wondering about a U.S. Army man going in there. How would it look? And how about our non-fraternization rule?"

"Oh, the Colonel decided to relax that rule, Major. As you know, sir, he's interested in establishing good relations with the civilians. Some of us have already been in the bar and it doesn't seem to be a problem for anybody. The Colonel knows that people are going to make friends, men and women are going to date, and there's not much need to try to suppress it."

At ten minutes past eight, in the evening of the same day, I walked into the bar Sergeant Newton had described. I felt uncomfortable. It was like I was out of place. Also, I was concerned that some of the civilians, knowing that I had been involved in a love affair with Ariane, and believing that she was dead, would see me as a very shallow person. But I had to put those thoughts aside—I had important matters to handle.

I had just stepped inside and looked around briefly when I saw Leni. It was fortunate. She was a familiar face in an otherwise unfamiliar set of circumstances. It made my presence there easier.

Leni was sitting at a table with two other young women. She saw me, smiled and waved, and then, she continued looking at me as if she was saying "come and join us." It was perfect.

I walked in the direction of her table. The large room, with tables and booths, was full of people, all civilians. There was another room, running off at a ninety degree angle, at the back of the main room, and it appeared there were many other people there. Music was being played, coming either from a radio or a record player, over loud speakers, and there was laughter and jovial talk among the people. It was typical of a bar, or even a small night club, back in the States. I smiled as I greeted Leni.

"So this is how you spend your time away from the office?"

"You bet your life, Herr Major. It's fun here. Oh, bitte, my friends are Heidi and Gertrude."

I shook hands with each and we exchanged smiles. Leni spoke again.

"Major, would you like to join us?"

"Yes, thanks."

There was an empty chair next to the table and I sat in it. I felt that I needed to make some sort of explanation about being there.

"I haven't been here before and I wanted to see how it is working out. Some of our men are telling me that it might help us forget that we were shooting at each other a few months ago."

All three smiled in agreement. Heidi was first to respond.

"I think it is good for Germans and Americans to relax now, forget about the past and think of the future."

Gertrude agreed. "Yes! Who knows, maybe we will even get to be friends soon." And finally, Leni commented, "We haven't had a place like this to go to in a long time . . . I think it is good that the Americans can come, too."

I agreed and responded to Leni.

"Where do they get the drinks they serve, the wine? I didn't realize that things of that sort are still available."

Leni, an attractive young woman who was groomed neatly, smiled broadly.

"Oh, Herr Major, we have plenty of wine. No new clothes or houses or automobiles, but, plenty of wine!"

Again, we each smiled. From previous experiences I knew the civilians did not like to discuss the war, the Hitler years, and I tried to steer our conversation into a neutral zone.

"Is Bad Welmsburg home for each of you, or have you lived in other cities?"

Leni answered. "Yes, it is our home. Each of us was born here and we went to school together."

It gave me a chance to ask about their school years and the curriculum for German students. They described it, saying among other things that six years of English was required, and it explained why so many of the civilians were able to speak English so well.

The waiter brought a glass for me and poured the remnants of a bottle of wine that was on the table in our glasses. I asked him to bring another bottle.

We discussed various things for a while, schools in the U.S., and requirements to get degrees. They wanted to know about Hollywood, resort cities, and other glamorous aspects of America.

About two hours later, we had talked our way through three bottles of wine. Leni and her friends had loosened up considerably. At one point, Leni talked about music.

"Major, I love your American songs. I listen to your radio broadcasting station, and . . ." she stopped and listened momentarily, then continued, "yes, it is the program that we can hear now. The music is so schön."

I had already heard the music in the background, coming from the loudspeakers, and I recognized it as the American Armed Forces Broadcasting Station. Like Leni, I had listened to the station previously and enjoyed it. From nine to twelve each night there was a mix of songs popular in the U.S., as well as the beautiful songs of Europe.

At ten twenty-five, I was speaking directly to Leni but noticed that Heidi said something quietly to Gertrude. Then, as I paused, Heidi spoke. "Leni, we must go. We have to be up for work in the morning."

Leni had been affected by the wine more than the others and she quickly responded, good naturedly.

"No! I'm having a good time. I want to stay."

Heidi and Gertrude looked at each other and smiled. Then they made preparations to leave. Leni looked at me.

"Major, can you stay longer?"

"Sure, Leni, why not?"

Heidi and Gertrude stood, and as they did, I stood. They offered to pay for their share of the wine. I told them I would take care of it. They thanked me and I shook hands with each of them. They said goodnight to Leni and me, and left.

Now, I would be where I wanted to be, alone with Leni. The wine was beginning to make her talk more freely and I thought that she might tell me more than she would otherwise. After I was seated, she spoke.

"Thank you, Major. You know, there are times when I don't know if I am happy or sad . . . and I just want to be happy. Is it the same with you?"

"Yes, Leni, it is. Many of us are in the same boat now."

"Why did all of these things happen? It seems like a bad dream."

"I know. And we can't really be happy because we remember so many things that make us sad."

"And . . . the future seems . . . we don't have . . ."

"Maybe it will be better in the future. I think you have to believe that."

She smiled and maintained a lingering stare into my eyes.

"You are a very nice man, Major. I know why Ariane was in love."

I could sense, of course, that she was being drawn to me, possibly with a romantic inclination. I didn't want to deceive her, or use the situation wrongly, though I did hope that she could tell me more than she had previously about the men who were involved with Karl Wegner in the escape plan. She would know about the SS men who were there, all of the civilians would know. In Bad Welmsburg, a small city of about eighteen thousand people, it would be impossible for the three assassins to conceal themselves, or disguise their motive in being there. I had to try to draw out as much information as possible from Leni.

There was just enough wine in the bottle for me to refill Leni's glass, and pour an ounce or two in my glass. She raised her glass in a toast.

"We will be good friends forever!"

"Absolutely! Good friends forever."

We touched glasses and sipped the wine. I tried to think of a way to get her into a subject that would help me.

"Leni, I heard about the pilot who was here. The man who flew General Kranz to Berchtesgaden. I know he was your friend. I'm sorry he was killed."

It was a statement that I thought would cause a surprising reaction from her. It didn't. The wine had softened her and she didn't question how I knew about the death of her boyfriend, Rudi. Instead she responded calmly.

"Thank you, Major. We were . . . I don't really know what we were . . . I thought we would be married, but changes come so often, and now, I don't know if it would have been right or wrong."

"You will meet someone in the future. You're a beautiful young woman."

She was pleased, and she stared back into my eyes, longingly for a few moments, and then she formed an alluring expression.

"Major, would you dance with me?"

She caught me by surprise. I looked over the room and there was no space for people to dance. I thought she must have been thinking about some time in the future.

"Sure, I will. Some day we will find a place and dance the evening away."

"No, I mean now. The other room, here, is for dancing."

I looked toward the back where another room ran off at a ninety degree angle from the main room. I couldn't see what was inside but it was apparently what Leni had meant. I looked back to her.

"You mean the room back there?" And I nodded toward the back. "Is it a room where people dance?"

"Yes. I want to dance . . . I want you to hold me."

The wine obviously was having an effect on her. I had no choice, and I had to agree. I looked around the room and about half of the people were gone, and I hoped it would be the same in the other room. I still had an uneasy feeling about being seen with Leni by the civilians, but I had to use the time with her as best I could. Also, she was an enjoyable companion and during the course of the evening we had become good friends, so I stood and held my hand out to her.

"It will be my pleasure."

She stood and took my hand, and we walked toward the back room. She was slightly unsteady on her feet when she stood. Then, as we walked, she seemed to be all right. One or two people glanced up as we walked by; otherwise, no one was interested. In the room where there was dancing there were a few tables with people. In the space set aside for dancing, an area that was about twenty feet square, there were two couples on the floor. The two men and two women looked to be older, the men appeared to be in their sixties and that would explain their presence there. The younger men, the ones who would eventually return from war service, were still away. Again, the room was half filled and I guessed that a lot of people had gone home.

There was a slow song coming over the loudspeakers. I took Leni's right hand in my left, and put my right arm around her waist. She put her left hand on my right shoulder and moved in close to me so that we were touching from the waist up. As we began moving, keeping time with the music, she leaned in and put her face against my upper chest. I could feel her relax, and touching me seemed comforting and emotionally uplifting for her. But it was because she was like a million other women, millions in fact. She was longing to feel the arms of a man around her, touching her and comforting her after the lonely and tragic years of war. Appropriately, I suppose, the song was *You'll Never Know*, a love song. I was concerned about the way it would look, holding each other closely, but I couldn't bring myself to back away, or pull apart from her. And she was, after all, only a lonely young woman.

We danced for about fifteen minutes. I felt it was time to leave. She, too, appeared ready to go, and she agreed when I suggested it to her. We walked back to our table, she got her small handbag, I left some money on the table, and we walked out.

The air was cool and refreshing outside. I offered to drive Leni home and she accepted. The ride in the open jeep, with the chilly breeze striking us in the face, would reduce the effect of the wine and I was hoping that Leni would be refreshed enough to talk some when we arrived at her home.

I followed her directions and in about ten minutes she pointed out a house and I stopped. She had told me earlier that she lived in a house with her grandmother. She turned and spoke.

"Major, can you come in for a short visit?"

"Yes, I can come in for a few minutes, Leni, then I think you better hop in bed."

She grinned. It had worked out the way I wanted, I would have a chance to talk to her in a quiet and private place. I took her hand to help her down from the jeep, and as we walked to the door, she held on to my hand.

On the inside we walked into a nicely furnished living room. She told me that her grandmother would be upstairs, asleep. She turned on the radio, playing it softly, and it was already programmed to receive the music from the American Armed Forces Radio Station. She took off her jacket, and, once again, she took my hand and we walked to a couch where we were seated. When she spoke, she made a statement that came as a complete surprise.

"Major, I know about some of the information you are seeking and possibly I can help you."

"I really appreciate that, Leni. I hope you don't feel I am trying to use you."

"I don't. I know you are like nearly everyone else, you need a friend because of the sad things that have happened. And, in addition, you are doing the work that has to be done."

The ride in the jeep had removed most of the effect of the wine and she obviously was beginning to think clearly. She continued.

"I can tell you more than I did in your office today. It was so sudden when you asked this morning, I felt it was better to wait."

"I understand."

"Rudi, my boyfriend who was the pilot, came here each month during the last five or six months. He flew a small plane and brought important people to see General Wegner. He stayed each time in the hotel and that is how I came to know him."

"Who were the people he brought?"

"Some were generals, others were important men in the Nazi Party. They were planning the escape . . . they knew Germany was losing the war and they did not want to be captured."

"And they were to go from here to Flensburg?"

"Yes. And from there they were to board a ship off the coast of Denmark. We are not certain but we believe some did board the ship, the ship that later sank in the English Channel. I believe it hit a floating mine that was still there."

"So, from what you have heard, none of the men actually escaped?"

"Rudi did not know, and after he was killed, it was all a matter of guessing."

"Can you tell me anything else?"

"Not about those men . . . except, there was someone else, someone very important . . . it was such a great secret that Rudi could not tell me."

"And you have no thoughts about who it might have been?"

"Only that he was with Rudi when a flight was made from Bad Welmsburg to Flensburg."

I thought about it, and tried to reason who it might have been. Bormann? Possibly. Goering, and most of the others who were high ranking, had been captured. Hitler had committed suicide, as had Goebbels. I asked Leni for more details.

"Where do you think the person came from, and when, the one who was very important?"

"Maybe it was Berlin. Rudi flew to Berlin with General Wegner on April 30, and returned here that night. It could have been someone who came at that time."

April 30. The day the Russians overran the area around Hitler's bunker. It would have been someone high in the organization, someone who had stayed with Hitler until the last moment. I would have to get the list in my office and check the names. It would be, most likely, the highest-ranking Nazi who was unaccounted for and still missing. I asked Leni if she knew of other flights.

"There was only the flight to Flensburg, the one that I mentioned before. Dr. Voss, Hitler's physician, and one other person was aboard the plane. I believe the second person was the one who was brought from Berlin."

"And then, of course, the last flight was the one to Berchtesgaden. Why did Rudi take General Kranz to Berchtesgaden when the others were going to Flensburg?"

"He said General Kranz had to see about some documents, destroy them. And then Rudi was to come back to Bad Welmsburg."

That would explain why Kranz had gone to Hitler's teahouse, there must have been papers there. I thought next about the three SS men who had come to Bad Welmsburg, and I asked Leni if others had come.

"For a while, others were here. But now, I think it is only the three."

"Where are they?"

"I do not know. They have been very careful and only a few people have seen them. It seems ridiculous that they are here, no one is left who knows about the escape plan."

What she said suddenly brought into focus her own situation. She was most likely in danger. Because of Rudi she knew many details and it was surprising that they had not already come for her. I had to warn her.

"Leni, do you realize that you, too, could be in danger?"

"Yes, I have thought about that, Major. And maybe I don't care. It has been so long . . . so much has been lost, so many people are dead . . . even my parents were killed in the Dresden raid. They were there to visit the parents of my father, and all were killed. And so, at times when I am sad, I feel I have nothing to live for."

"You've got to get rid of that feeling. You have a lot to live for, things will be better for you. I promise you that."

Obviously pleased, she responded pleasantly.

"Major, you are a kind man. And you seem . . . it is the same for me as it would be if you were a German man and there was no war. You even look like a German. Clear blue eyes, a strong face with fine features, and I must say, very handsome."

Her sincerity made her appealing. With greenish blue eyes and medium blond hair, she was a pretty young woman. She was almost childish at times, and then passive, but altogether attractive with an overall alluring image.

"Thanks, Leni, it's nice of you to say that. But, back to you, be very alert and careful. I don't think it's a good idea for you to go out alone at night. If you ever need me, call at any time."

"I will. And thank you, Major."

It was time for me to go and I told her. She walked with me to the door. There, she reached up and put her arms around my neck and kissed me, fully on the lips. I held her closely for a few moments and then pulled away. She smiled sweetly, we each said goodnight, and I walked out.

3.

THE NEXT MORNING I was in the office at seven forty-five. Colonel Margolies had arrived early, too. Each of us was there for the same reason; there was urgent business to be taken care of in Bad Welmsburg.

I brought him up to date on everything I had learned from Leni. We talked about security and our plans to look for the three SS men. I was uncertain about telling Colonel Margolies about Ariane. I felt sure it would be safe to tell him but I held back, looking for the right opportunity to bring it up, and the longer we talked the more reluctant I became to mention her name. I would tell him, I would not withhold information from him. It just seemed that I was caught temporarily with a cautious attitude. And before I got around to it, Sergeant Newton came to the door, escorting a captain in a U.S. paratrooper's uniform. Newton spoke to the Colonel.

"Sir, this is Captan LeTourneau."

The Colonel smiled and responded.

"Oh, yes, Captain, I've been expecting you. Come in."

LeTourneau smiled, and it was big, a natural expression that I felt people would see often. He stepped up to the Colonel, after a sharp salute, and extended his hand. He and the Colonel shook hands, and the Colonel turned in my direction and spoke to the Captain.

"Captain LeTourneau, this is Major Gordon. You will be working for him." And then the Colonel looked at me. "Max, about a week ago Colonel Mason of Division offered us some help because of our situation here. Eddie . . . ah, Captain LeTourneau, had transferred from the 82nd Airborne to our Division and they decided to send him here to help us." Then, turning back to the Captain, "and we're glad to have you Captain. We can use all the help we can get right now."

"Thank you, sir. I'm glad to be here."

LeTourneau seemed likeable, the kind of man who would promote friendships.He smiled constantly. He was large and robust, and I wondered how he made it as a paratrooper. He must have been six-four or six-five, and he would weigh about two-fifty or two-sixty. I asked him about it.

"Captain, how did they find a parachute big enough to keep you afloat?"

He laughed.

"They didn't. I was assigned to the ground. I had to wait until the rest of the guys jumped and then go and catch up with them."

"Sounds like you might have been in administrative."

"Yeah, pretty much. It wasn't what I had in mind when I joined, but at least I'm still here."

"I know. It wasn't all glamour like we thought back in the States. I remember thinking if I could just get a uniform with a pair of those boots I would be a real stud. But we sure didn't know what was waiting for us, did we?"

"No, sir, we didn't. I believe you were with the hundred and first weren't you, sir?"

"Yes. But combat for me was short term, only two days in Holland. I had a minor wound and was evacuated. They were going to send me back to the States, I think it was my age . . . I'm forty-five . . . but I was able to transfer to Military Government instead."

"Yes, sir, I heard about you at Division."

From that point on we talked about the current situation in Bad Welmsburg and the work we needed to do. LeTourneau seemed eager and very cooperative. I was glad to have him working with us.

Our conversation had drifted along for about an hour. The little clock the Colonel had on a table near his desk, a gift from his wife, was almost directly in line with my view as I looked into his face during our conversation. At eight forty-five, Sergeant Newton suddenly appeared at the door, and at a glance I knew there was trouble. He spoke, excitedly.

"Excuse me, Colonel. We just got bad news. Maria in the office downstairs got a call from Chief Swartz. Leni Schoenbrun is dead."

I was stunned. I stood immediately.

"What did you say, Glenn?"

"Leni is dead, Major. Her grandmother called Chief Swartz and he called us. It sounds like she has been murdered."

It was an unbelievable jolt, a great shock. I asked Newton about her.

"Where is she . . . where did it happen?"

"At her home. Jim Polofski and Maria are on the way over there now."

I couldn't believe it. It had come too quickly and I couldn't make myself accept it. I turned to the Colonel.

"Colonel, I'm going over there."

"Yeah, Max, you need to do that. Do you want to take Captain LeTourneau with you?"

"Yes."

I turned to LeTourneau who was already on his feet and motioned to the door. "Let's go."

We walked hurriedly to the outside. I was almost running. LeTourneau was following closely behind me, and when we got to the jeep we got in and moved out quickly.

On the way he spoke.

"Who is the woman, Major?"

"She worked for us. A secretary. A young German woman about twenty years old. It's a hell of a thing and I'm going to make somebody pay dearly for it."

"Why would anyone kill her?"

"She knew things about the Nazis, you know, this whole thing that's going on here now. I talked to her last evening and she told me a lot about it. Damn! Somebody must have seen us together! It's the same men, the SS, it has to be. I'm going to find those bastards quick, and I'll sure as hell save the Army some time in dealing with them."

Riding in the jeep beside me Eddie LeTourneau was quiet, and I preferred it that way. I thought about Leni, and being with her in the bar, and I knew the wrong person had seen us together there. Somebody like Braun, the man who had given information to the SS about Ariane, would be responsible. In addition to a combination of sorrow and anger, I was beginning to feel guilty. I should have known better than to be seen in a bar with her. It didn't occur to me that she was in jeopardy until we got back to her house. Then it was too late. Even so, I should have been more careful.

At Leni's home people were gathered in small groups in front of the house. I saw the car that belonged to the civilian Chief of Police, Chief Swartz, and I recognized one of his men talking to a woman on the porch. LeTourneau and I got out of the jeep and made our way through the people to the inside. There, we found Jim Polofski, a corporal who was a member of our Military Government team, and Maria, a young German woman who worked in our office. They, and Chief Swartz, were in the living room, as was an elderly woman sitting in a chair, weeping quietly. Maria was attempting to comfort her. I looked at Jim Polofski.

"Where is she?"

"In the bedroom, sir, through that door." And he nodded to a nearby door.

I walked into the room. Doctor Reuss was there, as was Wiedermann, a civilian policeman who worked for Swartz. Leni was on the bed. Her throat had been cut. There was blood, pools of blood, around her upper body. Her face was beginning to take on a bluish appearance. Sweet little Leni. I felt an overwhelming sorrow. She was so young, so pretty. And she had wanted so much to help us. I felt compassion, deep sorrow, and I was very nearly distraught. I turned to Doctor Reuss.

"Doctor, can you tell me what time it happened?"

"Not exactly, not yet, but I believe it was about four or five this morning."

"Are there other wounds, other than the neck?"

"No, no other wounds. No sex. It was a murder." He then pointed to a mirror where words were spelled out in blood: Death To Traitors. The words, in English, were, I was sure, for my benefit. Wiedermann offered some information.

"Herr Major, it appears the killer came through the rear door. The lock is broken."

"Okay, let's take a good look inside and out, and see if there is anything that will help us. Be extremely careful and search for any object that could be a clue. Also, Wiedermann, go out and look for footprints . . . and look in the street, all around the house. Find something for me!"

"Yavold, Herr Major!"

I walked back into the living room. I went over and took both hands of Leni's grandmother in mine and spoke to her softly.

"Dear Frau, I am so sorry."

She looked up through tearful eyes and nodded. I asked Maria if she thought the elderly lady understood what I had said.

"She doesn't understand English, sir, but she knows what you meant to say."

"Tell her we will help her. If she needs anything, let us know."

Maria spoke to her in German, and she managed a slight smile and nodded. I turned then and spoke to LeTourneau.

"We're going all out to nail these people. As far as I am concerned, Leni was one of our own."

I called Chief Swartz to one side of the room and told him I felt it was the SS. He agreed. I told him I wanted the name of every person who had been in the bar the previous evening, and I wanted to set up a time and place to interview each one as quickly as possible. He had taken out a small notebook and was writing. Next, I said, the owner and employees of the bar were to come to our offices for questioning. All were to be rounded up during the day. In addition, anyone in the city who was known to have seen the three SS men was to be brought in . . . we would turn the city upside down before nightfall. He was ready to leave but paused to speak.

"Thank you, Herr Major. It is good that we can work together, Germans and Americans."

"We have a common cause this time, Chief. And now, a few final instructions. I want the airstrip staked out. I want at least one of your men at the rail station at all times. When the trains arrive, I want four men there, two on each side of the train. If necessary, hold up the trains until you can be sure it is okay. If you need it, hire more men. I want everybody stopped, whether they are walking or riding. All civilian vehicles are to be stopped and searched thoroughly. We will stop all military vehicles. I want you to notify the townspeople that anyone who shelters these men will go to prison. Anyone who has knowledge of these men must disclose it to us at once or face time in prison. I'm counting on you, Chief. We have to be quick, and we have to be thorough. Call me at any time if you need me."

"I will do that Herr Major. And now, I go to work!"

He walked out. I talked to Maria and told her to stay with Leni's grandmother. I also told her to do whatever was needed to help her. Then, I told Jim Polofski to go over everything in the house and look for clues. I asked Wiedermann to question every resident in the area—go to each house and ask if anyone had been seen in the early morning hours. I told him to question the people in a forceful way.

"Be persistent. Go in and talk to the people, go inside their homes. Take your time and make notes. Ask if a dog barked or if a car was heard or if a gate squeaked. There might have been a noise when the back door lock was broken—maybe a neighbor heard it and looked out. If you have doubts about anyone, come and get me. Now, are you all set?"

"Yes, Herr Major. And thank you, sir, for your confidence in us." He turned and left.

I did have confidence in them. They were efficient and reliable. I had found that the Germans took great pride in their work. It was good to have them as an ally.

Suddenly I thought of Frau Erhlich, Ariane's aunt, who was in the Wegner mansion. The three assassins seemed to be certain that Ariane was alive, and they would no doubt go after anyone who could give them information. It was a situation that was somewhat similar to that of Leni, and obviously they would attack Frau Erhlich for the same reason. I had to go there, to the Wegner mansion, as quickly as possible.

Before leaving the home of Leni, I tried to think if I had covered everything. I asked Eddie LeTourneau to stay and take over the crime scene activities. I also told him to assist Wiedermann in the door-to-door search, the questioning of residents in the surrounding neighborhood, and finally, I asked that he assist Maria in whatever was needed in handling final arrangements for Leni.

As I drove away, the whole thing seemed incredible. Some ten or twelve hours earlier I had been there with a vibrant young woman who was now dead. It was, in my mind, a tragic event, and I was drained. But to the Germans it was different. Death no longer was shocking to them. They had seen too much of it. They could become angry, or resentful, or they could think in terms of revenge; otherwise, the loss of life did not arouse the same painful emotions that we felt. And, with millions of their people dead, I suppose it was understandable that they were more conditioned to it.

At the entrance of the Wegner home, Frau Erhlich answered my knock quickly, and I was quite relieved to see her. I explained briefly about Leni and how we were dealing with the investigation. Next, I wanted to find out about Ariane.

"Have you heard from Rolfe, or Ariane?"

"No, nothing more. But I have confidence in Rolfe, he will take good care of her."

"I'm trusting that he will do that, Frau Erhlich. In the meantime, you must be very careful. These men want revenge, and they will kill again. Be sure all of your doors and windows are locked."

"We are already doing that, Major. Also, an older man who is known to Else, who now lives alone, will move in with us later today."

"Good. I was going to send someone to stay with you, or move you, but that does not seem necessary now."

I spent the next ten minutes reviewing the things she would have to remember. I told her not to move around alone. And she was not to leave the house at night. Then I offered her my support.

"Call me at any time."

"Thank you, Major. I will only do that if it is necessary."

On the way back to town I thought of Gertrude and Heidi, the friends of Leni who had been with us in the bar. I wanted to talk to each of them. The chances were good that they would remember most of the people who had been in the bar. I would arrange to see them in a private place and it would not place them in danger.

I spent most of the afternoon in my office, making assignments for our men and talking by telephone to Chief Swartz and others who were involved in our search. Chief Swartz advised that the citywide sweep was going well and he was confident that no one had left the city without clearance by his men. He was bringing in the men and women who had been in the bar the previous evening and questioning each of them individually. He told me that anyone who appeared suspicious would be held for additional questioning.

Late in the afternoon, just before six, my phone rang and it was Heidi. I was not surprised by her call. In fact, I had been expecting it.

"Major, I am so sorry about Leni. Is there anything I can do?"

"I think we have everything taken care of, Heidi. But thanks. Oh! There is, however, one thing I would like to mention. I would like to talk to you and Gertrude. Do you remember who was in the bar last evening . . . or maybe I should ask if you can identify most of the people who were there?"

"Yes! I can remember almost everyone who was there."

"Very good. Can you make a list for me? And if you know anything about them put a note by each name. Will you do that?"

"Yes, of course, Major. I can have it done in a short while. When do you wish to have it?"

"As soon as possible. Can you do it this evening?"

"I will have it ready within an hour."

"That's great. I'll stop by to pick it up. Would eight-thirty or nine be okay?"

"It will be fine. Do you know where I live?"
"No."
She told me, giving me the address and then giving me directions on how to get there. I would have time to go by the gym first and talk to Chief Swartz. He was questioning people there, and I was hoping he would have some leads. It was getting late in the day and so far we had nothing. On the phone, Chief Swartz had told me that he had already talked to Gertrude and she could only remember a small number of people who were in the bar.
When I got to the gym, the Chief looked perplexed and tired. I knew before we spoke that he had no leads. People were there who were still waiting to be questioned, and there were others who had been released to go home. The Chief was a proud man, usually wearing a tie and coat, and I was certain he had used his position in the best possible way to try to help. I decided to try to encourage him rather than speaking to him about the negative aspects of the case. I smiled as I greeted him.
"Good evening, Chief. I appreciate the good effort by you and your men today."
"Well, we did put forth a good effort, Major, but I regret to say that we have no leads."
"Don't be discouraged yet. I think you have put a lid on this city that will make it impossible for anyone to get away."
He smiled faintly. Then, we talked for ten or fifteen minutes about key locations that should be given extra attention. As we talked, a woman who was possibly fifty approached us. She was followed by an elderly man, and standing back was a young woman who was accompanying them. The older woman spoke in German to the Chief and I didn't understand what she had said. He turned to me.
"Major, this woman asks if it is all right for her to speak with you."
"Certainly she can. Will you interpret for me?"
"She can speak in English."
He nodded to her and she looked at me.
"Sir, we wish to see this trouble end. We have come here before . . . during the years before the Americans came . . . to be questioned. Many times. Can you please let us now have peace?"
"Yes. It's what we all want. I didn't realize you had been brought here so many times in the past. I'm sorry for the inconvenience. But as you know, a young German girl has been murdered, we think by German men, and we want to find them. We appreciate your cooperation."
She shook her head and walked away. She and the elderly man walked with the young woman in the direction of the door, and the Chief looked back to me.
"Her daughter was in the bar last evening. That is why they were here. But she has been excused and they will go home now. I know it is difficult for an American to understand, Major, but the German peo-

ple, most of the people, only wish to have peace. We were foolish at first, then it was too late, and we all became prisoners of Hitler. I hope you can understand."

"I do. And I hope we can live side by side in peace very soon."

"Yes, so do I, and I believe we can do that, Major."

He had other things to do and so did I. In fact, I mentioned that I would go by to see Heidi and pick up a list of names from her, names of people who were in the bar. As I talked about Heidi he looked at me in a puzzling way, or at least it seemed to have brought out a questionable thought in him. He didn't speak and it aroused my curiosity.

"Is there something you want to tell me about Heidi, Chief?"

"Actually, I think you must know about her by now, from the records in your office. As you probably are aware she has lived here all her life except for a short period in the summer of last year. She was at that time with her parents in Hannover."

"Her parents are in Hannover?"

"Yes. Her father was wounded and when he recovered he was sent to an assignment there. His wife went there, but Heidi remained here in their home."

It still seemed strange, the way he had looked at me.

"And you have nothing more to tell me about her or her parents?"

"No, Major, I have nothing more to tell you."

I suspected he did but I didn't push it. There would be other ways to find out. I didn't want to tear down my relationship with him by being too persistent on a subject that he obviously didn't want to discuss. He was too valuable, too good in his job. We talked about other things for a few more minutes, after which I moved away to talk to one of his men. Eventually I left the building and went outside to my jeep with the intention of driving to the home of Heidi.

Heidi was friendly when she met me at the door and extended a warm welcome as she invited me to walk with her to the living room. There, we were seated, and she expressed again her sorrow about Leni. After a few minutes I asked about the list she had said she would prepare for me, and she responded at once.

"Oh, yes, of course. I have it right here, Major."

She got up and walked to a table and came back across the room to the couch where I was seated. She sat down next to me and I assumed she did so because she wanted to discuss the names. She positioned herself very near to me, in fact, we were touching, with our legs and upper bodies rubbing together. It was by her design and she clearly had something in mind in addition to the names on the list. I didn't move, mainly because I didn't think it was necessary at that point, and I wanted to find out what was motivating her. If it had not been for the comments of Chief Swartz I would have assumed that it was most likely a move by a lonely young woman. Now, I wasn't so sure, so I would give her time, and the opportunity, to do whatever it was she wanted to do.

She held the paper with the list of names out in front of us and made a few comments about each person. It was meaningless information in regard to our investigation. After about ten or fifteen minutes, she stopped and suddenly turned to look at me.

"Oh, Major, please excuse me, would you like something to drink, maybe a glass of schnapps?"

I preferred not to have schnapps because it was a powerful drink, but I accepted and told her it would be nice. She got up at once and walked out of the room, and as she did, I thought about her. She was twenty years old, the same age as Leni. She was different from Leni, both in appearance and personality. She was a brunette, which was somewhat rare in Germany, and she not only had dark hair, she also had brownish green eyes. She was very attractive. Her eyes, fully rounded, conveyed a mischievousness, and her other facial features were appealing with no flaws. She had beautiful lips and teeth, and it seemed to put the finishing touch on a face that was, as I was now able to see, superb. During the time I had spent with her the previous evening with Gertrude and Leni in the bar, I had not assessed her as completely and I had not been able to determine that she was such an unusual woman. I had now seen enough of her, however, to see her as a vivacious and fun-loving person. I suspected that, with a few drinks, she could easily become the life of any party. And she was, as our GIs would have said, stacked like a brick outhouse. With all of her attributes I had to wonder why she would focus her attention on me. Did she want a job? Did she want some special favor, maybe something to do with her parents? Would she, for whatever reason, be trying to get information from me? And finally, could it be the first thing I had imagined—was she simply another young lonely German woman? Whatever it was, I would try to go along with her as far as possible to find out.

Soon she was back, carrying a tray with glasses and a bottle, and she was smiling broadly. She knew perfectly well that she had an exceptional body, and she very confidently walked to a small table in front of me where she placed the tray, looking all the while quite seductive.

"Here we are, Major. I didn't bring a mix because most people prefer to sip schnapps without it, or straight, as I believe they used to say in your movies."

I grinned at her.

"Yeah, I think you're right, most people drink it straight."

She poured for both of us and we touched glasses. She spoke.

"And now, Major, you can make the first toast."

"Very good. Let's see. Oh, I know. For Leni!"

"Yes! For dear Leni!"

We remained silent for a few moments to pay the respect to Leni that we had proposed. Then, Heidi got up and turned on a radio on a nearby table, and it was, once again, the American Armed Forces Broadcasting Station. She grinned as she came back to the couch.

"Wouldn't it be great fun, Major, to be in a place where there would be a nice orchestra, good food, pleasant surroundings, and all the other things that go with that?"

"You bet! Have you been to places like that in the past?"

"No, not really. I have only seen it in the movies. The war stopped everything for us. How about you, have you been to places like that?"

"Yes, before the war. And even after the war was under way we still had some places that were able to keep going."

She had the seductive look in her eyes again as she answered.

"Tell me about the women you took there."

"Well, I was married you know, so I took my wife in recent years."

"How about before that . . . did you take brunettes or blondes?"

"Now, you're going to make me think. It was quite a while ago, you know. But, let's see, I remember Jean, my first year in college. She was a brunette."

"And your wife, what was she?"

"Kind of blondish."

"And I think during the inquest it was said that you and your wife were getting a divorce?"

"Yes. But let's talk some about you. Tell me about the men you have dated."

"There were not many because all of the men were in Russia, or France, or some other place. We spent most of our time writing letters instead of having dates."

"I'm sure that will change soon. I think a few of the young German soldiers have already come back and others will be home at some time in the future."

She was different compared to Leni, and more carefree. She looked to the future with enthusiasm. She was undaunted by the past. She was beautiful, and she knew it. I had the feeling that her confidence was borne out by some connection to powerful people, some friendships with individuals who were among the elite in Germany: high-ranking Nazis, the SS, others. It was very unlikely that a young woman with such a beautiful face and marvelous body would be overlooked. While in Hannover with her parents she would have been exposed to many high-ranking Germans, and with her outgoing personality, plus the desire to move up, or apparently gain entry to the higher echelon of the German power structure, I was very certain that she knew a great deal more than she would be willing to tell me.

The schnapps had a powerful effect. Even though I was sipping it slowly, I could feel myself becoming warm inside and relaxed. It was having the same effect on Heidi, and she had moved in close to me so that our bodies were touching again. She wanted to continue the same discussion she had started earlier.

"Well, Major, you knew at least one brunette, and your wife was blonde. What is your real preference?"

I thought it might be a good idea to tell her what I knew she wanted to hear.

"I think maybe it would be brunettes. And you, you haven't told me much about your preferences."

She stared into my eyes, alluringly.

"I think I would like a man like you."

"That's nice, Heidi, and I appreciate it. But I'm too old for you. You need a nice young man who is about twenty-one years old."

"You're not old, Major. I know your age. Forty-five. And you appear to be only about thirty-five. So, don't tell me that you are too old. All of the women in Bad Welmsburg talk about you."

"That's probably because nobody else is around. Wait until your men come home, then you will be talking differently."

She had kicked off her shoes and she pulled her left leg up and put it under her right leg. As she did her skirt came up, and she left it with about half of her upper legs exposed. She continued talking.

"Major, I would like to ask, and if you do not wish to speak about it I will understand. I would like to ask about Ariane."

"Okay. If there is anything I don't want to discuss, I'll let you know."

"When she was shot, you were not there—is that correct?"

"That's correct."

"I know it was a great shock to you to learn about it. Did you return at once from your office to the hospital?"

"I returned to the front of the hospital, to the spot where it happened."

"But you didn't go in the hospital?"

I paused and looked at her with a questioning stare. She continued quickly.

"I only . . . you were so much in shock, I think to have seen her would have been bad, so bad. I know that you went away . . . to England . . . but, did you . . . I am wondering why you would leave, and perhaps . . . why you did not see her?"

I paused, trying to reason the purpose of her question. After a few seconds I answered.

"She was dead, Heidi. It was confirmed by the doctor and our men. There was nothing for me to do and I wanted to remember her as I had known her. I thought it was possible that she had been struck in the face and disfigured, and I did not want to see her like that."

"I understand, Major. Yes, I heard that arrangements were made for her and she was quickly taken away by Doctor Reuss."

"That's right, arrangements for her were made by others and I was told it had been done."

"Well, possibly it is best that you did not see her."

"I think so."

"And, I think . . . she was taken . . . were you told where she was taken, Major?"

"No."

I was extending the conversation to try to determine her motives. She spoke again.

"Well, maybe some day you will know. But at least you can be sure that Doctor Reuss did all possible to save her."

She did not make the statement in the form of a question; however, she did have a questioning look on her face as she finished the comment, and I answered.

"Yes, I am sure that he did all possible. But it was hopeless. And now, Heidi, can we discuss other things?"

"Of course, Major," and she continued, "Oh, back to what you were saying about our men coming home, I don't care for them. We have already waited for an eternity and I want to be happy now. Do you want to be happy too, Major?"

We both had started on a second glass of schnapps and she obviously was feeling the effect of it. Maybe things were about to get out of hand, drift too far in the wrong direction, and I decided that I would leave soon. I was still uncertain about her motives, but it was looking more like she only wanted to have a male companion. I answered the question she had asked.

"Yes, I do want to be happy, Heidi. I hope we can all be happy."

She drew herself up even closer to me as she responded.

"You could make me happy, Major. And I can make you happy . . . I know that you like my body, and you would like . . . tell me what you would like, Major. No! Tell me, Max, what you would like."

"Heidi, we have to hold up, here. You're a beautiful young woman, but it's not a good idea for us to become involved in the way you are suggesting. Let's talk about your list a little more and then I have to be going."

"Oh, to hell with the list, I want to be loved. And I think you want it, too. If that is not true, why did you dance so closely with Leni? Now, I will show you something."

She stood and pulled her slip-on sweater over her head and took it off, leaving only a bra covering the upper part of her body. She put the sweater on a table, and moving quickly, she reached around to her back and unsnapped her bra. She removed it too, and her breasts were bare. She had moved so fast and unexpectedly, I hardly had time to even speak. She looked down at me and smiled.

"Do you like my breasts, Max?"

"Yes, of course," and I smiled, "They're very nice . . . but you should put your clothes on, Heidi, we can't do this."

She smiled, confident and self-assured, leaving herself bare for a lingering view, and then she accepted what I had said, and reached for her bra. I think she had accomplished what she had planned to do, at least she had completed the tantalizing beginning of what she wanted to do. She grinned as she picked up her clothing to dress.

"Well, okay, but I think you will be sorry later."

"I'm sure I will."

I might have dug a hole for myself with her. I had let it go too far, trying to determine her motives. Now, by turning away from her, I might antagonize her if she really was attempting to seduce me.

After she was dressed her attitude seemed to be fine. She showed no resentment and she did not appear to be angry or upset because I had not accepted her offer of "love." We talked for five or ten minutes about the rest of the names on her list, and it was time for me to go. I took the list with me and at the door she reached out and shook hands. She made no other effort to move in close and we parted by saying goodnight.

During the ride home I remembered something Heidi had said that I missed at the time she said it, at least I missed the significance of it. She had said, "Why did you dance so closely with Leni?" Now, in considering it, I wondered how she had come to know that . . . it was after she and Gertrude had left when Leni and I had danced. It meant that someone in the bar had seen us and had told Heidi.

In the office the next morning I arranged to meet with Colonel Margolies privately. I told him I had confidential information, and he readily agreed to meet in his office with the door closed.

I told him what I had learned about Ariane, that she was alive. He was extremely happy for me. He could hardly believe it and he kept asking that I repeat almost every detail. He said he understood my reluctance to disclose the information, even to him, and he assured me it would remain highly confidential. He couldn't get over it.

"Max, I'm so happy for you. I know it must have been wonderful news when you pulled it out of Doctor Reuss."

"It was, Colonel. It was like the beginning of a new life. Now, all I have to do is find her and be sure she's safe."

"We will sure as hell do that. How's it coming with Chief Swartz, has he made any progress, anything worthwhile?"

"He has done a good job of shutting down the city. He's got men stationed at all key points. I don't believe anybody can get by him."

"Good. What else is going on, Max—are you getting close to anything?"

"No, I don't have anything yet. I have a new idea but I don't know at this time if it's worth while. I'll need a little more time. And along that line, I might need Eddie LeTourneau today. Is he available to me?"

"Absolutely. Use him however you need him, that's what he is here for."

"Thanks, Colonel. Now I better get to work. See you later in the day."

"Fine. And once again, Max, it was great news about Ariane."

A few minutes later, downstairs, I asked Glenn Newton to find Eddie LeTourneau and send him to my office. He got up to look for Captain LeTourneau, and I walked back up the stairs to my office. In less than five minutes, Eddie walked in, flashing the big smile that always seemed to be on his face. We exchanged the usual small talk and then I got to the point I wanted to discuss.

"Eddie, I've got a hunch that I want to prove or disprove. At this point I want to keep it quiet and confidential. I need your help in checking on a young woman here, and her family. What have you got planned today?"

"Not a thing. I was waiting to talk to you."

"Good. I met a young woman who was with Leni in the bar night before last, whose name is Heidi Dittmann. I'm getting some mixed signals from her. Also, Chief Swartz seems to know something about her, or her family, that he is not telling me. It's possible that they may be clean, but I can't be sure. I know Chief Swartz would tell me if he had solid information, but I'm guessing that he suspects something and just doesn't want to accuse them."

"How can I help?"

"Heidi's parents live in Hannover at present. Her father was sent there by the German Army on an assignment after he recovered from a wound. He and his wife moved there. Heidi stayed here, although she did go there last summer to visit them. One of the concentration camps was located in that area and I am wondering if he was assigned to work there. I would like for you to check it out, go over and ask a lot of questions. You can start with our people—we probably have infantry units scattered through the area, and you might want to talk to civilians as well."

"What are their names?"

"Horst and Anna Dittmann. Maybe you can get some help from a Military Government unit in the area. I think they will have a list of names of the people who worked in the concentration camp. In fact, I'm pretty sure the guards, and others who worked there, are being detained. And while you are there, check on the three SS men who are in our area, Hueber, Stelling, and Augenberg. Maybe they worked at the camp too but got out before the Allies got there. Can you drive over there today?"

"I sure can, Max. I'll head out as quick as possible. How long should I plan to stay?"

"As long as it takes. Try to get a message to me and let me know how you are doing. The Signal Corps can help you get through on a radio."

"Anything else?"

"That's it."

"Well, Major . . ." and he flashed one final big grin, "I'm out of here."

Later in the morning, I called Gertrude, the other woman who was with Heidi and Leni in the bar. I had first called the place where she worked and was told that she was out due to an illness. I then called her home and she answered. She told me that she was not feeling well, that she was still upset about Leni, and she had stayed at home for that reason.

I had decided before calling that I would be very careful not to alarm her or give her reason to think that anything out of the ordinary was involved. And our conversation seemed to go well. She was a little nervous at first but eventually overcame it. She told me the same thing she had told Chief Swartz, that she could only remember a few of the people who were in the bar that night. I wanted to get Heidi's name in the conversation and finally I did.

"Gertrude, maybe it will help if you can think of the people that Heidi knew who were there, the people she spoke to, or spoke about. Does that bring back the memory of anyone?"

She mentioned several names. I had the list Heidi had given me on my desk and I found each of the names. She had paused, and then she suddenly remembered another person.

"And there was Herr Kurth. Heidi spoke to him."

"Could you hear what was said?"

"No, sir, they were standing away from me."

"How long did they talk?"

"Oh. . . . for only a minute or so, a very short while."

I looked on Heidi's list and his name was not there. It was probably left off on purpose, and I wanted to find out about him.

"Let's see, I believe Heidi did mention him . . . is he the man who works at the rail station?"

"Oh no, he doesn't work there, he does something at the large garage. I am not certain what he does but I believe Heidi can tell you, Major."

"I'm sure she can. When did you see him?"

"At the door as we were leaving. He was just going in."

"I see. Well, you have been very good to assist us. I hope you will feel better."

"Thank you, sir."

It was the end of our conversation. I immediately began thinking about Herr Kurth and how I would go about investigating him. Kurth would have been the person who saw me dancing with Leni. He must have called the killer, who in turn talked to Heidi at some point that night or the next day. Either way, it meant that Heidi was possibly involved, even if it was only through her knowledge of the crime. It was disappointing to think that Heidi would be sitting at a table in a bar with Leni, having fun, perhaps be acquainted with the killers, and not come forward. The only explanation would be fear; she might have been threatened by the people who were responsible. In that case she would be very frightened . . . she might even have been told that she could easily end up like Leni.

4.

JUST AFTER LUNCH I went into the office of Colonel Margolies to attend a prearranged meeting. I felt sure he was hoping that I might have new information concerning the death of Leni, at least I assumed it was the reason he wanted to see me. And it was. We talked, and I explained in detail all that I knew, the questions I had about Heidi, and the information I had gotten from Gertrude about the man named Kurth. He was interested in Kurth, and like me, he wanted to know more.

"Max, who is this son-of-a-bitch, Kurth? Do we have anything on him?"

"No, sir. He's not known as a big wheel in the Nazi Party locally. My guess is, he is a plant. As you know, the SS did that, they had people set up to watch the civilians and it was usually somebody who seemed to be a legitimate businessman."

"What did Kurth do here in town?"

"He operated the local Opel dealership which included a large repair garage. Apparently in recent years the repair business was what kept the business going because they had no new cars to sell. He must have been doing okay before we got here, and then he came in and requested permission to continue to operate under our guidelines. It looked okay to Major Fisher and approval was granted."

"Yeah, if he was clean, I can see how Fisher would have approved it. Okay, what's your next move?"

"I want to go in his place with some excuse, maybe take one of our civilian cars in there and ask for a repair. It will give me a chance to meet him and size him up. I don't want him to know we are suspicious. Also, I don't want Heidi to get suspicious."

"Yeah. . . . okay . . . but you better be careful. These people are not stupid and you can't afford to make the wrong move."

"I know, Colonel, they're sharp. But this one is important to me—I'm going to settle this one in a hurry."

He grinned.

"I know you will, Max. I sure as hell wouldn't want you on my case."

"Thank you, sir."

I left his office and went back to my own office to reason things out. I thought of Chief Swartz. He might be a good source of information about Kurth. The Chief had lived in Bad Welmsburg all of his life. He had worked in the field of education and he had been in charge of the school system in Bad Welmsburg during the thirties. In addition to taking care of the classroom needs for young people in the city he had been in charge of physical fitness for them. The Germans had considered him to be an excellent instructor and the Nazis left him to do his job rather than have him serve in the Wehrmacht. He was clean as far as we were concerned, and we were happy to appoint him as head of police. He had told me privately that he had no desire to be a soldier, and apparently, because of the good work he was doing in the community, he never lost respect and was well liked by the people of the city. He was an ideal choice to work for us.

In my jeep, riding in the direction of the gym, I had thoughts, repeating thoughts, of Ariane. I could see her in all ways, all of her joys, disappointments, and in each of her moods. And I could remember her in all places where we had been together. I thought of the time we met at her friend's apartment, for the lack of a better place to meet. It was soon after I had met her. I had called, saying I wanted to meet and she suggested Lottie's apartment. She had confided in Lottie, a good friend, and Lottie left so that we could be alone. As soon as I got there and went inside, we embraced immediately, and neither of us could control our emotions, our desire for each other. We kissed repeatedly in a starved way and I had never felt such an overwhelming desire to touch and feel the nearness of a woman, a feeling born from deep endearment and love.

At three in the afternoon I went inside the gym to find Chief Swartz. He was there, finishing up the interviews with the people who were in the bar the night Leni was later killed. He had a list of the people who had been interviewed and he showed it to me. Walter Kurth was among the names on the list. He had a check mark beside his name, which meant that he had been released. I wanted to find out about him from the Chief, although I did not want to name him specifically. Consequently, I went over all names on the list with him, taking much longer to discuss each name so that Kurth would not seem important to me. The Chief surprised me when we discussed Kurth, giving me quite a lot of information voluntarily. He may have felt suspicious of Kurth, but he had no reason to hold him or accuse him. At four-fifteen I concluded my discussion with the Chief about the names on the list and was preparing to leave.

I shook hands with Swartz and paused. It was because of the way he was looking at me. Then I remembered. It was the look he assumed when he had information he was not certain he should disclose, not sure he should tell me. After recognizing the facial expression, I had to know what it was.

"What is it, Chief—I know you have something to tell me."

"Major . . . you must understand that what I will say is only . . . it is only a . . . perhaps a coincidence."

"All right, I'll consider it in that way."

He hesitatingly continued.

"A man who lives near Leni, two houses away, told Wiedermann that he saw a man just before dawn the night she was killed. He was on the street near Leni's home. The man walked under the street light as he was leaving. He moved on around the corner, and then one of your jeeps could be heard as it was started and moved away."

"What is the name of the man who talked to Wiedermann?"

"Strassel."

"What did the man look like, the man seen by Strassel?"

"He was wearing an American uniform, I believe they are called fatigues."

"Did you get a description—how big was he?"

"He was a large man."

"How large?"

"He was three or four inches taller than you, and he was not fat, but big through his body."

"And you say it was about 4 or 5 in the morning, about the time Doctor Reuss estimated Leni was killed?"

"Yes."

This was, indeed, a new wrinkle. Could it be a German in GI clothing? Where would he have secured a jeep? And how would he be moving around, if it was a German disguised as an American, in a U.S. Army vehicle with our tightened security? I questioned the Chief further.

"How well did Strassel see this man?"

"Not well in the face. He was wearing a cap that was pulled down. He could only be sure of the size, very large."

"Chief, can you think of any of our men, anyone who is assigned to our team or any of the men who have come from Division Headquarters, who would fit this description?"

He paused, not because he didn't have a name, but because he was reluctant to answer. I had to prod him.

"It's important, Chief. I assure you I will keep it confidential."

He knew he could trust me, and he knew I would keep my word. He spoke, somewhat solemnly.

"The new man, Captain LeTourneau."

LeTourneau! How could it be? He had come that same morning with his papers from Division, saying that he had driven during the night, the same night that Leni had been killed. I thought of everything about him and I could remember nothing suspicious. How could he possibly be an imposter? He looked rather tired that morning, as anyone would who had driven all night. I simply could not believe it could be him, the man who had killed Leni. But, I knew Chief Swartz. He had never given me bad information. It would have to be checked out immediately and I wanted to talk to Strassel. I turned back to Swartz.

"When can I talk to Strassel?"

"At once, but we must pick a place that will be safe for him."

"Yes, I agree. Okay, go ahead and set it up. Meanwhile, I will go back to Leni's home to see one thing. I remember the printing in blood on the mirror, just vaguely, and it seemed to have been done by someone familiar with printing in English. Even though the thought flashed through my mind at the time that it did not look like the work of a German, there were other things that needed to be done quickly and I moved on. Do you think the words might still be there?"

"No. I think the grandmother of Leni would have removed them. I can call and find out."

"Yes, do that, and let me know as soon as possible."

"I will do that and call you as soon as I have the information."

We continued our discussion and I learned from Swartz that Walter Kurth had been a resident of Bad Welmsburg for four years. The Chief described him to me as a middle-aged man who had not served in the Wehrmacht. That seemed strange and I asked about it. He responded with an expression I had come to recognize, and with a slight twinkle in his eyes, he told me that individuals with close connections to Berlin were given more "important" work to do. It meant, of course, that Kurth was assigned by the SS to monitor the attitude of the local population. It was a method used by Hitler from the beginning to keep the people in line. Spies were everywhere. If a person made the wrong remark, didn't show up for Nazi-sponsored meetings, speeches, and parades, he was put on a list and watched closely. And it was a ruthless system. People who were turned in by the network of spies disappeared, were killed in accidents, or were "promoted" to assignments in other areas, from which they never returned. To resist Hitler, and the Nazi Party, was suicide. And the system could be used by those in command to require the people to do anything. Their power over the citizens was unlimited. And so, the people had a choice of either showing an enthusiastic support for Hitler or face a tragic change. Before I learned about the "system," I wondered why there was no opposition to Hitler. After details were given to me by a number of credible Germans, I understood. Hitler was in total and complete command, and to oppose him would bring about an immediate, and deadly, response.

I learned from talking to the Chief that Kurth had operated in the background, had appeared to be a legitimate businessman. He had been set up by the Nazis as an automobile dealer and it had seemed that no one was suspicious of him. The previous owner had been "promoted" to another location and had not been heard from since Kurth took over.

While the Chief would be checking on the printing on the mirror in Leni's home, I would go on to see Kurth. I told Swartz that I would be waiting to hear from him and we separated, going in different directions to continue the work we had planned.

It was easy to locate the garage that was operated by Kurth. I had passed the building frequently and it took less than ten minutes for me to get there. I was wearing fatigues rather than a dress uniform. Under the jacket, which extended down below my waist, I had on a wide web belt, and my loaded forty five automatic was in a holster attached to the belt. Knowing that Kurth had seen me in the bar and had reported it to the killer, I felt it was wise to take a weapon. Actually, I took along two weapons.

Even though Kurth was my top priority at the moment, I kept having thoughts about LeTourneau, disturbing thoughts. From what Swartz had said, it sounded like there was a distinct possibility that LeTourneau was involved in the death of Leni. And, for the present at least, I could not imagine why.

At the garage operated by Kurth there was an ominous atmosphere about the place. My instincts told me that there would be danger inside. It was unexplainable, the warning that was brought about in my mind. I had learned, though, not to ignore it, even if it was an unidentifiable cause of concern. And very rarely were my instincts wrong.

I parked in front of the garage and got out of the Opel. The building was large, stretching some one hundred fifty feet across the side which faced the street. An office and a showroom that was no longer needed were to my left, and the doors that would open for cars to enter the garage were to my right. I could see no one, inside or out, and that added to the mystique of the place.

I walked to the door leading to the showroom and tried to open it. Not surprisingly it was locked. The showroom was visible through the glass door and I could see only the remnants of what would have been at one time a flourishing business. I stepped away from the building to get a better overall view and noticed that there was a second floor above the area where the garage was located. It occurred to me that someone was probably living in that part of the building.

The garage doors were solid and did not provide an opportunity to see beyond them into the shop. I decided that if anyone was there, they would be in the shop, so I walked to one of the large doors and pushed against it. A vibration of metal against metal caused a considerable noise as I pushed. I kept it going for about thirty seconds and stopped. After a brief pause I was ready to push again when I heard a man from the inside.

"Ein moment, bitte."

Soon the door was moving upward on rollers in a track on each side, and then, as the door was opened to the uppermost point, a man stood before me. He smiled and spoke.

"Ah, good day to you, Herr Major. I am Walter Kurth."

He extended his arm and we shook hands. I returned his smile.

"Good day to you, Herr Kurth. Tell me, have we met? You seem to know me."

"No, Major, we have not met. But all people in Bad Welmsburg know you and the other Americans who are here."

"You don't seem to be very busy today, Herr Kurth."

"Oh, yes, Major, we have been busy. It is only that we have completed our work. You see, we start early and we close early. That is why the doors were closed."

He was jovial and making an attempt to be pleasant. I stepped inside and glanced around the large shop and turned back to Kurth. I wanted to follow up on my first question.

"Possibly you saw me at the bar several nights ago."

I looked at him with a questioning stare. It caught him by surprise, although when he spoke he had recovered.

"Yes! Of course! I was there. But I don't remember that you . . . were you there too?"

I didn't answer immediately. I turned and looked over the shop, pausing for a few seconds before speaking.

"Yes, I was there. We were there at the same time," and I turned and looked hard into his eyes, "I know that you saw me."

It was only slightly disturbing to him. He would have preferred not to admit it, although he was well experienced, I felt sure, in conversational exchanges that would require quick thoughts. He looked confident as he responded.

"Yes, certainly, it was you! I can remember you. It was a little confusing in my mind. You had on a different uniform that night. Was it more of what you would call a dress uniform?"

"Yes, it was a dress uniform. Herr Kurth, did you know Leni?"

"I did know her, Major."

He didn't go beyond answering the question, didn't volunteer anything. I continued.

"Tell me all that you know about her."

I had observed him enough to form an initial impression and opinion. He was clever and quick-witted. He appeared to be fifty, about my height and medium weight. His eyes were brownish and clear, and he would be perceptive and hard to pin down. He was slightly balding, otherwise a man who would be considered handsome. He was well kept, and he obviously had suffered no hardships in recent years. His demeanor and general attitude was that of a typical well-fed Nazi type. He began talking about Leni.

"She was, you know, the friend of Rudi, the pilot. This was common knowledge among the people. I think she would have known some of the things that . . . ah . . . involved Rudi, and what he was doing."

He knew that I already knew what he was telling me, and I believe he wanted it to appear that he was being very cooperative. I answered.

"You are right, Herr Kurth, what you have just said is common knowledge. What else did you know about her? How much did Rudi tell her?"

"Ah, Major, I am not sure what you are asking about Rudi."

"Tell me what you know about Rudi."

"He was a skilled pilot in the Luftwaffe, assigned to fly important people. As we have all learned in the last few weeks some of these people who came here, flew here with Rudi . . . were . . . well, as we know, Karl Wegner was their host."

He avoided saying anything about the escape plan. I responded to his last statement.

"Yes, that is what we have all learned. Did you know Karl Wegner?"

"Yes, I knew him."

"How well did you know him? Would you say that you were good friends?"

"Hardly good friends, Major. You see, I would repair his automobiles, and in that way we would talk and we were, as one might say, casual friends. He would sometimes come in his car to have a repair done."

"And that is how you came to know him?"

"Yes."

"Were you ever in his home?"

"Sometimes . . . I would drive his car there to return it, and, I would perhaps go inside briefly."

"Did you know his wife?"

"Yes, I knew his wife." He smiled slightly. "Perhaps, though, I did not know her as well as you."

He had stepped out of line with that remark and I let him know.

"My relationship with Frau Wegner is none of your concern. I advise you to remember that, now and in the future.

For the first time I had penetrated his tough exterior. He responded quickly.

"Of course, of course, Herr Major. It was a thoughtless comment. I apologize."

My attitude changed, and I no longer smiled as I talked.

"The man Rombach, the man who killed her, how well did you know him?"

He responded immediately.

"Major, I did not know Rombach! I would have personally killed that swine because of what he did to her. He came to an end that was appropriate, hanging by his feet from a tree in the square. The people of Bad Welmsburg took good care of him, and you must believe me, it was the same with me, I felt the same as all of the other people."

He was talking about the way Rombach died. The people of the city were so incensed when he shot Ariane, they overtook him as he attempted to flee and beat him to death. Then they took his body to the public square and strung him up like a slaughtered pig. So far, Kurth had told me nothing, and it was time to go in another direction.

"What was your connection to the Nazi Party?"

He didn't flinch.

"I had no connection, Major. I was simply a businessman who was fortunate enough to be able to perform a service in the city, and I was, you might say, neutral, or not an active participant in the Party."

"Are you saying you were never a member of the Party?"

"I was never a member of the Party."

I let it go. I had already gotten too far off track with my original plan. I didn't want him to believe that I had come to question him only about his political background. He was too experienced to be confused or trapped in such a conversation. So, I returned to my original approach.

"I came today, Herr Kurth, because we might be able to use your repair service. The Opel I have here needs a few repairs. Can you handle it?"

"Of course, Herr Major. May we bring it into the shop and take a look?"

"Yes."

He walked quickly to a phone and pushed a button. There was an immediate response on the other end of the line and Kurth spoke with authority in German. He extended the conversation longer than necessary and I could sense that my position could easily become dangerous. If he should be connected to the three SS men, and if he felt that he was becoming vulnerable, he would want to eliminate me. After he finished the phone conversation he came back near me.

"Albert will come at once, Major, and we will see about your car."

"Albert is a mechanic?"

"Albert is a mechanic, a very good mechanic."

"How long has he worked here?"

He thought for a second or two before answering. He made it appear that he was attempting to recall the right date to be precise.

"Let's see, Major, I think it is now about six weeks."

"Where did he come from?"

"From the East."

I would take a good look at his papers. Many of the fake identification papers found on the Germans had come out of the Kassel American Military Government office and we were able to recognize them—they no longer fooled us.

I told Kurth I would drive the Opel into the garage and he nodded. He remained where he was and waited. I parked near him and just as I did a man appeared, coming through the doorway of the stairs that would lead to the upstairs area of the garage. Immediately when I saw him I remembered the description by Doctor Reuss of the three SS men . . . one of them had a pock-marked face. Heuber. And the man standing before me, next to Kurth, had a pock-marked face. I was certain it was Hueber.

I was still sitting in the car. On the passenger's seat I had a Thompson submachine gun. I spoke from the car, leaning slightly through the window, and addressed the man who was called Albert by Kurth.

"Let me see your papers."

He turned and spoke quietly to Kurth, who then turned and spoke to me.

"He will bring them down from upstairs, Major, one moment if you please."

Kurth walked with him over to the door leading to the stairs. There was a quiet conversation between them as they walked along. Then, the man went through the doorway and Kurth waited, standing a few feet from the door but in line with the stairs, and in a position where he could look up the stairs and see me at the same time. I reached over and pulled the Thompson in position to be sure I could take hold of it easily, and I pulled the cocking knob back so that it would be ready to fire.

Kurth was quiet. He did not ask me to get out of the car. It was as if he was waiting for Hueber to come down with a weapon. It was a dead giveaway—he might as well have told me to expect Hueber to come back ready to fight. Kurth looked uneasy, and I decided that he felt he was in imminent danger, possibly from Hueber.

I decided to show my hand. I took hold of the Thompson and got out of the car. I pointed the weapon in the direction of Kurth, and with my finger across my lips I let him know that he was to be quiet. He was, for the first time, nervous. He glanced at me and then up the stairs. I thought it was time to bring things to a head, and I yelled up the stairs.

"Hueber! Come down at once if you want to live!"

There was no response and no movements from above that I could detect. I spoke to Kurth.

"Is the man upstairs Hueber?"

He didn't speak. I moved the Thompson two or three feet to his side and fired a burst, the bullets hitting a brick wall just behind him. He had an immediate reaction, showing great anxiety, and he yelled out.

"Yes! Yes! He is Hueber."

"Tell him to come down, without a weapon, or you will both die."

He yelled up the stairway, in German, and I recognized enough of the words to know that he had done as I had asked. Still, there was no response. I spoke to Kurth again.

"Who killed Leni Schoenbrun? Was it Hueber?"

"Nein, nein, it was not Hueber! He was there, Major, but she was already . . ."

Just then a Schmeisser fired from the stairway above and I could see the bullets hitting Kurth. He fell to the floor and didn't move. I moved quickly to a tractor and stood behind the large front wheels. It would give me some protection if Hueber came down the stairs and out of the doorway.

There were no sounds from above. Hueber was trying to decide what to do next. He knew he was trapped and would have to come down the stairs to get out. I heard Kurth moan slightly, otherwise there were no sounds. I yelled up the stairway loudly enough so that Hueber could hear me from where he was standing.

"Come down Hueber! You're trapped! Other men will be here soon and we will use grenades. Your only chance to live is to come down with your hands over your head!"

Still no sounds. It meant that he would fight to the end. I looked around to find the best position I could, and I decided to move to the rear of the big tractor where the wheels were larger, and where the main body of the big vehicle would be between me and the doorway of the stairs where Hueber would have to come out.

I waited and so did he, although I knew, and he knew, that time was on my side. I felt that he would, at some point, come out shooting and run for cover. I didn't really want to kill him, I needed him for a witness to find out about Leni. So, when he did make his move, I would attempt to wound him and not make it fatal.

In a few seconds I heard squeaking on wooden steps and I knew he was coming down the stairs. And suddenly he burst through the door, firing his Schmeisser in a wide semicircle as he ran to a large metal desk to take cover. I didn't fire and he still didn't know where I was, but he was desperate, and he raised up to look over the top of the desk and saw me. He fired a short burst in my direction, hitting the heavy metal body of the tractor. I pointed the Thompson at the desk where Hueber was hiding and waited. Knowing he was trapped, and knowing his time was short, he would have to come directly at me and get by me to escape. It would be his only logical means of reasoning. And so, I planned on receiving a frontal attack by Hueber within a few seconds.

I waited and so did he. Then, as I knew he would, he raised up and ran directly toward the front of the tractor, firing as he ran. His bullets pinged against the tractor. I could have easily hit him from my position but I wanted to take him alive. He raced to the front of the tractor and crouched there, withholding his fire until he could get a view of me. I, too, was low, and I had actually more cover than he did because of the heavy frame of the tractor and the two big rear wheels. And then, on an impulse I raised up with the Thompson pointed in his direction. A moment later he stood up and for a split second we looked into each other's eyes. I had the Thompson aimed directly into his face, and as he made a motion to raise the Schmeisser, I fired. I saw blood, skin, and bones fly outward from his face. The big slugs from the submachine gun literally tore his face and head apart. He fell backward, the Schmeisser dropping out of his hands and clattering as it slid away from him on the concrete floor.

There were no other sounds coming from overhead, or the steps. I think Hueber had been upstairs alone, and if there had been others, they would have come down with him. We would, however, make a thorough search later.

I walked toward him. He was on his back, motionless, with his face upward toward the ceiling. Except, of course, there was no face left. He was without doubt, dead and beyond any help.

I walked over to Kurth who was still alive. He was lying on his right side, moaning, and I turned him over and placed him lengthwise on his back. I took my jacket off and rolled it up and put it under his head. I had seen men in his condition before and I knew it was only a matter of a few minutes before he would be gone. He could, however, still talk, and he made an effort to say something to me, gasping and wheezing as he labored with his words.

"Major . . . I did not . . . they came, and I had no choice . . . ," he paused and tried to get a better supply of air in his lungs, then continued, "They were to kill everyone . . . it was to protect the . . . but, Hueber . . . did not kill her . . ." and he began to fade into his final moments, "it was, it was . . . " and then he closed his eyes and was gone.

Soon I heard a jeep and a few seconds later it was at the doorway to the garage. Jim Polofski and Virgil jumped out, both with Thompson machine guns. They saw me and ran in my direction. Jim yelled out.

"Are you okay, sir?"

"Yeah, I'm okay, Jim. How did you guys know about it?"

"A civilian called it in . . . said there was gunfire in the garage, and we knew you were coming here."

"I appreciate your quick reaction, both of you. I'm not sure anyone else is in the building and we will have to check the upstairs. Both men here are dead."

They took time to look at Hueber and Kurth. Virgil spoke.

"Who are these guys, Major?"

"The one with his face gone is Hueber, one of the three SS men we wanted. The other one is Kurth, the man who operated the garage."

Polofski asked a question.

"What happened, sir?"

"I came to see Kurth. Hueber was upstairs and when Kurth identified him, he shot Kurth. He waited a while and came downstairs—he had fired on Kurth from the top of the stairs—and he wanted to shoot it out with me."

Polofski, who had walked to where Hueber was lying and was standing over him, commented.

"Well, sir, I would say that he came out second best."

I felt no joy over killing Hueber and I let Jim know.

"I didn't want to kill him, it just ended up that way. He knew details about the death of Leni and I wanted him alive. But I just couldn't manage it."

"I understand, sir." And after a reflective pause, Jim continued. "Considering all we have heard about him I think the world will be better off without him."

I agreed, and then we talked about the upstairs and the fact that it would have to be searched. We moved cautiously to the stairway and went up together. After a careful look we found no one, and it was as I had thought—Hueber had been there alone.

Soon Chief Swartz arrived, as did one of his men in a separate car. They were also reacting quickly, as had Jim and Virgil. I explained everything to the Chief and he said he would take over, see that the two bodies were removed. He told me he would padlock the garage and see that it was kept closed for a few days.

I left the scene and went back to our offices. I asked Glenn Newton if any messages had been received from LeTourneau. He said there were none. I asked another question.

"Glenn, did you issue an order for him before he left?"

"Yes, sir."

"What destination did you put on the order?"

"The Military Government office in Hannover."

"Okay, get in touch with them and see if LeTourneau is there. If he is, have him contact me at once."

"Yes, sir."

Next, I would have to think of a way to concentrate on Heidi. I think she must have known everything. The details of the escape plan, the activities of the three SS men, the person responsible for the death of Leni, and possibly the location of the other two SS men, Stelling and Augenberg. I thought about bringing her in, arresting her. But, the two men I could have used as witnesses, Kurth and Hueber, were dead. The only thing I could hope to do was scare the hell out of her, and knowing her type, I was not sure I could do that.

I drove home, took a shower and changed clothes. All the while I was thinking of Heidi, and finally, I realized it was time to lay out all of the cards and be direct, I would plan to go to her home immediately and question her forcefully.

I called her. It was eight-fifteen in the evening. She sounded slightly different, and it was obvious that she knew about all that had happened during the day. I told her I wanted to come to her home to talk.

"When, Herr Major?"

"Now. I can be there in fifteen minutes."

"Yes . . . I . . . all right, I will be here."

I could imagine that she was not eager to see me—it was easy to sense it in her tone. She knew, however, that she was in trouble, deeply involved in serious matters, and she could easily guess that I knew much about her.

When she opened the door to let me in at her home, Heidi managed a wide smile. She had prepared herself to talk to me, perhaps tell a slanted story. And she would, I was quite sure, attempt once again at some point to use her physical appeal to try to persuade me. And it struck me as strange, how women would do that, believing that they could overcome problems with men in that way. Maybe in most cases it worked.

She escorted me to the living room and we were there alone, as I had expected we would be. She smiled at me again.

"Major, please, be seated. May I offered you something?"

"No thanks, Heidi. I have to talk to you concerning serious matters this evening. I believe you know the reason."

"Well, Major, I can tell you that I am like everyone else in Bad Welmsburg this evening. We heard what happened at the garage, but I am not certain how I am involved."

"I'll explain that to you. But first, I want to emphasize that it is important to tell me the truth, and I want answers to all of my questions."

I could tell by her expression that she realized I knew about her background. It seemed to change her attitude and she was a little more solemn. When she spoke it was with less confidence, and she apparently had made a decision.

"Major, if you will, please let me give you some information that will take a minute or so, and then I will answer your questions."

"Okay."

"When I was sixteen Herr Kurth came to Bad Welmsburg. He saw me one day walking on the street. He was passing in his car. Believe it or not, he stopped and came over to me and started talking. I knew who he was, everyone did, and he was well respected, and I could not be rude, and, in fact, I felt that I had to be friendly." She paused, thinking, and I asked a question.

"What did he want?"

"He . . . when I was sixteen, many men spoke to me and asked me for dates. My body was well developed, and I think I must have appeared to be twenty, twenty-five. He wanted the same thing that all men wanted from me . . . except . . . I knew him to be powerful, and I knew that I could not refuse him, and that day, I got in his car and we drove to a place where we were together."

"You had sex with him?"

"Yes. And then it was all the time. He would come and get me or send for me. It was so often I spent a great deal of time in his home. I heard many conversations that he had on the phone, sometimes as we were lying in bed. And there were times when important men would come from Berlin, or other places, and I knew about many things that others did not know. It was mostly about the people here in Bad Welmsburg. And, strangely enough, he . . . it was almost as if he wanted me to know, it was, I suppose, like I was his possession, almost like a wife. Then, after the invasion of Normandy, he began to change and he no longer wanted me as much, or it was like he was always thinking of other things. And it was during that time that he became worried about the future, and he made attempts to talk to the important men who would come to see Karl Wegner. He learned that some men were planning an escape and he wanted to become a part of it. He made me do things for these men, men who came to see Karl Wegner who were very powerful. He found out who they were and when they were here he used me, and even though he did this I do not think they included him in their plans."

She paused, then continued.

"On one occasion there were four men in his home. They had come from the hunting lodge on the Wegner estate. I don't know their names, except I know they were powerful men. They were drinking and talked freely at times. Walter . . . Herr Kurth . . . told me to come into the living room where they were, and he told me to undress, take off all of my clothes. And so, I had to do that, in front of them, and then . . . he told me . . . I had to . . ."

"Okay, Heidi, you don't need to describe that. Tell me about the escape plan, what did you hear, and who was involved?"

"Actually, I heard nothing specific that was important. They might say, 'When we go' and so forth . . . and once I heard a remark about the total number of men who would go and it was seven, which is the same number that everyone heard later, and so it means there were no others."

"Are you sure?"

"Yes. Walter knew the names later—he found out from the SS. There were no others, your men knew about all of them."

It was becoming painful for her and she made a pleading request.

"I don't want to be arrested. Please Max, promise me that . . . I'll tell you everything I know . . . I'll do anything for you . . . but, I don't want to go to jail."

"Heidi, I have to know everything before I make promises. Just be sure you tell me the truth."

She was encouraged and answered enthusiastically.

"Yes, okay, I will do that. Now, what do you wish to know?"

"Who killed Leni?"

"Major, you must believe me, I do not really know. The night she was killed Kurth and Hueber came here and said it was to be done. I begged them not to do it. She had been my lifelong friend, but they said she knew too much, and after she was seen dancing with you and drinking the wine, they felt she would talk. They waited here for another man who came at approximately four in the morning. He didn't come in and I did not see him. When there was a knock on the door Hueber said, 'That's Planet. Let's go,' and Hueber was to go with Planet, Kurth was to go home. And so, I don't know if it was Hueber or Planet. And, of course, it could have been Stelling or Augenberg."

"Do you know anything about Planet?"

"No. I was told nothing. He operates in a top secret way. But, Hueber did say one thing about him . . . he said, 'he is the top man in Germany,' and I think that he meant that Planet would go to the most important assignment that was still to be done."

I thought about Kurth and what he had said only moments before dying—"Hueber didn't do it." That would mean someone else was the killer. Possibly Stelling or Augenberg. I spoke to Heidi again.

"Can you think of anything else about Planet? Where he came from, where he was to go?"

"No. As I said, they were very careful not to talk about him."

"Rudi brought someone important here on April 30. Did he tell Leni who it was?"

"No. And yes, it was someone important because it was the only thing he never told Leni. At least, from what we have learned in the last few weeks he told her everything else."

"Do you have any thoughts on who it was? Could it have been Bormann?"

"No, I don't believe it was Bormann. During this whole time I have not heard his name mentioned and he is almost like a forgotten man."

"Could it have been the man called Planet?"

"Yes. . . . I suppose . . . but I don't think so, I don't think he was that important. The man who came with Rudi on April 30 would have been almost like Hitler, he was that important."

"You said the men who came from Wegner's lodge to visit Kurth talked freely. What did you mean by that?"

"They talked about women, their wives in a disgusting way, the places they had been in the past. Nothing about the escape plan or anyone in the hunting lodge."

"The other two SS men, Stelling and Augenberg. Where are they?"

"I don't know. I don't believe anyone knows. They may already be in another city. They too, operated in a very secretive fashion."

"Hueber must have been staying on the second floor of Kurth's garage. Do you think the other two might have been there at one time?"

"Yes, I think that is possible."

"Did you ever see them?"

"No. Walter didn't want me to see them, he didn't want anyone to see them."

"Do you think it is possible that Augenberg went to Fulda?"

She hesitated before answering.

"Maybe."

"Why?"

"Because he is not sure that Ariane is dead. And he believes that she knows the details of the escape plan."

"What do you think?"

"At first, I thought there might be a possibility that she was alive. But then, when you went to England, I thought, 'he would not do that, he would stay close by,' and so, I feel that she is actually dead. And I am sure that she would not know the details of the escape plan anyway."

"How do you know that?"

"Because if she had known, you, too, would have known."

I smiled at her for the first time. She returned the smile, and I could see that she was feeling better, not as anxious. I was beginning to believe that she was telling me the truth. What she was saying was making sense. Augenberg probably was in Fulda, and Stelling could be anywhere. I turned back to Heidi with a pleasant expression. I needed a few more answers before making a final decision about her.

"Did you talk to Kurth after Leni was killed?"

"No! He gave me strict orders. He told me not to call and he said he would not come for a while."

"You left his name off of the list you gave me of the people who were in the bar the night Leni was killed. Why?"

"Because he told me not to mention him or give his name to anyone, the Americans, or the German Police. He said, 'you can very easily end up like her if you do not follow my instructions', and it was disturbing . . . I was quite fearful."

"So, if you have not talked to Kurth, he was not able to describe Planet to you?"

"That is correct, Major. And I did not talk to Hueber. They would not have described Planet anyway, they fear him too much, or, perhaps I should say at this time, they feared him while they were alive."

"Is Planet a real name or a nickname?"

"Oh, I am sure it is a nickname."

For a short period, maybe ten or fifteen seconds, I was silent before speaking.

"I'm not going to take you in, Heidi. You had a close call. You were mixed up with some real bad characters, but I think it was because of the circumstances—I think you were drawn into it."

She stared with an appreciative expression, and spoke.

"Thank you, Max. I hope you will let me repay you."

"I will."

And I smiled again. She was joyful as she spoke.

"You will? When? Right now?"

"Yes, but not in the way you are thinking about. I want you to help me. I think this man, Planet, or one of the two others, Stelling and Augenberg, will come back, and I think they will use you as their focal point. I want you to help me catch them."

"Okay . . . but I'm really disappointed."

And she smiled widely again. "It won't be nearly as much fun trying to catch somebody."

"I know. But you're quite a beautiful young lady, Heidi, and I'm sure there are plenty of young men who would be happy to spend the night with you."

"Major . . . I've always had a . . . you appeal to me more than other men, Max. If you ever change your mind, I'll be waiting."

"Thanks, that's a nice offer and I'll remember it. But, back to business. You will have to be careful. These men are ruthless. They will eliminate anyone who knows too much, and they know you were Leni's friend. They may believe that you are a danger to them because of Leni. If you ever need me, call me at any time."

The key to getting Stelling, Augenberg, and Planet would now seem to rest with Heidi. The problem would be, keeping her alive. I would have to give it some thought and come up with a plan. I could possibly hide her, although they would have to be drawn to her for me to find them. I would keep thinking about it and hope that nothing happened to her in the meantime. But she seemed completely oblivious to her dangerous position and she only wanted to continue to have romantic thoughts.

She had a very devilish grin on her face.

"How about if I call you around three in the morning—will you come running to save me?"

I grinned back.

"Yes, I'll come running and save you."

"Good. Then you will have to spend the rest of the night with me to protect me."

We exchanged further smiles. In thinking about her, and her experiences with men, being introduced to sex at an age no more than sixteen by a man who was using her, I could understand that she would be drawn to someone she could trust, someone who did not plan to take advantage of her. Nonetheless, there would be countless stories like the one of Heidi in Europe. It had been a time when conquering armies would overrun the land of their enemies and rape would be as common as the rising sun. Even the power-structured governments like the one in Germany would bring about a drastic change in sexual behavior. I had heard that young men in Wehrmacht uniforms had almost complete freedom in picking young women as sexual partners. There were no rules or regulations to protect the women, at least none that would be enforced. To imagine that a young woman in Germany during the Hitler years would be a virgin beyond the age of fifteen or sixteen would be, most likely, completely unreal.

I thought of another question for Heidi.

"When Planet came, did you hear a car?"

"No. I think he would have parked away from here so that he could not be seen in a car or near a car."

"How about Hueber and Kurth?"

"They came in Walter's car. But he was here almost daily and no one would think it was unusual."

"Try to think for a moment, Heidi, and tell me anything you can remember about Stelling and Augenberg."

"There is nothing more because I knew very little about them. Why is it so important for you to get them? There must be thousands of other SS men who are still free."

"It's important because it was imperative for them to be here. Now that the escape plan has been carried out and is all over, why would they still be so concerned about concealing the details? We know nearly all of the details and a lot of time has already gone by. It has to be, I think, because of the person who was so important who came with Rudi from Berlin on April 30. They still want to protect that person. Who could it be?"

"You mentioned Bormann . . . I suppose he is the only high-ranking person who is still missing."

"Even if it was Bormann, I don't believe he was that important. In fact, I think the only person who would have been that important would have been Hitler."

"But he was found, his body, in the bunker by the Russians. It would be ridiculous to think it could have been Hitler."

"Yeah, I know. I just don't understand why Planet, the so-called top man in Germany, would be told to come here to eliminate people a long time after something is over and done with. Can you tell me why?"

"No, I can't. Is there any possibility at all that it could have been Hitler?"

"I don't know. The Russians are very secretive. They would, naturally, for the benefit of the world, want to report that Hitler was dead, which they did. As you said, there are thousands of German men who are free who would be considered dangerous, and, there is not a big effort to conceal them. It's too bad all of the key players are dead. Rudi, for instance. Whomever it was who came from Berlin with Rudi is the person who is creating all of the excitement, but Rudi is no longer here and can't tell us anything."

"That's right. But Max, are you forgetting what was happening? People were being killed like roaches. It was nothing for people to kill each other. Russian soldiers, German soldiers, all of the soldiers, the Gestapo and the SS, there was no end to it. After months and years of killing people, what difference did it make?"

"None."

I had extended the conversation with Heidi because I knew her feelings and instincts would most likely provide me with thoughts I would not have had otherwise. She would be a good contact for me if she could stay alive.

"Okay now, here is something important. Remember what you just said. Planet doesn't know what Kurth told you and he may come back for you. Is your house secure, or could someone get in?"

"Oh, they could get in. And I think a man who is so good at killing would not have to get in anyway. He could do it some other place."

"You don't have a weapon, do you?"

"No."

I was tempted to give her a pistol. It would violate our rules, however, and it would send her to jail if she was caught with it. So, I couldn't risk it, although I was certain they would come for her. She was reading my mind and she smiled.

"See, you will have to move in to protect me because you need me. Do you want to begin tonight, Max?"

"Heidi, get your mind off of sex for a change. We've got a serious problem here to think about."

She was enjoying herself. She was a spirited young woman and like many others she ignored the dangers I was trying to point out.

It was time for me to go. I advised her to be very careful, warning her to stay alert at all times. I knew, though, that she wouldn't have a chance with a man like Planet. And I would not be in a position to protect her. Then, a thought occurred to me that I had somehow ignored. Was it possible that LeTourneau could be Planet? It had to be a thought that was far-fetched and unrealistic, but I would look into it as quickly as possible. In the meantime, I would try to stay in touch with Heidi as often as I could manage.

I stood and told her I would leave. She walked with me to the door. There, she looked at me with a tenderness that I had not seen in many women. She spoke.

"Max, will you hold me and kiss me?"

"Heidi . . . ."

She put her hands on my shoulders in a tentative motion. When I did not move she reached around my neck with both arms and held me tightly, and she then kissed me fully on the lips. She pushed her body against me and held on for a long time. Finally, she backed away, smiled sweetly, and we each said "goodnight."

5.

THE NEXT MORNING I had a quick breakfast and went directly to our offices. Glenn Newton was there and I talked to him.

"Anything from Military Government in Hannover?"

"No, sir. They haven't responded."

"Where did you find quarters for LeTourneau?"

"That house near the lake, the one just evacuated by the displaced persons."

"Oh yeah, I know the place. Glenn, were you here in the office when LeTourneau arrived?"

"Yes, sir."

"Did he come in a jeep?"

"He did. And there was an enlisted man with him, an odd looking character."

"How so?"

"He had long hair, not like a GI. And his uniform didn't fit him very well. He brought in two bags and a trunk for Captain LeTourneau, got back in the jeep, and left without speaking a word."

"Yeah, that does seem odd. Did LeTourneau comment?"

"He said the guy was anxious to get started back to Division."

"Do you have a key to LeTourneau's house?"

"I have a key to all the houses, Major."

"Okay, we're going over there later in the morning. First I want to make a phone call and possibly run an errand. Let's plan to go to LeTourneau's house in about two hours."

"I'll be ready, sir." He looked a little puzzled, which was to be expected. I had no intention of accusing LeTourneau of anything, however, and I certainly did not want anyone to alert him that I might be suspicious of him.

I called Frau Erhlich and told her I would like to come by within the hour. She said it would be fine. Our conversation on the phone was brief and Ariane's name was not mentioned. It was early and back in the States it might have been an imposition to visit that early, but not for the Germans. They were up early each day and by nine A.M. they were fully organized and hard at work.

Next, from my office, I called Chief Swartz and told him that I would like to meet Strassel, the man who had seen a large man walking on the street at approximately five A.M. the night Leni was killed. The Chief said he would arrange to pick up Strassel on a street in an area near his home when it would not be conspicuous. I told Swartz where I was going, to the Wegner mansion, and he suggested a rendezvous on the Wegner estate. We could each drive a short distance from the main road on the private driveway and meet in a location that would be out of sight from the mansion, as well as the public highway. And so, we were set.

I arrived on the Wegner estate just before the Chief, and I was out of my jeep, waiting, as he drove up. When he stopped near my jeep, I motioned that he and Strassel were to remain in his car. Even though no one else was present, it would offer more safety for Strassel.

After greeting Chief Swartz from outside on the driver's side of the car, I reached across and shook hands with Strassel. Immediately I thanked him for coming and he nodded.

He was a man perhaps in his early seventies. I noticed he did not wear glasses. I began my conversation with him.

"Chief Swartz tells me you saw a man walking on the street near your home early in the morning of the same night Leni Schoenbrun was killed. Is that correct?"

The Chief had to translate. The answer came back "yes" and I continued.

"Will you please describe the man as best you can . . . his size, his clothing, everything you can remember?"

He talked at length to Swartz. It was, I learned from the Chief, almost the same information that we had already been given, including the fact that a cap was pulled down low over the man's face. I asked him to describe the cap, which he did, and it sounded like one of the knit-type caps worn by GIs under their helmets during cold weather. I asked if the man was in a rush and the answer was "no." Strassel also volunteered a description of the clothing on the man and it was, without a doubt, an American fatigue outfit, the same as was originally reported.

Strassel seemed very positive in his comments and was responding convincingly. In summary, the description of what he saw was that of a white male, large, possibly six-five and two-hundred forty pounds. He could not see the face well. The man had nothing in his hands, and he walked as would a man perhaps thirty years old. Shortly after he vanished from view, Strassel heard a jeep start and leave the area. I asked Strassel why he was up at five A.M. and he responded, through Swartz, "I am always up at five A.M." I smiled at him and he smiled in return. I said, "If you saw this man, face to face, could you identify him?" The answer, after a lengthy statement to Swartz, was, "No, I do not believe I could identify him by looking into his face. On the other hand, if I saw him walking, wearing the same clothes, walking at the same place, I believe it would be possible. He had a smooth and even gait, like that of a person who is physically well fit."

I wanted to check one final thing. My jeep was approximately forty feet away, and on the rear bumper there were five numbers, printed in a small size, white numbers that were used by the army to identify the vehicle. I could hardly make them out from where I was standing, and, if I had not known the numbers anyway, I might not have been able to read them. I asked Strassel if he would be kind enough to read the numbers to me. He looked, and the numbers rolled out easily from him, all correct. I smiled and said, "Very good!" I thanked him again for coming, and then I asked the Chief to return him to an area near his home.

I watched them move away and reflected on our conversation. A picture of LeTourneau kept popping into my mind . . . a man six-five and two hundred forty pounds wearing a fatigue outfit and in an American jeep. It had to make him a suspect, regardless of how ridiculous it might seem.

Ten minutes later I was standing in the doorway of the Wegner mansion talking to Frau Erhlich. I asked immediately if she had heard from Ariane or her son, Rolfe. She said she had not and I asked her opinion of what it would mean.

"I think, perhaps, Rolfe is concerned for some reason. Even though he has taken her to another city, I believe they are in danger. And so many people are left, Germans, who would turn against them, I am sure he cannot trust anyone. A telephone call, one that might be intercepted, could put an end to everything for them, and I know he will not call until it is safe."

It was disappointing and frustrating. There were, as she said, people left among the Germans who would turn them in to the SS, people who were frustrated with losing the war, angry at each other and the rest of the world, people living in misery who would welcome a chance to put someone else in misery, and many other various reasons. The only thing we could do would be to wait, and I told her.

"Yes, Herr Major, we must wait. I will contact you immediately if I hear from Rolfe."

"Thank you, Frau Ehrlich." Then, I spoke to her about the one question that was still bothersome to me.

"Frau Ehrlich, the escape has been accomplished—it is over and the men are gone. We've even heard that it most likely failed. The ship that was to take them to South America sank in the English Channel. Why would it still be so important to the SS to kill everyone who might have known about it?"

"Herr Major, that is, indeed, a question that is very difficult to answer. I think there may be some hatred and resentment involved, but it is too much, I cannot believe that such a mission would be carried on for that reason for so long a time."

"Someone was with the group of men who was very important. Can you guess who it might have been?"

"No, I cannot. If it was someone very important I think they might have been concerned about keeping the destination secret. And even if that is true, we have heard that the ship sank, and unless they were picked up by another ship, it would not matter about the destination. No, I cannot imagine why it is so important to these terrible men."

"Could something else be involved, something we have not considered? Can you think of anything Ariane might have said, even long ago, that might help us?"

"Nothing, Major. I am as puzzled as you."

There was no need to extend the conversation and I asked her to call if she heard anything. She said that she would, we shook hands, and I left.

I drove back to the office and picked up Newton. It took fifteen minutes to reach the house where LeTourneau was billeted.

I searched the house thoroughly, even going through LeTourneau's personal belongings. At one point Glenn stared at me and I felt I should give him at least a partial reason for carrying out the search.

"Glenn, I have a reason to be doing this but I can't discuss it, okay?"

"Sure, Major, I understand."

"And we have to keep it secret, don't mention it to anyone."

"All right, I'll do as you say, Major. I've come a long way with you, sir, and I don't have any reason to doubt you now."

"Thanks, Glenn."

There was nothing in the house to help me. If he had fatigues or a cap, he had disposed of them. Newton and I rearranged everything so that it looked the same as when we had arrived, and we left. I dropped Glenn off at the office and went home.

My phone ran at eight-forty-five P.M. It was Chief Swartz.

"Major, I regret it is necessary to call this late. Please forgive me."

"No problem, Chief. What have you got?"

"A man who is at the hospital. A Russian. He is very near death. He was shot some time ago and was cared for by a German farm family. It was obvious that he was getting worse but he would not agree to let them bring him to a doctor. Now, he is in the hospital, and they have waited too long, and he will soon die."

"It's regrettable . . . but how is this a matter for me to become involved . . . is there more to the story?"

"Yes. He was working on the Wegner estate. Karl Wegner was using him and three other Russians to handle large wooden crates. They were being placed in a location on the Wegner estate. While he was working on the last occasion, after the crates had been put in place, Wegner shot them all. The other three men were killed and Wegner thought the fourth man . . . the one who is now dying . . . was killed as well. But, he survived, and he was able to get to a farmhouse not too far away, and the people helped him. He was very fearful and would not tell them where he had come from, and he would not agree for them to tell anyone that he was there. He was afraid that Wegner would return and kill him."

"When did this happen?"

"Just before Wegner, himself, was killed."

"I see. I'm sorry about the Russian man, Chief, but I still don't understand how I would be involved. Does the man know that he is no longer in danger from Wegner?"

"Yes. It is something else. He says he has information that he will only give to you. He does not trust anyone else."

"How does he know me, or about me?"

"Because he worked on the Wegner farm, and . . ."

"Yes?"

"I think he must have known that you came there."

"Okay, I'll come at once. Are you at the hospital?"

"I will meet you there. I will be at the entrance."

Twenty minutes later I parked in front of the hospital and walked to the entrance where Swartz was standing. We shook hands without speaking and he turned to lead the way inside.

We walked along a corridor for a short distance and entered a large room. There were many patients in the room, lying on cots pushed closely together. The room was packed and I realized for the first time about the shortage of bed space and treatment facilities that were available to the people.

I walked behind Swartz to the far end of the room. The Chief turned once and spoke.

"He has been placed at the end of the room because he is dying."

Apparently it would be easy to remove him from that point and the others in the room would not be affected as much by his death. As we came near to the man I could see that there was a German doctor standing over him and he was being assisted by two nurses. The doctor turned to us and spoke.

"He has been asking for the Major. He is hanging on, just barely, and I am not sure he can speak. Major, if you plan to speak to him you must do so quickly."

The man, about forty-five, was still breathing, although he was trying to draw in air laboriously, and it was obvious that he was within the throes of death. The doctor leaned over close to his face and said, in German, "Here is the Major."

The man had an amazing reaction. He opened his eyes widely and looked at me and he was both relieved and gratified.

I leaned over very close to his face. My ear was less than an inch from his lips. He spoke in a low whisper, and actually, I could only barely make out what he said.

"Geld . . . sehr Geld . . ."

"Money? Gold? Where? Wo?"

"Millions . . . millions . . . yes, gold bars. . . ." He had used three words in English, possibly he had learned them to be able to tell me. I asked him again how to find it.

"Wo?"

"A cave . . .", and he paused, struggling to breathe, then he continued, "hundred million Marks . . . or more . . . Wegner . . ." He was speaking English again and I knew he had been helped by someone, awaiting the moment, or time, when he would be able to talk to me. Now he was gasping, and struggling, and I believed it was to be his last words.

And I was right. He was finished. He had spoken so quietly I was certain that none of the others nearby had heard him. The doctor leaned over and put a stethoscope on his chest, leaving it for ten or fifteen seconds. He then shook his head. The man was gone.

Gold. Millions of dollars in gold. There had been a rumor, coming from some distant place, that there was a large cache of gold hidden by the Nazis. It was like a hundred other rumors and landed on us with no particular interest. We had no reason to think that it would be near us. Now, in thinking about it, I decided that it would make sense that such a treasure would be connected to Wegner. All of the other important activities were somehow tied to him, and he had been shielding some of the most important men left in the Third Reich.

The nurses pulled a sheet over the man and prepared to remove him. The doctor, seeing death almost daily, looked at me and Chief Swartz, said "good evening," and turned and walked away. The Chief and I also walked away.

On the outside I asked the Chief about the family who had cared for the Russian man who had just died.

"Major, believe it or not, they are gone. They had become quite fearful. They had learned something from the man, not a lot, just enough to make them desperately afraid of the SS. Their nephew is taking care of the farm and even he was not told where they would go. I have talked to their nephew and he believes they are somewhere south of Munich but it is only a guess, and I believe him when he says that he does not know where to find them."

"I see. The Russian man made a statement to me that was related to a fear of the SS . . . I know that you were unable to hear him . . . and so that goes with what you have learned from the nephew. I think we can consider it a closed matter."

I wanted to close out the conversation as quickly as possible. I had many new things to consider, and I needed time—time alone to have a chance to think clearly.

He nodded and accepted what I had said without further questions. He was not convinced that I had told him the whole story, that was obvious, and I knew him to be too wise to think otherwise. I also knew him to be a man who would not pursue a subject with me at the wrong time, or under the wrong circumstances. And I respected him for that.

During the ride back home I realized for the first time what was really happening in Bad Welmsburg. The SS had completed their work involved with the escape plan long ago. Now, they were concerned about the gold. Wegner, even if he had tried, was unable to keep the gold a secret from the highest-ranking members of the SS. It was because there would have been millions of Marks involved, possibly as much as a hundred million dollars, and it would be top priority, a key prize for any and all people who knew about it or even suspected the existence of such a tremendous amount of money. And it explained about Ariane, why she was so important to them. They must have felt assured that she knew the location of the gold, or some hint as to where it might be, although anyone who knew Wegner would know that he would not tell her any specific details. And, actually, I was convinced that he would not even tell her about the existence of the gold. Poor Leni, killed without a doubt because of her relationship with Rudi, and the possibility that Rudi somehow would have known about the gold.

My mind was flooded with questions. Such a huge amount of gold could attract people from all directions . . . even the U.S. Could LeTourneau know about the gold, and could others in the U.S. Army know? If LeTourneau did, in fact, kill Leni, he would have done so because of the gold and not the escape plan as I had first imagined. He could be a plant in the U.S. Army from years back. We knew it had been done. The Germans, in the late thirties, very carefully picked a selected number of men who were first-generation descendants of German families who were living in the U.S. They were citizens of the U.S. and subject to the draft when the war began. A few were caught, both at home and abroad. It became a difficult task for our intelligence units, and it was impossible to know, or be certain, about the total number involved. After arriving in Germany with the U.S. Army, as soldiers, they would be in a good position to work for the Germans, or even become double agents. It would be conceivable, of course, that a soldier in such a position could become "the top man in Germany," as the man Planet had been called.

How did Wegner accumulate the gold? It must have been through the men who escaped. Did they trust him to bring the gold to South America at some future time? It would have been impossible to move it during the time of the escape. There was too much weight, and it would have been too difficult to handle. Their first priority would have been the escape to South America, and then, possibly it would have been the responsibility of Wegner to move the gold at a later time. The only flaw in that theory was the death of Wegner. And yet, the escape plan could have been in progress at the time he was killed and there would have been no opportunity to change the plan. The gold would have been kept highly secret, although I had never known of a case involving a large sum of money that was successfully concealed. And a hundred million dollars was unheard of—I had no knowledge of anything even close to it. One million dollars back in the U.S. would have been considered a ton of money, and only the very wealthy people would have had such an amount. At the end of the thirties in the U.S. I would guess that less than five hundred people would have had a million dollars.

Now, with a completely new set of circumstances in progress, my thinking would have to change. Should I continue to work alone, or should I call in the U.S. Army? Greed and the scramble for a huge amount of money could change people and trust would become a huge gamble, a very big risk. I would be facing the greatest challenge of my life in dealing with it. I could go to Division Headquarters and tell the Commanding General about the gold . . . but . . . I had the feeling, because of LeTourneau, that the Division Commander might already know about the gold.

At home I was up late, thinking about Ariane, the gold, everything. I was having a very difficult time. The phone rang at twelve-thirty-five A.M. It was Frau Erhlich, and she was quite upset, almost in a panic as she yelled into the phone.

"They have her, Major, they have her!"

"Who? Do you mean Ariane?"

"Yes! They have Ariane!"

"How do you know?"

"They called . . . a man called and said, "Listen," and then Ariane spoke to me."

"What did she say?"

"It is me, Auntie."

"What happened next?"

"The man came back on and said, 'tell the Major,' and that was all."

"He hung up?"

"Yes."

"This sounds bad, Frau Erhlich. They have us in a . . . we will have to do whatever they ask. I don't think they will harm Ariane—they will use her to bargain for something. We will hear from them again, soon, I am quite sure of that, I just don't know what can be done in the meantime. If they call you, be sure you speak to Ariane each time and we will know she is safe."

"It seems you could do something, Major."

"I'll try to think of everything possible, Frau Erhlich. If they were going to harm Ariane they would not have called, they would have done it already. No, I think they want something and will use Ariane to get it. So, let's be hopeful and believe that they will call again soon. And I believe Rolfe will be safe too, for the same reason."

"All right, Herr Major, I will follow your instructions, and when I receive a call I will let you know at once."

"Very good."

I wanted to get her off of the line as quickly as possible without telling her anymore than was necessary. After hanging up the telephone I ran to my jeep and drove to the office of the main telephone exchange. All long distance calls were put through manually and no automated system was used. Inside the office I found two people, two women. One was working at a switchboard, the other was sitting nearby. I asked a question, looking alternately at both of them.

"There was a long distance call, about thirty minutes ago, to the residence of Karl Wegner. Which of you handled that call?"

The woman at the switchboard answered.

"I did sir."

"Where did the call come from?"

"Frankenberg Eder."

"You are sure? How can you be sure?"

"Because that is the way it works, sir. A call comes in and the operator states, 'Here is a call from Frankenberg Eder. Connect to Karl Wegner,' and that is the way the call was received."

"What time did the call come in?"

She looked at a document, a log, and responded.

"At twenty four hundred hours, plus twenty nine minutes, sir."

"Did you hear any part of the discussion, any voices?"

"No sir, only the operator from Frankenberg Eder."

"I am Major Gordon. There is a serious matter involved here and I am requesting your assistance by following my instructions. Do you understand?

"Yes, Herr Major."

I continued.

"Call back, at once, to Frankenberg Eder and ask the source of the call that was made. Or better, ask the operator if she can speak English and I will talk to her."

"Yes, sir."

She immediately went through the process I had requested, spoke briefly to someone in German, and turned to me.

"Sir, if you will pick up that telephone," and she pointed to a phone on a desk nearby, "I will connect you with the operator."

I did as she suggested and said 'hello.' A female voice answered, saying, 'yes, bitte.' I spoke again.

"This is Major Gordon with the U.S. Army in Bad Welmsburg. I am calling about a very serious matter and I am requesting your assistance. Is that clear?"

"Yes, sir."

"A call was placed at twenty four hundred hours, plus twenty nine minutes from Frankenberg Eder to Bad Welmsburg. Did you handle that call?"

"Yes, sir."

"Where did the call originate?"

"From the Romantic Inn here in the city."

"Was it placed from a room at the Inn, or from the office?"

"Sir, the call was placed by the desk manager for someone in a room. When the person in the room was on the line I heard nothing further."

"How do you know the call was placed in that manner?"

"Because I could hear two men, the desk manager and a second man. I assumed the second man was placing the call from the room because of his instructions to the desk manager."

"And both were speaking in German?"

"Yes, sir."

"And the German accent that you heard, it sounded like a true German?"

"Yes, it was a German man, I am sure of that."

"All right, call back to the Romantic Inn and get the desk manager on the line for me."

"I can do that, Major, but I must call you on a different line. Is that all right, sir?"

"It is all right if there are no mistakes. Call back as quickly as possible. I will wait five minutes, no longer."

"I will do it at once, sir."

In about three minutes a call came in and the operator at the switchboard turned and nodded to me. I picked up the telephone on the desk and said, "Hello."

"Ah, yes, Major Gordon, I am Kurt, the desk manager at the Romantic Inn. How can I help you, sir?"

"You placed a call for a man there about an hour ago to the home of Karl Wegner in Bad Welmsburg. Who was the man?"

"He gave me the name of Herman Grote."

"Did he have a room at the Inn?"

"Yes, he had a room."

"Who was with him?"

"No one that I saw, sir."

"What did he look like? Give me your very best description of him."

"He was German, blonde hair and blue eyes. He was about six feet in height and one hundred eighty pounds. He was, perhaps, forty-five years old."

Augenberg. It fit the description I had gotten from both Doctor Reuss and Braun. I was sure it was him. I spoke again.

"Okay, listen carefully. I want you to carry out some important instructions. Put the telephone down and leave the line open. Go to the room where the man is located. You can take a tray with a bottle of beer and a glass. Knock on the door and see if he is there. If there is no answer, use your master key to go inside. If he questions you, you can say you have the wrong room. I want you to be absolutely sure if he is there or not. Come back to the phone and tell me and I will tell you what to do next. And, do not make a mistake. I must know if he is there. Are you clear on that?"

"Yes, sir, I understand. I will go at once."

I waited. Five minutes. Ten minutes. Twelve minutes, and I was beginning to think of trying some alternative action. I could alert the American Military Government, which I would do at some point anyway, but I felt I would be wasting precious time, and it would be best to locate Augenberg first if at all possible.

Finally, Kurt was back and picked up the phone on his end.

"Herr Major?"

"Yes, Kurt, what did you find?"

"Sir, he is not there. No one is there. The room has not been used. It appears that he only wanted to make the telephone call from the room."

"Did he have a car?"

"I did not see a car."

"When did he rent the room?"

"Today, at noon. He said he wanted a private location and he walked back to the room and he could see that there was an entrance from the rear. It seemed to be what he was looking for and he paid for the room at that time."

"And he did not come by car?"

"No sir, there was no car."

I paused to think about it. He most likely parked nearby when the call was made. He would want to be able to leave in a hurry. If Stelling was with him they could force Ariane to do as they asked, and all three could have left the room after the call and walked to a car that would have been concealed from the Inn. I spoke to the desk manager again.

"Kurt, thank you for assisting me. If you see the man again, call the American Military Government office at once. He is dangerous and is wanted by both the German Police and the American Army. Be sure to let us know immediately if you see him."

"Yes, Herr Major, I will cooperate fully. Thank you, sir, and good evening."

It was the end of the conversation. I told the switchboard operator to place a call to the American Military Government office in Frankenberg next, and about three minutes later I was speaking to the sergeant on duty. I explained everything to him and he said he would call at once and tell Captain Brown, the team commander. He also said that he would get patrols on the street quickly, both German and American, and men would be stationed at all key points in the city, including the railroad station. During a pause he asked a question.

"Do you think they are still in town, sir?"

"Yeah, I think so. It would be too dangerous for them out on the highway. And I think they must have walked away from the Inn . . . the desk manager there said he did not hear a car. Tell your men to concentrate on the area near the Romantic Inn. They could still be there, in a house close by. If it is possible for me, I will come to Frankenberg tomorrow and I will see you at that time."

"Yes, sir."

I had done all that I could. I left the telephone exchange office to go back home. I glanced at my watch and it was one-fifty A.M.

When I arrived at my house there was an envelope tacked to the front door. I took it down, went inside and turned on a light, and opened the envelope. There was a printed message, in English, on a plain white sheet of paper. It read:

> Be careful, Major. You are getting in over your head. People will die. One person will die tonight. If you continue to make trouble, one person will be killed each night. You will learn in the morning that we are serious.

It was written by someone familiar with English, and the expressions that were used would have been by English-speaking people. I was reasonably sure, even though some Germans could simulate our writing very well, that it was done by an American, or a person familiar with terms only Americans would use.

It brought about a new problem. It meant that there were people in Bad Welmsburg who were actively involved working against us, possibly not only the SS, but maybe even Americans.

I thought of Heidi. Would they go for her? Yes, she would be a likely candidate. I decided to call her, and if she was still alive I would help her, keep her with me for the time being.

I dialed her number. It rang three times and she answered. I was glad to hear her voice, I had already formed a vision in my mind similar to seeing Leni lying in a pool of blood and I wanted to prevent it from happening again if possible. I let her know right away that she might be in danger.

"Heidi, you have to get out of that house tonight. You may be in serious danger. I will come in ten minutes and pick you up and you can stay here with me. In the meantime, be very careful."

"Yes, I will. Thank you, Max. I will be ready."

When Heidi opened the door at her house fifteen minutes later, I was more than happy to see her and to know that she was still alive. She, too, was glad to see me. I think I had impressed her enough on the phone about the situation to let her know that a serious condition was prevalent, and she was ready to leave with me at once. She picked up a small travel bag, pulled the door closed behind her, and we walked quickly to the jeep. There, I looked at her.

"Heidi, wait until we get to my place and I'll explain."

"Yes, okay, I understand."

At my home I pulled the jeep into the garage, which was actually under the house in the basement area. Normally I parked in the driveway above, but to have more security, I drove into the basement and locked the garage doors.

Heidi and I went up the basement stairs into the house above. She remained quiet, sensing from my attitude that there was danger involved. Once we were inside, I moved through each room, looking into closets, and in any and all places where a person could hide. After satisfying myself that no one was there, I closed all of the windows and doors leading to the outside and I made sure that all were locked. Heidi had walked along with me silently, and then, finally, I spoke to her.

"Let's go into the middle room and I'll explain." After we were seated I began talking.

"I got information tonight that explains many things to me. A threat was made that caused the concern I had about you. You were not named specifically but I am sure you were to be a target. You will have to stay with me for a while . . . possibly we can get you on a train to Hannover soon and you can join your parents."

She had become even more serious.

"But, Max, what is it? What has happened so quickly to change things in this way?"

"I can't give you all the details, Heidi. You will have to trust me. I'm going to make sure you are okay, that's the important thing."

She smiled.

"Thank you, Max. How would I have managed without you?"

"I don't know, but don't worry about it. Now I will take you up to your room. I'm totally exhausted and I'm not sure at this point that I am thinking straight. Try not to worry, you will be safe here. We will talk again in the morning."

She nodded. She followed me up the steps and into a room next to the room where I would sleep. There were sheets, blankets, and other items she would need, and a bathroom was close by. Before going to my room I spoke to her again.

"I'm going to leave the lights on downstairs. Also, I'll leave the light on in the bathroom up here. If you hear anything, come and wake me." And I smiled slightly. "Can you scream very loud?"

And finally, she answered with her normal vigor.

"You bet!"

"Good. Hope you sleep well."

"You too, Max. And thank you again."

After looking at her with a pleasant expression to acknowledge the remark, I walked out of the room. In my room I sat on the bed and removed my shoes and socks. Then I stood and removed my clothing, except my underwear. After that I crawled into the bed, a wonderfully soft and comfortable bed. I tried to remember . . . I thought of . . . things that had happened . . . Ariane . . . and . . .

The next morning a ringing awakened me. I wanted it to stop. It was a vague nuisance, and I was still tired and sleepy. Then, I realized it was the phone downstairs. I thought, "let it ring," whoever it is can wait, I'm too tired to get up.

But then, I realized that I was not alone in the bed. Heidi was beside me, still asleep. She apparently had come in during the night without awakening me. That made me decide to get up. It was no time to have her wake up and roll over on me.

Downstairs I answered the phone. It was a familiar voice.

"Hello, Max. Sleeping a little late this morning?"

It was Eddie LeTourneau.

"Yeah, you might say that. Where are you?"

"Here in town. I never left."

"Oh? Why not?"

"I don't have time to play games, Max. I'm here because of the gold. I've got contacts with the U.S. Army, the Russians, the Germans, and the longer it goes on the longer the list will get."

"What do you want from me?"

"What did the Russian man tell you?"

"He told me there was gold, million of Marks."

"Where?"

"He couldn't tell me. He tried, but he only spoke about five words before he died."

"I don't believe you. Why would he tell you about the gold, and not tell you where it is?"

"Like I said, he tried, but I got there too late."

"Okay, if you want to play it that way, you can. Even if you're telling me the truth, you and the gold are not going anywhere, anyway. This town is full of people, disguised as Germans, who know about the gold. The Russians found that German farm couple who took care of the Russian man, the one at the hospital who spoke to you before dying, and they killed them. The stupid jerks. Those German farmers could have told us more than anybody."

"Eddie, how did you get yourself involved in this?"

"Oh, easy. I've had German contacts for years. I'm with an organization that is big and powerful. So listen to me, pal, and listen carefully. I've got people in the army protecting me, people in high places. If you tried to take this to somebody in the U.S. Army you wouldn't last five minutes. In addition, I've got contacts with the Russians and the Germans. We've agreed to a split, three ways. Hell, there's a hundred and twenty million dollars in pure gold bars and its enough for everybody. I've heard that the British and Chinese may move in, too, so we need to move fast. Now, think about it. It's worth one million dollars to you. Tell me what the Russian man told you. Where is it?"

"I told you, Eddie, he was dying. Whoever your contact is could see that . . . I'm sure it was somebody in the room where he died at the hospital . . . he was only able to speak enough to tell me about the gold, he said, 'hundreds of millions of Marks', and that was it."

"Okay, we will leave it like that. Are you straight on how things are going to work?"

I didn't answer. Heidi had come into the room and sat in a chair near me. After no response from me, Eddie spoke.

"Max, you're stupid. People are going to be wiped out. You beat us to Heidi last night, but Gertrude wasn't that lucky. And we can still get Heidi. You better think about your own ass, too."

"Okay, okay. Hold up the killing. What do you want me to do?"

"Just act normal. Margolies and all of the others with the team don't know about the gold. Once we find it, we will move it and be gone. And by the way, don't go to Frankenberg. Augenberg would like nothing better than slicing the throat of dear little Frau Wegner. So . . . as you can see, Max . . . I'm holding all the cards."

"Yeah, I can see that. All right, I'll do as you say. I'll continue to operate as I would normally. But, when it's over, the woman in Frankenberg comes home. Do you agree?"

"It all depends on you, Max."

He hung up. I looked across at Heidi and she was puzzled, waiting for an explanation, so I decided to tell her as much as I could.

"We're in a hell of a mess, Heidi. Right now, I don't know what I'm going to do. You will have to stay with me for a while."

Normally she would have smiled. She didn't—she knew it was too serious. She spoke.

"Can you tell me anymore?"

"I think . . . and I'm sorry to tell you this . . . they might have killed Gertrude last night."

She stared in disbelief, and soon small tears formed in her eyes. I stood, and she did too, and we embraced. I held her and rubbed her back, and she remained in my arms for a long time. She cried the whole time, at one point almost out of control. Finally, she was better, and the crying seemed to have helped her release the emotional jolt she had received. She backed away, taking her arms from around me, and spoke.

"When will this ever stop? It is like the war is still going on and there will be no end to it."

"I know. I'm sorry, Heidi. I know she was a good friend."

She nodded, affirmatively, and was silent. I took her arm and walked with her to a chair, and after she was seated, I sat in a chair near her. After a moment or so she spoke.

"They were coming to get me, weren't they?"

I didn't want to tell her so I didn't speak. She knew the answer, anyway.

"Thank you, Max. You saved my life. I heard part of what you were saying . . . will it stop now?"

"Yes, he agreed to stop."

"Thank God for that. What about you, are you in danger, too?"

"Yes. And at the moment, I can't think of any way to handle it."

"Oh, Max, please, let's get on the train and go away."

"I can't. I'm in the army and I would be a deserter. I don't want to run, anyway. There has to be a way to deal with it."

"I just can't . . . why, why is this happening?"

"I can't tell you, Heidi. All I can tell you is, if they want to they can overpower us at any time, and for now at least, we will just have to do as they say."

"Can I stay with you until it is over? Or will it ever be over?

"It will be over, probably soon. And yes, you can stay here."

Although I was still speaking in a serious tone, she forced a grin.

"Good! And I know, no sex, right?"

"Right. And by the way, what were you doing in my bed this morning?"

She could sense that my mood was changing and that I was not as tense.

"I couldn't go to sleep. And you were so sleepy I knew it wouldn't matter, anyway."

I managed to smile as I answered.

"Well, just don't make things . . . you know, difficult."

"I won't. But . . . I know you like me . . . and, someday you may change your mind."

She was watching to see if I would smile, and I did. I got up and told her I would go up to get dressed. I told her there was food in the kitchen and she could prepare breakfast. She said she would and I continued up the stairs, trying in my thoughts to solve what had suddenly become an extremely difficult problem.

When I came down a few minutes later, Heidi was feeling better. She had prepared breakfast for me and she was drinking coffee. I told her what I would do.

"I'm going to the office and carry out business as usual. That's what I've been told to do. Stay here and keep the door locked. Don't let anyone in, and don't even go near the door."

"All right. When will you be back? I will need more things from my house."

"At noon. I'll come at noon and we will go to your house. We should be back here by two. Heidi, there is a pistol in the footlocker in my room upstairs. Don't touch it unless you have to. Will you promise me that?"

"Yes, I promise. And I will be ready at noon."

During the morning I heard about the murder of Gertrude. Chief Swartz came to my office, very concerned. I couldn't tell him anything, I just advised him as best I could about the investigation that was needed.

At noon I took Heidi to her home and she gathered up the things she needed. I helped her get them into the jeep and we returned to my house. In thinking about LeTourneau I felt we were reasonably safe. The timing involved would be the critical part. If he found the gold, he would want to eliminate me and anyone else who had knowledge of it. And so, I, too, would have to search for the gold and hope to find it first.

When Heidi and I unloaded her things at my house, it was three-thirty and I decided not to return to the office. I called Sergeant Newton and told him I was working on something and would be in the next morning.

Heidi and I sat in the middle room of the house. We were both somewhat solemn. Each of us knew that we were in a serious predicament, and even though she didn't know all the details she knew from my attitude that we were in trouble. Neither of us had spoken for a while, then she looked directly at me and asked a question.

"When you were on the phone this morning, you said, 'When it is over, the woman in Frankenberg comes home.' Who did you mean?"

"It's a hostage. A woman from Bad Welmsburg."

"And you were trying to be sure she gets back safely?"

"Yes."

She seemed to believe me. And it was, in fact, true. I just continued to feel it was important to keep the information about Ariane secret until the whole thing could be settled. She, too, was in great danger, and the less that was known about her the better it would be.

I began to consider the gold, and how I might go about searching for it. If the Russian man who was shot by Wegner and left for dead eventually made his way from the cave to the German farmhouse, the cave most likely was near the farmhouse. The only problem with that theory was LeTourneau would have realized the same thing, at least he would realize that the Russian man, being wounded seriously, could not have gone very far to get to the farmhouse. Consequently, the area around the farmhouse would have been explored thoroughly by LeTourneau and the others who were looking for the gold. But maybe they didn't know about the cave. And Wegner, in his attempt to conceal a tremendous amount of gold, could have done an expert job of covering up the entrance to a cave. He could have used other Russians to construct an artificial covering, and then, of course, he would have shot the Russians. I knew the location of the farmhouse—Chief Swartz had told me—and it was about a mile from the Wegner property. I couldn't go there because I knew LeToureau and the Russians would have surveillance teams set up covering the area. How could it be done without going there? What information would be available? Would any record of caves be on hand? If not, would there be topographical maps that might indicate the most likely places for caves to exist? Possibly. A shot in the dark that might work.

Heidi brought my thoughts back to her.

"What are you thinking about? Your mind seems to be a million kilometers away."

"I suppose I was thinking, Heidi, how we will overcome the problems we have, but, you're right, no need to dwell on that at the moment. Okay, let's see, what can we talk about? Oh, I know, what are our plans for dinner? Can you cook?"

"Oh, to hell with dinner, let's talk about running away," and she had a pretty smile on her face, "will you run away with me? We could go to the U.S. I've always wanted to go there and see Hollywood."

"Oh, that's a great idea. There's only one problem . . . they lock up deserters from the army. They would grab me as soon as I stepped off of the ship. And you would be left standing on the dock in New York with nobody to take care of you."

"I could manage."

She was enjoying the conversation and was watching me closely for an answer.

"Yeah, I think you could. In fact, you might even make it big with your looks."

"Oh, so you have noticed?"

"Yes, I've noticed. And while we're on that subject, let's set some ground rules for around here," and I was smiling. "Don't walk around half dressed or undressed. And don't come and get in my bed any more."

She was smiling broadly.

"Okay."

"It's bad enough watching you walk around with your clothes on . . . I don't think there's another woman in Bad Welmsburg with a body like yours."

She laughed.

"Well, Max, if someone put a dish of ice cream in front of you, you would eat it, wouldn't you?"

"No." And I continued to smile. "I'm on a diet."

She became smug and mischievous.

"Well, we'll see. Why is it so important to you?"

I was a little more serious.

"I've always been a one woman man. It's important because it involves trust, reliability, credibility, and a lot of other things. In college they called me 'one-woman Max.' It involves loyalty. If we can't believe people, especially the ones we like, or love, there's nothing left. If you could not believe in me now, my loyalty to protect you, how would you feel?"

"Terrible."

"Okay, it's the same thing. I don't want to go to . . ." and I almost forgot, I almost said Ariane, "well, I just don't want to go to bed with a woman, unless," and I got stuck again, "unless it means more than just having sex." It was the best explanation I could think of, and she laughed again.

"Max, you are so funny. I like you, and it would be easy to love you. Okay, you can be a monk if that pleases you. I will just be like an object in the house."

"Good!" And she knew that it was a good-natured response.

"And I suppose I should start calling you Father?"

"No, that won't be necessary."

"Fine, because I wouldn't do it anyway. I'll always call you Max.

And someday," and she had the devilish grin on her face again, "you will come and get in bed with me."

She obviously was being drawn to me, and it seemed to be sincere. I wanted her to know that I appreciated it.

"Heidi, believe me, I'm flattered by your interest in me. It's really amazing, hard to believe that you are attracted to me, an older man, in the way you describe. Maybe it's the war, and all of the things that go with a war. People have been torn apart, their lives have been disrupted, and, it's been very difficult and different in many ways. And I know you've had some experiences during the past four years that were not good, and I think that must have given you a different outlook about men. Don't you agree?"

"No. It's not the war. But, yes, I can say that my attitude about men was in the past based on my experiences during the time you mentioned. Now, my attitude has changed . . . since I have come to know you so well. I thought that men were the same, I thought they only wanted to have a satisfaction with a woman because of sex. I didn't know about the loyalty you spoke about. I thought that every man goes from one woman to another, whether he is married or not."

She paused and looked at me with a tender expression, and continued.

"You will always be dear to me, Max, and I think I must be in love with you at this moment."

6.

HEIDI AND I had continued our discussion until five-thirty, at which time I suggested that we consider what we should prepare for an evening meal. She asked about supplies, and what I would like. I told her.

"How about an omelette? I can cook a great omelette."

"Oh, so you will be the cook? Wonderful. Yes, chef Max, I would love to have an omelette."

We moved into the kitchen and I began gathering the things I would need. I had a few cans of food on hand, ham, cheese, boxes of army-issue nourishment, and I had picked up a few items locally—onions, potatoes, eggs, and milk. I kept it for occasions when I wanted to stay in on Sundays, or during evenings when I did not make it to the officer's dining room in a house that was located in another part of the city. I glanced at Heidi.

"When you were in school, did you take classes in cooking?"

"No. We were taught about that at home."

"What did you take? What were you interested in, what subjects?"

"I liked the subjects that told us about the other countries of the world, their people, the unusual things about their country. And I would imagine how it would be to go there."

"You could envision high mountains, or large rivers, and maybe even something like the North Pole?"

"Yes."

"Did you take geology?"

I was talking with a casual attitude as would a person attempting to maintain an interesting conversation. She was sitting in a chair close by, watching as I worked with the food.

"Sure, we had to take geology."

"Yeah, so did we. We used to go on field trips and look at rock formations, go in caves and explore them. Did you do that?"

"Most of our work was in the classroom. We didn't go on many field trips."

"So, if you and I wanted to head out and explore a cave, you wouldn't be much help?"

"No, I don't like caves. I told Herr Gruber that once and he became angry with me."

"Herr Gruber was your teacher?"

"Yes."

"And he was going to take your class in a cave?"

"He was until I told him I did not want to go. And some of the others didn't want to go either."

"Where was the cave?"

"I don't know, I can't remember, I never got there anyway."

"Did Herr Gruber forgive you later?"

"Oh, yeah, he was a nice old gentleman."

I dropped it. I didn't want to carry it too far. Herr Gruber, however, might be a good resource on caves in the area if I could figure out a way to find him and get the information from him.

I had put forth my best effort with the omelette and Heidi said it was great. I had come to like her. She was pleasing in her manner and her personality. I was very fascinated by her and I liked having her with me. I think, possibly, she was somewhat like a daughter . . . but . . . she was also an appealing young woman. If my feelings for Ariane were not so strong I would most likely find myself being drawn to Heidi with a different motivation. She was, without doubt, a very beautiful young woman.

We continued the bantering about sex to create humorous remarks and she knew that it was not my intention to become involved with her in bed. She was enjoying herself, and at times she was completely oblivious to the precarious situation surrounding us. For me, it wasn't that easy. I had grave concerns about Ariane, the gold, and how to handle everything. I had no plan, at least no workable plan, and I was in limbo, hanging out in space, and it was making me uncomfortable. LeTourneau was right when he said that he "was holding all of the cards," and it would take time for me to solve his puzzle. I felt that we were safe temporarily but everything would depend on who could find the gold first.

After the meal and kitchen clean-up, we moved back into the middle room. Heidi was in top form.

"Now, Max, what can we do? Let me think . . . if you're stranded with a monk, who also is a chef part time, what does that leave for the rest of the time? Maybe I should read Shakespeare."

"We'll have to think about that. By the way, your English is pretty good. Are you sure you haven't been keeping company with some other American soldier?"

"Aha! Are you jealous?"

I smiled and she continued.

"No, I don't know any other Americans. I don't want to know any others." And she became a little more serious temporarily. "I just want to keep the one I'm with now."

"That's nice but how long would you stay? You would soon get tired of me. You would walk away and leave me."

We were both grinning.

"No way, Max. You know that would never happen."

"Well, let's think about a few things. When I'm seventy, you would be forty-five. How would you feel about that?"

"Oh, to hell with seventy. I'm not interested in seventy, I'm interested in now. How can we go through a war and start worrying about seventy?"

"You're right, we won't worry about that."

We talked, had a few glasses of wine, listened to the music on the radio coming from the American Broadcasting Station, and it was time for bed. Without any prompting she went to her room, and I went to mine.

As usual, I had thoughts during the night when I would awaken briefly. I didn't sleep too well and I was awake almost as much as I slept. Finally, about five A.M. I made a decision. I would go to Frankenberg, disguised, and try to find Ariane. The gold would stay put, I was sure of that because of the expert way Wegner would have hidden it. And so, if I could get Ariane out of the hands of Augenberg, it would be the first step to take. I could deal with LeTourneau and the Russians later.

If I could make my plan work, get Ariane back to Bad Welmsburg safely and hide her, I had another thought concerning the gold that might be a possibility. Why not go to "Ike"? It was big enough, one hundred twenty million dollars in gold. Possibly it would be claimed by the Allies as a prize of war. It would be, after all, a confiscation of money accumulated by the Nazis. And, if the Allied Supreme Commander should so choose he could send a regiment of infantry soldiers, supported by armored vehicles, into the area, which would be more than adequate to overcome any resistance. And the army, being able to work openly, could use sophisticated equipment to find the gold. After the action could be planned, the army could put in motion an investigation of LeTourneau and his friends. I would save Augenberg and Stelling for myself—the army wouldn't have to worry about them.

I felt good and in excellent spirits. I was downstairs, drinking coffee, and as is the case when I had what I considered good thoughts, I wanted to share them. I looked at my watch and it was ten past six. Heidi was still in bed upstairs. I think she normally would have slept a little later, but I wanted her to come down and be with me, talk to me.

I went up to her room and she was, as I had imagined, still asleep. I walked over to the bed and touched her on the shoulder, speaking at the same time.

"Hey, what's going on here? Are you going to sleep all day? It's time to get up and go milk the cows."

She opened her eyes and grinned. Then she curled up and pulled the cover over her head. She knew what I would do, pull the cover back and take hold of her. And that's what I did. She was curled up tight, almost in a ball with her knees pulled up against her chest. I reached over with both hands and tickled her, beginning around her neck and moving down her back and upper left arm. She started laughing and as she began getting out of bed, she spoke.

"Okay, Major Monk, you're asking for it!"

She stood and playfully reached up in the area of my arms as if she would tickle me in return, and then, she stopped and gazed into my eyes, and in a sudden move she put her arms around my neck, and pressed herself against me. She was holding on tightly and I could see that I had probably made a mistake, and I told her.

"Hey, hey, I'm just trying to wake you up. I didn't mean it any other way."

"I know. I just thought it would be a good chance for me to get a hug."

She backed away, grinning, and was ready to go with me downstairs. She was in a thin, knee-length sleeping gown, and as we walked toward the door, I reminded her to put on her robe.

"I don't have a robe with me. I don't want to wear a robe anyway."

She said she would stop in the bathroom and meet me downstairs. I told her I would have a cup of coffee ready for her. Were my thoughts about Heidi becoming too serious? She was, to some extent, getting "under my skin." Was it because she was with me and Ariane was not? Obviously I was on the edge of no man's land, and I was having strong feelings about two women. It was not yet a dilemma for me. It was conceivable to me, though, that I might be moving in that direction, and my reputation in college as a "one-woman man" might be hitting the skids.

It was disturbing. Ariane and I had been as much in love as any couple could be; now, there was something pulling at me that I couldn't control, couldn't understand how far it would go, or where it would end. It violated my principles of the past and the loyalty I had talked about with Heidi in a past conversation. And actually, it didn't make sense. Heidi was far too young for me to become involved with her. Maybe I could blame it on the war. The traumatic events that are observed and encountered as people are killed, seeing cities and homes destroyed, people uprooted and in despair, looking in almost any direction and finding only horrible scenes, had brought about, for me, a different set of emotions and mental attitudes. As Heidi had said, how can we go through a war and continue to have the same thoughts we had before, be the same people we once were?

When Heidi came into the kitchen she had her hair neatly in place, and she had completed the first phase of grooming herself. She looked

. . . cute? No, beautiful would be a better word. She was still in the thin gown and the outline of her body was prominently displayed, the garment clinging closely around her. She sat in a chair near the table with her legs crossed, and the gown flowed upward to the top of her legs.

When I spoke I intended that a good mood would be reflected in my voice.

"Madam, would you mind pulling down your gown?"

She laughed.

"What's wrong? Are you afraid you might change your mind about things?"

"I won't comment on that, I'm just suggesting . . . "

"Yes? Suggesting what?"

"You know."

"No, I don't know. I might even take my gown off."

I looked at her quickly.

"Heidi, don't do that. You know what the ground rules are."

"Okay. But I don't agree with your ground rules. Who do you think you are—Hitler?"

We both smiled. I sat in a chair at the table across from her. I wanted to tell her, as much as I could, about my plan to go to Frankenberg.

"Listen, I'm going on a trip to another city. It involves the problem we have, the danger that is here. I thought about it last night and this morning, and I think it will help me get us out of trouble."

"What city? And what about me, are you planning to leave me here alone?"

"No, you're going with me."

She was very pleased.

"Good! Now we will do something different, and we can be together."

"Yeah. Heidi, I want you to go with me because it is the only way I can be sure you will be safe. And maybe we should talk a little more about what is happening here . . . between us . . . we have to be . . . careful."

Her intuition and perception went into action immediately. I could see it in her expression. The instinct that every woman seemed to have in detecting the thoughts and feelings of men became obvious as she answered.

"I know that you like me. And you will like me even more in the future. But we will do as you say, we will stay away from each other until you wish to do otherwise."

"Thanks. That helps. I can't do all of the other things that have to be done and . . ."

She flashed another grin.

"It's not going to be a problem. Don't worry about it, I'm just happy that we are going to be together."

We talked about other things. It gave me a chance to watch her and think about her. Her vivaciousness and strong-willed characteristics popped out frequently. She would have been able to "hold her own" in almost any situation. Her face and body were both unique. She smiled a lot, showing white teeth that were perfectly aligned. Her eyes, nearly always portraying her mischievousness, were brownish green and matched her medium dark hair with an enhancing blend. For a twenty year old, she was far advanced beyond her years. It was due, I was sure, to the life she had been exposed to after she became the mistress of Kurth. I wanted to know more about Kurth and I brought up his name.

"How did you explain Kurth to your family and friends?"

She looked at me like I was ten years old.

"Listen, you're talking about the system that was working here in Germany. We didn't say yes or no whenever we pleased, you should know that much about us by now."

"You're right, and I do know, I suppose I just forgot temporarily. How did Kurth treat you?"

"Okay, at first. Then he became terrible, and I began to hate him."

"You were telling me about the time that the four men came to his home and you had to undress before them. What else did you have to do?"

She was touched by my concern.

"Nothing, my darling Max, that was terrible. He wanted me to dance, and then some of them put their hands on me and said things, but that was all."

"You didn't have to . . ."

"No, I didn't have sex with them."

"Well, thank heavens for that."

"You're kind to be concerned. Actually, I think I am like a woman who has been married and becomes a widow. Believe it or not, Walter Kurth was the only man I ever slept with, the first and the last."

That came as a surprise.

"That day you were walking on the street and he picked you up, that was it?"

"That was it. I had just become sixteen and I got educated in a hurry."

So, she was not as I had imagined, not experienced with a lot of men. And maybe it explained her attitude toward me. She apparently was having deep feelings about me, rather than only pushing the idea of sex, as I had assumed. And too, I had felt that she was like countless other young women after the war, left without male companionship, and I had come to believe that she might be searching for someone who could fill that void. Now, I realized it was different.

She stood and walked to the sink to empty the remnants of coffee in her cup. I sized her up and decided that she must be five-five or five-six in height. She was smaller than Ariane. Her posture was ideal, and it complimented her other physical attributes. She turned from the sink and smiled. She wanted to come to me, and, although it was a little troublesome to me, I wanted it too. But she would not come, she would keep her promise. She moved back to her chair and spoke.

"You thought I was like a—what are they called in English, the women who are with men and get paid?"

"Prostitutes. No, it never occurred to me that you were a prostitute. The only surprise was Kurth, that he was your only lover. How did you manage with the other men who were in the Wehrmacht? I thought they could have whoever they wanted."

"It was because of Kurth. Everyone knew, at least everyone suspected, that he had high contacts and they were afraid to bother me because of him."

"Maybe if there was a good side of the story, that was it."

"I think so. And now we have, as I believe they would say in your movies, a triangle affair. It is at least a triangle because of the feelings you still have for Ariane, even though she is not here. And I admire you for that. It is, as you explained, loyalty, something I have never seen before."

She was looking at me with compassion, and, possibly, love. It was shaping up as tough duty for me. Regardless of her age, regardless of everything else and my love for Ariane notwithstanding, I was being drawn to her with serious feelings.

It was time for me to go to the office. I would explain to Colonel Margolies that I had received a tip about Ariane and that Augenberg might be holding her in Frankenberg. He would readily agree with my plan to go there and it would only be a matter of working out details. I stood and told Heidi that I would have to be gone for a while, saying too, that I would set aside some time later in the day to make final plans.

"When I get back we can decide about how and when we will leave. We're going to Frankenberg, and I think it will be best to travel in a civilian car. I can get one from our motor pool. And it probably will be best if we leave here after dark. I suspect this house is being watched, and if it is, we can move out at night better."

She had a question to ask and I paused. She took longer than usual to speak.

"Max, can I ask you . . . the day you were speaking to someone on the phone and I came into the room, you asked the person to stop the killing and they agreed. And then you asked a question. You said, 'When everything is settled, the woman comes home.' Do you remember?"

"Yes, I remember."

"Was the woman . . . is it Ariane?"

I didn't answer immediately because I was not expecting that kind of question. I had thought about it, however, and I knew I would have to tell Heidi at some point. After a few seconds of gazing into her eyes, I spoke.

"Yes."
She smiled faintly.
"I thought so. I believed at the time you were on the phone that you were talking about her, I just didn't want to say anything. I'm happy that she is still alive."
"Thank you, Heidi. It's . . . we will have to talk, okay? And be sure you don't tell anyone about Ariane, she could still be killed very easily."
"Oh, of course, I would not do that. Can we talk about it again soon?"
"Sure, we will. We can talk tonight in the car on the way to Frankenberg. You know . . . it's . . . complicated. The first thing we have to do is try to save her."
"I understand and I agree. Thank you for telling me."
As I walked by her to leave I reached down and touched her on the shoulder. She recognized it to be an affectionate gesture.
Some hours later, at ten-forty P.M., I backed out of the basement garage of my house in a black Mercedes sedan that I had brought from our motor pool. The late-model car, confiscated when we arrived in Bad Welmsburg from a man who was a local high-ranking Nazi, had been serviced during the afternoon by the German mechanic who worked in our garage. I had a full tank of gas, which was adequate to get us to Frankenberg. Heidi was grinning the whole time as we loaded up, and she could have cared less about the surveillance of our house that had troubled me. I drove slowly, with the headlights off, watching carefully for movements of any kind as we reached the street. There were none, and after moving for approximately a mile, I turned on the headlights and increased the speed.
Soon we were on the highway leading in a westward direction, riding along on the road that would take us to Frankenberg. I saw no other vehicles and it seemed we were in the clear. Heidi had remained silent as she usually did when I was tense or uncertain about a situation. Suddenly she spoke.
"Now! Can we turn on the radio?"
"Why not?"
She reached over and pushed a button and at first there was static, then she found by turning a knob, the American Broadcasting Station where she set the dial. She turned to me.
"You know, you look like a German man. With your clothes, the civilian clothes as you called them, makes it the same for me if I was driving away at some different time, maybe five years ago. You came to my house, asked me to run away with you, and here I am."
"And so you think I can pass for a German man in my outfit?"
"Absolutely. Your face has a strong Nordic appearance. Deep blue eyes, blondish hair, thin lips, and a perfectly shaped nose. Yes, Hitler would have been proud of you."

"You forgot to say that I am handsome."

"Oh, really? How could I forget that? Well, yes, Max, I think you are a very handsome man. And when I am with you I feel safe. You are tall and muscular, and I think any other man would make a mistake to challenge you."

"Thanks, that was quite a compliment. Now, may I say what I think about you?"

"I would love for you to do that."

"You're quite a beautiful young woman. It's very pleasing, and comforting to be with you. I find myself missing you when you are out of the room. And when I'm away, I think of you often."

She was sincerely impressed.

"Thank you, Max. That means so very much to me. Do you . . . how do you . . . no, I can't ask. I will wait."

Obviously she was going to mention Ariane. And it would have been hard to handle. I had reached the dilemma I had thought about previously. I was still in love with Ariane, but Heidi had taken possession of me, and I could not escape my feeling for her. She had asked, earlier in the day, if we could talk about our situation, and I had said we could. Now, I felt it was too soon, I couldn't tell her how we would be able to solve the question she would want to know about—the triangle, as she had termed it. Heidi had moved into my life so quickly and so overwhelmingly. I had not had an experience like it previously. I had asked myself a dozen times during the day if it was real. And the answer always came back the same . . . real or not, I could not give her up.

She must have realized my predicament because she didn't mention it. Instead she moved over and leaned on me as I drove, and I put my right arm around her shoulder. The music on the radio was nice, and as she had said, it was easy for me also to let my mind wander back, back to college or some other time, and she was my date during a perfect evening.

We arrived in Frankenberg at two forty-five A.M. I had been there before and I knew where a hotel was located. I drove up the hill to reach the hotel. The city was shaped like a great mound and the old part of the small town, including the hotel, was located on top of the mound. I told Heidi to talk to the attendant at the desk because I would not be able to speak German. She said she could handle it, and she also said she would do as I asked and get two adjoining rooms.

I parked the car and we went inside. She handled things well and soon we were in the rooms. There was a door that opened on the inside to connect the rooms and we left it open. We were both tired and agreed that we would separate and get to bed. She had a request before we parted.

"Max, will you kiss me goodnight?"

"Yes."

And we embraced. We were both emotional, and we kissed repeatedly with great passion. But soon, I brought it to an end. I had to. I knew where it would lead and I wasn't ready to compromise myself and surrender to animal-like instincts. We backed away from each other, we both smiled, and she walked to her room. As she entered the room she spoke over her shoulder.

"I'll leave the door open if that is all right."

"It's fine. And sleep late if you want to, I know you must be tired."

"Okay, and you do the same. Goodnight."

"Goodnight."

It would have been easy for me to go into her room and sleep with her, and most men would call me a lunatic. I could just hear the comments of our GIs. Even so, I was still holding on to a thread of the loyalty I had spoken about, and I decided then and there that I would at least try to make a choice between Ariane and Heidi before sleeping with either.

7.

THE NEXT MORNING at seven-twenty I was awake. Still in bed, relaxing, I could hear activity on the street outside, people talking and moving about. It would be getting late for most working Germans, and sounds from the street would increase for a while before the people would disappear into buildings and go to work.

There were no sounds coming from Heidi's room and I thought that she must be sleeping. It would give me a chance to think about how we would conduct our search during the day. I had papers for both of us that would protect us in any situation if we were stopped and questioned. Also, I had an order signed by Colonel Margolies authorizing me to be in Frankenberg on official duty. I would let Heidi talk for us when we encountered German people. She could use any number of reasons for the muteness I would display. I told her the best reason might be to describe me as a soldier from the Wehrmacht who was suffering from the trauma of being shell-shocked. In that way I could not only remain silent, I could be dumb if spoken to.

Where should we start in the city? The Romantic Inn, the place where Augenberg had made the call to Frau Erhlich? I wasn't sure. It would be risky, although nearly all places would fall into that category. If we checked into the Inn we might be able to talk to Kurt, the night desk manager, the man who had seen Augenberg. If we could learn something from him without disclosing our identification, it would be ideal. I thought about the local American Military Government office and I would at some point contact them. I would wait on that and go as far as possible on my own. Information had a way of seeping out of the American offices because of the civilians who worked there. I would probably use that contact only as a last resort.

I heard a movement in the next room and it sounded like Heidi was getting out of bed. I was right, and she appeared in the connecting doorway, grinning as she greeted me.

"Now don't panic. I'm just going to get in your bed on top of the covers so we can talk, okay?"
"Yeah, okay."
She did as she said and nestled herself up next to me with the cover separating our bodies. She kissed me on the cheek and spoke.
"Did you sleep well?"
"Like a rock. How about you?"
"I slept very good. Did you miss me and dream about me?"
"Yes and yes. How could I do otherwise?"
She was on her side and was facing me. She was thinking serious thoughts, I could always tell.
"Max, when we find Ariane and get her home safely, what will happen next?"
It was a tough question and I really didn't know how to answer it. I told her the truth.
"I don't know. You've become . . . someone in my life . . . that I cannot let go. I can't answer your question now, and I think it is going to take time. Let's do what we have to do here, try to get Ariane home, and then we will settle things. Does that sound like a good plan?"
"I think so. I just hope each of us will be happy, and I hope it will be possible that no one will be badly hurt."
"That's a very sweet thought and I feel the same. Why can't life be more simple? It's a time when we should all be out in the street celebrating the end of the war, with no worries or complications. Instead, we've got ourselves messed up."
"I'm not messed up, at least I know what I want."
"I know. You've told me and I believe you. I hope you will be patient with me. And you know, even if I haven't said it, how I will always feel."
"Will you say it?"
"Heidi . . . I . . . yes, I will say it. I love you."
She smiled and kissed me on the mouth. It was an emotional moment for her, and for me. I think I had only said that to one other woman, Ariane, and really meant it. Did I really mean it now, or did it just "pop out"? They were easy words to say, and men had said them a million times when it was not true. Was it too quick? Had I really come to that point with her while having similar feelings about another woman? And all of it happening within such a short period of time; could I honestly stand behind those words? Yes. Even though my feeling for her had come about in a matter of days, and even though there was another woman in my life, Heidi was now a part of me that would remain, an imprint that would be indelible. She pulled away and turned over on her back.
"Thank you, Max. That was wonderful to hear. And now, I will get up so that I will keep my promise and not make it difficult for you. And by the way, what are we going to do today?"
"I've been thinking about that and I'm not sure. What do you think about going to the Romantic Inn?"

"What would we do there?"

"Try to talk to Kurt, the night manager who saw Augenberg. We might even have to get rooms there."

"Do you think we can fool him?"

"Maybe. You can describe Augenberg and tell him you are his friend or relative. Say that you got separated and you're trying to find him. Ask him if he will keep it confidential—try to think of some reason for that. What do you think?"

"It might work. What will you do if you find Augenberg?"

"It depends on where he has Ariane. It would be no problem if we could get to Ariane first. Otherwise it would be dangerous. Do you think Augenberg would know you or recognize you?"

"No, because I never saw him."

"Let's think about it to be sure. If he was living with Kurth for a while, would he have known enough about you to identify you?"

"Again, I don't think so. I think Walter told everyone about us but perhaps he would not describe me in a way that would be so complete."

"How much can you learn by talking to people who are strangers? I don't know the habits of the German people well enough to understand what can be learned in that way."

"You can learn a lot. It became common during the war, and while Hitler was alive people talked continuously and they would tell each other everything. And in small towns it was impossible to conceal anything."

"That sounds good. Maybe we will have good luck."

After we had breakfast and walked out onto the sidewalk of the street in front of the hotel, a tremendous shock occurred. A man who was walking ahead of us spoke to another man a few steps ahead of him, asking him to wait. He addressed the man as Augenberg.

Heidi and I turned and looked at each other in amazement. The man called Augenberg was walking toward the Mercedes we had driven from Bad Welmsburg. It was parked on the street about sixty feet from the entrance of the hotel, and Augenberg seemed to have a special interest in it.

I tried to see the man well enough to see if he matched the description I had been given of Augenberg, and, as he reached the Mercedes and turned in a different direction to look at the car closely, I could see him better. He did appear to be the man who had been described to me and I was almost certain it was him. The second man did not match the description of Stelling. They were keenly interested in the car and looked at it from all angles. I took Heidi's arm and guided her to a position where we would not be conspicuous, while continuing to watch the two men. I told her to make it appear that we were having a conversation.

At one point, Augenberg took hold of the handle and tried to open the door of the car. It was locked and he could not gain entry. He leaned over then and put his face against the glass of the window, shading the light by placing both hands on his face next to his eyes. Did he recognize the car? Maybe he knew the previous owner. Although there were no tags or other identification on the car, if he had known the owner well enough he might be able to determine that the car had come from Bad Welmsburg.

After looking at the car for at least five minutes, Augenberg turned his attention to people on the street. Fortunately, Heidi and I had moved inside a camera shop and he could not see us. Heidi talked to the owner of the shop and I remained near the entrance watching Augenberg. The second man was younger, twenty-eight or so, and I had no previous description of him. I had to find out about the two men; I had to take a chance.

I called Heidi over and whispered to her. I told her we couldn't let them out of sight, and I asked her which of us she felt Augenberg would be most likely to recognize. She said it would probably be me because everyone in Bad Welmsburg knew the American soldiers. She told me not to go near Augenberg, it would be too dangerous. She offered to go. I wasn't sure.

"He might know you or remember Kurth's description of you. No, I can't let you take a chance like that. I think he already knows about the car—he seems to recognize it. He may suspect someone is here from Bad Welmsburg."

"I can do it, Max. He has never seen me. And I have changed my hairstyle. Just before I knew you I styled it differently, I did it before I met you in the bar that evening, and I think Augenberg had already left Bad Welmsburg."

"What would you do?"

"I can go to that shop near the car and look in the window. I will keep my back turned and try to hear what they are saying."

We had to make a move quickly. They would only be near the car for a short while longer. They were already looking occasionally in the direction of the hotel, and they seemed to be in serious conversation.

I told Heidi to go. I would be nearby and could get to her quickly. She grinned and walked out the door of the camera shop.

She made it to the shop near the two men and stopped. They glanced at her but she had done as she had said and turned her back to them. They continued to talk, looked briefly at the car again, and turned toward the hotel. I felt there was a good chance that Heidi would hear part of their conversation because she was only a few feet away.

The two men abruptly decided to walk in the direction of the hotel. Heidi waited briefly and came back to the camera shop. I listened eagerly to learn what she had heard.

"I could only hear a few words. They were upset. And you were right, they must have decided that the car had come from Bad Welmsburg."

"Anything else?"
"They were going into the hotel to see if they could find out who was driving the car."
"Did you hear the name of the second man?"
"Yes. He was called Rolfe."
Rolfe! I couldn't believe it. It would be the son of Frau Erhlich. Could he have been a part of the scheme from the beginning? Could Frau Erhlich be a part of the group as well? It was an amazing development. We would have to follow Augenberg and Rolfe on foot and the Mercedes would have to be left in the same place until we could return at a safe time to drive it away.
I had to make quick decisions. It was imperative that we somehow contain Augenberg and Rolfe. They were most likely going to become alerted, based on the possibility of information that would come from the hotel employees, and they would be more difficult to follow. They had already gotten a glimpse of Heidi on the street so I could not let her go alone to become exposed to them again. She would arouse their suspicions immediately.
It would become my responsibility to follow them—whether they saw me would not matter. If they should split up, I would let Heidi follow Rolfe from a distance. He had seemed less interested when he and Augenberg had glanced at her on the street, and he would be less likely to be observant enough to remember her. I told her what we should do.
"When they come out of the hotel, I'll give them some room and follow them. I want you to follow me, but stay back as far as you can. If they separate, I will motion to you. I will follow Augenberg, you can follow Rolfe. If we lose each other, come back to the Rathaus and go inside. You can wait for me there and you will be safe."
She was worried.
"How about you, Max, will you be safe?"
"Yes. I've got my forty-five hidden under my coat. Don't worry, we'll be all right, just don't take chances. If you have to decide on safety or losing Rolfe, go for safety. Will you promise me that?"
"I promise."
Just as she finished speaking, Augenberg and Rolfe came out of the hotel. They were concerned and looked in all directions. They saw us and Augenberg focused on us. He spoke quickly to Rolfe, turned, and walked away to his right. Rolfe came down a few steps that led to the sidewalk and came toward us. He must have believed that we would not know him. He passed by us and continued down the hill that led away from the hotel.
I turned to Heidi and spoke hurriedly.
"Follow Rolfe but stay back. I'm going after Augenberg. Be careful, Heidi."
"I will, and please Max, you be careful too!"
We parted. Augenberg had walked up the hill away from the hotel

and he had turned the corner. I ran after him. When I reached the corner, I could see him heading into a park. He looked back and saw me coming and increased his pace, and so did I. As we entered the park he was about twenty paces ahead of me.

He ran toward the far end of the park. I had been in that park before when Ariane and I were in Frankenberg, and I knew that the far side of the park would contain him. On that side there was a drop, several hundred feet straight down, and when he reached that point he would have no place to go.

I saw no other people as I raced after him. The park was empty and that was good because we would cause no concern by others who might call the police. Augenberg reached the far end, looked over the guardrail and saw that he was trapped. Knowing that he was cornered I slowed my pace to catch my breath. He set himself in a position that indicated he would fight with his hands and I assumed he had no weapon.

When I walked up to him I stopped five feet away and spoke.

"Are you Augenberg, a member of the SS?"

He didn't answer. He looked beyond me to see how he might move away. He could see it was hopeless, and I think at that moment he decided to try to fight his way past me. He moved slightly to his left, faking a move to make a run for it and I stepped in more closely to him. I was only an arm's length from him. He made a sudden movement with his left hand, reaching down into his pocket. I knew it had to be a weapon, and while his guard was down, I hit him on the left side of his face, hard, with a right-hand punch. It smacked loudly, and stunned him. He had withdrawn a knife and snapped it open by pushing a release and a long blade was exposed. He swung the knife toward the middle part of my body with the best effort he could muster, but the point hit against my forty-five which I had stuck down inside my trousers, and the heavy metal of the weapon prevented the blade from penetrating into my stomach. I moved in and used both fists, going for his stomach and his face repeatedly. He staggered back and I kept pounding him. He had been hurt by the first punch and he had not been able to recover enough to defend himself. He continued to swing the knife at me in wild motions which were harmless to me, and he was becoming weaker with each movement. He obviously was very tired.

He appeared ready to drop and at that point I stepped in close, placing myself to his rear so that I could lock my left arm around his neck. I took my right hand and put it around my left wrist and pulled hard. He was gasping for air and I eased up some on the neck hold and spoke.

"Where is Ariane Wegner?"

He could barely speak but I heard him mumble the word "nein."

I pulled hard again with the arm lock. He tried to move. He couldn't because he was too weak, and he began sagging so that I not only was using force on his neck, I was partially holding him up. I repeated the two questions, asking about Ariane and if he was with the SS, and I eased my hold around his neck so he could answer. Again, weakly, but in a voice that was a little more audible, he said, "Nein, nein."

I tightened the hold again and this time he went down. I stayed with him, keeping the same arm lock. When we landed on the ground I was on top of him and I put my knee against his back. He managed to get the knife in his hand again but he was not able to use it effectively, and he was only brushing me slightly with it. I gave him another chance to tell me where to find Ariane, and the result was the same, nothing. I was furious with him, and temporarily I lost control. I squeezed his neck with all of my strength and pulled upward at the same time. And then, without realizing what I was doing, I heard a pop and suddenly his head fell forward. I had broken his neck.

I released my hold on him and he was lifeless on the ground. He was either dying or dead. I regretted it immediately, I had taken away what I had come for, the opportunity to find Ariane. I waited for a few moments, maybe as much as twenty or twenty-five seconds, and then I felt the veins in his neck. There was some slight movement for a second or so and then it stopped. He was dead.

I had made a mistake. I had been too frustrated and angry. I had no regrets about Augenberg, although I was always sorry to see, or be responsible for, the loss of life.

I looked around the park to see if there were witnesses. There were none. I quickly went through his pockets and was able to verify that he was the man I thought him to be. He had retained his SS identification, apparently believing it would be safe to do so because he could be too elusive to be caught. I was hoping to find an address or telephone number, anything that might help. There was nothing, only a few coins and some paper money. I took the SS identification and left everything else in his pockets.

He was lying about ten feet from the guardrail, and two feet beyond that was the drop. I grabbed him under the arms and pulled him to the drop. I looked downward and there were many trees in the area some two or three hundred feet below. I pulled him parallel to the edge, got behind him and pushed. He rolled over rather easily and was gone. I threw the knife over after him. It was the end of a ruthless man.

I turned around and looked again over the park. It was still empty. A church and a house were some distance away at the entrance to the park—otherwise, nothing. I moved out, walking back the way I had come in. I felt there was a good chance that no one had seen me.

Back at the Rathaus I went inside and waited for Heidi. I was concerned about her. Twenty minutes passed, then thirty. I avoided people so that I would not have to speak. I gave them a hard look when they came in my direction and they left me alone. Finally, the large wooden door that served as the entrance opened, and it was her. I smiled with relief and so did she, and we walked hurriedly to meet. I embraced her and she clung to me, and spoke,

"Thank God, Max, I was so worried about you."

"I'm glad to see you, too."

We backed away from each other and moved toward the door. She told me about Rolfe.

"He knew I was following him, and he went so fast, he got away. I'm sorry."

"It's all right. We will find him."

I told her about Augenberg and what had happened. I told her I regretted that it had to end that way.

"Don't worry about it, Max, you did what you had to."

"I know. But in addition to losing the man we came to find, it is never a good feeling to take a life."

"You must not let yourself feel guilty or blame yourself about Augenberg. He was a terrible man and had taken the lives of many innocent people. I have heard about him from Walter Kurth and he was responsible for killing many good German people. Try not to think of him again. He is gone and we are better off without him, both Americans and Germans."

She was right and I would try to forget about him. In any event, we would still have our work cut out for us. Rolfe had escaped and would go to Stelling, who was probably in charge of watching Ariane. They would know that they were in danger and would plan to move out as soon as possible.

My thoughts took a very disturbing twist. How could Rolfe, the son of Frau Erhlich, be deeply involved with Augenberg without the knowledge of Frau Erhlich? And would it be possible . . . could it be possible . . . that Ariane would have knowledge of the gold? It was . . . almost . . . too incredible to consider.

Heidi and I went back to the hotel. In my room I told her there was no further need to try to conceal ourselves. I thought that we might want to get back out on the streets and hope to get another chance sighting of Rolfe or Stelling. Heidi disagreed, saying that it would be best to leave it to the Americans and the German Police . . . they had already been alerted by my previous call . . . they would know the city better and would know the most likely places to look.

After lunch in the hotel dining room we went back to my room. At two-fifteen there was a slight tap on the door. I took out my forty-five, went to the door, and opened it. There, standing before me, was Rolfe. He was quick to speak.

"Major, please, I must talk to you. May I come in?"

I motioned for him to move into the room while still pointing the forty-five at him. I closed the door and asked a question.

"Do you have a weapon on you?"

"No, sir. Please search me if you wish."

I did and found nothing. I told him to be seated. He spoke to Heidi, saying "good day" in German. I looked down at him and put the forty five back in my hip pocket.

"You are Rolfe Erhlich?"

"Yes."

"You are the cousin of Ariane Wegner?"

"Yes."

"Tell me where she is."

"She was here, Major. They found us and forced us to do as they said. We . . ."

I interrupted.

"You say they. Who do you mean?"

"Augenberg and Stelling. They found us in the home of my friend who lives here."

"Who is your friend? And where is Ariane now?"

"My friend is Odenbacher. They killed him. Ariane was there, in his home with me. But now, she has been taken away by Stelling."

"How?"

"They had a car. It was stolen from the American Military Government in Marburg. They can travel in the car because it is marked American Military Government on the outside."

"Describe the car."

"It is a black sedan, an Opel."

I stopped my interrogation and went to the phone. I called Captain Brown who was team leader of the American Military Government in Frankenberg and advised what I had been told by Rolfe. He said the information should help and he would alert his people at once. I completed the call and turned back to Rolfe.

"How is Ariane?"

"She is fine, sir. They did not harm either of us."

Was he telling me the truth? More questions would be needed to decide.

"Why did they take you and Ariane? What comments did they make while you were with them?"

"They did not say, sir. Ariane asked the same question and they would only tell her to be quiet."

"We saw you with Augenberg before you saw us. You seemed to be at ease with him. Were you friends?"

"Oh, no sir, of course not. He told me Ariane would be killed, and I as well, if we did not do exactly as he said. He is a terrible man and he killed my friend with no hesitation."

"How did he kill your friend?"

"With a knife. He keeps it with him at all times. When you find him, sir, you will have to be careful about the knife."

He had spoken in a way that made me feel that he was asking a question even though his words were not phrased in that way. I didn't comment about Augenberg. I still wanted to know more about Rolfe.

"How did Augenberg find you?"

"That I do not know, and please, sir, you must believe me."

"How did you get away from Stelling when you went back there to-day, after we had seen you?"

"He was excited, and he was more concerned with getting Ariane in the car. As he was doing this, I ran and he could not leave her to come after me."

"Did you think about staying to try to help her?"

"I thought I could help her more if I could get away and tell you or the other Americans."

"Where was he planning to take her, what did he say?"

"He said nothing. I think he wanted to find Augenberg."

Again he looked at me with a questioning expression and it was as if he wanted me to tell him what had happened with Augenberg, if he had been captured or had gotten away. I continued to question him.

"You heard nothing while you were with them to give you any thoughts on where they might go?"

"No, sir. I had the feeling that they were to wait here until someone called or contacted them with instructions."

I couldn't be sure about him. Heidi had heard everything and I wanted to get her opinion. I told Rolfe to sit where he was and I asked her to come with me to the doorway of the connecting rooms. We walked just inside her room, where I could still see Rolfe, and I talked to her in a low tone.

"Do you believe him?"

"No."

"Why?"

"I don't know exactly, there just seems to be something that is not right. I remember how they sounded as I stood near them on the street as they were looking at the car, and it did not seem that Rolfe was like a prisoner—it was more like he was a friend. And I think that Augenberg found them too easily. It doesn't make sense that he would have found them without help."

"And you think Rolfe might have provided the help?"

"Yes."

"I feel the same. I don't believe Rolfe about the car. Stelling wouldn't try to use the car if Rolfe got away. He would know that roadblocks would be set up, at least he would know that the local American and German authorities would be alerted, and he would not try to go far in the car."

"I agree."

I would question Rolfe further. In particular, I wanted to find out about his knowledge of the gold. Because Heidi did not know about the gold I preferred that she not be in the room. I told her what I would do.

"I'm going to question Rolfe again to determine if he is withholding information. Since we don't know if he might have others involved who might be nearby, I would like for you to go downstairs and watch people in the hotel lobby. If anyone looks suspicious, call me from the desk. You can speak in German, if it is necessary and I will understand. Don't take chances. Give me about twenty minutes and come back up. Can you do that?"

"I can and I will. I'll go at once."

She left and I went back into the room with Rolfe. He was beginning to show signs of anxiety, and I felt that would help me. He was about thirty years old, rather slender, and otherwise a nice-appearing young German man. Without speaking I walked to the window and looked out. He must have realized that I was undecided about him and he waited in silence. After a short pause I turned back in his direction. I asked if he had served in the Wehrmacht. He said that he was in the German navy. His ship had been called in to port as the war was coming to an end and he had been told to report to Fulda for home guard duty, which he did. He said he was to fight as a soldier when the Allies reached Fulda, but his unit fell apart before he was ever called upon to fight. I decided that I would try to back him into a corner.

"Rolfe, you are in a very serious situation. You may be arrested."

"Major! Please, I am trying to help you. Please sir, do not arrest me."

"I know that you are withholding information. Also, it appears that you were in a conspiracy with Augenberg and Stelling, and perhaps others. Unless you can provide information that will contradict that, I will have to recommend that you be placed in a camp with war criminals to be held for trial."

My statement had a grievous effect.

"Sir, I cannot go there. What is it that you wish to know?"

"There is a rumor that there is a large amount of gold near Bad Welmsburg. I think that Augenberg and Stelling know about it, and I think you know about it. Tell me what you know."

"I have heard that there is gold there, but I have not seen it and I do not know where it is."

"How long have you known about it?"

"For a few months. Ariane told my mother about it."

"Ariane knew the gold was there . . . a few months ago?"

"Yes. She did not know where it was or how much it was. She learned, somehow, from Karl Wegner, or possibly she learned about it from one of the Russians who was working for Karl, I am not sure about that. There was a Russian man who was disguised as a prisoner of war who was there and he may have been the one. He was working on the farm among the other Russians."

"And so you, your mother, and Ariane knew about the gold. Did anyone else know?"

"I do not know."

"What did Ariane say about the gold, what was to be done with it?"

"She . . . sir, I . . . she was planning I believe to tell you. Yes, I am sure she was planning to tell you."

"When? When did she plan to tell me? Wegner had been killed and she did not tell me. Can you explain that?"

"It was only that . . . everything was so uncertain, she knew that others, in addition to her husband would most likely know about the gold, and I believe she did not wish to have you involved because it would be dangerous for you."

That didn't seem likely. Was he lying about Ariane and her motives concerning the gold?

"I will remind you once again, Rolfe, if you lie to me you will go to prison. Now, think carefully and tell me if you ever heard any discussion between Augenberg, Stelling, and Ariane about the gold."

"Ah . . . possibly there was talk between them . . . I could not always hear what was being said."

"But, you believe that she was cooperating with them?"

"Major, you must remember that she was in the hands of men who would kill her. She had no choice."

"All right, then, let's talk about you and Ariane, before you were taken prisoners. What did Ariane want to do about the gold, and what did she tell you?"

"As I have told you, Herr Major, she planned to tell you at the right time, and I agreed with her."

It was obvious that I could not learn from him what I really wanted to know; what were the intentions of Ariane about the gold, and why had she delayed in telling me? I changed to another subject.

"Where would Stelling go in Frankenberg?"

"He could drive the car, he could leave the city, as I—"

I interrupted.

"No, he couldn't leave the city. The American Army and the German Police have been alerted. They would stop and search every moving vehicle. And I think you know that. So, tell me, where would he go in the city of Frankenberg?"

He didn't respond and looked a little frightened again. I pushed him to answer.

"Speak up, Rolfe, your future depends on it. You could very easily go to prison for the rest of your life."

He did speak up.

"I think others are here and in Bad Welmsburg—others who know about the gold. Stelling may have taken her to a location provided by others."

"Are Americans involved?"

"I believe at least one American is involved."

"Who is he? Describe him."

"I cannot because I have not seen him. I have only heard one or two references to him by Stelling and Augenberg."

"You heard no name?"

"No, I did not hear a name, or a description. They only refer to him as 'the American,' and he moves about very secretly."

In considering all of the statements he had made, I was almost certain he was lying. He might have said that Ariane had known about the gold "a few months ago" to reinforce his position. If he could persuade me that she was involved, it would help him. If it was decided later to eliminate her, his story would stand better, be more likely to be irrefutable. It would bring about a grave situation for her at present. Stelling might be awaiting word from Rolfe before making a decision about her. So, in summary, and in my best judgment, Stelling had moved Ariane a short distance from the original location to a second spot. This could have been accomplished easily if there was a second location available to them in Frankenberg. Rolfe, it appeared, had become involved with Augenberg and Stelling because of big money. They probably offered him a bribe, as LeTourneau had done with me. If Rolfe had told them that he suspected that Ariane knew about the gold, they might have offered him a million Marks, or more, to help them. And Ariane, after being taken prisoner, might have been wise enough to let them continue to think that she knew about the gold, to some extent, to prevent them from killing her.

I would have to release Rolfe. To hold him might be a death sentence for Ariane. I would release him under a house arrest arrangement. I wanted him to think that I believed him, and I used a conciliatory tone as I continued.

"Rolfe, I am going to release you on one condition. You must remain in the house of your friend, Odenbacher, until we have everything cleared up. I will advise the American Military forces here, as well as the German Police, that you are to remain in the house until you are advised otherwise. If you attempt to leave, you will go to prison. A method of surveillance will be used to enforce your containment. We will search every house in this town if we have to, and if Ariane is harmed, I will hold you responsible. Do you understand what I have said?"

"Yes, Herr Major."

"All right, tell me the address of Odenbacher's home and the telephone number. We will see that you have adequate supplies and there will be no reason for you to leave the house."

He gave me the information. Also, he gave me directions on how to locate the house. I told him I would be calling frequently to verify his presence there. I took his identification papers.

My objective was to place him in a position to communicate with Stelling, which he would be able to do by telephone. LeTourneau would soon learn all of the details and he would realize that he was no longer "holding all of the cards." The absence of Augenberg would alarm him. If he felt that we had Augenberg and would keep him safely hidden away to be used as a witness, he would know that his position had been weakened. And Augenberg's body was unlikely to be found. The location where I had pushed his body from the drop was inaccessible below and heavily wooded. He might never be found.

Heidi returned and I told her I was releasing Rolfe. She looked slightly puzzled, so I winked at her, being sure that Rolfe could not see me. She acknowledged with a tiny movement of her eyes that she understood. I turned to Rolfe.

"Thank you for cooperating. You are free to leave now."

He smiled, we shook hands, he said "good day" to Heidi and walked out.

8.

FOLLOWING THE DEPARTURE of Rolfe I told Heidi that I let him go because he was our only link to Ariane, and to hold him might place her in jeopardy. I told her we would restrict his movements but not his communication with Stelling and others. And, sooner or later, Stelling might come out in the open. She said she understood and thought it to be a good plan. I could tell that she was eager to let me know about something—she always had a different twinkle in her eyes.

"Max, you will not believe it! Guess what I was able to buy downstairs?"

I grinned.

"Let's see. Would it be a mink coat?"

She was enjoying herself.

"No. Make a real guess."

"A bottle of wine?"

"You can do better than that. There is plenty of wine. This is something I haven't seen for a year. Guess again."

"All right. I noticed the small bag you had so it has to be an item that is not too large. Candy! You found some chocolate candy."

"No, not right. But that was a better try. It is shampoo! We have had no shampoo for ages and they had some in the shop in the lobby."

I enjoyed it when she was happy and I liked to tease her.

"Hey, hey, you were on duty down there. What were you doing in the shop?"

"Are you going to arrest me? If so, I hope this room will be the jail."

I was fascinated by her and she knew it. She got up and moved toward the door, speaking as she walked.

"I am going to wash my hair. I'll be back soon, okay?"

"Okay."

I thought about her and Ariane. I considered their similarities and their differences. Heidi was more outgoing, more independent, and I think it would have been the same even if she had lived the same kind of lifestyle that I associated with Ariane. Both displayed compassion and a kindness for others. Ariane was more passive. Heidi had more "street" knowledge, due to the relationship with Kurth and his friends. Ariane, because of the wealth of Wegner, would have been exposed to a more elegant existence, and she would have known people who were a part of the highest level of German society. Neither was pretentious or presumptive. Both had expressed their love for me vividly, and each seemed to have the same desire for the ultimate consummation of love between a man and woman.

Ariane was slightly taller. Both were women of exceptional beauty. Ariane's hair flowed down perhaps more nearly to a shoulder length. Their coloring was similar, and each had facial features that were flawless. I think either could have become an instant success in Hollywood—their faces and bodies would have opened the necessary doors.

How did I come to know two such remarkable women so intimately? I had spent the previous adult years of my life without even coming close. Was it like so many other things that happen unexpectedly during a war? Countless numbers of people are thrown together who might have otherwise never known each other. The world had become a big melting pot, and we would see a broader range of people in a year than we would for the rest of our lives.

I called Captain Brown in the American Military Government office and told him about Rolfe. He said that he would offer whatever support I would need, and he was, in effect, allowing me to head the investigation and activities that were needed.

About an hour after leaving, Heidi came back. She had a different hairstyle. It looked great and I told her.

"Oh, I am glad you like it. Do I look . . . ah . . . more mature?"

"Oh, so that is what you had in mind? Yes, you look more mature, and more beautiful as well."

She had pulled her hair back and eliminated the slight curls that were previously around her face. And she did, in fact, look more sophisticated and as she had said, more mature. Her hair was parted in the middle and pulled straight back and I think she did want to make herself look more like a thirty-year-old woman rather than twenty. She was pleased that I liked it.

"I did it for you, I was hoping you would like it. So you see, Major, now it will not be easy for you to ever leave me."

I was a little more serious.

"No, that would not be easy for me to do, you've certainly taken care of that. I think it's the other way around, anyway, you'll go flying out the door some day."

"A fat chance!"

"Well, I must say, you're getting pretty sharp. You've picked up a lot of the common expressions that are used in English. And speaking of languages, I want you to continue to teach me German. So far, it seems to be working well for me."

"Okay. Are you doing as I said when you answer the phone?"

"Ja."

"Sehr gut. I think the only way you might get caught by the wrong person is during a telephone conversation with Captain Brown, if someone was able to cut in and listen."

"Yeah. It may not be as important anyway at this point. The people we are after know we are here, so, concealing ourselves might not be necessary."

"Oh, let's leave it like it is, I like you as a German man."

"All right, just for you, we will leave it that way. And now, madam, would you honor me with your presence at dinner this evening?"

"Yes! I will be happy to be with you for dinner," and there was a mischievous grin, "and the rest of the night, too, if you wish."

I didn't have to answer the second part of her statement. She knew from my previous resolve what I would do to maintain the position I had established. Also, she knew that it was borne from a feeling of endearment and not a lack of desire. I could only be with her if everything was right.

"Heidi, you will enjoy being in the dining room this evening. They change the atmosphere and make it nice. They even have music."

"You were here before . . . with her . . . and that is how you know. Am I right?"

"Yes, that is right. But now, this evening, I will be here with you."

"And I'm glad. I hope it will last forever."

We changed the subject and talked about other things. She would speak German often and I was beginning to pick up more of the language each day. It was easier to understand than pronounce, although Heidi said I was doing very well. I was concentrating on it in order that I would have a good understanding of the language if caught in certain circumstances that could occur.

We spent the rest of the afternoon in the room. I felt it had become a waiting game and it would be best to make myself available for the call I knew would come. LeTourneau would be calling soon.

Later, when it was time for dinner, Heidi appeared in the doorway of the connecting rooms. She had transformed herself into a glamorous woman and I told her.

"Heidi, you are beautiful. You look wonderful."

"Thank you, Max. I will always try to look beautiful for you. And you, in your nice German suit with a tie, are quite charming. So! We will be Herr and Frau Gordon this evening!"

"Sounds good to me. Let's go."

I got up and we walked out together. I had called Rolfe a few minutes earlier to let him know that I would be checking frequently as I had told him. And, with that done, I was ready to relax and enjoy the evening.

The large dining room was, as I had remembered, very nice in the evenings. People were dressed more formally and there was a different atmosphere. There was music. A woman was playing a piano accompanied by a man with a violin, and a second man with a bass fiddle. After we were seated by the hostess, Heidi looked at me from her seat directly across the table and grinned broadly. She spoke in German, saying it was wonderful. I glanced around to be sure no one could hear and responded in English.

"Yeah, it is for me too. Can you order for us? Our waiter will expect us to speak in German."

"Of course. And first, I am going to order wine, and we can relax and listen to the music while the food is being prepared. So, leave everything to me."

"Good."

The waiter came and greeted us in German. Heidi spoke to him and I nodded. She told him to bring the wine first and we would wait for a while to order. He turned away to follow her instructions.

Some of the songs being played were familiar to me, and most had the rhythm of a tango. We stopped talking for the most part so that we could better hear the music. The wine had come. We had a toast and it became a nice time for us. Heidi heard a song and spoke excitedly.

"Oh, it's *Bel amil,* one of my favorites."

As the song progressed she moved her upper body, her shoulders, keeping time with the music, and then she started clapping her hands. Others around her, mostly the women, did likewise, and soon the whole room was synchronized by the song. Over a hundred people were there, every seat taken, and all were reacting together as one. Heidi looked alternately over the room and back to me. Once she motioned to me and I, too, had to clap my hands in rhythm. I remembered her from the first night I went to her home in Bad Welmsburg, and as I had imagined she would do then, she was grasping each glorious moment as it came, loving to live, living to love, and holding on to each momentous occasion. Vivacious and fun loving, she was filled with an infectious enthusiasm for joyful moments. Bold and aggressive, she didn't try to conceal her pleasure, and she even stood momentarily so that she could move her whole body to keep pace with the music. After the song was finished she sat down and took a sip of wine. She grinned at me.

"I think we might turn this room upside down before the evening is over. I'm really having fun. How about you, Herr Major?"

"Yeah, I'm having fun too. Maybe we should stay up all night if we can keep this party going."

"Yes! I think that is a great idea!"

She turned and talked briefly to a young woman at the next table. The woman, who was about the same age as Heidi, laughed and agreed with several remarks Heidi made. I could well imagine what she was saying . . . I think she really did plan to turn the place "upside down." She looked back at me and spoke in English, keeping her voice low.

"After the food has been served we are going to ask the waiters to move some of the tables near the musicians so we can dance. You will have to dance with me, okay?"

"How do you know I can dance?"

"I don't care whether you can dance or not, you are going to have to get up and take me over there and try . . . do you understand, Herr Major?"

"Yes, I understand, my good Fraulein. Or should that be Frau?"

"It should be Frau. I have already told Freya, at the next table, that you are my husband."

I laughed. She was absolutely incomparable. A "take-over" type, she would leave everyone in an uncompromising position. She not only had grown on me, she had taken possession of me, and it would be next to impossible to refuse her anything.

Other songs were greeted with excitement by Heidi, and as we drank the wine we were both enjoying ourselves immensely. As each song began she told me the titles. *Nur Eine Stunde* was slow, followed by *Der Wind Hat Mir Ein Lied Erzahlt,* another tango; *Ich Will Nicht Vergessen,* apparently a love song; the same with *Ich Mochte So Sein Wie Du Mich Willst,* and many others that added enchanting sounds.

Our food came, and not surprisingly, it was good. The hotel must have been bringing in supplies of produce being harvested locally, and many vegetables were in season. Veal, a popular food with Germans, was served, and the flavor of a marinated sauce made it delicious.

From time to time I looked at the people in the large room. I would guess that possibly two-thirds or more were women. The men who were there were either older or very young. A few military-duty-aged men were among them, and I guessed they had come home as wounded soldiers and recovered. There were three American soldiers in the room, enlisted men, and they were escorting young German women. Young German women filled the seats around some tables and obviously they were there because of the lack of young German men who would have been there in normal times.

Everyone was having fun, and a unity had taken place with the people. It was due, of course, to the music and wine. It was a time for all of us to forget the past and enjoy life. Several people stopped by our table and wanted to shake hands with me. At first I didn't think it to be unusual, then I asked Heidi about it.

"You are a wounded German soldier! Don't you remember that we said you would play that part?"

"Sure I remember, but I didn't realize word would spread so fast."

"I told the desk manager when we came into the hotel the night we arrived and I suppose that is how it became known."

"Well, we better slow up on that story. You might have some disgruntled people on your hands if they find out the truth."

"Don't worry about it. I think only a few people would know. And they probably would not believe it in most cases because you certainly do not appear to be in bad condition. In fact, you look healthy and very strong."

"Thanks. And by the way, do you ever worry about anything?"

"No! Well, maybe . . ."

"What?"

"I worry about whether you will always love me."

"I'll always love you."

It was true, even though I was still in love with Ariane. Heidi smiled affectionately.

"That was nice. I like to hear you tell me things like that." Then, in a gleeful tone, she continued. "Now listen, Max, I love to dance to a tango. Can you do that?"

"Sure I can. I can dance to anything."

She was not certain about my answer even though she had a twinkle in her eyes.

"We will soon find out. Our waiter says they will clear out a square for dancing in about five more minutes."

At that moment, a woman from the audience was called by the woman who had been playing the piano, to come up near the musicians. Heidi said that she was going to sing.

The music began and the woman did sing. We could all understand at once why she had been asked. Her voice was exceptional. I remembered the song—it was a favorite among the people of Europe during the war. The German title was *Komm Zuruck.* During the second course the people in the room, most of whom were standing, began singing with her. Heidi came around our table and I stood. We held arms, and she sang. At the conclusion there was a loud and long applause by all.

The waiters moved tables and chairs back from the area in front of the musicians, and people crowded the open spot at once. Heidi held my hand and pulled me in that direction. When we got there people were jammed tightly together. The music began and I was happy to hear that it was a song with a slow pace. Anything else would have been a disaster. Heidi and I held on to each other and moved to the rhythm, and it felt good, holding her snugly in my arms. And she felt the same. I could sense it by touching her and feeling the movements of her body. She glanced up occasionally and I could see it in her eyes, the same thing, the tenderness of her love.

We danced for an hour and fifteen minutes without stopping. We had many chances to give each other an extra little squeeze, and touching her during that time, hugging her, gave me the opportunity to have the gratification I had been longing for as I had been near her each day. But it was getting late and the woman at the piano announced that the evening had come to an end for the musicians. There were a few groans, but it was good natured and the people knew it was time to go home. Heidi and I held hands and walked back to our table briefly. From there we went out of the large dining room and through the lobby to the stairs that led up to our rooms.

In my room we sat to relax and talk. She spoke first.

"Max, this has been the most wonderful evening of my life."

"I'm glad. It was great for me too. Did you—"

The phone rang. I picked up and it was the call I had been expecting. LeTourneau.

"Been out on the town, Max?"

"No, just here in the hotel. Where are you?"

"Here in town. I thought we might have a little talk."

"Okay. What do you suggest?"

"Meet me on the street in ten minutes. Go to your car and wait for me. We can sit in the car."

"Fine. I'll be there."

"Listen, Max, don't call any of your friends. You know we still have your lady."

"I know. I'll be alone."

He hung up. Heidi was eager to know about the call and I told her.

"It's the American who is involved. He wants to meet down on the street."

"No, Max, you can't. Don't you see, he will kill you."

"He can't, he doesn't know what I've got. I'm going to bluff him about Augenberg. I have to talk to him. Don't worry, I'll be safe."

She accepted what I said with some reservation.

"How long will you be gone?"

"Probably not more than thirty minutes."

I stood, touched her on the face with my fingers, and walked out.

Outside I walked to the black Mercedes sedan and sat in it. Within minutes, I saw in the rearview mirror a figure approaching up the hill, a large man. It would be LeTourneau. I was sitting on the driver's side of the car. I leaned over and pushed open the door on the passenger side, the door that would be next to the curb.

LeTourneau moved the door open wider to accommodate his large frame and got in. He greeted me in his normal manner.

"Hey, Max, I like your style. It's been a while since I've been in a Mercedes."

"What's on your mind, Eddie?"

"I came over to get you straightened out. You've got to get your mind right."

"And how is that?"

"Let's don't mess around, Max, I don't have time. Where is Augenberg?"

"In a place where you will never get to him."

"I don't believe you. You couldn't have taken him alive."

"We've got him, Eddie, and he's spilled his guts. He's told us enough about you to send you up the river for the rest of your life, if they don't decide to hang you."

"No way, Maxie. I know the boy and you would have to bury him before he would talk."

"Well, I guess you will just have to wait and find out, won't you?"

He paused, and it was not like his usual method of carrying out a conversation. I think I had struck a nerve. After about thirty seconds, he turned in my direction.

"You know, Max, you're about as stupid as anybody could be. What do you want, five million?"

"I want Ariane Wegner returned, unharmed. We're in a swap-off situation and you don't hold all of the cards anymore."

"Do you have any idea who you are up against?"

"No, and I don't really care. The documentation we have from Augenberg is detailed enough to hang you and the people you are working with."

Again, he thought about it. Then he spoke.

"No, I don't believe you. He's just not the type."

"We offered him a deal. He can walk—we will set him free in the Russian Zone when everything is over. We will hold him, however, until your trial is over."

His anger increased.

"You dumb bastard, you're throwing away a fortune. What the hell is wrong with you?"

"I want to see Ariane Wegner walk away from where she is being held. After that we can talk."

"Oh, hell, no! I won't do that! No deal, Max."

He turned to leave. I had one final comment.

"If she's harmed, Eddie, the army won't have to worry about you. Remember that."

He got out of the car and then leaned back in to respond.

"You don't worry me, Max. But I do need some time. I'll be in touch."

He closed the door and walked away. I got out and went back into the hotel.

Heidi grinned when I returned to my room where she had been waiting.

"Max! Tell me what happened."

"I intended to make him believe we captured Augenberg and I think I succeeded. If he believes Augenberg will tell us about LeTourneau's connections with the SS, I'm hoping he will release Ariane. Right now he is undecided and needs time. He will contact me when he is ready to talk."

"What if Augenberg's body is discovered?"

"That won't happen. His body went down into an inaccessible area that is wooded. I don't think he will ever be found."

"The American, who is he?"

"His name is LeTourneau. I suspect he is a first-generation son of a German woman who immigrated to the U.S. We know some of those people still had close ties to Germany. Also, we know that Hitler developed a plan to try to use them. After arriving in Germany as soldiers, they were used by the Germans. LeTourneau might be in that category."

"I'm not surprised. There were spies everywhere. Oh well, at least we will get to be together in Frankenberg for a while longer."

"Yeah, we can't do anything now except wait for his next move."

"Well, Herr Major, we can have fun while we wait."

"Absolutely. What can we do tomorrow?"

"We can go in the shop downstairs . . . if I am not on duty again."

"That's a good idea. Maybe I can find something in the shop, too."

I glanced at my watch and she noticed. She didn't move. She was sitting with a sweet look on her face, waiting for me to speak, and I did.

"Well, I guess we better hit the sack. We'll have another great day tomorrow, how about that?"

"It's fine."

She continued to sit. I stood up, still gazing into her eyes, and her eyes told me her inner thoughts; she wanted to be held. She stood and I moved to her and held her. We stayed in an embrace for a few moments, and then I kissed her on the cheek and her lips. She returned the kiss, and as before, we were locked together with a cherishing desire, and it quickly became passionate for each of us. I released her, and we backed away from each other.

"Goodnight, Heidi."

She smiled and turned to go to her room.

"Goodnight, Max."

After I was in bed I thought about her. Could it only be a "crush" as we used to say in high school? How could I really love two women at the same time? Was it like a book I read while in college, about a Russian doctor who was overwhelmed by his love for two women? He was a man with good character who placed great importance on loyalty and integrity, but he could not bring himself to leave either of the women. Now, I felt the same, and I could not imagine that I could leave either Ariane or Heidi. I ruled out the idea that it might be a simple "crush" with Heidi. I had come to love her. And I knew that I did not have an answer on how to handle the future.

While we were having breakfast in the dining room the next morning, I asked Heidi about her parents.

"They live in Hannover. My father was wounded and was sent to work at one of the camps after he recovered. He was not a guard and had no contacts with the prisoners. He worked in the office, doing paperwork."

"Will they return to Bad Welmsburg?"

"Yes, when they are released. They are under house arrest until the investigation of all people who worked at the camp is completed."

"Yeah, I had talked to Chief Swartz while we were investigating the death of Leni and your name was mentioned. I believe the Chief misinterpreted the status of your father and he might have believed that he would be held in Hannover for some reason."

"No. My father has been told that he will be released soon."

"I'm sure you will be glad to see them when they get home."

"Yes, indeed."

We left the dining room and Heidi showed me the shop in the lobby where she had bought the shampoo. It was too early and the shop was not open. I asked her if she would like to go for a walk and she answered with an enthusiastic "Yes."

On the outside we turned to the right and walked up the street. The Rathaus was nearby, as were many old buildings. The town apparently was like some of the others I had seen in Germany, and it had been there for many centuries. At the top of the hill we could see the entrance to the park about a hundred yards away. Heidi asked if we should go there, knowing it was where I had chased Augenberg.

"I think it will be okay. I don't believe anyone saw me when I was here before."

We continued straight ahead and soon we were in the park. Some other people were there, elderly men and women, and a few mothers with children. We found an empty bench and sat down. Heidi was more serious than usual.

"Max, what is going to happen . . . between us?"

"I don't know. I thought about it last night while in bed."

"How can it end?"

"I hope, as you said once, that no one will really be hurt."

"How can that be?"

I turned and grinned at her. I wanted to get her in a different mood.

"Hey, this is not you. You told me that you don't worry."

She smiled slightly.

"I lied. Max, please tell me that you will . . ."

"Heidi, don't worry. Let's take it a day at a time. You know that I cannot walk away from you."

"What about Ariane?"

"Let's don't try to settle it now."

She smiled and agreed. Although she would depend on me to settle things, I, too, was uncomfortable. As she had said, how could we all three end up happy? It was just as difficult for me as it was her. Even though she had indicated it would be my choice, I would still be hurt, badly. I decided to follow my own suggestion and change to another subject.

"Do you think it would be possible for us to walk to the spot where I pushed Augenberg over and look down below?"

"No, that would not be a good idea. Others might see us and become curious. I think we should leave well enough alone."

"You're right. I am certain that his body cannot be seen anyway. I was just thinking about LeTourneau, and how desperate he is, and if he knew that Augenberg is dead it would change his position."

"He will never find out. If what you say is true, about where his body is, Augenberg can never be found. What is so important to this man, LeTourneau?"

I would have to explain it to her as best I could. To protect her, I did not want to tell her about the gold. If anything happened to me, LeTourneau would take her and assume that she knew about the gold. I was certain he would torture her.

"There is something else involved, Heidi. To protect you, I cannot tell you about it. If anything happened to me, LeTourneau would take you and try to force you to talk."

"What do you mean by saying if anything happened to you? Is he crazy?"

"Yeah, in a way, he is. But, now that I've got him thinking about what Augenberg might have told us, he's in a different position. He will have to back off and try to negotiate with me."

"I don't understand it all, and I don't think I want to understand. I think I will just be happy while we are together and forget about everything else."

"Good. I was hoping you would say that."

It was pleasant in the park and relaxing. I would try to do as Heidi had said and forget the things that were troublesome, and concentrate on the happiness of the moment.

I did have two additional thoughts that had entered my mind since I had talked to LeTourneau. Would he try to take Heidi? He would know that she had become important to me. Her presence with me would tell him that. He would be turning over every stone for something he could use. I made a mental note to send a message to him through Rolfe. I would tell Rolfe that I had information for "the American" and that he should contact me. Then, I would tell LeTourneau that we had removed Augenberg to another city, a location where top security was in place. It should convince LeTourneau that Augenberg would be inaccessible and we would hold him for use in a trial. There was, however, one other alternative that he might try, and I wanted Heidi to know.

"Heidi, let me say a few additional things about LeTourneau, and then we will forget about him."

She nodded and waited for me to continue.

"There is a possibility that he might try to take you, and hold you. I'm not too concerned about it because he already has a hostage, and that would not be a new idea. The other thing I have thought of is more likely. And I'm saying this to you because of my military training; every good commander tries to anticipate what his enemy will do.

LeTourneau has high contacts in the U.S. Army. He would have no problem in having me transferred away from here, even back to the States. He might feel if he was able to remove me, it would make it easier for him. It's only a possibility, so don't be concerned yet. If Le-Tourneau is convinced that we have Augenberg, and that Augenberg has already made a detailed statement, he most likely would realize that removing me would not help."

"What a terrible thought. What would I do?"

"If I should happen to be removed, I will see that you are protected."

"No, Max, what would I do without you? Would I ever see you again?"

"Oh, sure. I could come back after a discharge from the army. Don't worry, it's not likely to happen anyway."

"Okay, I am not going to worry."

"Good! Now, let's forget about LeTourneau for a while. What would you like to do, stay here or go for a walk?"

"Go for a walk."

We stood, held hands, and walked in a direction to exit from the park. It was a pleasant day, typical I think, of a summer day in Germany. By mid-afternoon the temperature might go to the mid-seventies.

Heidi would speak to people as we passed, and so would I, using a few selected words that I could pronounce well in German. No one stopped to talk. We had decided that it would not be necessary for me to continue the masquerade as a former soldier suffering from shell shock who could not speak.

I liked to watch Heidi as she walked along, sometimes going away from me to the side for some reason, or walking ahead momentarily at times. Her body personified her personality, and even if I had not known her, I think I would have guessed accurately about her by watching her movements. She went along confidently, smiling most of the time. And now, of course, she was exhibiting the pleasure she felt from being in the middle of a new and exciting adventure. I had asked her what she had told her employer in Bad Welmsburg about her planned absence from work, what reason she had given for being away. She said she told them that she was going to be working temporarily for the American Military Government, and if there were questions they should be directed to Major Gordon. She said she felt sure there would be no questions asked.

We saw old houses as we walked along, three and four floors, houses that would have been constructed hundreds of years before. The Germans, it seemed, built homes to last forever. And Frankenberg had been spared during the war. There were only two air raids and our planes on those occasions had dropped bombs in the vicinity of the rail lines in the edge of the city. Most likely it was a "dump" by the pilots following a raid on a city or target, deeper in Germany, and to get rid of their remaining bombs during the return to England, they would pick less important sites, usually rail lines. Consequently, the people of the city were spared the destruction that had been so brutal in other parts of the country. And for that reason, I think it was easier for the people of Frankenberg, as well as cities in the same category, to accept our presence, even offer to become friends after we had lived among them for a while. And it was the same for us—it was easier to forgive and forget. And there was no question that we were all happy to be free of further deaths and devastation that accompany war.

Back in my room at the hotel I called Rolfe. I told him that I knew it would be possible for him to contact Stelling by telephone. At first he insisted that he could not, he had no way of knowing about the location of Stelling. Finally, he did admit that he received calls from Stelling, but could not return them because Stelling wanted to keep the telephone number and his location secret. I believed him. My advice to him at that time was to tell Stelling, the next time Rolfe received a call, to have the American contact me. Rolfe agreed.

In the afternoon, Heidi and I went into the shop in the hotel lobby. Surprisingly, quite a few items were on hand, a mix of clothing, personal care merchandise, jewelry, and various other things. Heidi was like a child in a candy store; she wanted to look at everything. She moved from counter to counter, completely enthralled. It was understandable. Many of the things were intriguing to her because she had not seen them for a long while. She stayed at the jewelry counter for a while and her eyes seemed to be glued to a silver chain necklace. I asked the lady behind the counter, in German, "How much?", and she told me. I had brought a large amount of money, not knowing how much I would need. In fact, I had brought much more than I anticipated I would need just to be on the safe side. The saleslady told me the price of the necklace in Marks, and it was the equivalent of approximately one hundred fifty dollars. I told her, again speaking in German, that I would take it. I had Marks on me, of course, and I counted out the amount and placed it on the counter.

Heidi was bursting with excitement and she could hardly contain herself. She looked at me with a sincere expression, truly appreciative, and she didn't have to speak—I could see it all in her eyes. She knew the necklace was for her.

After we were out of the shop she did speak.

"Oh, Max, thank you so much. It is so beautiful. I will treasure it forever."

"I'm glad. It was my pleasure. And by the way, how do you think I handled things with the lady? Did my German sound okay?"

"Yes! I was very proud of you."

We had been in my room for only a short while when the phone rang. It was LeTourneau. "Understand you want to talk, Max. Have you come to your senses?"

"I wanted to let you know your boy is in another part of Germany at this time. He left here with a heavy escort during the night and he is now in a top security prison where he will be watched twenty-four hours a day. I worked it out with the German Police, Eddie, so your buddies with the U.S. Army will have a tough time helping you."

"Well, now, that's a real fine story but I don't believe you."

"That's okay, I thought you would feel that way. So, let me tell you where you are. A copy of Augenberg's statement is in the hands of a reliable friend. The friend will go to the Allied Supreme Commander with it depending on how things turn out here. Eddie, you're a real con man, but I doubt you've been able to get to Ike. Think it over."

There was a long pause. I knew before hearing him speak that I had nailed him. It was possibly a full minute before he continued.

"What do you want, Max, the woman and the gold too?"

"I want the woman first. The other aspects of the matter can be settled in a different manner."

"How?"

"I don't know. Maybe they would let you off . . . they might even give you a finder's fee."

"Hell no! I'm not looking for something like a hundred thousand dollars, I want no less than twenty million. No, I'm not ready to settle like that. And I'm not convinced you've got Augenberg, anyway. You'll have to give me proof."

"I don't have to give you anything. You're the one who is in deep, deep trouble. I'll give you twenty-four hours to think it over."

"No, no way. You can't bluff me, Max. I can leave here and disappear into the Russian Zone any time I want to . . . and I can take the little lady with me. Or leave her here with her throat cut. No, you think it over, you've still got the same problem you started with so don't think you can push me around."

"All right, we've reached an impasse. What do you suggest?"

"Time. I suggest that we both take time to think. I'll be in touch."

He hung up. Heidi wanted to know what he had said and I explained to her.

"It's going to take more time. He's still trying to decide what to do. We will just have to wait for him."

Heidi, a little tired of LeTourneau, talked about other things and I was glad. She asked if we could go back to the hotel dining room for dinner and I said "yes." It quickly put her in a gleeful mood.

"We will have to go early. You know last evening was the first night of the week-end but tonight it will be more crowded because there is no work tomorrow. What do you think?"

"I think you should call down there now and make a reservation for us."

"Yes! Why didn't I think of that? I hope to see Freya again."

She made the call and was told that our table would be reserved. After she had finished the call she said she would go downstairs to the shop again, and would return in an hour. I told her it would be best not to go out on the street and she agreed.

After she left, my thoughts reverted to the present situation involving Ariane. I had talked to the local American Military Government Investigator previously, and he had German Police surveillance set up on the house where Rolfe was located. We were not equipped to trace, or hear, telephone calls to the house. It might be just as well. Even if we could locate the house where Ariane was being held it would be dangerous to rush it or try to move in with force. Stelling probably would kill Ariane and then shoot it out with our men. It was frustrating. We would have to continue the waiting game for a while.

Heidi was back at twenty minutes before six. She had a bag, larger than the one she had brought when she had bought the shampoo. She looked at me with the familiar expression that I had come to recognize when she was eager to convey an exciting message.

"Max, I bought something to wear tonight. Do you want to see it now or wait until I am dressed?"

"Ah . . . let's see . . . I'll wait until you put it on."

"Okay. I'm going into my room and get ready. Our reservation in the dining room is at six forty-five. Are you going to wear the black suit you brought?"

"Yes."

"Good. Maybe we will be like, . . . you know, matching together, I think, is what I am trying to think of."

She turned and walked away. It was one of the few times she had gotten tangled up a little with her English.

When she appeared some thirty-five or forty minutes later in the connecting room doorway, she looked glamourous. She had on a black skirt that was pleated. Her top had a soft blend of leopard-like colors, with full-length sleeves. Both garments appeared to be silk. A narrow scarf, made up of a combination of the colors of both the skirt and blouse, was tied neatly around her neck. The style and mix of colors made the outfit look expensive and classy. I told her.

"You look great, like a model or a movie star. I had no idea you could find such nice clothing in the shop."

"Thanks. I liked it the moment I saw it and I hoped you would too."

"I do, absolutely. I'll have to keep an eye on you tonight, you might leave with another man."

"Oh, no, not a chance. Maybe I should watch you. I saw women looking at you last evening when we were there."

"Good! That will keep you on your toes."

She laughed.

A few minutes later, we were downstairs in the large dining room. She had been correct earlier—already the room was crowded with people and without the reservation we might have had a problem. It was probably the most popular place in town, if not the one and only center for evening activities with a nice environment. The people of the city were showing that they were ready to return to normal, relax, and enjoy themselves. And I could sense a feeling of relief among them, even without words. Most were good natured and friendly. During the previous evening many of them had moved from table to table, laughing and talking.

After we were seated Heidi ordered white wine. Both of us preferred it. And, apparently there was nothing more plentiful in post-war Germany than wine. Possibly it had to do with storage facilities for the wine. Most likely they were located away from primary targets of Allied air raids. There were a number of German trucks left, which we allowed the civilians to keep in operation for many reasons, so transporting the wine could be accomplished by using the trucks on the autobahn. The rail system was functioning well, too, and with the exception of some few areas, people and materials were effectively moved from place to place.

Our wine came, and with a toast to each other . . . I said, "to you," Heidi said, "and to you, my love," . . . we began another wonderful time of being together. Heidi was in high spirits, and like the others who were there, she greeted people who passed or were seated near us with kind words.

The same three musicians were on hand and the instruments they played, the bass fiddle, violin, and piano, were coordinated to send out pleasing sounds. Heidi would always tell me the title of a song as it began and I could sense, of course, the nature of most of them; love songs, often a tango, and occasionally, an American song picked up from the American Radio Broadcasting Station. The BBC in London was heard loud and clear too in Germany, and at night, other radio stations located all across Europe could be heard because reception was better during that time. The tango seemed to be the favorite of people of all nations, judging from the frequency with which it was played.

Heidi heard a song and liked it.

"Max, this is a good song. It's called *So Liebt nur ein Zigeunerherz.*"

I remembered the song. I had heard it before, in the very same room, with Ariane. I did not tell Heidi. I didn't want to take anything away from her pleasure, or joy, by talking about Ariane.

I looked over the audience to see if the woman who sang during the previous evening was there. I wanted to hear her again. I couldn't spot her, but it did give me the opportunity to see the mix of people, and it seemed to be about the same as before. Four American soldiers in uniform were the escorts of young German women. Fraternization rules had been relaxed by the American commanders, and friendships were developing fast. And it seemed right. Why carry grief, hatred, and all of the other negative factors to our graves? All of us had been displaced, shot at, hurt, and had suffered a loss of time and pleasures for a period that would be taken out of our lives forever, but, as some would say, "it was time to move on."

Heidi was going through the same body motions she had displayed the previous night, and I knew she was getting warmed up to dance later. She was cute and beautiful, all in one, and I was looking forward to dancing with her.

We were sitting close together rather than being on opposite sides of the table, and it was easier to talk in English. Between songs I teased her.

"Do you really expect me to believe that you had no boyfriends, no one other than Kurth?"

She knew what I was doing and it was fun for her.

"Well, let's see, now that I think about it, there was Wilhelm."

"Wilhelm? Who was he?"

"Oh, he was very fond of me. He used to bring me an apple."

"Aha! Trying to persuade you by giving gifts. What happened?"

Her face was near mine and she had an intriguing glow in her eyes.

"When he became ten he liked another girl in school. So you see, Max, there really were no others."

She leaned over and kissed me on the lips. It was a brief encounter and she pulled away. The music started again and both of us turned back to face the musicians.

She was making it more difficult for me as each day passed. And staying in the room next to her each night, thinking about her and how much I wanted to be with her, wanting to hold her in my arms, was almost tearing me apart. Something out of the past, maybe it was the influence of my parents who had placed great importance on integrity and honor, kept me steadfast in holding to the ideals I had been taught and had come to respect. But it was not easy.

The background noises in the room, people talking and laughing, grew louder and it was easier for us to carry on our conversations in English. Heidi leaned over close and spoke.

"You want to know something, Max?"

"Sure. Tell me."

"I'm having fun!"

"I would have never guessed."

"How long will we get to stay in Frankenberg?"

"Maybe a few more days."

"And then we will go back to your house in Bad Welmsburg?"

"Yes."

I couldn't be sure about that but I didn't want her to know. I did want her to know something else.

"Heidi, when we leave here tonight to go to our rooms . . . when we get to the rooms, I hope we can just . . . separate, and go to our own rooms."

She turned to look at me.

"You're serious. What is it?"

"It's becoming more difficult for me. Do you understand?"

She gazed into my eyes with an expression of love.

"Yes, my darling Max, I understand. It is the loyalty you spoke about. Yes, we can do as you say. You must be one in a million to have such strong feelings about Ariane and me, and be so careful to be loyal."

"It has to be right in my mind, Heidi. If it was reversed and she was here, it would be the same."

"I know. I think I must have realized that the first night you came to my home in Bad Welmsburg. When I stood and showed you my breasts you did not become like a dog and reach for me. You were able to control your desires because of your love for Ariane. This is something new for me and I did not realize that any man would be like you."

"Thanks. Speaking of that night in Bad Welmsburg, what did you really hope to accomplish?"

"I knew you were the head of American security in Bad Welmsburg. I wanted you to become my friend and protect me. I knew about the background of Walter Kurth, and I knew that the SS men were there for some important mission. I could have become involved because of Walter, and either way, whether it might be the Americans or the German SS, it could have been bad for me."

I grinned at her.

"I hope you learned a good lesson. In the future, don't show everybody your breasts."

She smiled.

"I will never show my breasts to anyone but you, Max. Now, I know about the loyalty you have taught me, and I want to be the same way. Since I have come to know you so well I know the true meaning of love between a man and a woman. If you love someone you do not turn your back for a while to be with someone else."

"Right. I'm glad we feel the same."

At that moment I happened to think of my former wife, Moira, and the feeling I had for her. It was very different. When I had married her I think it was simply a time in life for it to be the right thing to do. For Moira, it was probably the same. And neither of us had feelings like I had experienced with Ariane and Heidi. Eventually, of course, we realized it was dull and not right, and while I was overseas in the army Moira took care of the necessary details of our divorce. I still thought of her in the same way I always had—as a friend. Now, I could see that there was much more involved in really caring for a woman.

Things were becoming a little more lively in the large dining room. Heidi saw Freya on the far side of the room and went over for a short visit. When she came back she told me about her conversation.

"Freya is married and she is waiting for her husband to come back. But he was in Russia and she . . . I don't think she will ever see him again. It must have been terrible there. So many German soldiers went there and were never heard from again."

"I'm sure it was a bad place to be, for both sides. The cold, along with the brutal warfare, would make it miserable."

"I'm glad the Americans got here first. I think it would have been quite different if it had been the Russians."

"I'm sure it would have been."

She grinned.

"And if you had not come here first I would have never seen you."

"Yeah, and that would have been bad news."

"Bad news?"

"It means terrible."

"Oh, yes, I agree, it would have been bad news."

Our food was served, and again, it was good. It was pork, red cabbage, and cooked apples. After we were finished our waiter cleared the dishes and brought another bottle of wine.

It was another delightful evening. At times I forgot about everything else and became absorbed with the nearness of Heidi and the gaiety of the environment around us. The music, the laughter, the presence of a beautiful and loving woman at my side made the time pass quickly, and suddenly the evening had faded and disappeared much like a beautiful sunset.

9.

WE SLEPT LATE on Sunday morning. For me, it was seven forty-five. Heidi was still asleep and I heard no activity from her room.

I thought about LeTourneau and what my next move should be. He had talked about proof concerning Augenberg. He wanted to verify that I actually had Augenberg. I thought of the perfect means of convincing him.

I would copy, in detail, the information from the SS identification I had taken from Augenberg's clothing following our fight. LeTourneau could show it to Stelling who would recognize it immediately as being authentic. I had carried the SS identification in my own wallet after taking it to be sure that it would be kept securely.

I got up immediately, took Augenberg's identification out of my wallet and sat in a chair next to a small desk. I copied everything that was written on the document, including dates and signatures, and I arranged it on the paper I was using in the same order that it appeared on the original document. It would leave no doubt that it had been taken from Augenberg—it would have been impossible for me to have it from any other source. It would be irrefutable.

Later in the morning after Heidi and I had returned from having breakfast, I called Rolfe. I told him to get a message to "the American" and have him call me.

Heidi and I went for a walk. We walked down the hill to get a look at the buildings in the lower part of the city. We walked down a long hill, which at the bottom bowed to the left. Soon we could see an American flag on a building and I assumed it would be the office of the American Military Government. And it was. We passed directly in front of the building, which formerly housed a bank, and we saw a sign near the entrance which listed the American unit. It was a proud moment for me, seeing our flag on the building.

We kept going. Heidi found out from people along the way that we could continue in a circle around the great mound on which the city had been built, and eventually it would lead us to a way to go up on the opposite side to reach the hotel. Perhaps a thousand years earlier, when the city first came into existence, the crest of the great mound would have provided a measure of safety and protection from the forces roving the area bent upon attacking and plundering the villages. Their defenses must have worked well because the old city was still intact.

Shortly after three in the afternoon, as Heidi and I were relaxing in my room, the telephone rang. I answered, saying "Ja."

"Hey, Max, it sounds like you might get to be a good German one of these days."

It was LeTourneau.

"You got my message, Eddie?"

"Yeah. What kind of cock and bull story have you got for me this time?"

"You said you wanted proof about Augenberg. I can give you proof. What will you give me in return?"

There was a long pause. It was typical of Eddie when he felt he was at a disadvantage.

"What kind of proof?"

"Something that is irrefutable."

"Okay, let's say you've got something. What do you want?"

"The release of Ariane Wegner."

Another long pause.

"How about the gold?"

"It's not the issue. The woman is the issue."

He seemed to be partly convinced about my proof, and he took more time.

"I'll have to see the proof."

"That's no problem."

"Why are you offering proof now, why not earlier?"

"I had to give the German Police time to place Augenberg in a top security location. They requested it."

"So, you're saying that no Americans are aware of this, you worked it out entirely with the Germans?"

"That's right."

"I don't believe it. They don't have the facilities, or the authorization to move like that. It would be impossible to conceal an operation like that from the U.S."

"We worked it out. Have you seen Augenberg lately? Has anybody seen or heard from him?"

He delayed a few moments before responding.

"No."

"What does that tell you?"

"I don't know . . . I don't know. Max, what the hell is wrong with you? Hell, man, you're not a boy scout, you're a paratrooper, you've killed people. You can have your woman and a big pile of gold. You wouldn't have another worry for the rest of your life. Why can't you get that through your thick skull?"

"We don't all think alike, Eddie. I want the woman, unharmed. If you send her back, I'll negotiate with you."

"No! Hell no! I'm not going to move first. Let me have your proof about Augenberg and I'll make a decision after that."

"This has gone on long enough. It has to be resolved quickly."

"Or you will do what? Hell, you're still up the creek."

"I want to talk to her. You want proof, I want proof."

"No, no way."

I thought about it briefly, then responded.

"Have her write me a note. Tell her to name the song she was playing on the piano the first day I went to her home. Bring it to me this evening. We can meet in the car in front of the hotel at ten. I'll bring the proof about Augenberg."

He thought about it and finally decided.

"Okay, it's a deal. And Max, let me warn you again, if you call in your friends, her throat will be cut in less than five minutes."

"I'll be alone."

"I'll see you."

Heidi had been listening and she spoke excitedly.

"What can you show him?"

"Augenberg's SS identification, or actually it will be a copy that I made from the real document. I took it off of him before rolling him off of the drop into the ravine. They will recognize it as valid information and I am sure it will convince them that we have him."

"Max, is this becoming more dangerous?"

"No, not really. In fact, we may be making some progress."

"What will happen if he releases Ariane?"

"You mean, with us?"

"Yes."

"Heidi . . . I . . . I've thought about it and I will tell her, but first, I want to greet her and let her feel happy for a while. She has been through a real ordeal. Then I will tell her the truth."

"What will she say, or do?"

"I don't know. What would you do if you were in her place?"

"I cannot say, but . . . I think that you must be with both of us for a while. In the end . . . it is going to be up to you."

"And I can't really think about that at this moment. I don't have the answer."

"Did you sleep with her?"

"Heidi, please . . . ."

"I would like to know. Can you please tell me?"

"Yes, I slept with her. Once."

She was disappointed. I tried to say something to help.

"It was after Karl was killed, and after my divorce."

"Was it here?"

"Yes."

"So, all of this with me is not new to you, you have already been here with her."

"Yes, Heidi, I have been here with her. But I have never lied to you, and now, I am in love with you. I'm sorry that it is complicated. It is something that is very disturbing to me. I don't want you to be hurt, you've been a wonderful companion and I have loved every minute of it."

She felt better. She came and put her arms around me and we held each other for a long while. Then she pulled away and spoke.

"What would I do if I lost you?"

"What would I do without you? As you said, it will take time and maybe that will heal everything."

The day seemed long to me. Even as Heidi and I went out for our usual walk, my thoughts remained unchanged, and I was more worried than usual. I tried to cover it up for Heidi's benefit, although I knew that her keen sense of perception was telling her the truth.

Finally, at five minutes before ten P.M. I left the room to go down to meet LeTourneau. Outside I walked to the black Mercedes sedan and got in on the driver's side. I didn't have long to wait and soon I saw Eddie in the rearview mirror approaching as he had before, coming up the hill. Then, he was there, and he opened the door and sat in the passenger seat beside me. I could tell by his facial expression that his mood was different. He did not have the easygoing attitude that I had seen during other meetings. He got down to business at once.

"Okay, let's see what you've got."

"Hold up the piece of paper you have for me. We will exchange at the same time."

He reached in his pocket and pulled out a small piece of paper. I took hold of a piece of paper in my shirt pocket that I had brought for him and held it up. Then, simultaneously, we exchanged the two pieces of paper.

I opened the folded paper he handed me at once. There was enough light coming from the street to allow me to read the writing easily. There was one word on the paper: *Jalousie.* It was the word I was looking for, the title of the song Ariane had played. I knew it had come from her.

LeTourneau was looking carefully at the information on the paper I had given him. He seemed puzzled by it.

"How the hell can I read all of this crap? It could be something you dreamed up."

"Take it to Stelling. He will recognize it. For example, a number was assigned to each member of the SS. Augenberg's number is on the paper you have."

He stared at it closely and reacted.

"Damn! Damn, damn. The lousy, no good, lying jerk!" He fussed and fumed and used some additional profanity and looked back to me.

"Tell me one thing, Max, how the hell were you able to take him alive?"

"That's not the point. The point is, he has torn down your little playhouse. You've got to do something, and do it quick. You can start by releasing Ariane Wegner."

"Man, you're crazy. I'm not ready to fold at this point."

"Eddie, you're in big trouble. The decision you make now will determine your future. The people you're calling your friends are expecting you to deliver the gold, and if you can't do that, you better head for the Russian Zone fast."

"I'll deliver the gold, don't worry about that, but right now, I need time."

He moved to get out of the car. I made one final suggestion.

"Don't wait too long."

He didn't respond, and obviously, he was upset. He had bought my story about Augenberg and he knew that my "boy scout" tendencies he had referred to earlier had backed him into a corner. The philosophy of LeTourneau was typical of the "me first" attitude of some men I had known. He was so deeply embedded in his own desires he was oblivious to others and he would step on people who were in his path in order to satisfy and achieve his self-serving motivations. For him, there was no honor, integrity, discipline or loyalty, and in his mind such characteristics were only for people who were stupid.

I was somewhat concerned about him . . . would he panic? If so, would he kill Ariane and try to escape? I had thought about it beforehand and had decided that he probably would not because of the gold. If Ariane had been wise enough, as I had assumed, to make him believe that she had some knowledge of the gold, he would not harm her. Still, it was risky. The whole matter was risky.

I returned to my room and brought Heidi up to date. If LeTourneau decided to run I would be ready. I would plan, the next day, to go by the American motor pool garage and fill up with gas. I had two five-gallon cans of gas in the trunk of the car, and that, along with the fill-up, would give me a range of about four hundred miles. I would tell Heidi to pack up, and I would do likewise so that we could leave quickly. I might even take our travel bags down to the car whether we checked out or not. I could always bring them back in if we decided to stay. My instincts were telling me that LeTourneau would make some sort of move quickly.

At nine forty A.M. the next morning, I drove the Mercedes into the American Military Government motor pool compound on the Marburg Road. I was met by a friendly sergeant, a fellow whose name was Randy Miller.

"Good morning, sir. It's a good thing Lieutenant Casteel called and told me about your civilian garb. I might have turned you down on the gas. Must be something pretty important you're working on."

"It is that, Sergeant, and thanks for your help. And by the way,

Lieutenant Casteel is due here at any time. He was to meet me at nine forty-five."

I had called Casteel earlier and had asked about weapons. In particular, I wanted a Thompson sub-machine gun. He said he could handle it, along with ammunition. In answer to another request he told me he would bring along six hand grenades.

I signed for the gasoline just as a jeep was pulling into the compound. An officer got out near me and started to salute, then, smiling broadly, he spoke.

"Excuse me, sir. I was about to give you away."

"No problem, Lieutenant. I appreciate your cooperation."

We talked for a while and I let him know that I might have to make a quick exit from the city, depending on new developments. He told me that he would continue the surveillance at key places in town, and he would contact me through my office in Bad Welmsburg if necessary. I put the machine gun and grenades in the trunk of the car and headed back to the hotel.

When I entered my room Heidi looked anxious. She explained.

"Max, your Colonel just called. He said you must leave at once."

"Why?"

"It is the American Army, they will come for you."

"Was it Colonel Margolies?"

"Yes! Yes, that was his name."

"What else did he say?"

"Not much. He said it was very important. You should leave at once and do not take time to try to call him."

"All right, let's go. Do you have everything ready?"

"I'm all set."

"Good. I'm going to give you some money. Go to the desk downstairs and pay the bill. While you are there be sure to say, in a casual way, that we are going to Marburg to see your aunt. Can you do that?"

"Yes, I can do that very easily."

"Fine. I'll take our bags to the car and wait for you there."

In less than fifteen minutes I had everything in the car and waited inside for Heidi to come out of the hotel. It gave me a moment to think. Apparently LeTourneau had used his contacts with top brass in the army to have me charged somehow so that I would be arrested. For what reason I could not imagine. But, once again, the gold was emerging as the reason for everything.

As she got in the car, Heidi smiled.

"The man at the desk asked if we would be coming back soon. I said, 'Oh, yes. We are going to Marburg for a few days to stay with my aunt. Perhaps we will return next week.' "

"Excellent."

I started the engine and we drove up the hill a short distance to the old part of the city. I turned left to get to the Marburg Road. After going less than a mile I came to a juncture in the streets. I took a right turn on to the street that would send us in the direction of Marburg. I stopped long enough to take a good look in all directions, including the rear. There was no one following us. And no other cars were present so I paused again to look at a map of the area. Ten miles south of Frankenberg on the Marburg Road there was a village where there was an intersection of the main highway with another road. The second highway circled back to the north, in a wide arc some fifteen miles from Frankenberg. It would lead us in the direction of Hannover without passing through Frankenberg. It was the route I would take.

When we passed the American motor pool on the Marburg Road, I slowed the speed of the Mercedes to about twenty-five miles per hour. As I had hoped, Randy Miller was outside, looking into the front part of a vehicle. I wanted him to see me. I pushed the horn and he turned in our direction. We waved to him. He recognized the black Mercedes and waved. I told Heidi that things were going well for us so far.

"I'm glad he saw us. He will be asked about us, as will the desk manager at the hotel, and it will send the people who are after us to Marburg."

"Max, please tell me what it is."

"I can't. Remember I told you previously that there is something important involved, and I cannot tell you to protect you."

"Yes, I remember."

"Just try to trust me. It's very big and important to many people, Americans, Germans and Russians. It's best that you don't know."

"I cannot imagine anything like that," and she smiled, "is world war three about to begin?"

"No, but it's just about that important to some people and you will be better off not to know the details."

We were silent for a few moments before I continued.

"I don't want you to be mixed up in this fight. We've got to get you to a safe place, and I will go on alone."

"No! Absolutely not! You can forget it, Max, I'm staying."

I turned and glanced at her and she obviously was dead serious. I began considering alternatives.

"Well, maybe we can delay that some. Let me ask you, how would a German farm family react, if we could tell them a good story and ask for shelter for a few days?"

"I don't know. The farmers don't have houses that are separate, they are all together in small villages. So, you would not only have to convince one farmer, you would have to persuade a whole village to hide us."

"Do you think that could be done?"

"Possibly. For a day or so. But there would always be someone who would tell."

"I know there will be roadblocks by our men. They may concentrate on Marburg but they will be checking all of the highways. I would like to find a place close by, maybe fifteen or twenty miles from Frankenberg, and sit tight for a few days. What do you think, can we do it?"

"Maybe. The German farmers will not be aware of what your army is doing, at least not for a while. What could we tell them?"

"You will have to say that I am a German. A wound or the shell-shock story we used before might work. It would explain why I cannot talk or understand things well. Possibly you could say that I escaped from an American prisoner of war camp and that I don't want to go back. Would that work?"

"Yes, it would work for a while. What about the car?"

"You can say that I come from a wealthy family and it is the car of my family."

"Of course! And how about us, are we married?"

"I don't think so. You can be my younger sister."

"Oh, all right, we can do it that way. But we might still be in the same room."

I grinned.

"Good. I'll get to be with you all day."

She grinned too.

"And all night."

"None of that, now, you know the rules."

"Okay, Hitler."

By twelve-thirty we had driven around Frankenberg on the highway I had found on my map, and we had reached the main road leading north from the city. I estimated that we were twelve to fourteen miles north of Frankenberg. The U.S. Army would be swarming toward Marburg, fifty to sixty miles to the south.

I began looking for side roads that would take us out into the countryside. After a few miles I turned left onto a paved road. I didn't know if it was a good road to take, I only knew that I had to get off of the highway. U.S. Military Police would have been alerted and would be all over the place. I had glanced frequently in the rearview mirror and as we rounded each bend I was preparing myself mentally to deal with a roadblock. I could not kill an American, and I did not know exactly what I would do. Try to go around the roadblock and use the powerful engine of the Mercedes to outrun them seemed like the best bet. Fortunately, we did not see any U.S. vehicles, nor did we see any civilian cars. We passed through a small village about two miles from the main highway. I felt it was too close and I continued on. After some seven or eight miles, and two other small villages, we came to another village. There were perhaps thirty houses grouped together and it was very quiet. It seemed perfect and should be a good haven for us. I parked on the side street. There were no people moving about, none to be seen, and Heidi said it was the time of day for the farmers to be out in the fields. I told her I would stay in the car and she could get out and try to find somebody to talk to, somebody who could steer us in the right direction, help us locate a place to stay.

When she left the car, leaving me alone in the village with Germans all around me, I realized how important Heidi had become in my current circumstances. Without her I would have been lost. I had glanced at a small sign as we entered the village and the name appeared to be Ederbringhausen.

For almost an hour and a half Heidi was gone. She was not in sight and I had no way of knowing how she was doing. I was confident about her, though; she was wise and capable of taking care of herself.

Finally, she was back. Another young woman was with her. When they got to the car Heidi spoke to me in German.

"Come! I have found a friend."

She and the other woman got in and Heidi spoke in German again.

"You can start the engine now."

And she held up her hands simulating a hold on the steering wheel. Then she turned to the other young woman who was in the back seat, and as before she spoke in German.

"He does not always understand at first. But he is all right, you don't have to worry."

"I understand," the other woman said.

We drove a short distance. Heidi did a good job of directing me in such a way to make it appear that care was needed in guiding me. I remained silent, and, at times, tried to look a little dumb. We arrived at a small two-story structure like those that were seen frequently in Germany: living quarters above, storage, or sometimes livestock, below. The young woman, whose name was Hanna, would be the occupant of the upstairs part of the building. She and Heidi got out of the car and opened two large swinging doors that were on the lower level. Heidi motioned for me to drive forward, which I did, and after I had the car inside she and Heidi closed the two swinging doors. It was perfect.

I got out of the car and Hanna showed us to two rooms nearby. There was a bathroom and kitchen adjoining the two rooms. Hanna told Heidi that it was to be an apartment for her cousin who would arrive from Berlin soon with her two children. The cousin was attempting to get out of the Russian Zone but was having difficulty. Hanna said she would rent the downstairs part of the building to us for a week or until such time as her cousin would arrive.

Hanna left and said she would bring bedclothing and other supplies in about an hour. It gave Heidi a chance, speaking softly in English, to bring me up to date on what she had told Hanna.

"I knew about the identification papers you had prepared for us so I told her we are in love and that is why we have different last names. And I told her that you were severely shell-shocked during an air raid, and that you had spent a number of months in a hospital. What city did you mention where there were so many German soldiers who were shell-shocked after an air raid?"

"St. Lo, in France."

"Yes, now I remember. So, to continue, I said that you were in the American hospital and after you were partially recovered you escaped. You were able to get back to Germany just ahead of the American Army. You have been on the move since then and I have been with you. The story is weak in some places, but she did not seem concerned. I think she is running, too. She came here from Munich, so she is sympathetic to us."

"Who else lives upstairs?"

"Only one other woman."

"What about food?"

"She says it is no problem. We can buy almost anything we need."

"This is great. You did a wonderful job."

She grinned mischievously.

"Do I get a kiss?"

"You bet!"

We embraced and kissed. It was long lasting and endearing. It was meaningful to each of us, and maybe being in a safe place allowed us to release our emotions more completely. After a half minute of a passionately consuming closeness, we pulled away slightly, and for a moment I stared into her eyes. It was a joyful time for us, and I think Heidi might have felt more gratified at that moment than she had on any other occasion. I had come to care for her more and more and it brought about an obvious question. Was I beginning to love her more than Ariane?

We looked around the apartment, which was closed off from the open area of the garage, and we found it to be neat and pleasant. I looked out a window and saw a stream nearby. I raised the window and could hear the soft, trickling sounds of the water. I decided that a Guardian Angel must have made the trip with us; we could not have found a more fitting place to be. Heidi was in love with the place, too.

"Let's stay here forever, Max. We could live here among these farmers and be happy, even if you do have to appear dumb part of the time."

I laughed.

"It would be nice, wouldn't it? But life is just too complicated to even dream about something like that."

"No, it's not too complicated. We will stay here, I have decided." And she was smiling. "Do you want me to cry and tell Hanna that you beat me?"

"Oh, that would be helpful . . . the first day we are here and we get in a fight."

And I was smiling, too.

"Well, you better be careful. But seriously, I love it. It will be quiet during the day and then the men will come in from the fields. Most are old so we don't have to worry too much. A few are young, in their teens, and they would be the ones most likely to cause trouble."

"I'm glad you told me. I'll be careful when I see them."

"Maybe we can just stay inside when they are here and it will be okay."

"Yeah, that sounds like a good plan."

Hanna was helpful. She seemed to enjoy our company, even though I would only nod my head occasionally as she spoke. I had the same impression about her that Heidi had mentioned, and I believed she felt secure with us because she was hiding from something as well. After a good conversation she went back upstairs.

We could hear the men as they came from the fields late in the day. There were no windows facing outward from the apartment toward the street, and the two large garage doors were solid wood, so that we had privacy as well as security. On the inside of the garage there was a rear door, and stairs were there on the outside leading to the apartment above.

I felt good about our circumstances. The Mercedes, an expensive car that would not normally be seen in the village, might have been seen as we came, and it would arouse some talk in the village. Hopefully, Hanna would explain to the people, using the story we had told her. In thinking ahead, I decided it would be safe to stay two days, maybe three. At that time, we would have to move on to another location.

Heidi was busy working with the vegetables Hanna had brought. Without looking at me she spoke.

"Do you like soup?" And before I could speak, she continued. "Yes, you like soup. Okay, let's see, we have five vegetables I can use. It will be delicious, Max."

"I'm sure it will."

It was typical of her. Answering the question for me and moving ahead. She liked doing that, and it was a likeable part of her personality. She could get by with more than other women and she knew it.

Later, when I tried the soup I found that she was right; it was delicious. I told her and she was pleased. After the meal was finished I helped with the clean up, and we moved into one of the rooms where there were chairs. There was a radio and we played it softly. It was a peaceful and relaxing time. Heidi found a station in Hungary that was coming through clearly and she left it there. At eleven we decided it was bedtime.

She took the front room, the one where we had been sitting, and I went to the other room. I raised the window again and listened to the water from the stream, and it was soothing.

I undressed and got in bed. I had been there only momentarily when Heidi appeared in the door.

"Max, I am going to sleep in your bed tonight."

She moved to the bed, took off her clothing, and got under the cover in the bed next to me. Touching her body was a sensational delight—an electrifying moment. Quickly, we were entwined as one. I was overwhelmed with a maddening desire, and I kissed her repeatedly. She, too, was ecstatic, and she let me know.

"Oh, Max, this is wonderful . . . and beautiful. I hope it lasts forever."

The next morning, early, there was a loud knock on the heavy wooden doors of the garage. I was up, and dressed, as was Heidi, and we went together to open the large doors. There, before us, were the farmers, the men of the village. Some had pitchforks.

Heidi spoke to them, asking what they wanted. One man, who appeared to be the leader, or elder of the group, exchanged words with her. His attitude was such that I felt we were in jeopardy. I could understand enough of the dialogue to realize that he was a dedicated German, and although he would not have been a Nazi, he was saying that he did not understand about the expensive car and how we happened to come to their village. He said all strong supporters of the "Homeland" would have been in other places instead of riding around in a fine car. It seemed to be getting out of hand and I couldn't judge where it would end. Suddenly I had a thought that might help us.

I raised my finger up to indicate that everyone should listen. The talking stopped and all of the farmers looked at me. I pointed to the leader and then motioned for him to come with me. He did. We walked to the rear of the garage and out the door and we were standing alone on the back side of the building. I reached into my pocket and withdrew my wallet. I found the SS identification of Augenberg and took it out. Then, I looked at the farmer and put my finger across my lips to indicate that I would show him something that was to remain a secret. He nodded. I unfolded Augenberg's identification and handed it to him. He studied it only briefly, and smiled as he spoke.

"Ah so!"

He had seen enough. He patted me on the shoulder several times, returned the document to me, and was ready to rejoin the others. He spoke briefly to them, and they all turned and left.

Heidi was astonished and looked at me for an explanation. I told her what I had done, after giving her some background information first.

"Do you remember that I told you the first description I was given of Augenberg was from Braun, the man who worked at the hospital?"

"Yes."

"Well Braun, as he was talking to me, said that Augenberg's appearance and age made him look very similar to me. And when I saw Augenberg in Frankenberg I could see that there was a similarity. So, just a few minutes ago, I showed the farmer Augenberg's identification. He believed, at once, that I was Augenberg. I believed if I could show him that I was a dedicated German it would solve the problem."

"And it did. It was a very good idea."

"Thank you. And now, do I get a kiss?"

"Yes, you get many kisses."

And she did come forward and kiss me, several times, on the lips. Then she moved back, still gazing into my eyes. It was a look that told me about her love, her devotion to me.

I felt better about our circumstances, being in the little village of Ederbringhausen. We might be safe for a longer period than I had first imagined. It would be less likely that one of the villagers would convey to anyone on the outside that we were there. And it was conceivable to me that we would be able to stay for as long as a week or more. If that turned out to be true it would be frustrating to the people who would be looking for me, and they would be more likely to give up the search much more quickly.

During the morning we were able to relax, sitting in the chairs in the front room. When a lull in our discussion came about, my mind became fixed on a distinct thought. I still had memories, flashing back intermittently to Ariane, and the cause of the problems that were presently surrounding her. I thought of her aunt, Frau Erhlich, the son of Frau Erhlich, Rolfe, and Doctor Reuss. Rolfe had said that Ariane had known about the gold and had told both him and his mother. Did Doctor Reuss also know about the gold? If so, was there a possibility of a union, and a conspiracy to conceal the matter of the gold? It was difficult for me to believe that Ariane would have withheld the information from me. And, as is the case when a serious matter is involved, I felt I wanted to discuss it. I decided to talk about it with Heidi. I didn't know exactly where to start, so I began with a question.

"Did Walter Kurth ever mention anything to you about a large amount of gold that might be in Bad Welmsburg?"

"No." And after a long stare, she continued. "Is this the thing that you have discussed before, the matter that you would protect me from knowing about?"

"Yes. The American, LeTourneau, is looking for the gold. He believes it is somewhere on the Wegner estate. He, and many others, Americans, Germans, and even Russians, are involved in a desperate effort to find it. They are ruthless men who will do anything, kill anyone who is in their way. LeTourneau has contacts high in the American Army who are secretly promoting his efforts, and they are protecting him."

"And that is the reason you have been accused of something, because of the high-ranking American officers who are involved with LeTourneau?"

"Yes. If the amount of gold I have heard about is true, it is an almost unbelievable sum of money."

"Max, I have just remembered. There was a time when Walter got a call and began talking. Suddenly, he said, "the gold!". And then he paused and asked me to leave the room."

"So he knew about it. The men who were being hidden by Karl Wegner, the ones who tried to escape to South America, had apparently accumulated the gold and planned for Wegner to hold it until it could be moved or otherwise used."

"And that explains all of the excitement about the so-called escape plan?"

"Yeah, the escape plan was over and done with a long time ago. It was simply being used as a ploy."

"But why would the men kill Wegner if he was left to protect the gold?"

"Who knows? It could be many reasons. Greed. Mistrust. A way to lower the number of people who would have access to the gold. And probably other reasons that I can't think of at the moment."

"How did you learn about the gold?"

"From a Russian man, as he was dying. He had been used as a laborer to help hide the gold. Wegner thought he had killed the man after the work was completed but he survived and got away. He was badly wounded, but he was afraid to get medical help because of Wegner, and he gradually got worse. Close to the end, a farm couple who had helped him brought him to the hospital in Bad Welmsburg. He asked for me, and just before he died he whispered in my ear and told me there was a large amount of gold that had been hidden by Wegner."

"And now it is the cause of all of your problems. Thank you, Max, for thinking of me, but I am glad that you have told me."

"Well, at this point, LeTourneau would kill both of us anyway because he thinks Augenberg has revealed everything. So, I decided there was no need to conceal it from you any longer. I guess we will sink or swim together."

"We will not sink, we will swim! We can hide, and we can get away. And I think there must be somebody left in your army who will help you."

"There is, the only problem is being able to get to them. Right now it would be suicide to travel in the car we have."

"I know." And she was thoughtful for a few seconds, then spoke. "Maybe there is another car here in the village . . . you could exchange the Mercedes for another car."

"That's a great idea. When you talk to Hanna try to find out if there is anyone in the village who has a car."

"I will do that today. I will tell her that you are afraid of being caught and returned to the prisoner of war camp, and in that way it will not change our original story."

"Very good. I think I'm feeling better already."

"I'm glad. I want to be able to help you."

"You might have to change your story some . . . now that I have identified myself as Augenberg . . . maybe you can discuss it in a different way."

"I can handle it. And Hanna will know how to help. I like her and we have become good friends."

"I felt like you might be able to handle it."

She grinned.
"Oh, so you think I am doing okay, then?"
"Yeah, you're doing okay."
After smiling for a few seconds she seemed to become wistful.
"Max, can we go away soon? Can we make this wonderful time last forever?"
"I can't run away, Heidi. There is too much to be done. But, I feel there is a good chance we can stay here in this village for a while."
Later in the day, as we were talking again, Heidi expressed a new thought.
"Max, let me ask you . . . and before you answer, think about it. I would like to go to Frankenberg and talk to Freya. We became good friends and she can tell me what is happening there."
I didn't wait to think about it.
"It's too dangerous. People saw you, a lot of people, in the dining room at the hotel. If the German Police have secured a description of you from Bad Welmsburg, they would stop you, and hold you. And besides, how would you get there?"
"I don't know. How about the telephone, could I use it to talk to her?"
"Wouldn't the operator announce the origin of the call?"
"Not if this village is within the Frankenberg exchange. I will ask Hanna, okay?"
"Do you really trust her?"
"Oh, I have no doubt about her, we don't have to worry about her."
"What would you ask Freya? And what would you tell her about your location?"
"I'm not sure yet, I just believe that I can learn something that will help if I talk to her."
I thought about it for a while. She was right, an update on events in Frankenberg would help. The civilians always seemed to know every detail of what was happening. I thought of a suggestion.
"I have two cans of gasoline in the trunk of the Mercedes. If there is a car in the village, and it can be done in the right way, we could furnish the fuel for someone to drive you to Frankenberg. And if we did that you would have to change your appearance, try to disguise yourself somehow. Can you do that?"
"Of course I can do that. Wait and see, even you will not know me."
After a few moments she looked at me with a quizzical expression.
"Max, do you mind if I cut my hair?"
"You mean to help with your disguise?"
"Yes."
"No, I don't mind, of course not. It will grow back anyway."
"And I might change the color. Hanna has a rinse, she uses it on her hair, and I will become a blonde. What will you think of me?"
"I'll think of you as I do now, nothing will change my feelings. Don't worry about it. You will still be beautiful, always."

She spent the rest of the day talking back and forth to Hanna. In the end, we learned that there were three cars in the village that were thought to be in running condition. Each of the owners jumped at the opportunity to go into the city.

Early the next morning two men came to get the five gallons of gasoline. I could tell by their attitude that they believed me to be a former member of the SS. They were polite and respectful.

At seven-forty the same two men came in an Opel sedan to pick up Heidi. She was ready. Even though she had changed her appearance by cutting her hair, changing the color and creating a new style, anyone taking a close look at her would recognize her. She had called Freya. Hanna had said that it was not a long distance call, and Heidi had made plans to meet Freya at the Rathaus in Frankenberg at ten. I waved to her as she left in the Opel, but I didn't feel good about it.

During the day I tried to think of things not associated with LeTourneau and the gold. Knowing the people of the village now held me in high esteem, I got out and walked. I covered the entire village, mainly to stay occupied. The people who saw me smiled, and would nod to me, or offer a brief greeting. Fortunately, none tried to talk to me.

I had time to think, once again, about my relationships with Ariane and Heidi. Were my feelings the result of the war and a long separation from women? No. I could easily rule that out. I had never had an experience that was similar, or even close, war or not. And reversing the situation, were the feelings of Ariane and Heidi attributable to the war? Many German women were obviously lonely, and a large number had either lost husbands or boyfriends. The agonizing hardships would naturally make them cling to others to be comforted.

It was very disturbing, and difficult, to imagine being without either one. During the time I had been with Ariane, I was certain that nothing else had ever occurred in my life that was comparable. And she felt the same. It was an ideal relationship, as much of a love affair as could be imagined.

And now, Heidi had come into my life in such a way that I could not give her up. I had tried to avoid sleeping with her because I knew that would be "the last straw." And finally it had happened, and it had consummated our love.

Although choosing between them was not a pressing matter, the time would come, possibly, when I would have to decide. There were still many unknowns: would Ariane survive, would I survive, would I be the victim of a rigged court martial, would Heidi be in trouble and sent to jail? And so on. LeTourneau had surprised me. I had felt that he might try to have me transferred back to the States, and I had not considered that he would have charges brought against me. What type of offense he could try to establish was a puzzle. My best guess would be a conspiracy charge in connection with Wegner and the escape plan. Because of my relationship with Ariane he might suggest to top brass who were supporting him that I knew about the escape plan and did nothing to stop it. Even though it would be circumstantial and literally false, it would serve their purpose in making a case. I would have the cooperation of Colonel Margolies in defending myself, although, it would take me out of circulation for a while.

I would await the return of Heidi to formulate a plan to cover our activities in the near future. My inclination would be to stay in the village for a week or more. The location was as safe as we could expect to have under the circumstances. Eventually we would have to move on, someone would turn us in to the police. It always happened.

By six-thirty I had experienced the first wave of anxiety about Heidi. She and the two men had not returned. I knew her to be "street wise," and it would not be easy for anyone to surprise her. My greatest concern was that she might be too bold, might go too far in trying to get information. She had mentioned once while discussing her plans that she might attempt to make contact with one of the civilian employees of the American Military Government. I told her not to go in their office and to be very careful about talking to anyone who worked there.

I was in the apartment just after nine when I heard a car. Immediately I went through the garage to the large wooden doors, and as I reached the outside, the Opel sedan pulled up. Heidi got out, turned and said "auf wiedersehen" to the two men, and walked with me to the inside. She was eager to talk.

"Max, I have learned some things. I had to stay until the American Military Government office was closed so that I could speak to Helene, who works there. She is a friend of Freya. We didn't want to go in the offices so we had to wait for Helene to come out at the end of her workday at five. That is the reason I am late."

"I'm just glad to see you. Did everything else go okay?"

"Yes, it went very well. I don't believe anyone saw me who recognized me. And no one followed as we came back."

"Good. Tell me what you learned."

"Helene said that Captain LeTourneau came into the Military Government office today. Another German worker heard most of what he had to say to Captain Brown. Captain LeTourneau said that you were wanted by the U.S. Army."

"Why?"

"Because of your connection to Ariane Wegner. He had a statement, a written document, which he said was in her handwriting, and he said it was dated before the time she was thought to be killed. In it, she expresses a fear for her life, and she says she is leaving information to be used in the event of her death." And she paused to give me time to speak. I did not and she continued. "She said that she had given information to you, Major Max Gordon, about her husband, and about other men who were high-ranking officials in the Nazi Party. The men were planning an escape and she revealed the names of the men. She said that Major Gordon told her to forget about the men and he would do likewise. And after that, of course, the men were able to escape from Bad Welmsburg."

My guess about LeTourneau had been correct. If he did, in fact, have a written statement by Ariane, he would have forced her to write it. And, with such a statement, he could use it to have charges brought against me. Heidi was looking at me for a response.

"Was the statement in English or German?"

"German. Captain Brown had to ask one of the civilian workers to interpret it for him."

"So, if one of the civilians read the entire statement they might be able to help us. Do you think that is logical?"

"I think so, yes."

"Was there anything else that was important?"

"I don't think so. Oh! They do believe we went to Marburg. Captain Brown said that he would cooperate by placing patrols on the road going in that direction. He thinks that you lied to him and he now believes LeTourneau is right and you are wrong."

"Naturally he would feel that way. And because of that it will give LeTourneau the opportunity to move around with no problem. This could be bad for Ariane. Now that he has forced her to make the statement, and it incriminates me, he no longer needs her."

"I'm sorry, Max. I sincerely hope that she will not be harmed."

"Thanks, Heidi. I know you mean that." My mind drifted back to LeTourneau. "Did you really get the feeling that they will be looking for us in Marburg?"

"Very definitely."

"Well, that's one break for us. When we were en route here, after we turned off of the Marburg Road and headed back to the north, we did not pass another vehicle, I was careful to watch. The problem we may have now is with the people here in the village and whether anyone will notify the police. How about the two men who were with you, do you trust them?"

"I think so. They know nothing about what I have told you."

"We might have to move on. I think it has become a risk for us here now."

"Where can we go, and how?"

"I'll have to think about that for a while."

We were silent for a few moments. Suddenly she had a thought.

"Do you have your American uniform with you?"

"Yes."

"Could we go from here into the British Zone . . . would that help?"

"Wear my uniform and be an American officer on leave?"

"Yes! Why not?"

"It might work. Let's think about it. I have enough gas to get us there. Actually, if there was a way to pass through the last checkpoint in the

American Zone, I could probably get us to Hamburg. We could travel at night. That could be a risk, too, because they know about the Mercedes. Maybe we should abandon the car at some point and get on a train."

"Max, it seems the car would be better. How many people in your army know about LeTourneau and what he has said?"

"Not many at present. It's known in Frankenberg; otherwise, probably not too many people have been alerted. On a charge like they have invented against me the army doesn't move too quickly. Most likely it will be left to LeTourneau and his friends at Division Headquarters to establish a local investigation as the first step."

"I think we should leave now, go to Hamburg tonight."

"What about Ariane?"

"You can't help her, Max, you would be arrested. If he was going to harm her he would have already done it. I think he will continue to hold her until everything is settled."

She was right. I could not expose myself to continue the search for Ariane. I would have to leave the area temporarily to avoid being caught and held. LeTourneau would have a reasonably strong case if it was sent to a court martial trial. The handwriting in the note could be verified—other samples of Ariane's writing could be found and used. And so, even as badly as it made me feel, we would have to make a run for the British Zone. I told Heidi that I felt she was right, we should use the car.

"Let's get ready as quickly as possible. We will have to drive all night. Do you want to let Hanna know that we are leaving?"

"Oh, of course," and she grinned, "she might even want to go with us."

"Well, be sure you don't tell her anything about our plans."

"I would not do that, Max, you have taught me to be careful about such things."

At eleven we were packed and ready to leave. I had a feeling of relief, as well as reluctance. I was relieved because I felt that we were making the best move we could to get away. I was reluctant because our hideaway had seemed perfect, and it would have been nice to stay there if the conditions had been right.

Hanna came down, hugged Heidi, and shook hands with me. Heidi and I got in the Mercedes, Hanna stood by the big wooden doors that were open, and we backed out. Heidi and Hanna touched hands as the car moved slowly by, and she waved to us as I straightened up and moved forward. Soon, we were on the outskirts of the village, passing through the lonely farm countryside with only our headlights piercing the darkness.

Driving, with thoughts racing through my mind about roadblocks, an explanation at the final American checkpoint, and various other obstacles, I must have had a grim look on my face. Heidi moved over on the seat next to me, pushed herself up closely against my body, and spoke joyfully.

"Let's sing a song!"

"Good idea. You start it."

She began humming, then singing in German, a beautiful song that I recognized. It was *Komm zuruck.*

She had a nice voice and hearing her sing gave me a good feeling. I let her continue to sing alone. She stopped once and asked me to sing along with her.

"I just want to hear you, okay?"

She nodded and continued to sing.

Within a few minutes we reached the main highway, the road leading north to Korbach. It was deserted as I had expected.

I used the powerful engine of the Mercedes to increase our speed. I anticipated that no one would be out at that hour. The civilians were restricted from traveling at night by our curfews. And our people would be moving only near the cities, other than possibly a rare occasion when a special assignment was involved.

While looking at a map before we started I had estimated that we could get to Paderborn between one and two A.M. From there we would go to Hamein, and on to Braunschweig, bypassing Hannover. From that point we would have a straight shot to Luneburg, a small town near the outskirts of Hamburg. I decided the best time to pass through the last remaining American checkpoint would be mid-morning. It would raise fewer eyebrows. Depending on our progress, we might have to pull off of the highway and wait for a while in order that our timing would be right.

After a night of stopping and stretching, eating snacks Heidi had brought, using the woods for a bathroom, singing, embracing, and kissing when we had the opportunity, we arrived in a small village not far from the American checkpoint. I had changed to my American Army uniform during one of the stops. I had brought papers with me to cover almost every conceivable situation, and the papers I would use would show that I was on leave. I had papers for Heidi that were standard travel permits for the civilians. There should be no question regarding our papers.

Now, it would seem that our only problem would be whether there would already be an alert out for me. Heidi and I had stopped and we were standing beside the car on a street in the small village a short distance from the last American checkpoint. We discussed the danger of our next move and what some of the alternatives would be. I took some money out of my wallet and handed it to her. She didn't take it.

"I don't want that, Max. If they take you, I am going where you go."

"You might need it. They might take me and leave you. You probably wouldn't even have a car."

"I don't care!" And she repeated, more emphatically, her earlier statement. "I am going where you go!"

I put the money back in my wallet. I had been thinking about it and I wanted to say something to her while I still had the chance.

"Before we go, I want to tell you something. You've been wonderful. I can't describe how much it has meant to me, I can only tell you how I have come to feel . . . I love you, I want you, and I hope I will never lose you."

It surprised her, caught her unexpectedly. She couldn't speak because she was too emotional. She was deeply affected and it took her a few seconds to recover.

"Thank you . . . my love . . ." and there was a pause before she could continue, "I want to say something, too . . . but I can't . . . right now."

I helped her.

"It's okay, I know what you want to say."

In other countries, including the States, terms of endearment were used both casually and to express sincere affection. In Germany it was different. If a German woman, in speaking to a man, said "my love," or "my darling," or, "my dearest," she would be telling him, or letting him know, that she was in love. And I knew when Heidi had used words of that nature to me, she was saying "I love you."

After waiting a few moments, during which time she smiled passively, it was time to go and I let her know.

"Ready?"

"Yes, I'm ready."

We got in the Mercedes. I still had a third of a tank of gas, plus the full five-gallon container in the trunk. We were only a short distance from the checkpoint. It would give me another three or four minutes to review in my mind the possibilities that might occur. Heidi, being very perceptive, remained silent, and it was purposely intended by her to give me the opportunity during that time to concentrate.

My plan was to go through the checkpoint in a normal way, using a casual manner in talking as would an officer on leave with a pretty young woman. Our success in getting through would depend on how quickly, and to what extent, LeTourneau would have activated the charges against me. I had thought about trying to go around the checkpoint on another road but after some talk and research by Heidi with local residents I decided against it. Heidi had learned that the side roads were being patrolled by both American and British, and to be caught in an attempt to take such a route would be trouble.

During the night at one of our stops I had removed the Thompson submachine gun and the grenades from the car. I placed them in a heavy canvas bag, along with my forty-five, Augenberg's identification, and all other papers that we did not need. I walked approximately one hundred yards from the highway into the woods and left the bag well covered with brush. I made a mental note about the location so that I would have a reasonably good chance to recover the bag at a later time if I should so choose. The bag, waterproof and tied securely, would protect the contents from the environment.

Moving along with the checkpoint in view in the distance, I felt some anxiety. If the army had moved quickly, it could be the end of our trip and I could not be certain about Heidi, what would happen to her. Either way, we would be separated, and it could be a long time before I would see her again.

As we approached the checkpoint, I looked at Heidi. She grinned and held up her right hand, touching her thumb and forefinger together to form a circle, giving the signal she had learned from me to indicate that we would be okay. I smiled and lifted my right hand, using the same gesture to agree with her.

When we were about two hundred feet from the checkpoint I slowed the speed of the car and took in the view before me. There were two small structures just off of the paved surface of the highway, one on each side of the road. The small buildings, which were about eight feet wide and twelve to fourteen feet in length, were there to provide shelter for the U.S. soldiers on duty. On beyond, some one hundred feet, were similar buildings which were there for the British. I could see U.S. soldiers near the first two buildings, as many as three men on each side of the road, and perhaps a total of six altogether. Also, there were British soldiers near their own buildings.

I eased up slowly in the northbound lane of the highway. A corporal wearing an MP armband over his U.S. uniform motioned for me to pull off of the highway over to the right. I did so and he walked in our direction. When he was near enough to see me and recognize my uniform with the insignia of a major, he smiled and saluted. I returned his salute and he spoke at once.

"Good morning, sir. Didn't recognize you for a moment."

"No problem, Corporal. Would you like to see my papers!"

"Yes sir. And begging your pardon, sir, can you tell me the purpose of your trip?"

He was friendly and appeared to be carrying out routine duties. My initial impression was that he was not looking for me specifically.

"Yes, of course, Corporal. I'm on leave," and I paused as I withdrew my papers, "and I have a friend who is traveling with me."

He took my papers and responded.

"Very good, sir. And may I please see her papers as well?"

Heidi already had her identification and travel papers in hand and I gave them to the Corporal. He smiled.

"It will be just one moment, sir."

He turned and walked back in the direction of the small building. Heidi and I glanced at each other and I spoke.

"I think it is routine so far. Keep your fingers crossed."

"I already did that," and she laughed.

We could see the Corporal as he walked inside the building. The structure was glass from about a waist-high level and it allowed observations of the people on the inside. The Corporal was talking to two other men in uniform, one of whom appeared to be an officer. They talked for a minute or so and at one point the officer looked in our direction for what seemed like a long, hard stare. Their discussion continued. Heidi and I were silent as we watched them. After three or four minutes the Corporal, accompanied by a First Lieutenant and a Sergeant, came out and walked in our direction. The Lieutenant saluted when he was near me. The Sergeant walked in front of the car and continued by the passenger side to the rear. The Lieutenant spoke.

"Major, the Corporal tells me you are planning to go on leave into the British Zone."

"That's correct, Lieutenant."

"Well, Major, we don't have any regulations covering this type of situation. Can you tell us a little more?"

The Sergeant had circled the car, and he, along with the Corporal, were standing beside the Lieutenant. I decided to get out of the car, believing that it might add some firmness to my position if we were standing eye to eye. I spoke, looking at the Lieutenant.

"Lieutenant, I have a standard leave form. It is the same form I used when I traveled to England a few weeks ago. Are you saying that you have never had an officer pass through here on leave?"

"Not many, Major, not many. What is your destination?"

"Hamburg."

"Major, how is it that you happen to be traveling in this car?"

"By permission of my commanding officer."

"And he would be?"

"Colonel Margolies, Team Commander of the Military Government unit in Bad Welmsburg."

He glanced at the Corporal, who was taking notes. Then he walked around the car and back near me before speaking.

"And I imagine the car was impounded, or taken from the civilians in Bad Welmsburg?"

"That's correct."

"Major, you certainly should be aware that any vehicle used by U.S. personnel should have identification on it."

"I understand your point, Lieutenant, and this particular car just happened not to have been scheduled with Ordinance to get the work done before it was time for me to be away on leave."

"Well, I'm sorry, Major, it would be a violation for us to let you pass. We certainly could not allow you to travel in the British Zone in this car."

"I see. All right, Lieutenant, we can change our plans. We're flexible and we can turn back with no problem."

He was now looking for other answers.

"Major, where did you come from to get here?"

"Bad Welmsburg."

"You came here directly from Bad Welmsburg?"

"Oh, I see what you are asking. No, we stopped off at a couple of other places."

"Where was your last stop?"

"Lieutenant, let me remind you, I have valid papers and I am your superior officer. Now, tell me the purpose of your questions."

"With all due respect, sir, I am the ranking officer in this zone and it is within my authority to question you. Now, once again, sir, what city did you come from?"

"Frankenberg."

"And I would assume that you refueled there?"

"That's correct."

"All right, Major, if you will give us a few minutes to use our radio we will try to clear things up."

"Are you telling me I am being detained?"

"Yes, sir. Because you are in an unidentified vehicle our regulations require verification. So, if you will, remain in your vehicle until we complete what we have to do."

He turned and walked back into the small building. The Sergeant and the Corporal went with him. I got in the car and looked over at Heidi.

"We might have a problem. If he contacts Captain Brown in Frankenberg I'm sure he will hold us based on what Brown will tell him. Our only chance of being able to drive away would be a contact with Colonel Margolies. If he is able to talk to Margolies, we will be okay and we can turn back."

"Max, will he arrest you?"

"No, I don't think so. He might send us back to Frankenberg under escort if he contacts Brown. Otherwise, I think we can leave on our own."

She wasn't too happy with the answer. And I didn't feel good about it either. In her eyes I could see the fear and anxiety she had shown a few times recently. I wanted to make her feel better.

"Try not to worry. If we should have to go back it will only be for the purpose of clearing up the questions they have about me, and Colonel Margolies can take care of that in about five minutes. Okay?"

"I suppose it is okay, Max. I'm just tired of running away or being fearful. It was bad enough before the Americans came, and now I still feel it."

What I had tried to do—help her overcome the worrisome attitude— had failed. I thought of one other way to reassure her.

"Heidi, remember the day Colonel Margolies called our room in the hotel in Frankenberg and talked to you?"

"Yes."

"And he told you at that time that I should get away as quickly as possible?"

"Yes, I remember that as well."

"Okay, what that meant was, Colonel Margolies had just heard about the false charges that had been made against me. He knew it was wrong and he was warning me so that I could get away."

“I can understand that, Max, but why didn’t he do something?”
“I’m not sure what he would have done at that point. If he talked to the officers at Division who had made the charges, the ones who were protecting LeTourneau, they would have confirmed the charges. Colonel Margolies is sharp enough, however, to know that something is not right but he probably felt that he wanted to talk to me before going to someone higher up, a high-ranking officer he could rely on and trust. Does that make sense to you?”
She smiled.
“Yes, I think so.”
“Good. Let’s talk about other things. What will we do after this is all over?”
“We will have a happy home. You will go to your work each day and I will have a wonderful meal when you come home at night. We will have children, and we will sit around the table at the evening meal and hold hands before we eat. And we will laugh and have fun and talk about what we have done during the day. Then, the children will go to bed, and later, you and I will make love when we are in bed.”
“That sounds like a great plan. And maybe I can become a normal human being again. I think all of the experiences I have had during the last year or so have changed me . . . killing people, hurting others, and sometimes, I was doing it with not so many regrets. I trust God will forgive me.”
“Max, you must not punish yourself in this way. You did what you were asked and what was expected of you. You are a sweet and kind man who was asked by your government to do what is done in a war. And some of the men like Stelling and Augenberg were terrible, both guilty of killing their own countrymen. And the people they killed were not only the Jews, they were innocent people like Leni and Gertrude, and I think they enjoyed what they did. And now, you must not let this worry you, you did what was best for Germans and Americans.”
“Thanks. You always seem to be able to make me feel better.”

10.

WE CONTINUED to sit in the car, looking ahead most of the time to the small building in front of us where the three Military Policemen could be seen as they talked. Heidi and I talked about various things, forced a few laughs and tried to avoid mentioning our present situation, but finally, after some twenty or twenty-five minutes, she turned to me.

"Max, why is it taking so long?"

"They're checking my story and maybe it's difficult to get in touch with the right people. But let's talk some more. Tell me about your whole family, and what happened when you visited your grandparents when you were young."

She had a pleasant expression on her face.

"You can't fool me, Major, you're really trying to keep me from worrying about those soldiers in that building over there."

I grinned and I lied.

"No, I know you're okay. I just thought it would be a good time for me to learn all about you."

"Well, okay. My grandparents, who lived in Dortmund, were kind to me when I would visit. At the end of the visit, my grandmother would say, "You can't go back home, you must stay and live with me." And my grandfather would always make me sit on his lap so he could hug me."

"They were the parents of your mother?"

"Yes. I didn't see my father's parents very often. They lived a great distance away."

"And what was your favorite meal, or dish, at your grandmother's home?"

"Chocolate cake. Oh, it was so good! I wish I had some right now and I would share it with you."

I looked back in the direction of the small building and the men were stilling talking. Heidi changed to another subject.

"Do you really think Ariane knew about the gold and where it was being kept?"

"I can't be sure. I think she would have told me, unless she really did believe it would place me in jeopardy as Rolfe told us."

"And so you feel Rolfe might have been attempting to protect her when he talked to us in the hotel?"

"I can't be certain about Rolfe, either. But, yes, I think he lied to us in the hotel room. Maybe both he and Ariane were afraid because of the danger of being held by the SS and LeTourneau, and they were trying to survive by staying in the middle of the road. Otherwise, if he was being truthful, it would mean that there were circumstances that I cannot be sure about."

I glanced at my watch. We had been detained for thirty-five minutes. Many different scenarios had been flashing through my mind. I could be arrested on the spot and taken to the nearest Military Police facility. Heidi might also be held, and that was more worrisome. She would have no one to represent her, and she might be sent to jail or a camp for women who were either known criminals or under suspicion of being criminals. She could get lost in the mix. Her destiny would be entirely dependent upon me, and should I be held in tight security I would be unable to help her. Adding to her problems, our people would learn that her father had worked at the Bergen-Belsen concentration camp, and although at last report he had been cleared, it wouldn't help matters. I was concerned for her, so much so that I momentarily thought about making a run for it in the Mercedes. I quickly ruled that out, however, because common sense told me that it would be a disaster.

The MP officer and two enlisted men were still in conference in the small building. Heidi looked in that direction and back to me.

"Will they let me stay with you?"

"Oh, sure. The worst thing that will happen will be a return to some location in our car."

I couldn't really be sure of that, but she did seem to feel better.

"When this is over, let's go away for a while. Will you do that, Max?"

"You bet I will! Where do you want to go?"

"I think I would like to get out of Germany for a holiday. Could we go to Switzerland?"

"I believe so. Maybe I can get papers for you, place you on special assignment with the American Military Government. Now, tell me, what would we do in Switzerland?"

"Make love." And she grinned.

"That's an offer I can't refuse. Let's plan on it."

The Lieutenant came out of the building and walked in our direction. He appeared to have a determined look on his face, and when he reached the car a firmness was reflected in his voice.

"Major, will you and the woman step out of the car?"

I turned and nodded to Heidi, and we both got out. Heidi walked around the car and stood near me. The Sergeant and Corporal, who had followed the Lieutenant to our car, began searching the car. I looked at the Lieutenant.

"What's going on, Lieutenant?"

He ignored my question and spoke quietly to the Corporal, who, in turn, approached me and made a request.

"Begging your pardon, sir, would you unbutton your jacket and hold it out so that I can see around your waist?"

I did as he asked. He took a good look and turned to Heidi.

"Ma'am, do you have any kind of weapon in your possession?"

"No."

The search of the car was completed in about ten minutes.

After looking through the car and our personal belongings, nothing was found that was a concern to them. The Lieutenant looked at me.

"Major, I have been instructed by Colonel John B. Mason of Division Headquarters to have you returned to Frankenberg. You can travel in your own vehicle. There will be two of our escort vehicles accompanying you, one in your front, and one in your rear. These orders have been issued directly by Colonel Mason, and he will be on hand when you arrive in Frankenberg. Do you have any questions?"

"Did you contact Colonel Margolies?"

"We made an attempt but we were unable to reach him."

"Did you talk to anyone in that office?"

"A Sergeant Glenn Newton. He did vouch for you."

"Okay, Lieutenant, I guess we can't argue with what you have done."

"I'm just doing my job, Major." And for the first time he showed a conciliatory attitude. "I hope you have a pleasant return trip, sir. Sorry to interrupt your plans."

"Thanks, Lieutenant, and I understand your position."

He stood at attention and saluted.

"Good luck to you, sir."

I returned the salute and smiled. I took Heidi's arm and walked around the car with her where I opened the door on the passenger's side. She got in, looking quickly into my face to show her appreciation, and I closed the door.

Five minutes later a jeep with two Military Policemen inside came and pulled into the southbound lane of the highway opposite us. It was followed by a weapons carrier with two other soldiers, and the driver parked about thirty feet behind the jeep in the southbound lane. The Corporal we had seen earlier, motioned from where he was standing on the highway for me to make a U-turn and position the Mercedes between the two army vehicles.

I started the engine and slowly moved into the spot that was assigned to us. The Corporal, smiling, walked up to the window of the car.

"My apologies, sir, but here are some instructions for you from the Lieutenant."

He handed me a folded piece of paper. I was impressed by the polite manner of the Corporal, and spoke to him.

"Thank you, Corporal. By the way, where is your home back in the States?"

"Lexington, Virginia, sir."

"Oh, yes, I know that area, that's good country. Hope you get back there soon."

We exchanged salutes and I was ready to move out. I glanced briefly at the paper the Corporal had given me. On it was a one sentence, handwritten statement: "Major Gordon, you are requested by Colonel John B. Mason to return to Frankenberg under Military Police escort. Paul E. Johnson, 1st Lieutenant, Military Police, Checkpoint Zone B-26."

The drive back to Frankenberg, sandwiched between the two Military Police vehicles, was uneventful. We made the necessary stops, to refuel, go to the bathroom, and eat a meal that was provided by our escorts. All supplies were in the rear compartment of the weapons carrier. The Military Policemen were polite when we stopped, and we were treated with respect and courtesy.

Heidi and I talked some but not consistently. I could see that she was still worried and occasionally I would try to cheer her up with a wisecrack remark. I was not too successful and I believed that she must have thought it was going to be the end of everything for us.

Once, I looked at Heidi and thought about the difference in her appearance that was created when she cut her hair, and used the dye on it before going into Frankenberg. Now, it was shortened and blondish, reaching just barely below her ears. In front she had long bangs, separated somehow into strands so that it did not fall solidly across her forehead. There was not an obvious part in her hair, it was simply pulled over, left to right, with no distinct line formed at the starting point. Her eyebrows were only slightly obvious possibly because she might have used some of the same rinse to change the color when she did her hair. Her teeth were white and even. Her face was rather full, but it added to her attractiveness, especially when she smiled. Her nose and mouth were shaped perfectly and were contoured to embrace enchantingly her other features. Possibly the most imposing part of her appearance was the expression in her eyes; a mischievousness which was extended to a greater degree when she laughed. It created a contagious friendliness, making her even more desirable and appealing. Her body was unique, and I could not imagine a female physique that could be more attractively formed. She was, beyond any doubt, the most beautiful woman I had ever seen.

At eight-forty P.M. we were within three or four miles of Frankenberg. I knew because I remembered the road. The jeep in front of us began slowing and eventually the driver pulled off of the highway. He had motioned to me to do likewise. The weapons carrier followed us, and soon all three vehicles were brought to a stop just off of the pavement. All four of the Military Policemen got out and walked to the Mercedes. They gathered beside my door. For a split second, I thought, is this going to be an execution? But just at that moment, the Sergeant in charge spoke.

"Major Gordon, our orders are to escort you to the outskirts of Frankenberg. According to my map, sir, I believe we are now within five miles of the city. Would you say, sir, from your knowledge of the area, that I am correct?"

"Yes, Sergeant, I would say that you are correct."

"Well, sir, you are now under your own recognizance. My orders are to inform you that you are to report to the Military Government office in Frankenberg. You are to report to Colonel John B. Mason who is there from Division Headquarters. Do you understand the orders, sir?"

"Yes, Sergeant. We will proceed directly to that point."

"Very good, sir. And now, we will leave you. Good luck, sir."

Heidi looked at me in amazement and could hardly believe what was happening. The four soldiers returned to their two vehicles, started engines, moved out by making a U-turn in the road, and headed back to the north. I explained it to Heidi.

"Colonel Mason from Division wants to create a friendly atmosphere. He wants it to appear that there has been a mistake and that I am not to be charged. In return, he will try to find out what I know about Augenberg and the gold."

"But Max, I don't understand, I . . ."

I turned and looked at her with a pleasant expression.

"Don't worry. This is better than I thought we would get. I have to think now about how to handle it. They won't hold either of us but I have to be careful. I have to convince them, somehow, that I will cooperate."

She wasn't convinced. Unlike her usual moods she was anxious. I reached out and touched her hand.

"Trust me."

She smiled slightly.

"Okay."

I started the motor of the Mercedes and pulled out in the direction of Frankenberg. Ten minutes later I stopped in front of the bank building where the Military Government office was located. I made a final comment to Heidi.

"Remember, it's okay. I think it will all be over soon and we can be together."

She looked somewhat relieved and it appeared that she believed me. I got out and went around the car to open the door for her. I held her arm as we walked into the bank building.

On the lower level of the Military Government offices we were met by an enlisted man. It was obvious that he knew who we were, and before I could speak, he came in our direction with a friendly look on his face.

"Good evening, sir. Captain Brown and Colonel Mason are waiting for you upstairs. Captain LeTourneau is there also. Would you follow me up the steps, sir?"

"Yes, of course, Corporal."

Colonel Mason and Captain Brown had been anticipating our arrival. I felt that some sort of communication was used by the Military Police to let them know about our presence in the area. Colonel Mason, a man who looked to be fifty, could have come directly from Wall Street. He was big money. A take-charge, high-level executive type who would negotiate on his own terms. I could sense it at a glance. He smiled as we walked near him, attempting to exude a graciousness, and he extended his hand to me as he spoke.

"Major Gordon! It's good of you to interrupt your plans to come in. I hope we can get you on your way soon." Then he turned to face Heidi. "And I must say, mademoiselle, it is my pleasure to meet you."

Heidi responded, barely above a whisper.

"Thank you."

I looked at Mason.

"What seems to be the trouble, Colonel?"

Again, he formed a pleasant expression while speaking.

"I believe there has been a huge mistake. I think we can get everything straightened out quickly. Captain Brown has agreed to let us use his office for a while to talk. Major, do you have any objection to a private conference with me and Captain LeTourneau at this time?"

"None whatsoever, Colonel. How about my companion, will she be allowed to remain in the room with us?"

"Of course, Major, of course."

LeTourneau spoke.

"Colonel, if I may make a suggestion, possibly the fraulein will be more comfortable at the hotel."

The Colonel readily agreed.

"All right, Captain, we can send her along up there and get her settled in a nice room. Is that agreeable, Major?"

"I prefer for her to remain here."

He was a little more firm.

"Let's don't quibble, Major. She will be fine at the hotel."

I looked at Heidi and she appeared uncomfortable. I turned back to the Colonel.

"I'll agree on one condition. She is to be allowed to call me as soon as she is in the room at the hotel."

"No problem, Major."

He turned to Brown and instructed the Captain to personally escort Heidi to the hotel. Heidi stood and looked at me. I knew the situation was making her uneasy. She was anxious, and she wanted me to give her some sort of assurance. It was a dreaded feeling, I felt sure, that was brought about from the past, the many days during the war when people in Europe had a last visit with a loved one who never returned. She needed a boost and I grinned at her.

"It's okay, I'll be there soon."

Obviously feeling a little better, she nodded and walked out with Brown. Mason immediately went over and closed the door. Only he, LeTourneau, and I were left in the room. Mason's attitude changed at once and he stared hard at me.

"Listen, you bastard, we're here to settle up quickly. I hope, for your sake, you understand that. First of all, let's go over your story about Augenberg. Where is he?"

"Can't tell you that, Colonel, I would lose my ace in the hole."

"The way it stands now, you may lose your ass. We don't believe you have him. We've interviewed every German civilian policeman in town and none of them took part in his removal to another location as you claim. Can you explain that?"

"Certainly, I said I worked it out through the German Police, not with them. Secondly, do you think for a moment that they would incriminate themselves by telling you anything?"

He turned and scowled at LeTourneau.

"What the hell is going on, Eddie?"

Eddie answered.

"He told me, Colonel, that he had Augenberg and that the German Police removed him to another location."

Mason looked back to me.

"Okay, to hell with this play on words. Tell us where he is."

"I told you, Colonel, I won't disclose that information at this point. Maybe LeTourneau didn't tell you but I have a written statement from Augenberg that is stashed away in a safe place. Even if the man could be found and killed I still have enough in that statement to nail everybody."

Mason looked at LeTourneau.

"You dumb ass, you didn't tell me that. You know, Eddie, you're getting yourself on thin ice. What else do you need to tell me?"

"Nothing, Colonel, nothing. I didn't believe him and that's the reason I didn't mention it."

Mason looked in my direction.

"I'm going to get straight to the point, so listen carefully. We've got a solid case against you and we can send you up the river for life. We've got one of your women, and we can get the other one any time we want to . . . hell, man, what do you hope to gain?"

"My freedom, and the freedom of the two women."

"And you will do what?"

"Cooperate with you any way I can."

He thought about it and he seemed to be appeased. He became more conciliatory in his next statement.

"All right, let's get some ground rules established. First, I want every detail you have about the gold."

"The only thing I know about the gold is what a Russian man whispered in my ear as he was dying. Prior to that I had no knowledge of the gold."

"Frau Wegner nor anyone else had not told you about the gold?"

"No."

"Exactly what did the Russian man tell you?"

"He said, 'much gold,' and then he mumbled something about Wegner. I couldn't judge the significance of that, whether he was telling me Wegner had shot him, or if Wegner was connected to the gold."

"That's it? He told you nothing else? What about the location of the gold?"

"He told me nothing else. He just slipped away immediately."

"Okay, let's say that's true. Who have you told about the gold?"

"No one, I have told no other person about the gold."

"Why not?"

"Well, for one thing, time was a factor. I had to get out of town fast, I knew that LeTourneau and others were involved, and I assumed that they had high-ranking people protecting them. Also, LeTourneau threatened to kill people if I talked. I suspected that he had Frau Wegner, which I eventually learned was true, so I had to do as he said, act normal, carry on business as usual, and keep my mouth shut."

"And that was smart. Okay, let's talk about a deal. You keep your mouth shut, give us Augenberg, and accept a transfer back to the States. In return, no charges will be filed against you."

"What about Frau Wegner?"

"She stays in Germany. And if you talk after you get back in the States, we kill her. And I might add, your life wouldn't be worth two cents at that point either."

I paused, trying to think of an answer. I couldn't decide how to respond, and Mason spoke again.

"Take your time, Gordon. But we have to have your answer, here, tonight."

I looked at LeTourneau.

"How do I know Frau Wegner is alive?"

"You got the message from her, the title of the song. Also, I have a statement she wrote for us just in the last forty-eight hours."

"Where is she?"

"Can't tell you that, Max."

"Can we work out an exchange, Augenberg for Frau Wegner?"

Even though that would be an impossibility, I was attempting to probe in all directions, get any concession from them that would help me. Mason answered.

"No. No exchange. Everything is on our terms."

"That seems a little one-sided. You get everything you want, I get nothing."

"You get to save your ass. You don't seem to follow things too well. You really don't have any choice. And there's one thing I haven't mentioned. Sometimes, accidents happen. A man runs and he is shot by a trigger-happy GI. Of course it would be a tragedy, and a mistake, but I believe you follow my thinking."

"Yeah, I follow your thinking. Looks like you may be holding all of the cards. Will you give me a few minutes to think about my position?"

"Oh, sure. But about five minutes should do it. LeTourneau and I will walk over to the other side of the room and give you some privacy, some time to think . . . okay?"

"Yes, okay."

The phone rang and LeTourneau answered. He handed me the phone. It was Heidi.

"Max, are you all right?"

"Yes. Where are you?"

"In a room at the hotel."

"Are you alone?"

"Yes. Everything is all right. When will you come?"

"Soon. Don't worry, okay?"

"Yes, okay."

It was the end of our conversation.

To give me the time I had asked for, Mason and LeTourneau had walked to the other side of the room, about twenty-five feet away. I began to formulate my plans.

First, I would try to convince them that Heidi was with me only for sex. I would tell them, if asked, that she knew nothing about the gold. I had drilled her repeatedly on how she should respond if questioned, tell them she knew absolutely nothing about gold, and I believed that her story would hold up. Under those conditions they might be willing to set her free and that would take care of one of my problems. Next, I would try to work out something to protect Ariane. Even if I did as Mason said and returned to the States, I would need proof that she was all right. Some sort of communication with her on a regular basis would have to be established. Also, I would have to convince them that I would not reveal anything even remotely connected to the gold when back in the States. Finally, I would have to cover myself concerning Augenberg. They would be asking for more details about him. But I would have to withhold that information until everything else could be agreed upon. In fact, I might not tell them that he was dead. It was the only real advantage I had, and I would not give it up easily.

LeTourneau and Mason were talking quietly on the other side of the room. Occasionally they glanced in my direction. After three or four minutes, I spoke.

"Okay, Colonel, I'm ready to talk."

He and LeTourneau walked in my direction. The Colonel formed a slight smile on his face. When he spoke, however, it was with a somewhat cynical tone.

"Well, that didn't take too long. I hope you have come to your senses."

In response, I used a firm manner.

"I've decided to accept your offer, Colonel, and take the transfer back to the States. In return, I will ask for your agreement to cooperate with me on several issues."

"Talk."

"First, the young woman with me has to be released. She knows nothing. It was simply a chance for me to enjoy sex with her. I will have to see her on a train leaving for Bad Welmsburg, or drive her there myself."

Mason grinned.

"No problem, Max. We already knew what you were doing with her. What's next?"

"I have to be assured about Frau Wegner. I want to know she is safe, and will be safe in the future."

He and LeTourneau glanced at each other, and the Colonel looked quickly back to me.

"Of course, Max. We don't want any harm to come to her."

"LeTourneau says she knows about the gold. Is that true?"

Mason looked at LeTourneau, who spoke.

"Naw, Max, I was just using that, she doesn't know anything."

He was lying. I was sure of it because of Rolfe. Rolfe had said that Ariane knew about the gold "several months ago." I answered LeTourneau.

"I want to talk to her. It could be by telephone."

Mason looked at LeTourneau with a questioning glance, and it seemed he was in favor. LeTourneau got his message and responded to me.

"Well, it has to be set up in the right way. It might take time."

"How much time?"

"I don't know—"

Mason interrupted.

"Okay, okay. It can be done. Move on with what you've got to say, Max."

"If I talk to Frau Wegner, and she is okay, I'll be ready to take the transfer back to the States. But if I do that I will have to communicate with her on a regular basis, hear her voice."

"And if we agree to that, what is your position regarding the gold?"

"The gold is yours. I'll say nothing."

"Let me remind you that we have friends in the U.S. If your memory goes bad and you fail to keep your promise, you won't last five minutes."

"I know. That's why I have made these decisions."

Mason was pleased.

"Well, looks like we might be getting somewhere. All right, we need to know about Augenberg and get his statement back."

"Can't do that, Colonel. He's the only thing I've got left and I have to be sure you keep your promises."

He frowned.

"Hell, Max, we can find him. You don't really have a bargaining point there. Give it up."

"Yeah, Colonel, you might find him. But I'll guarantee you that his statement will never be found."

Mason looked at LeTourneau and spoke harshly.

"You dumb son-of-a-bitch, what about that?"

"I'm telling you, Colonel, he's lying. If he had a statement, why wouldn't he use it, show us a copy?"

I interjected a thought.

"I was protecting my position, Colonel, as I am doing now. The subject never came up about a copy, I was never asked for a copy."

The Colonel was disgusted. He turned and took two or three steps away from us. Obviously, he was assessing the information about the statement of Augenberg. After a minute or so he turned to me.

"Where is the statement?"

"You know I'm not going to tell you that at this point, Colonel."

LeTourneau attempted to make a statement.

"He's lying, Colonel. He—"

The Colonel interrupted.

"Shut the hell up, LeTourneau. You've really screwed this up. You may get bounced out of here when the people higher up find out about this. If I were you I wouldn't turn my back on too many people." Mason turned back to me. "Okay, let's say you've got a statement from Augenberg. And let's say, too, that we find him, and he has an unfortunate accident. How good is your statement?"

"I think we would just have to wait and see. You're not named because he didn't know anything about you. He does name LeTourneau and he tells details about the gold. Also, he states that LeTourneau has the protection of high-ranking U.S. Army officers."

Mason had to think about it. He was silent, as was LeTourneau. Finally, Mason spoke to me.

"How do I know there is a statement?"

"You don't. But I'll tell you what I did. I sent it by the army courier from here to a reliable friend. He has it and will hold it until I tell him what to do."

He smiled.

"That ought to be easy enough to check. We will see if you brought in something for the courier in the last few days."

"You can save yourself the time. I waited outside and while he was in the office I put my envelope, which was U.S. Army issue, in his vehicle. Then I watched from across the street as he came out and drove away."

Mason's expression seemed to indicate that he was finally accepting what I was saying.

"Okay, Max, looks like you've done your homework. I'm going to let you go on up to the hotel and join your girlfriend for the night. We'll meet again tomorrow and come to some agreement. Don't try to run. That would be stupid and you know it."

"How about the car?"

"You can keep the damn car."

I walked out immediately. At the hotel I used my limited ability to speak German with the man at the reception counter. He gave me the room number where Heidi would be and I climbed the steps quickly to the second floor. After locating the room I tapped on the door.

She was there and quickly opened the door. She reached out and we embraced. It was an unusual moment, unlike some of the other occasions when we had reached for each other. Now, there was more of a feeling of comfort from being safely reunited. Being apart with the uncertainties that were involved brought our union into focus more meaningfully. Then, as we kissed, passionately, it was different, more endearing and affectionate than sexually arousing.

Soon we were inside the room with the door closed. We walked to chairs and sat down. She was eager to hear about things.

"Tell me what happened."

"It's not really settled. They still don't know what to do about Augenberg. But it's not all bad . . . they did agree to let you go. I told them we were only together for sex and they believed me. You're going to be safe."

"But what about you?"

"I don't know yet. I've got them convinced about Augenberg, that I have his statement in a safe place. They know it could be very damaging. They want to meet again tomorrow to try to make a deal."

"What can you do?"

"I'm not sure. I might tell them to go ahead and charge me and I would take my chances in a court martial. The only problem is, they have threatened to kill me and I might never get to a court martial. So, I will probably have to think of something else."

"Max, can't you get help from someone? Is your whole army bad?"

"No. It's only a few people, the men who know about the gold. The problem is, some of those people are high ranking and I don't have any way of knowing who they are. If I could get through to Colonel Margolies he would help. But, it might be like putting a contract on him, signing his execution papers, to involve him."

"I will think about it too and before tomorrow we will know what to do."

I smiled.

"You know, you're great to have around. You never give up."

She was pleased but she wanted to tease me.

"Oh, so that is why you keep me around?"

"Yeah, of course, did you think there was something else?"
She grinned.
"Okay, the next time we are in bed together I will remind you."
"I take it back."
"That's better. Seriously Max, I will always want to be near you and help you, you know that . . . I love you."
"I know. And I love you."
Later, as we were lying in bed, she asked a question.
"If you did go back to the U.S. as they have offered, could I come there too?"
It was a tough question and I wanted to be truthful without discouraging her.
"Probably, over a period of time. It would be complicated. It's difficult to get any German out of the country right now, and because of your connection with Kurth, it would be even more difficult. And, depending on what happens with Mason and LeTourneau, how they are able to settle things with me, they probably would want you to be left in Germany simply because of your relationship with me and the possible knowledge you might have gained from our relationship."
"Max, I . . . don't want you to go back to the States without me."
"And I don't want to do that."
She snuggled over close to me and we embraced. Then she moved her leg over on me, and gradually, she had her whole body on top of me, and kissed me passionately. She always got in bed with me without her clothes, and in between kisses, I teased her.
"Do you always go to bed with men with no clothes on?"
She laughed.
"Not always, just when I am with you."
Later, after she had dropped off to sleep, the same troubling thought came back. The time might be getting close when I would have to choose between Heidi and Ariane, assuming Ariane would be released unharmed. It would be the most difficult decision I would ever have to make . . . how could I say "goodbye" to either? It was almost unbelievable, and rare, that I could love two women so immensely. Most people spent their whole lives without even one real love affair.
The next morning Heidi was lying on my right arm while still sleeping. Her right leg was across my lower body and her right arm was around my neck. It was time for me to wake her. I rubbed her back gently with my left hand, and she signed contentedly. Just at that moment, the phone rang.
I got up and answered. It was Colonel Mason.
"Something happened overnight, Max. We need to talk. Meet me in front of the Military Government office in thirty minutes. Don't go inside. We will take a walk on the street."
"Okay, Colonel, I'll be there."
I explained the conversation to Heidi and prepared myself to go. She looked at me with some anxiety.

"Max, my greatest fear is that you will sometime leave and never come back. Promise me that will never happen."

I touched her face with my fingers and smiled.

"I promise it will never happen."

As I approached the Military Government offices I saw Mason standing in front. When he saw my car he turned and walked in a direction away from the American offices. I drove past him, half a block, and stopped. I got out and stood on the sidewalk until he reached me.

"Max, it's a new ballgame. I'm in a different position. I'm going to try to work out something that will be agreeable to both of us."

"Sounds fine to me, Colonel."

"Okay, here's the picture. Some time during the night, that dumb ass LeTourneau left town. I know he's got contacts with the Russians and I think he is making a run for it to join them. He knew he was in trouble with us, and he was right, the guys up above would have had him taken out. So it's easy to see why he didn't want to hang around any longer."

"How about Frau Wegner and the others?"

"He took her. We've got the other SS guy, Stelling, and the man whose name is Rolfe."

"How did he leave town?"

"We had the house under surveillance by German Police. He shot the man on duty at the house, the German Policeman, took a wild shot at Stelling, and then he and Frau Wegner left in his jeep. It was around midnight and we didn't find out about it until this morning. So, with that much head start, he could be anywhere by now."

"How can he travel and operate without papers?"

"Oh, hell, he's in an American vehicle in a captain's uniform and it would be easy, especially for a con artist like him. He may already be getting close to the Russian Zone, I don't know how far it is to the nearest border."

"Why would he take Frau Wegner?"

He turned and stared at me.

"According to Rolfe there may have been more than just a casual relationship between them."

"No! That's not right! I don't believe it. What reason did Rolfe give for saying that?"

"He has talked to Stelling, Stelling has talked to me."

"You are holding both Stelling and Rolfe?"

"Yes."

"I want to talk to both of them."

"You can do that. In the meantime, we will need to work out something. Since this dumb bastard LeTourneau has pulled out, the position of the U.S. is in trouble."

"When you say the U.S. position, you mean your position and the people who are supporting you?"

"Yes, of course! Hell, Major, the Russians, or even the Germans, can walk away with the gold and leave us nothing."

I thought of a possibility.

"Colonel, you've lost some ground and you're going to have to settle for less than what you thought originally. Would you be willing to accept a finder's fee if we can get to the gold first?"

"A finder's fee? Who the hell would give me a finder's fee?"

"Maybe the army. If you convinced them you were keeping it quiet to protect the gold . . . keep the Russians and Germans from getting to it first . . . they might reward you."

"No . . . no . . . it wouldn't work. Too many people in high places already know too much."

"Then how about a deal?"

"A deal? A deal with you?"

"Yes, a deal with me."

"Do you know more about the gold than you have told us so far?"

"There is one thing I haven't told anyone. I don't know the exact location of the gold but I do know, in general, how to pinpoint the area."

He became excited and showed interest at once.

"Max, you take me to that gold and I'll give you anything you want. Anything! You name it and you've got it."

"I can't take you to the gold, I don't know where it is, I only have a hint about the general location."

"Tell me what you want from me, Max."

"I want Frau Wegner returned to Bad Welmsburg, unharmed."

"How the hell can I do that? We can't go into the Russian Zone."

"Use your top brass friends. Make some concessions. Tell them we will make an exchange. There must be some way to negotiate with them."

"Why is this woman so important to you? It sounds like she has already turned her back on you."

"I don't think so. I want to hear what Stelling and Rolfe have to say about that."

"Fine. Let's go see them right now."

We got in the Mercedes and he directed me along a route to a house on the north side of town. It was located across the river. The house sat back from the road and was almost isolated from view by trees in the middle of a wooded area. I parked near the entrance and we got out. Two jeeps were there, as were two civilian automobiles which were marked Polizei.

Inside, Rolfe and another man were in seats in the front room. I assumed the second man to be Stelling, the man who was a former member of the SS. Others were present, German Policemen and three U.S. enlisted men. After returning salutes to the U.S. personnel and greeting the German Police, the Colonel turned to me.

"All right, Max, do whatever you want to. Do you want to talk to Rolfe first, or Stelling?"

"Stelling. And I want to be alone with him."

"You've got it."

The Colonel turned to the U.S. enlisted man and pointed to Stelling, speaking with a gruffy tone.

"Does that son-of-a-bitch speak English?"

The enlisted man spoke to a German policeman and the answer came back "yes." I moved forward and told the Americans that I would interview Stelling and I would need a room where he and I would have privacy. Two of the German policemen spoke to Stelling, telling him to stand and go with them. He did so, and the two policemen, after glancing at me to be sure they were carrying out orders correctly, took him toward the rear of the house. I went along too and we ended up in what seemed to be a utility room with two chairs and a table. A German policeman ordered Stelling to sit and then looked at me for further instructions. I said, "You can go. And lock the door behind you."

Stelling sat with a sullen and defiant look on his face. He was younger than Augenberg. He was still arrogant, and I could sense that he had complete confidence in himself. Being a typical SS soldier he would be difficult. It was no longer a time to have picnics, however, and I was prepared to do whatever was necessary to get him to talk.

I left him sitting and remained on my feet. I walked over near him and spoke.

"I am going to ask you some questions. I know you speak English and I am expecting you to answer. Will you cooperate?"

"Nein!", he said, speaking loudly. And then, amazingly, he raised up and came at me. I was near him, within the reach of my arm. I hit him on the left side of his face with a right-hand punch as hard as I could deliver. He went flying backward, and he, along with the chair where he had been sitting, were down and on the floor, the chair ending up a few feet away from him. He was dazed but attempted to get up and I could see in his eyes that he would come at me again. I moved in with another hard right, hitting him in the middle of his face. Again, he went backwards, this time groaning as he fell to the floor on his back. While he was still down I moved in over him. Leni and Gertrude flashed through my mind, I knew he had killed them and many others, and now, if he wanted it, I would return the favor. He was not out and he was able to move a little and speak.

"Wait! Wait, Major."

"Are you ready to talk?"

"Yes. I will talk. But please, give me a moment."

He struggled and was eventually able to get up on his knees. He looked around for a place to sit. I picked up the straight-back wooden chair and sat it beside him. Gradually he pulled himself up into a sitting position on the chair. He was bleeding profusely, mostly from his nose and mouth. The side of his face was beginning to swell, the result of the first blow I had landed. I gave him about thirty seconds to recover, then spoke.

"If you don't give me the answers I'm looking for, you may not leave this room alive. How do you feel about that?"

"Bitte, Herr Major, please, no more strikes. I will answer truthfully whatever you ask."

He couldn't get his nose to stop bleeding and it was pouring. There was a sink in the room and a towel. I took the towel, ran water over it, and handed it to him. He held it up to his nose and it prevented the blood from spilling on to his clothing. The towel was soon soaked and I found another one for him. This time he mumbled, "danke."

After a few minutes the bleeding slowed and I felt he had recovered enough to continue with my questions.

"Okay, Stelling, we're going to talk now. And remember what I said, don't lie to me."

"I will not lie."

"How long were you with Frau Wegner?"

"It was, I believe sir, five or six days."

"Where did you first see her?"

"We learned that she was in Fulda, but we did not take her until she was here in Frankenberg."

"Were you in this house?"

"Yes."

"Who else was here?"

"Only the American, LeTourneau."

"LeTourneau and Frau Wegner, did they appear to be friendly?"

"They appeared to be friendly."

"Where did you sleep, and where did they sleep?"

"I slept in one room, they slept in another."

"Did he force her to sleep with him?"

"No."

"How can you be sure? Did you see them go together into the same room?"

"Yes."

"How did they act . . . what was their behavior . . . while in your presence? Was it like a man and woman who care for each other?"

"Herr Major, I cannot answer, I do not know."

"Did they embrace, and kiss, in your presence?"

"Yes."

"I am going to ask a question and I want you to think about it before answering. Take your time and be sure that you give me your very best response. Do you feel that Frau Wegner, realizing that she was in a situation that might result in her death, could have been friendly to LeTourneau in the way you described in an effort to save her life?"

Remembering what I had said, he paused as if to think carefully before speaking.

"Major, I do not know the answer to that question. Please sir, you must know that I cannot determine such an answer."

He was right. It would be difficult to determine. Ariane, knowing LeTourneau to be a ruthless man, would have realized that her life would be hanging by a thread. Under those circumstances she might have faked a friendly attitude toward LeTourneau. I looked back to Stelling.

"When they left here last night, did she go freely with him?"

"There was confusion, Major. He killed Otto, the German policeman who was here on duty. When I saw it happen I ran out the door. He shot at me as I went toward the forest. Then he returned to the inside, and while I watched from about two hundred meters away as I hid among the trees, he brought out some things and put them in his jeep. About five minutes later he and Frau Wegner got in the jeep and left."

"Did he force her?"

"No, he did not force her. But, there was something else—"

"Yes?"

"She was dressed as a man. She was wearing the duty uniform of an American soldier."

"Like fatigues? Do you know how a fatigue uniform looks?"

"Yes, it was a fatigue uniform and she had on a cap that covered her hair."

Dressing her as a man in the uniform of a U.S. soldier would give him the opportunity to move through the American Zone with no problem. He would easily be able to make it into the Russian Zone if that was, as Mason had speculated, his objective. At least he apparently had no intention of killing Ariane. I spoke to Stelling.

"The man who is here, Rolfe, where did you first meet him?"

"In Fulda. LeTourneau told Augenberg to contact him and it was approximately three or four weeks ago."

"Why did Augenberg contact Rolfe?"

"I do not know, Herr Major."

I took a step in his direction and he quickly spoke.

"There was some talk about gold."

"And Rolfe knew, about the gold?"

"Yes, he knew about the gold."

"Did he say that Frau Wegner also knew about the gold?"

"I . . . I believe at that time Frau Wegner knew about the gold."

"Do you believe Karl Wegner told his wife about the location of the gold?"

"He did not tell her. He told no one. He killed all people who knew about the location."

"He didn't kill the Russian man."

"No, not as he did the others but it was only by a miracle that he escaped and lived for a short while. And now the German farm couple is no longer there, they too, are dead."

"Yes, that is true." After a pause I continued. "I am going to ask one more question and then you will be allowed to return to the front room of the house. Do you think LeTourneau is holding Frau Wegner because he feels she can locate the gold, or do you feel that she might actually know the location? I'm asking you this because you were with them, you saw them together for long periods, and I feel you should be able to give an accurate answer to my question."

He took some time, probably to impress me. After nearly half a minute he gave his answer.

"Sir, as I said, Karl Wegner told no one about the location. If she knew, she would have found out by some other means. Maybe a careless mistake was made by Herr Wegner and she discovered it in that way. And yes, I believe LeTourneau is holding her because of the gold, no other reason. She has possibly given him some reason to think she knows the location."

I considered what he had said. Maybe, as he stated, Ariane did try to convince LeTourneau she knew the location of the gold to save herself. It was almost impossible for me to think that she would have been close to him, as described by Stelling, or for any other reason. And now they were gone and it would be futile to try to guess how to follow them. We could send out an alert by radio and describe them, although it most likely would be a meaningless effort. Still, I had to cling to some hope about Ariane. And the way Stelling had described her relationship with LeTourneau, I had to know about that. At least I had to try to find out. Realistically, I knew that I might never know the true details about it because I might never find her.

I decided to let Stelling return to the front room and have Rolfe sent back. I wanted Rolfe to get a good look at Stelling's face before coming in. I tapped the door and it was unlocked by the American Corporal. I told him to take Stelling to the front room and send Rolfe back. In answer to my question the Corporal said that Colonel Mason had already put out an alert for LeTourneau.

When Rolfe entered the room I could see at once the dismay he was feeling. I pointed to the wooden chair and he sat down. I spoke in a low-key, casual tone.

"Rolfe, you will most likely leave here within the hour and be sent to our prison at Darmstadt. You will be kept there temporarily and then be transferred to a permanent location to await trial. Because of the gold you will now be considered a war criminal. Are these things clear to you?"

He was greatly shaken. I had detected when talking to him a few days before that he had a horror of being sent to prison. He was eager to speak.

"Herr Major, I will cooperate in any way that is possible. Please tell me, sir, how I can assist you and possibly it will help me."

"Possibly. I need facts from you, Rolfe, and if you lie there will be no help."

"I understand, Herr Major."

"Tell me exactly how Ariane Wegner felt about LeTourneau."

"Major, I . . . it is difficult for me to make that conclusion. I know that she was fearful and believed that her life was in danger. How she actually felt about LeTourneau, sir, I can only guess. There is no other way for me to state it."

"You saw them together on many occasions. You must have a good opinion on how she felt."

"I saw them together only a few times and then I was moved to the other house, the house of my friend here in Frankenberg."

"When did she meet LeTourneau for the first time?"

"In Fulda while she was recovering from the gun shot wound."

"Did you ever hear him speak about her?"

"No, I did not hear him speak about her."

"You told me, when I talked to you at the hotel, that Frau Wegner had known about the gold for several months. She told you and your mother. Why would she do that?"

"Again, she was fearful. She might have thought that her husband knew, and it would place her in danger. I believe it made her feel better to share the knowledge with us."

"And you believe she withheld the information from me only to protect me?"

"Yes, I believe that is the reason, Herr Major. She was in love with you."

"How can it be, then, that she is now, perhaps, in love with LeTourneau?"

"I did not say that, sir. I said that I could not be certain about her feelings for him."

He was silent and so was I. Actually, I did not believe that she was in love with LeTourneau, I was simply probing for additional comments from Rolfe.

I turned and walked to a window. There was a forest nearby, and the shaded area under the trees looked mysterious, and I thought, many things are hidden there, including small animals, and large animals. I stood there, looking out, and I was hurting. Faint doubts were beginning to come into my mind about Ariane. Did she really love me in the way I had imagined? After a few moments I turned back to Rolfe.

"We will hold you here temporarily, Rolfe. You will be under house arrest as you were before. Don't try to run."

"Oh, I will not do that, Herr Major, and thank you, sir."

We walked out together. I told a German policeman that Rolfe was to be held in the same house as before. Then I spoke to the Colonel.

"I'm finished, Colonel."

He nodded. He was ready to go and we moved toward the door. Outside, he spoke.

"Do you believe it now, the story about your lady and LeTourneau?"

"No. She was trying to protect herself. But it's a futile point anyway, Colonel. They're gone and I don't believe we will ever see either of them again."

"Yeah, unfortunately, I would say that is correct. Oh well, it's time to move on anyway. Now can you help me with the gold?"

"I haven't decided what I will do. I would like to return to Bad Welmsburg and have a day or two to think about it."

"Oh, hell no, we're going to settle this now. I want your answer here, today."

I looked hard into his eyes.

"Or you will do what?"

I surprised him and he was speechless, so I continued.

"I've still got Augenberg and his statement. No, Colonel, you don't give me orders anymore, so don't give me any deadlines."

He was silent until we got inside the Mercedes. After we were underway he turned to look at me.

"Tell me what you want to do, Max. Hell, we can forget about the charges against you. You've got no problems. Why don't you go on home and get on with your life back there?"

"I don't like your plans for the gold, Colonel, it isn't right. Otherwise you and I can part company here and now."

"I'm not going to give up the gold. I couldn't even if I wanted to. There are powerful people involved in this and we are all in the same boat."

"Okay, so right now we've got an impasse. I'll agree to stay here in Frankenberg another day or so. Who knows, maybe something will turn up on LeTourneau."

"All right, it's agreed. Drop me off at the Military Government office and check in with me tomorrow. I assume you will be at the hotel?"

"Yes."

Heidi was glad to see me. We embraced and held on for a long while. Then, we pulled away and sat down. I gave her the details of what had happened during the day and I told her we would be staying on in the hotel for a day or so. She was thrilled.

"Oh! Wonderful! We can go to the dining room and listen to the music tonight, okay?"

She was like a pretty little girl in a toy store, and naturally, I agreed.

At seven-thirty we were in the dining room. It wasn't crowded. Most of the people who came there on weekends were missing. Even so, the musicians were playing, and it was nice and quiet, and more peaceful. And it seemed to fit my mood. Heidi noticed.

"Do you think that LeTourneau . . . and Ariane . . . will be found?"

"It doesn't look good."

"Do you think it is possible that she went with him because . . ."

She didn't want to finish the question and paused to let me speak.

"She might have been forced to go. I'm sure she must have been fearful, but . . . I can't be sure about everything at this point."

"It might be a time to . . . maybe you should try to forget it now. It may be over. It's like the people I knew who were killed—they are no longer here, the war took them away. And it may be the same for you. I know you are hurt, I can see it. But when it happened in the war we tried to think of the things that were left. We have to go on, and . . . Max, will you tell me again . . . please . . . that you love me?"

"Yes, I do love you, Heidi. It's not easy for a man sometimes to say that to a woman, and I don't know exactly why. But with you, it's easy for me. You've become a part of my life that I can never give up and I hope that I can be near you, always."

My words made her happy and she formed a sweet expression.

"Thank you, Max. That means so much to me. I have loved you almost from the first moment that we met. In the beginning I was looking for security, and then, as I came to know you, I felt differently because you are a good man, a man like I had never known before." And then there was her mischievous smile. "And I thought, here is this very handsome man, who women in Bad Welmsburg talk about all the time who is showing some interest in me. I felt very proud and happy."

I smiled in return.

"Thanks, Heidi. I can say some of the same things about you. I thought that I was very fortunate to have such a beautiful woman attracted to me. And I am comforted by your nearness, I miss you very much when we are separated."

11.

NO OTHER PEOPLE were sitting near us and we were able to speak in English openly. I continued.

"There have been so many things I haven't said to you. Little things sometimes, like your hair, when you changed it to disguise yourself. I thought you were real cute and I should have told you. It just seems that I have been so preoccupied and I don't say as much as I should."

"It's okay, Max. I can see a lot in your eyes, you don't always have to tell me."

"I know. But now that I have the chance I want to say a few other things. You've been completely unselfish. You've given me all of your love at a time when most other women would have walked away. And, as beautiful as you are, you didn't have to do that, I'm sure there must be many other men who would like to take my place."

She was grinning and I could tell she would probably start teasing me.

"Yes, that is right, and I think I have stayed with you long enough."

I wanted to keep her good-natured mood going.

"Don't even think about it. You're stuck right where you are."

"Oh? I don't know, I might go away. Yes! I might go to Paris! I will find another man who will take me there."

We both smiled. We were drinking the white wine that had been served as we first arrived, and our waiter stopped by again. Heidi spoke to him in German and he readily agreed with her, assured her that whatever she had said would be done. He walked away and she spoke in English again.

"We are going to dance, Major. I spoke to our waiter and he says it will be fine. We can use the open space in front of the musicians. And you want to know what else we will do?"

"I'm afraid to ask."

"I requested that they play a waltz and he says they will do it. So, we are going to dance to a waltz. And don't tell me you can't dance to a waltz."

She had me laughing.

"I told you before, I can dance to anything."

We sipped the wine and enjoyed the pleasant surroundings. I think she was as happy as I had ever seen her. And it made me feel good. I had never been able to tell her that "I only have eyes for you," although I had shown her, and told her, how much I cared for her. Even so, she would still know that I had Ariane in the back of my mind, and I regretted it for her, I was sorry that it was making her uncomfortable because I only wanted to make her happy. Heidi was different from most Germans, at least she was unlike most I had observed. Normally a German would not become involved in a triangle. Maybe it had to do with their discipline and pride. Also, they were not as prone to become as emotionally involved with others. But it was not true with Heidi—she was determined to have what she wanted.

I saw the woman at the piano look in our direction and nod to Heidi. Heidi stood, smiling, and took my hand and I, too, stood. We walked to the part of the room that was considered the dance floor, an area just in front of the musicians. We stood facing each other, about a foot apart. I took her right hand in my left, and put my right hand at the side of her waist on the left, only lightly touching her there. She placed her left hand on my shoulder and we were poised to begin dancing. The woman at the piano nodded to the other two musicians and the music began. It was a German waltz, a song that I vaguely remembered. We had plenty of room and we took the long steps that were needed to go with the rhythm of the song.

It was fun. It had been years since I had danced to a waltz and even after so much time it was coming back quickly. And Heidi seemed to be having the time of her life, looking up at me as we made the wide turns with a huge grin on her face.

No one else was dancing and when the song was finished, a few people sitting at the tables clapped. The woman at the piano smiled at me and made a slight motion with her little finger, and obviously it was a gesture for me to be ready for another song. She spoke to the two men accompanying her and they were ready.

She began alone on the piano and I recognized the song at once. It was *Moonlight Serenade,* a song made famous in the U.S. by the Glenn Miller band. It was nice to hear. Heidi was pleased too and reached for me to begin dancing again. I spoke as we moved over the floor.

"We didn't fool anybody, did we?"

"No, of course not. They're not stupid, they always knew who you were."

"Even when we first came, when I had on my German outfit?"

"Yes, even then they knew."

"And you let me think I had everybody fooled."

"It was more fun that way. I wanted to pretend that you were a German man and we were here together, to . . . we were together because we belonged together and it would remain that way and nothing would happen to prevent it."

We danced for a while and eventually returned to our table. The room had a few more people present and there was slightly more noise, pleasant sounds of people laughing and talking.

Our meal had been served and I asked Heidi if she would like to go for a walk.

"Yes! We can go to the park and sit on a bench."

On the way out I caught the eye of the woman at the piano and formed the words "thank you," silently sending her a message across the room. She smiled graciously and nodded.

We walked through the lobby of the hotel to the outside. When we got to the sidewalk I reached down and took Heidi's hand.

Being with her and knowing how she felt was nice. I think she must have felt the same and we were content to walk along in silence, and maybe it was the time she had been waiting for. She glanced at me occasionally, and although she didn't speak, I could sense her feeling of happiness and contentment.

We went into the park and it looked deserted. There were benches throughout, scattered some fifty to one hundred feet apart. I let her pick a spot and soon we were settled, sitting close together. I put my right arm around her shoulders and she leaned her head over so that it was resting against my neck. Her hair felt good next to my chin, and it enriched my feeling of love for her, and it was also a sexually arousing sensation, the touching of her hair against my face. She made a comment, in the form of a question, that seemed unusual.

"Max, tell me about your philosophy."

"You mean how I feel about life?"

"Yes."

"Well, let's see, how do I start? Okay . . . I believe right is better than wrong. People should strive to have truthfulness instead of deception. And I think it is disgusting to have too much pride. We should concentrate on helping others, not hurting them. How am I doing so far?"

"Fine. What else? What about men and women?

"They should get married and be loyal to each other. And live happily ever after, of course."

"What if it is not always that simple?"

"Yeah, I know. As we go through life, I think most people have two personalties. For a man, I suppose the swashbuckling-type individual he sees who sleeps with many different women, all beautiful of course in the Hollywood version, is a tempting character to copy. The other personality is different, honorable and steadfast, and deep down, I think we almost always like him the best. And, personally, I think the most important thing for a man as he has a relationship with a woman is his intent. Whether married or not, if he treats her with kindness and honors her, I believe in the eyes of God it is a blessed union. Now, tell me about your intent."

"I don't have to tell you, you already know my intent."

When we were lying in bed together, much later, Heidi as usual dropped off to sleep first. It gave me a chance to think about the current situation and how I could manage it.

I considered the facts. Colonel Mason no longer had control of me by using Ariane. He no longer had her and he was not likely to have her again. He still had enough to carry out his threat of charging me, or maintaining the charges of negligence and conspiracy already made, and following up with a court martial. That scenario, however, though limited, had one good possibility. If I could talk Mason into releasing Heidi, she could return to Bad Welmsburg and talk to Colonel Margolies. She was now familiar with all details and could fill him in on everything. He was a career army man and would have some long-time friends in high places who would be reliable. If he could get to them, Mason and his friends could be stopped. The issue of the gold could be settled jointly by the leaders of the Allies. The risk in such a plan would involve timing and how quickly Mason might learn what was happening. He, and the people above him, would order the execution of everyone even remotely connected to a move to block their plans. And even though he might agree to release Heidi, he might be suspicious and order an "accident" for her. And so, I would have to remember, even with LeTourneau and Ariane out of reach for Mason, he still had enough firepower left to make it risky. Maybe I would discuss it with Heidi. She always considered things in a way that was level-headed.

The next morning after breakfast in the dining room, Heidi and I returned to our room upstairs. We sat in the chairs that were there and relaxed. Following a brief period, I told her that I had something important to discuss. She was surprised but looked at me eagerly to hear what I would say.

I told her, in complete detail, about my plan and followed up with a question.

"Do you think you can do it?"

"Yes, I can do it, except I don't know if I want to do it. I don't want to leave you."

"And I don't want you to leave. It just seems like the best plan I can come up with."

She was thoughtful for a while before speaking again.

"If I should decide to go, do you think Mason would allow it?"

"I don't know. And even if he did there would be some risk. I don't trust him, and so I am actually undecided whether it is a good idea."

Her wheels were still turning so I continued.

"I can't think of anything else, Heidi. We're both at risk, whether we stay or go. It's not safe either way. If you do decide to go, I am going to do everything possible to make it safe for you."

This time she didn't wait—she had decided.

"Okay! Let's do it!"

During the early morning I drove the Mercedes to the Military Government motor pool garage and filled up with gas. It was no problem; I had simply called the office and said I was running low on fuel. I knew Mason had people scattered through the city watching me, so I was given limited freedom to move about as I desired.

I was back in our hotel room at mid-morning. I called the office of Captain Brown and asked for Colonel Mason. He was soon on the line.

"Good morning, Colonel."

"Good morning, Major. What's up?"

"Have you heard from LeTourneau?"

"No. We'll never catch that bastard. He's probably in Moscow by now. And I'm sure your little lady is with him."

I was glad he mentioned Ariane. It gave me a chance, in an insignificant way, to bring Heidi into the conversation.

"Yeah, Colonel, unfortunately, I think you are right. Speaking of women, I am ready to get rid of the one who is with me. I'd like to send her back to Bad Welmsburg."

There was a long pause before he answered.

"I don't think so, Max. She knows too much."

"She doesn't know anything, Colonel. Do you think I would risk everything by spilling my guts to a prostitute?"

"She's been here, she's heard things."

"The only thing she's heard is the jingle of my money. I want to get her out of here."

Again, a long pause.

"What do you want to do, put her on a train?"

"Yes, I'd like to do that and it will rid me of some excess baggage."

"Well . . . I guess we can do it. I can send somebody with her, you know."

"Oh sure, that's no problem. I just want to get her out of my way while we settle things."

"Okay. Put her on a train. But remember, Max, we've got people everywhere and the wrong move will be curtains for you."

"I know. I've very aware that we are being watched, and I know that our telephone calls are being monitored, incoming and outgoing."

He laughed.

"How the hell did you find that out? That was supposed to be kept secret."

"I've been in this business for a while too, Colonel, and I know how surveillance is handled."

I didn't actually know our calls were monitored, I only suspected it. He chuckled again and spoke.

"Okay, let your little whore go on home. But you stay put here in town and I'll be in touch."

After hanging up I told Heidi that our plan was going to work. She already knew because she had heard my end of the conversation and she was able to judge that it was going well.

We spent the next hour going over details of her train ride, including such things as being alert and watching people around her. Next, we went over all of the information she was to convey to Colonel Margolies. She was very clear on everything and I felt good about her.

At eleven twenty-five the phone rang. It was Mason and his voice was a little more animated than usual.

"Max, we've got some new information. Come on in to the office and I'll tell you about it."

"Okay. Can you give me a hint about it?"

"Yeah. After you beat hell out of Stelling yesterday, we told him this morning that you were coming back today. He opened up some. But wait until you get here and I'll explain."

Thirty minutes later, the Colonel and I were in Captain Brown's office. We were alone. Mason spoke.

"Stelling knew more than we realized. LeTourneau didn't plan to go to the Russian Zone. He had lost his position with them and he knew they would kill him. Stelling says he had talked just recently about where he would go if he got in a jam. He wanted to stay in the U.S. Zone, but close to another country. Stelling says he is ninety-nine percent sure that LeTourneau is in Berchtesgaden. LeTourneau's reasoning for that was the nearby borders of Austria and Italy—he could very easily move into one of those two countries if it got hot for him. Also, by staying in that area he would be able to use his rank and privileges."

"So, what's your next move?"

"We have to take him out. He knows too much. And he might turn to the Germans now and try to make a deal. I'm telling you this but it has to be kept quiet. If you talk we will have to take out the lady, too. Do you understand?"

"Yes, I understand. How will you do it?"

"Don't worry about it. It's already under way."

"How about Frau Wegner?"

"She will be returned."

"How do I know that? She's in the middle—she could easily be taken out with him. I have to be involved in this. I want to be in Berchtesgaden when it happens."

"No! No way. Why the hell do you have to be there?"

"To be sure she isn't killed."

He turned away and walked to the other side of the room. He was silent for a long while, maybe a minute, before turning back in my direction.

"Okay, you can be there. You'll have to move fast. In fact, you need to fly down there today. Are there any planes in the area?"

"Yes, there's an artillery outfit about thirty miles from here on the road to Bad Welmsburg. If you get an order for me I'll get a pilot to fly me in one of their observer planes. I can be in Berchtesgaden late today."

"We'll do it that way on one condition. When you return with the woman I want to know everything about the gold. Are you straight on that?"

"Yeah, I'm straight."

"And listen, Max, don't mess with me, don't run."

"I can't run, you're covered down there. All I want is to get her back to Bad Welmsburg safely."

"You've got a deal. Now, go back to the hotel and get your things and come on by the office and pick up your order. I've got a hell of a lot to do today, a lot of calls to make, but I'll have you ready to go."

On the way back to the hotel I thought of a different angle that might work better than a train ride back home for Heidi. Heidi could go with me in the car and drop me off at the artillery outfit where I would be going to get the flight to Berchtesgaden. She could continue on from there in the car to Bad Welmsburg. In that way she could travel more safely. Mason wouldn't notice because he would be too involved in making telephone calls to his "associates," and to everyone else it would look legitimate because they would know that Mason had given me permission to leave.

When I got to the room Heidi was anxious to hear about everything and I began.

"Heidi, we have to be separated for a short while."

"I know."

"It's different from the way we talked."

She knew what I would say next and she mentioned it first.

"It's LeTourneau and Ariane, isn't it? Have they been found?"

"Not found but Mason got information out of Stelling that gives him the name of the city where they are located."

"What city?"

"Berchtesgaden. I have to go there . . . today."

She didn't speak. She smiled slightly and walked over to a chair and sat. I moved over to the other chair and sat close to her. I continued to explain what we were to do.

"We have to pack up and get ready to leave. Mason will let us go with no problems. Can you be ready in a short while?"

"Yes, I can be ready."

She appeared to be passively accepting what I had said, and she got up and began gathering her things. Within an hour we were ready to go. Heidi didn't talk much and it was distressing. I knew she was hurting, as was I.

We checked out at the counter and put our things in the Mercedes. We pulled away from the curb and headed in the direction of the Military Government headquarters in the bank building. When we got there I parked at the curb, and on the inside I was taken to an office where Mason was sitting alone. He was at a desk, in the process of reaching for a phone, when he saw me. He stopped and quickly reached for a piece of paper, which would be my order, handed it to me and spoke at the same time.

"Okay, take off. And remember, no funny business."

"Tell me who your people are in Berchtesgaden. How will I know them?"

"You don't need to know them."

"How will I know what's going on?"

"They will find you. Check into a hotel and wait. Don't worry about it. From what I have learned Frau Wegner may know the location of the gold, and I want her back here as much as you do. Now, get the hell out of here, I'm busy."

In the car I told Heidi about my conversation with Mason. I wanted her to know every detail of what was happening. It would be important when she talked to Colonel Margolies. I had brought it up as we headed out in an eastern direction. I continued the discussion with an attempt to be more personal.

"You should be in Bad Welmsburg by mid to late afternoon. Contact Colonel Margolies immediately and tell him everything. Can you do that?"

"Yes, of course. Do you think he will see me without a problem, is he the type to do that?"

"He's very definitely the type. He will go into action quickly and I think the end will come for Mason and his friends as early as tomorrow."

"And you will return to Bad Welmsburg soon?"

"Yes."

After that she became silent. I didn't know exactly what to say so I became silent, too. I had been that way for several hours, since I told her about going to Berchtesgaden, and it seemed that neither of us could find the right words to talk. I thought it might help so I turned on the radio and we listened to the American Broadcasting Station in Paris.

In a short while we were nearing the location of the American unit where I would get out of the car and leave Heidi. I told her and she began talking.

"Max, it will be best . . . you will soon see Ariane again. If it is to be her, I will understand, and I will only say that you have been the most wonderful thing that has ever happened to me. I can never forget you, there will never be another man for me . . . I believe I was born to love only you. It would not be fair to another man, I could not feel in my heart the same for anyone else. You don't have to say anything now, in fact, I don't want you to say anything. I have only one request. If it is to be Ariane, you don't need to come and tell me. If it is to be me, come back to me in Bad Welmsburg."

Again, I didn't know what to say. I smiled at her, and she smiled sweetly in return.

At the field artillery unit headquarters building it took me about twenty minutes to get to the right officer and explain my needs. He looked at my order and spoke.

"Major, we'll have you under way in about ten minutes. You can drive around to the field next to the planes and wait in your car."

I did as he said and parked at the edge of an air strip near six small planes. It was time to make a few final comments to Heidi.

"You won't have any trouble with directions from here to Bad Welmsburg, will you?"

"No. I will go back to the main highway and continue east."

"Right. Do you have enough money?"

"I have some money at home, and I have the money you gave me this morning for unexpected expenses."

"Good. I'll be thinking of you. I probably can't contact you from Berchtesgaden—the distance is too great for a phone call."

"I know. I'll be thinking of you, too."

A Corporal came to my side of the car and spoke.

"Okay, sir, the pilot is ready." And he pointed to a plane with the propeller turning.

"Thanks, Corporal, I'll be right there."

The Corporal reached down and picked up the two bags I had placed beside the car and moved away toward the plane. Heidi and I looked at each other. She forced a smile, and so did I. I got out of the car and walked around to her side and opened the door. She stepped out and stood facing me. We reached for each other spontaneously. I held her tightly, rubbing my cheek over her hair. Then, we were kissing. I felt love, passion, tenderness . . . mixed with a forlorn feeling that goes with a solemn goodbye. She was returning my kisses with all of her love, and it continued for maybe half a minute. Finally we pulled away and I looked into her eyes. She was somber, and I knew that I must have appeared the same to her. I took her hand and walked around the car to the driver's side and opened the door for her. She made a move to get in, and then she turned back and put her arms around my neck. I reached around her with both arms and pulled her to me again, and our bodies were pressed together tightly as before. We both were feeling the same emotions and it was almost impossible for me to let her go. It was tearing our hearts out, and for a split second I thought that I could not leave. We were kissing again, even more affectionately, and it was a mixture of our tenacious love and the passion we had known during the times that we had slept together. I couldn't turn loose. She was so dear to me, and I was so deeply in love with her, it took everything else away, and I only wanted to continue holding her.

I felt a tap on my shoulder and it was the Corporal. He was smiling.

"Sorry to interrupt, sir, but the pilot is ready to take off."

I had to go, there was no other choice. I backed away. Heidi and I took a long look at each other, and I turned to walk in the direction of the plane. Near the small plane I stopped and looked back and she was standing by the car. I waved, and so did she.

The pilot, a young man who looked to be in his mid-twenties, had a wide grin on his face. He glanced toward Heidi and back to me before speaking.

"Are you sure you want to leave here, sir?"

"No, Lieutenant, I'm not sure, I just don't have a choice."

He laughed.

"I'm Jim Johnston, Major, and I'm happy to be your pilot today."

"Thanks, Jim. My name is Max Gordon."

He directed me toward the plane as he spoke again.

"You might have a tight squeeze, today, Major. You know these planes were actually designed to accommodate only one person, the pilot. I think there's enough space behind my seat for you and your gear but you won't be able to get up and walk around."

"No problem, Jim."

Soon we were in the air headed in a southeastern direction. Jim told me we would fly over Schweinfurt and Nurnberg, and I thought about our pilots who would have flown over the two cities under different circumstances. I had heard that Schweinfurt had been horrible for our planes during the war, and we had lost many airmen in that area.

We didn't talk much during the flight. The engine was loud, and I was not in a talkative mood anyway. After at least two hours, Jim did turn and speak.

"Sir, my orders are to get you as close to Berchtesgaden as possible. I can't land in Berchtesgaden because of the topography, I'll have to pick a level spot on the highway and I'm hoping I can find something within twenty miles or so of the city. Can you manage like that, sir?"

"Oh, sure. There should be plenty of our vehicles on the road and I can catch a ride."

Just a few minutes later, Jim turned his head sidewise and spoke.

"Sir, we are approaching the area north of Berchtesgaden. I'm going to follow the highway all the way in to the city and look for a level stretch of road. By doing that I can get you in as close as possible."

"Sounds good to me, Jim."

By looking downward I could see what he had meant about the topography. There were mountains in all directions. The highway curved in and out of the crevices formed by the valleys, and getting down, even in his small plane, would not be simple.

Suddenly he turned and yelled back at me.

"There it is, sir! We can use that stretch of the highway straight ahead. See it?"

I looked and saw what he was describing, at least a quarter of a mile of the highway that was straight. I told him it looked good.

He flew on in over the city. The highway "airport" we had just passed over was about ten miles north of Berchtesgaden. He made a wide circle and headed back to the area where he would bring the plane down. When he got there he circled twice to be sure no vehicles were approaching the spot, and then he very quickly took us down for a smooth landing.

We got out and stretched and it felt good. I had been in a rather cramped position during the flight and it took a minute or so to walk off the tightness in my legs.

Within five minutes we heard a truck approaching from the north. When it came into view I recognized one of our U.S. two-and-a-half-ton "Red Ball Express" vehicles. The driver slowed immediately when he saw us and Jim stepped out into the middle of the road and held up his hand. The enlisted man who was driving was surprised to see us and the plane, but he was glad to help us. I told him I needed a ride into town and he said it would be no problem. Next, Jim asked him to back up and block the road to prevent another vehicle from getting in the way while he took off for his return trip.

I shook hands with Jim, thanked him, and got in the big truck. We backed up to the spot Jim had pointed out and in about thirty seconds he took off, passing directly over us.

The driver asked me where I would like to go in Berchtesgaden and I told him a hotel. He said he knew a good place where other Americans were staying.

The mountain village of Berchtesgaden, made famous in recent years as the retreat of Hitler, was actually a tourist attraction even before the Nazi leader came into power. Many gift and hobby shops lined the sloping streets, and there were numerous hotels and inns. The driver of the truck took me to the lower part of the city, not too far away from the rail station, and there he let me off at a nice-looking hotel that appeared to be modern and clean.

Inside, in the lobby, I saw several other American officers, two with women. At the counter I asked the young German woman if she had a vacancy.

"Yes, we do have a vacancy, Major. How many in your party?"

"One, only me."

She smiled broadly.

"Oh, what a shame. Well, maybe that will change."

She was well experienced in dealing with Americans. She recognized my rank, and she had learned that she could share a little humor with most of us. And it would be easy for her to learn about Americans judging from the number of others who were there. She gave me a key, told me how to find my room, and after a pleasant look at her I picked up my two bags and walked away.

The room was nice. At one end there was a large window and it provided a panoramic view of the mountains. Oddly enough, there were a few magazines printed in English on a table. Whether placed there by the hotel employees or left behind by other Americans, they would come in handy. I was preparing myself for a wait, and it would be different from other times when I was more aggressively on the move.

I had dinner in the hotel dining room. Quite a few people were there, mostly American Army officers, many of whom were accompanied by German women. The meal was good, as usual, which didn't surprise me. The Germans seemed to take great pride in preparing food.

After dinner I went back to my room. It would be important to make myself available for the contact I was expecting.

Nothing happened during the evening. I read the magazines until midnight and then got in bed.

The next morning after breakfast I went outside to take a walk. In thinking about it, I believed that whoever would contact me would be reluctant to come into the hotel. So, I would give them other opportunities, let them see me on the streets or in the shops. There were countless gift and hobby shops.

At the end of the day no one had approached me. Many questions were beginning to form in my mind. Did LeTourneau really come to Berchtesgaden? If so, was Ariane still with him? Would Mason have sent me off on a "wild goose chase" to get me out of the way? Were new people involved, now that Heidi would have had time to explain everything to Colonel Margolies? The risk to all of the players would have doubled, or tripled, in the last twenty-four hours.

I missed Heidi, her humor and reassuring attitude when I had doubts and uncertainties. It was impossible for me to let my thoughts drift away from her for even a few minutes.

While walking during the day, occasionally stopping in a shop, my thoughts were focused on Ariane, as well. And it was still amazing when I considered how I had come to love two women at the same time so intensely. I had spent my life without having similar feelings; what I now knew to be real love. With Moira, my former wife, I'm sure that I must have said at some point, "I love you," because it was typical of what people do, and it was the right thing to say when getting married. Maybe I felt I was in love, and it could have been the same for Moira, but when I met Ariane, and was in love with her, I knew for the first time about the assuredness of being in love. And then, miraculously, it was the same with Heidi. I had asked myself over and over if it was the war, were my emotions all tangled up, had I changed so much that I would have felt the same about other women as well? Going for months, and years, without a relationship with a woman . . . did it give me an entirely new and different perspective? I leaned over backwards to convince myself that it could not be, I could not love these two women as much as my mind was telling me. In the end, however, my heart told me there could be no doubt, my love for each was indisputable.

I had become obsessed with a need to find Ariane and talk to her. I had to know how she felt. I was being moved by the deep love I had known in the past, a love that was still with me to the extent that I could not remove it from my mind. Maybe talking to her would resolve it; maybe she had changed and she would let me know. Her emotions might have been tangled at the time she knew me, because she was, after all, subjected to various tragic events that were taking place at the time. I was not concerned about LeTourneau. She was not in love with him, he was not her type. Obviously she was fighting for her life during the time she had been with him. I think my only doubt about her was the gold and why she withheld that information from me. Did it mean that she had some future plan that did not include me?

12.

THE NEXT DAY it was the same. Nothing. It was frustrating and I was not sure what I should do. Not knowing the status of Mason and LeTourneau made it worse. If they were both still free, and active, the wrong move by me could jeopardize the countermoves that might be taking place. And I could not even be certain that Heidi had been able to reach Colonel Margolies. I decided to wait another day before asking for assistance from local U.S. Army personnel.

There was a popular bar across the street from the hotel. I had seen many people going there in the evenings. Would the people Mason had sent to get LeTourneau, the assassins, be more likely to approach me in a bar? Bars usually had a wide mix of characters, and the ones who were devious felt more comfortable in such surroundings. They could mingle among the people without too much risk, mainly because others would be there who would be in the same category. I thought it would be worth a try to go there, and after dinner I walked across the street and went inside.

As I had assumed, there was a general mix of people in the bar. People in military uniforms, mostly American and British, both men and women were there, but it was predominately women. The civilian men, older of course, were in the minority, and obviously it was primarily a gathering place for Allied soldiers, either on leave or stationed in Berchtesgaden. The original proclamation, banning fraternization with the Germans, had long ago flown out the window. Both the military men, and the German women, having spent months and years apart from relationships, were not going to be further denied regardless of the rules that were established by the Allied leaders. The people in the bar, numbering some one hundred and twenty five, were mostly women, more than fifty percent of the total I was sure. It was not surprising. German women not only were looking for a relationship with a man for love, they were looking for security. Suddenly all of their things were gone: food, clothing, and for some, even housing.

British and American military men could change that and the women were quick to realize it. And again, there was a broad mix of types among the women. Some were even elderly, looking to be in their sixties. Some, who were younger, looked glamourous and they would have obviously used all of their resources to present themselves in the best possible way. The men would be having a field day—hardly any woman would turn down a friendly approach by a prospective date. The only problem for the men would be getting to the best, first. The "left-overs," though less attractive, would also be taken at some point, and I could see after being there only briefly that constant movements were being made back and forth by the men jockeying for the most beautiful women.

I saw an empty seat at the bar and headed for it at once. After I was seated and had a chance to look around the room I believed that I might have gotten the last empty seat in the place.

I ordered a glass of wine. While waiting, I turned on the swivel seat and watched the people. There was a lot of loud talk and laughter. Music was coming from loudspeakers, and, in general, a high level of sounds could be heard. Two British officers were sitting next to me at the bar and they were completely absorbed in analyzing every woman in the room. I could hear their comments occasionally: "Oh, look at that one in the gold dress!", and the response by the other officer, "Yeah! What a build!".

My seat was at the end of the bar and there was a slight space between me and the wall. The waitresses would come to that location frequently to pick up trays of drinks to take to the tables. The space was to my right and the two British officers were on my left. Glancing in their direction I could see that they were quite interested in something that was apparently just behind my right shoulder. I turned and was surprised. A woman was there. She spoke.

"Do you have a light, Major?"

She was about thirty, smiling, and holding up a cigarette. She was very pretty. She had on an expensive-looking dress, and actually, she seemed to be out of place. I would have been less surprised to have found her in a different surrounding, like a formal dinner in the home of a wealthy person back in the States. I told her I didn't have a light but would get one, which I did from the British officer next to me, and as I held the lighter up to her cigarette, it occurred to me that she might be the contact I was looking for and I grinned at her, speaking at the same time.

"Are you alone?"

She took her time. She lit the cigarette and blew out smoke, all the while gazing into my eyes with a rather seductive expression. Then she answered.

"Yes. Unfortunately my date didn't show up."

"That's surprising. He must be nuts. If you . . . would you mind if I join you?"

She was not the average barroom type woman; I could tell at a glance. It made me reasonably certain she had picked me for a reason, and it could only be one thing. She would be the contact I was seeking. She smiled and answered in a friendly tone.

"Yes, that would be very nice. That's my table over next to the wall."

I got up, took her by the arm, and accompanied her to the table. She was very poised, and a woman of "class." I held her chair and after she was seated I took a place in a chair opposite her at the table. I began a conversation with her.

"I can't imagine that you are here alone. What happened, do you think your date was somehow delayed?"

"No. We had agreed to meet here when we were together last evening. Then, we had an argument and he left. Even though he was angry at the time I felt he would still keep the date tonight."

"I see. Does he live here, or is he stationed here?"

"It doesn't matter, Major. We are finished. It was simply a passing friendship and I do not plan to see him again."

"How about you, is this your home? You don't seem to be the type to be living here in a small village."

"Oh, it's nice here. But you are right, my home was Berlin. When the Russians were coming, and it was obvious that they would take Berlin, it was easy for me to decide to come here to our mountain villa."

"You were married?"

"Yes. He was killed two years ago. I've been on my own since that time, and actually, I have been on my own for a long time because he was away all of the time."

"You were very fortunate to be able to come here. Your husband was a soldier?"

"Yes, a doctor, but assigned to the Wehrmacht."

"Are you sure about his death? So many men are still missing."

"He is dead. I received official notification. It was when the Russian Army pushed forward temporarily and was then pushed back. My husband's body was found."

"That's too bad. Do you have children?"

"No. My husband, we . . . we didn't think alike, and we didn't want to be tied together by children."

"You certainly speak English fluently. How did you get to be so proficient?"

"My husband and I were both educated in the United States. We were in New York."

"Oh, so that explains it. Well, maybe we will have something in common and we can talk about things that involve New York, or the States. I think we are all tired of talking about the war at this point anyway."

"I agree. Tell me about yourself and your family."

"I'm not married and I don't have children. I was married for quite a few years but it never was right, even from the beginning."

She was charming. Not pushy, not giggling or laughing at the wrong time, and not tense. Her appearance was typical German, blue eyes and blonde hair. Her bearing indicated a lifetime of luxurious living. And it was puzzling. It would take more time, and more talk, for me to find out about her. She spoke first after the slight pause.

"Are you here on leave?"

"Ah . . . yes and no. I do have some work to do, and after that I can relax for a few days."

"That's nice. I hope you enjoy your stay."

My instincts had failed me completely. I had to lie about being able to relax for a few days because I was not sure of her, or how she planned to handle the situation. On the other hand, she knew who I was—we had introduced ourselves as we had walked to her table. And so, if she was the contact for Mason, why wouldn't she go ahead and tell me? Maybe she was being conservative, afraid she might be arrested if Mason was caught. It would be a reasonable assumption if LeTourneau was still missing. And, of course, she might not be the person I thought she was—she might not even know Mason. I would have to ask more questions, and I decided to start at the beginning.

"Were you born in Berlin?"

"Yes."

"How did you happen to be educated in the United States?"

"My husband wanted to go to school at Columbia University. And because we had been . . . sweethearts, I suppose you would say . . . I wanted to go there too."

"And there was no problem from your government about going to school in America?"

"Oh, I believe some strings might have been pulled. Anyway, we were there for six years."

"Did you enjoy the time you were there?"

"Very much. But our families, and our homes, were in Germany and we had to return. Just in time for the war, unfortunately."

We talked about various things for a long while, more than an hour. She was content to talk and drink the wine, and she did not give the impression that she was looking for a relationship with a man. But, over a period of time, I did come to know that she had some reason to seek me out, and gradually I got the feeling that she was somehow on my side. I took advantage of it to address her more intimately.

"Erika, if you lived in the U.S. for six years, you must feel a loyalty and a closeness to us."

She looked at me without speaking, and I could sense that she knew all about me. Without taking her eyes away from my inquisitive stare, she eventually spoke.

"Max, I can't tell you anything at this time. Don't ask me. It's not settled. Nobody is safe. Do you understand?"

"Yes, I believe so. Is that all you can tell me, do you know about—"

She interrupted.

"I know about everything. I just can't discuss it now. My purpose in meeting you tonight is to tell you to be careful. Don't try to get involved. Stay away."

"Okay, I can do that. Will you contact me at the hotel?"

"I'll be in touch. Just be sure you stay out of the way."

"Will you answer one question?"

"No."

"Who are you working for? Is it Mason?"

She didn't answer. I asked again.

"Do you know Colonel Mason?"

"No."

"Are you connected to the Russians or the Germans?"

"No. It should be over soon, maybe tomorrow. I have to go now. Goodnight."

She put some money on the table for the wine, stood up, and without speaking again walked away and quickly disappeared through the door leading to the outside.

I was certain she had no connection to Mason. Who could it be? The Russians? Not likely. The Germans? Possibly, but again, not too likely. It actually seemed more like the U.S., but how could a German woman from Berlin be on our side, be involved with the Army investigating Mason and the gold?

The next morning I was restless. After breakfast I went by the reception counter in the lobby and picked up some different magazines. I walked outside and stayed briefly, breathing the fresh and crisp mountain air.

Back in the room I began what I disliked more than anything else, waiting. The magazines, *Life, Yank,* and several others, would have been interesting under normal circumstances. On this day I was only able to scan them quickly and look at the pictures. I read very little.

At noon I had a quick lunch in the hotel and returned to the room. Finally, at one forty-five the phone rang. It was Erika.

"Major, I am here in the hotel, in the lobby. We can have a talk now if you wish."

"Very good! Would you like to come to my room?"

"That will be fine. There is another person with me, Captain Barksdale of the U.S. Army."

"Okay, I'll be waiting."

I gave her the room number and location. Captain Barksdale with the U.S. Army? My hunch was right; she was on our side. Also, it meant that things were settled, and I began to feel excited about seeing Ariane soon.

In less than five minutes there was a tap on my door. I moved quickly and opened the door. Erika was there, as well as a captain in a U.S. uniform. I invited them in, closed the door, and we stood facing each other. The captain spoke.

"Major, I am Allen Barksdale with G-2. It's my pleasure, sir, to meet you."

He extended his arm and we shook hands. He was about thirty-five, medium built, and a clean-cut, nice-looking individual. His uniform and shoes were immaculate, and his face conveyed to me honesty and reliability. His unique facial appearance was unmistakable, and I knew before we began our conversation that I would believe whatever he told me.

"Thanks, Captain, I am happy to know you, too. I hope you have good news for me."

"I can tell you, Major, that Frau Wegner is alive and well. Sir, we need to have a talk, and an understanding, and then you will be able to see her."

"Sounds great. Let's be seated. You and Erika take the chairs and I will sit on the edge of the bed."

After we were settled, Barksdale spoke.

"Major, we've just completed a quick, but monumental investigation. Well, let me change that slightly. We've had an extensive investigation going on for months but it was brought to a quick conclusion by the action you took in sending information to Colonel Margolies a few days ago. It solved something that had been driving us crazy for months."

"You're talking about Heidi and what she told Colonel Margolies about the gold? You've known about the gold all that time?"

"Yes," and he glanced at Erika, "we knew. We just didn't have a clue as to where to look and it was extremely frustrating."

"How did you know about the gold?"

He became a little more serious.

"Major, at this point, sir, I have to have a commitment from you. What is said in this room must never be repeated. Can we agree on that, sir?"

"Yes."

"Thank you, Major. And I might tell you, sir, we have checked you backward and forward, and just about every other way, and we have no reluctance to give you the information that will be discussed here."

"That's nice to know."

"Okay, now, where do we begin? Well, it seems logical to tell you about Erika first. She has been working with us since 1943. While she was in the States, during the time she was at Columbia University, she had . . . a friendship with another student. The student went on to Washington after graduation, and rather quickly moved up to a high position with our Intelligence Department. He and Erika were able to maintain their . . . friendship, after she returned to Germany, and even after the war began. I can't use names or specific details, you will have to accept what I am saying without it. Is that agreeable?"

"Absolutely."

"Erika began working for us in the fall of 1943 after her husband was killed. She was unable to secure military information for us; however, she did let us know about German morale, how the people felt about Hitler, and many other important things. Erika will continue to live in Germany, Major, and I cannot overemphasize the importance of keeping everything confidential."

"I understand Captain, and there is no problem whatsoever."

"Thank you, sir. Now, back to your question about the gold. After the Normandy invasion, and later in the summer of that year, Erika first heard about the gold." And he turned to face her. "Do you want to take it from here?"

She nodded.

"Yes, I can do that. Hitler realized that his position and the future of Germany was becoming weaker. And as you probably remember, there was an unsuccessful attempt on his life that summer. After he recovered from the slight wounds he received he decided to have a glorious ball in Berlin. Everyone was to come in their finest clothes prepared to have a wonderful evening, and it was to reassure everyone, be a big morale booster. I was invited and attended. Late that night, maybe it was two or three in the morning, a man named Wassermann began making advances to me. He was high ranking, next to Himmler I think, and I encouraged him, believing that I might get some useful information. It worked and we ended up in his hotel room. He was older, late fifties or sixty, and he seemed to be thrilled to be with me. He wanted it to continue. I said that we could not be secure, nothing would be left in Germany. I'll never forget his answer: 'Don't worry about that, my dear, we are collecting gold, pure gold, and there will be more than enough for us.' And when I asked how much, he said, 'If it is exchanged for American currency, it will be over one hundred million dollars in all.' But I could not find out where it was or any other details."

She looked back to Barksdale and he spoke.

"We were able to verify the story in other ways. Even so, we could not determine if the gold had been shipped out of the country or was hidden in Germany. And then, when we got the break from your involvement, and the message by Heidi to Colonel Margolies, we were able to move."

"Who did Colonel Margolies contact?"

"He had a friend at the American Supreme Headquarters, a general. As soon as Heidi got to the Colonel, the same day you flew to Berchtesgaden, Margolies contacted his friend and we went to work immediately."

"Is the gold secure at this time?"

“Yes. There is a regiment of our infantry in Bad Welmsburg, and the entire Wegner estate is occupied.”

“Do you know the specific location of the gold?”

“It’s in a cave. The entrance was covered in such a way that no one would suspect it was there. Wegner and his friends did an outstanding job of concealing it.”

“How did you know where to look?”

“Frau Wegner told us. We have detained her for two days, and we have spent most of that time interrogating her.”

“Where is she?”

“Here, in Berchtesgaden.”

“And LeTourneau?”

“We have him, too. We’ve also questioned him extensively and we have the names of the U.S. officers who were involved in trying to get to the gold. We may not have them all yet, but we have the core of the operation.”

“Including Colonel Mason?”

“Oh, yeah, he has been detained and I would say that his future is not too bright right now.”

“Okay, can we talk about Frau Wegner now?”

“Yes, we need to do that. And by the way, Major, I hope you won’t feel that your privacy was invaded—it was simply so big we had to do a thorough and complete investigation. It was carried out by a team of many of us, and we had to work fast. We didn’t have time to be diplomatic in every situation. I hope you understand.”

“I do, Captain, and I don’t feel that you would have done anything that was not required.”

“Very good. Okay, let’s talk about Ariane Wegner. She found out about the gold eight or ten weeks ago, accidentally. And incidentally, our team concurs that she is a credible person and we believe she has been truthful with us.” He paused to let me speak, and when I did not, he continued. “She told us that one evening when her husband had been drinking, more than usual, he went up to bed first. She followed soon after, and when she passed his room on the second floor she saw that he had his safe open. He kept everything in that safe. She continued on to her room on the third floor. The next day while he was away, she said that she somehow felt an impulse to go into his room and try the door to the safe. Amazingly, and much to her surprise, he had closed the door to the safe the night before but had neglected to turn the combination knob and when she pulled the door opened. She looked inside and found a diagram, or drawing, showing the location of the cave where the gold was stored. She also saw a listing of the amount collected, at least she saw enough to realize it was a tremendous amount. She was afraid of being seen, or caught, and she quickly put the documents back in place as she had found them, closed the door and turned the knob of the safe to lock it. We learned later that Wegner was the focal point of everything, the escape plan as well as the gold. Apparently he was to keep the gold until the others were safe in South America, and then it could be moved or used in some way. We don't have details on that and Frau Wegner could not help us because no one was aware that she even knew about the gold."

He paused again and looked into my eyes.

"Major, do you have any questions up to this point?"

"No, let's go through the whole story and then we can discuss it."

"Fine. Okay, to proceed. Frau Wegner felt that she had come upon something that she didn't know how to handle. She knew it would be dangerous to discuss with anyone. She told us, over and over, that she was afraid to involve you because it would not be safe for you. She knew it was wrong, and she had no designs on it for herself, she only wanted to be away from it and be sure that you were not hurt."

He thought for a while before continuing.

"We had to determine the truthfulness of everything she told us. And in that process, we had to consider the personal aspects of it, her feelings for you, and based on our best estimates, your feelings for her. Also, we considered the statements of others with regard to the relationship. I'm sorry, sir, and I hope you understand that it was necessary."

"No problem, Captain."

"We believe she was sincere when she stated she was in love with you and did not wish to see you hurt. I don't know where we would be if she had not been shot, even though unfortunate for her, it seemed to open up the whole matter of the gold. We speculated that Rombach might have shot her because of the gold, he might have suspected that she knew about the gold. And then, of course, it was just a little later when Mason and LeTourneau got involved. LeTourneau was the go-between with the Russians who had somehow already learned about the gold, as well as the remaining Germans who were knowledgeable about it. There was to be a three-way split, Russians, Germans, and the U.S. people who were involved. LeTourneau admitted, while being interrogated by us, that the real intention of the U.S. group was to take the gold and leave the Russians and Germans out. Frau Wegner was able to convince LeTourneau that she had some knowledge of the location of the gold, and he kept her with him for that reason. Their real problem, in addition to actually finding the gold, was logistics. How would they move it without being seen? Small lots would have been the only way and that would have created a lot of traffic and the possibility of being caught. They needed time, and after you became involved, Major, they didn't have time so it became more complicated at that point."

He paused to let me ask a question.

"When did you get LeTourneau?"

"The day after Heidi talked to Colonel Margolies."

"And it was here in Berchtesgaden?"

"Yes."

"Did you know that Mason had put a contract on him?"
"We were able to surmise that early in our interrogation of Mason."
"And Ariane was with LeTourneau at the time he was taken?"
"She was. And she is fine."
"What will happen to her now?"
"It has become a problem because of the Russians. Although we are convinced that she did not intend to keep any of the gold for herself, she did not report it to you, and so, to the Russians, this makes her a war criminal. They want her to be prosecuted. They say the gold was taken by the Nazis from people all over Europe, including Russia. We've talked them out of prosecuting her, but we had to make a concession. She is to be deported to Switzerland, and she can never return to Germany. All of the Wegner assets in Germany are to be confiscated and she is to be removed from the country immediately. We agreed because it was the best deal we could get for her. The gold will be divided, or used, by the Allies in a manner that is agreed upon at high levels."
"What about her Aunt, Frau Erhlich, and Rolfe?"
"The Russians seem to be unaware that they had knowledge of the gold. They will not be deported."
"What was your conclusion about Rolfe and Frau Erhlich?"
"They are borderline. Especially Rolfe. I think it would have been easy for him to become a part of the scheme with Mason and LeTourneau. We decided to let it go, mainly because it would have stirred up more trouble from the Russians. And they actually had no part in collecting the gold, or taking it from others as the Nazis did, so we will not prosecute them."
"Where is Ariane now?"
"Here, in the hotel, in a room. We arranged it this morning. Two of our men are with her. Unfortunately, as part of the deal with the Russians, we have to keep her in sight until she is delivered to the destination in Switzerland. After that she is on her own. I guess that's about it. Do you have any further question, sir?"
"No. Will I be able to see Ariane now?"
"Yes. In the lobby. We will let you sit apart with her but we will have to keep her in sight. She will leave in about two hours on the train to Switzerland. We will let you know when it it time. And Major, when she leaves, she will have to be alone. In other words, sir, you will not be allowed to accompany her on the train. And that is not my idea, Major, it came from the top."
"I understand, Captain. Okay, if we're all set, I'd like to go down to the lobby now."
We stood and moved toward the door. I was feeling more of the excitement I had felt from the beginning, and it was building to a peak. To see Ariane again after all that had happened was bringing back a little of each of the emotions I had experienced: hope, fear, uncertainties, gratitude and disappointment, the whole range.

At the door, Barksdale paused, and we all three stopped. He turned to Erika and spoke.

"Erika, would you mind giving me five minutes with the Major? We'll be right down."

"Of course," she answered. She walked out and closed the door. Barksdale spoke.

"Major, I hope you will forgive me for sticking my nose in where it might not belong. I've come to know Frau Wegner quite well and I would like to make a few comments that are personal if you don't object."

"I don't mind, Captain. I will welcome anything you would like to say."

"It's a little difficult, so cut me off at any time. Frau Wegner knows about your . . . situation . . . with Heidi. We had to go over everything so thoroughly during her interrogation it was brought out. I thought, perhaps, you would want to know that, Major."

"Thanks for telling me, Captain. How did you describe the relationship to her, the relationship with Heidi?"

"We gave her all of the facts we had, which included the amount of time you were with Heidi. We didn't make any guesses, or speculate, we only told her what we knew or had heard from others."

"Did she question you about it?"

"Not too much. But, going on my gut feeling, I believe she knows all she wants to know."

"And she didn't comment in any way, to maybe . . . give you a clue . . . or give you some thought on how she might feel?"

"No, sir."

"Did she know, from the information you got from Heidi, how Heidi feels?"

"Yes, she did ask about that and we told her. She was being truthful with us and I felt we should be truthful with her."

"Captain, do you happen to remember exactly what you said about Heidi, and her feelings for me?"

"I can remember very well, Major. Heidi didn't attempt to cover up anything and she expressed a very sincere love for you."

"Did Ariane comment on that?"

"No."

"Do you have a feel, Captain, about the effect it had on Ariane?"

"No sir, not really. She stayed composed the whole time. I think, though, she may have formed some conclusion in her mind at that point—it seems I could detect it to some slight degree as we talked further. She's an exceptional woman, Major, but I'm sure you already know that."

I paused to think. Knowing Ariane as I did, I suspected that I knew what conclusion she would have reached. I spoke to Barksdale again.

"What will happen to her in Switzerland? How will she live?"

"She told me that her husband had transferred money from Wegner

Brothers to a Swiss bank beginning early in 1942. It was not money taken by the Nazis, it was money earned by Wegner Brothers, and her husband had a legitimate reason to take it. He felt, after the U.S. entered the war in December of 1941, that Germany would eventually be defeated, and he wanted to be prepared for it. He set up a joint account at the Swiss bank and Ariane now has clear title to it. She said it was probably the only real considerate thing he ever did for her."

"How much money is there?"

"He had Marks converted to U.S. currency as it was being deposited. The account is now worth two million dollars."

"Oh, that's great. She will never have financial problems."

"That's true. I think the information should remain secret, though, Major. It would be tragic if someone tried to take it. I've told no one else about it."

"That's good, Captain, very good."

"Well, she's an unusual woman. You are very fortunate, Major. She would make any man happy. And Heidi would as well. You know, Major, I think something astounding has happened with you. Hollywood would have a hard time believing your story."

"I've been fortunate, Captain. The two women who have come into my life in the last two months are both truly exceptional. And that makes it very difficult for me. Both are beautiful, as you know from having seen them, and each one has given me the same thing, a sincere and dedicated love. I've had a relationship with two women that most men don't have with even one during their lifetimes."

"I agree. And you are right, both are beautiful, and both are sincerely loyal in their love for you. All I can say, sir, is good luck, and I hope you make the right choice."

"Thanks again, Captain. I'm ready to go down to the lobby now."

Before we could move, he remembered something else.

"Oh, Major, I need to make one other statement. It would be very difficult for you, sir, right now, to have a relationship with Frau Wegner. She's in the spotlight with Allied Supreme Headquarters due to the reaction of the Russians. And because she knew you at the time that she knew about the gold, and since both of you were in the area where the gold was hidden, our people say you have to stay away from her. It's from the top, sir."

I didn't speak and he continued.

"There could be some surveillance initially, but maybe that will change at some point in the future. Nothing stays the same forever." And he smiled as if he wanted to end his comments with a note of encouragement.

It seemed that a decision I had thought I would have to make was being taken out of my hands. Even so, as Barksdale had said, "Nothing stays the same forever." But was it right, was it the decision that was already buried deeply inside of me? Maybe. I was not sure, and I might never be.

In the lobby two U.S. enlisted men were in chairs near the entrance. Erika was in a seat at one end of the rather large room. On the opposite side, the hotel reception counter was located some thirty to forty feet from where four or five chairs, along with a sofa, were grouped in a corner near Erika. Erika stood and walked to meet us. The two enlisted men stood as well but stayed nearby where they had been sitting.

Erika spoke to Barksdale.

"Are we ready for Frau Wegner?"

"Yes." Then he spoke to me.

"Major, if you will wait over there by the sofa and chairs, I will go and get Frau Wegner. We are going to make it private for you over there, I have already spoken to the manager of the hotel."

I nodded and smiled. He turned and walked in the direction of a hallway leading to the rooms for guests, and I stood with Erika. She knew my state of mind and smiled knowingly as she spoke.

"Major, I think I will use this opportunity to go out for a breath of fresh air. See you a little later."

"Okay, Erika, see you later."

I didn't know how to prepare myself for the meeting with Ariane, or plan what to say. I was a little nervous, and excited too, of course. So many things had happened since I had seen her. Many pictures of her were flashing through my mind. The times she had said "I love you," the times when I had made her laugh with silly remarks, the beautiful smile she had on the occasions that she had passively gazed deeply into my eyes. Her beautiful face and body. Her need to have me hold her at times, and the comfort it gave her. I remembered the first time we met when we were alone at the lake. We were drawn together in a passionate embrace immediately, and we kissed repeatedly. From that beginning we began meeting almost daily, and it was the same for both of us—we had to be with each other.

13.

I WALKED OVER to the area of the lobby that had been set aside for us to be alone and sat in a chair. I stayed put only a few seconds and moved to the sofa. I did it, I think, because it would give us a chance to sit side by side and be near each other. But I was not sure of myself, and soon I got up and stood nearby.

I tried to think of a way to greet Ariane, how to use the right words. I was struggling, and I wasn't sure what was causing it. It might have been Heidi; dealing with my feeling for her, and that, along with the knowledge that Ariane knew about her. I decided that I would just be natural, and let my true feelings take over.

Soon she came into view from the hallway, along with Barksdale. I smiled and so did she. We walked toward each other and met in the middle of the lobby. We embraced, lightly, and then we kissed. It was done only briefly and we backed away. I told her she looked wonderful, and she responded with a similar statement.

"So do you, Max! I can't believe you are standing here before me."

"I know. It seems like a million years have gone by."

"Yes, indeed! How are you?"

"Fine. And I understand your wound has healed. How are you otherwise?"

"Right now, I am great."

"And you look great. It's wonderful to finally see you again."

She smiled broadly. Then I suggested that we go to the area of the lobby that had been reserved for us, and as we moved over to the sofa and chairs I held her hand. We both sat on the sofa. I spoke first.

"So much has happened I don't know what to ask about first. Captain Barksdale has filled me in on many things, the events that have happened recently. He seems to know all about you at this point."

"He has been very nice, both he and Erika. They even bought a dress for me, the one I am wearing," and she grinned, "so at least I can look a little better than I would have if I had worn the fatigue outfit."

We both smiled and she continued.

"He is kind in other ways. And he has so much power it seems. A plane is at his disposal at all times, and he has many of your people assisting him. I think he has been very active in the last two or three days and he has talked with many people."

"It was because of the gold. It was such a large amount it could have caused an international incident if not handled properly."

"He says you will receive a letter of commendation from the Allied Supreme Headquarters."

"That's nice. I only wanted to be sure you were safe, though. The gold was important, but everything I did was done in a way to ensure your safety, as best I could, of course."

"Thank you, Max."

"Were you treated okay?"

"I was treated okay. I'm just glad it is over."

There was a pause as we stared at each other. Neither of us could think of what to say next. Then, she spoke.

"Max, let's talk about some of our best memories! Do you remember when we first walked into the hotel room in Frankenberg? I think we were both embarrassed. Then, you said something very sweet, and I . . ."

"You cried."

She laughed.

"Yes, that's right, I did. And you came and put your arms around me and I felt wonderful." She waited a moment, and continued. "And remember Boris? And the party? It was so funny when you danced with the Russian women."

"Yeah, I can still see you and Boris watching, and laughing. But we had a great evening. I was sorry to leave when it was time."

"So was I. I remember telling you later, on the train as we were returning to Bad Welmsburg, that being with you in Frankenberg was the best time of my life."

"I can remember that too, so well. And even though I knew we would see each other again soon after we returned home, I still felt it would be difficult to leave you at the station in Bad Welmsburg."

"I know. I wanted it to be the same as it was in Frankenberg, forever."

She looked into my eyes with the same passive allure, the same love I had seen before. I thought it best to try to think of something humorous.

"Hey, do you remember the outfit Boris was wearing when you first saw him on the street in Frankenberg? The odd-colored mismatched coat and trousers, with the coat about two sizes too large? But he was a likeable character, and I enjoyed him from the very beginning."

"Oh, he was so funny! He would say, in English, quite often, 'We drink now, okay?', and I think he must have been surviving on vodka and cigarettes."

"You're right, and I believe the only other two words he attempted to say were vodka and party."

"And what a party he arranged for us. He wanted it to go on all night and we couldn't get away. How did we finally do it?"

"We told him we would plan another party soon."

"Oh yes, I remember. But even then he was very disappointed."

There was another slight pause before I continued.

"I'll never forget the first time I saw you, when you came late at night to tell me about seeing Rombach at the station. I thought you were the most beautiful woman I had ever seen, and I could hardly believe my eyes as you stood there at my door."

"I could tell that you . . . you could never hide anything. I could always tell by your eyes. And then, as I was leaving that night, you said, 'you're quite a beautiful lady,' and it was a very exciting moment for me."

"I was uncertain about what I should say. I wanted you to know how I felt, but under the circumstances I was not sure of myself."

She grinned and continued.

"Well, for someone who was uncertain, you certainly did okay the day we met at the lake."

"Yeah, I think we both did. For two people who hadn't had a relationship for a while, we moved along pretty good."

"It was so new, and happened so quickly, and it was different. Karl and I had become so distant it was actually no longer a marriage."

"It was almost the same in my case. My wife and I realized we were not right for each other several years earlier, and she had started the divorce proceedings. We were still friends, and I think that was the only thing it ever was, a friendship."

We had moved into a little more serious-type conversation, and she waited briefly, and spoke.

"Max, so many things have happened recently . . . to each of us. And I suppose we must . . . continue . . . in the best way . . ."

It was the first hint of what she might have decided about us. I changed the subject at once, and we continued to talk about the happy times of the past, and the people who were known by each of us. She was unchanged, both in appearance and manner. And I had the same feeling for her I had always had; I still loved her. I didn't know how to handle it or what to say about it. We kept talking about other things, laughing some, and remembering the exciting moments that had taken place between us. We both avoided talking about the future.

Before I had realized it, the time had flown by and Barksdale walked over as Ariane and I were talking. He waited politely for a break in our conversation before speaking.

"We've got about ten more minutes, Major."

"Oh! Thanks, Captain."

He turned and walked back to the other side of the big room where

Erika was sitting. Ariane and I looked at each other rather solemnly, and each of us knew what had to be said. I spoke first.

"Ariane, I know that you will be going to Switzerland. Captain Barksdale explained everything to me."

"Yes, I will be living there. I will be in a hotel in Zurich for a while, and then I will probably move into a house."

"Do you know anyone there?"

"I know both some German people and Swiss people. I met them when my sister was there for two years."

"I'm glad."

Then, there was another pause. Neither of us wanted to say anything. Finally, she stood, and so did I. She spoke.

"Max, my darling . . ."

She stared into my eyes for a long while, and I think small tears were forming in her eyes.

I didn't know what to say, so she continued.

"I didn't want it to end this way. I'll always love you. You don't have to say anything."

I reached down and took her hand. We turned together and slowly walked toward the door. I asked her a question.

"Do you want me to come to the station, or should we say goodbye here?"

She waited a moment or so before answering.

"I think it will be best here."

"Yes . . . maybe that is best. Ariane, there is something I want you to know. It's very important to me. There is no greater love in my life than you. Please remember that always."

"Thank you, my dearest. And you were the best thing that ever happened to me. I can never care for anyone as much."

She moved forward and we embraced. I held her tightly for a long while. Then, I kissed her, and it was a complete and fulfilling culmination of the tender feeling of affection that we each shared.

We moved apart. She smiled and so did I. Barksdale was nearby and spoke.

"Major, will you be here later in the day?"

"Yes."

"Good. I'll be back after I see Frau Wegner off. I want to talk to you. Maybe we can have dinner together."

"Okay."

Ariane moved away. Barksdale, Erika, and the two enlisted men, followed in the same direction. At the door, Ariane stopped and looked back. She smiled at me beautifully, and I returned it as best as I could. Then, they were gone.

14.

I WATCHED as they walked to the vehicle waiting at the curb. Ariane didn't look back again. I believe she was resigned to a decision she had made, a decision that was actually the one that was necessary for both of us.

They pulled away and headed in a direction toward the rail station which was not too far from the hotel. For a fleeting moment, I considered going after them, going after Ariane. Something about the finality of seeing them leave had hit a nerve. Although the words were not spoken by either of us, I knew it was the end for me with Ariane. It was the same as the time when she had been shot in Bad Welmsburg and was reported to be dead, and I was saying goodbye again.

I turned and walked slowly toward the reception counter, possibly thinking in the back of my mind that I would pick up a magazine to read. The woman who was there on duty at the counter, the owner of the hotel, smiled at me and spoke.

"Good day to you, Major."

"Good day, Frau Verner."

"Ah, Major, it's time for me to take a break. I'm going out for a walk. Would you like . . . I am wondering, sir, if you will walk with me?"

She had seen everything that had happened in the lobby. I knew she wanted to talk about it. At first, I thought, no, I don't want to talk to anyone. Then, I changed my mind and answered.

"Yes, Frau Verner, I would enjoy a walk with you."

"Good! It will be just one moment."

She disappeared to another part of the hotel but returned shortly with her son, Albert. He took her place behind the counter and she came toward me. Together, we walked outside.

It was pleasant, and although the crisp mountain air could always be felt, it was the time when the temperature would reach a high for the day. She guided us up the hill, which was the opposite direction from the rail station. I was silent because I was hurting, and she knew it. She began a conversation.

"You know, Major, we saw so many tragic things in Germany in recent years we almost expected some new disaster each day. I think, in a way, we almost became immune to it. It reached the point that we just considered it a success to get through a day without some new troublesome event. Your people in the U.S. were fortunate to be so far removed from the war."

"That's true, Frau Verner. I've had the same thought, and I'm very thankful that we did not have the same sort of turmoil there that took place here in Europe."

"I still have my son, Albert, but my husband was killed early in the war. I was only forty years old at the time, and I didn't think I could go on. He was the only man in my life, and it will, of course, remain that way. We were sweethearts at an early age and when I became seventeen we were married. It has not occurred to me, since his death, to think of another man."

"That's very admirable, Frau Verner. I know that you and your husband must have been very devoted to each other."

"We were. And I know, for all people who are devoted, it is heartbreaking when a separation occurs."

She paused, glanced quickly at me, and continued.

"We must always find a desire to continue. In my case, it was Albert. And now, we are happy. We made it through the war, and we are doing well with the hotel. So, many times when there is a storm it is soon followed by a time of peace, a day of sunshine."

We kept moving along. I turned to look at her as I spoke.

"You know about me, don't you?"

"Yes. I talked to Erika and she explained about you in detail. I hope you do not mind, sir."

"No, I don't mind. In fact, I appreciate your interest."

"Major, something unusual has happened in your life, and I'm sure you have been told the same by others. And I know at this moment your heart is filled with sorrow. When I received the news about the death of my husband, I had to focus my thoughts on other things, something that was left that I could cling to, and that is what I did. It was Albert, of course, and he has remained by my side these five years since my husband was lost."

She stopped talking temporarily to give me a chance to speak. I did not and she continued.

"From my discussion with Erika I learned that you were exceptionally fortunate. You had the almost unbelievable experience of having a love affair with two women who were eager to devote their lives to you. And now, at this moment, half of you belongs to the one who was here today and the other half belongs to the second woman. So, it leaves you with a broken heart. And once again, sir, I hope that my comments are not becoming too personal."

"Not at all. I need to talk about it. And you're right, it is a sad time for me."

"I saw what took place in the lobby today. I know you have deep feelings for this woman, and it is the same with her—she loves you. But she knows there is another woman and she has decided to remove herself. You did not stop her, or pursue her, and now, you must find a desire to continue, as I did, and you must go to the other woman. The woman who was here made a decision for you that you could not bring yourself to make, and I think it was best."

"I appreciate your thoughts and comments, Frau Verner, and I think you are right, I believe it is best."

We continued the walk, talking about other things. She described seeing Hitler several times when he was in Berchtesgaden. She told me some of the history of the small city and the surroundings. She turned out to be a very interesting person. After twenty-five minutes, she turned and said it was time for her to return to the hotel to supervise preparation of the evening meal in the dining room. We turned back at that point and headed down the hill in the direction of the hotel.

Just before six, in my room, the phone rang. It was Barksdale.

"How about chow, Major?"

"Sounds fine, Captain. I'll be right down."

"Erika will join us if it is okay."

"No problem, Captain, she's welcome."

In the dining room we were met by the smiling hostess, who just happened to be Frau Verner. She greeted us warmly. The large dining room was nearly full of people, and the crowd was made up mostly of men in American uniforms, some of whom were accompanied by German women. Frau Verner seated us at a table in a far corner where it was away from the flow of traffic and a little more private. I smiled at her and said, "Thanks." She graciously responded, speaking as she moved away.

"It's my pleasure, Major."

A waiter came at once and asked about wine. I asked Erika her preference.

"Red."

Barksdale said that was fine with him, too. I told the waiter to bring two bottles, one red and one white. After he left I turned to Erika.

"It's nice to have you join us. Is there any problem for you, being seen with American soldiers?"

"No, Major. Look around. I will be considered like the other German women who are here."

"I was thinking more about you possibly being considered a collaborator."

"Not here, not in Berchtesgaden. In other places, it might be a little dangerous. Although now that the matter of the gold has been settled,

I think everyone will forget it and there will be no more trouble. I believe the time has come when we can finally relax."

We all smiled in agreement. Barksdale spoke next.

"Major, I will explain our position with Erika. We are keeping no secrets from her. She has been an integral part of this investigation and she knows just about every detail that is involved. You can speak freely with her."

"I had assumed as much. And I want to thank you, Erika, for buying the dress for Ariane. It was beautiful," and I smiled at Barksdale, "I know the Captain, here, didn't have that kind of taste."

She grinned.

"Well, he was at least with me at the time."

I continued.

"Did you get her off on the train okay?"

Barksdale answered.

"Yes, we did. She is being accompanied by five of our people. Two WACs, two enlisted men, and one officer, a first Lieutenant. They have been instructed to give her everything she needs, and make her as comfortable as possible. They will get her settled in the hotel in Zurich and the two WACs will remain with her in the hotel for a week. At that point, Frau Wegner will be on her own."

"Sounds like you have done all you can to assist her."

"We did, Major. She deserved it. By pinpointing the location of the gold she saved the U.S. a lot of trouble, possibly a confrontation with the Russians. We screened the people who are with her and they are some of our best."

The waiter came and poured red wine for Erika and Barksdale, white for me. Barksdale made a toast.

"To happier days."

We touched glasses and sipped the wine. I looked at Barksdale.

"How was she at the station?"

"She was composed. I think she had cried a little during the ride, but when we got there she was okay. She shook hands with me and said that she appreciated my kindness."

It was typical of her, never forgetting to thank people. I commented on it.

"Yeah, that's her. Did she . . . do you feel she was settled emotionally . . . and in good shape mentally?"

Barksdale and Erika looked at each other quickly, and Erika spoke.

"Yes, Major, I believe her attitude was good. This was a difficult day for her, maybe the most difficult of her life, and naturally she will need a little time to recover, but I think she will be fine."

She glanced at Barksdale, who seemed to give her his agreement of her assessment. We were silent for a few moments, then Barksdale changed the subject.

"Major, do you have any names of U.S. personnel who might have been involved with Mason and LeTourneau in the search for the gold?"

"No. I never heard any names. LeTourneau was careful to keep them secret. There is one person, apparently an American, who had the code name Planet. Even though I never found out much about him, I wondered if it could have been LeTourneau."

"It wasn't LeTourneau. We heard about Planet some time ago, and some of the Germans did confuse LeTourneau with him. Planet was much more extensively involved with activities in Germany, and we are not sure what happened to him. We believe he is dead, most likely killed by the Russians."

We talked about other things. Both he and Erika seemed to be putting forth an effort to keep Ariane out of the conversation. At one point, Barksdale asked about my immediate plans.

"I plan to leave tomorrow to return to Bad Welmsburg."

"I'll be glad to give you a lift. I have a plane in Salzburg."

"That would be great. I think a train would take all day."

Erika had a pleasant look on her face and I wanted to say something that would bring her back into the conversation.

"Are you planning to stay in Berchtesgaden?"

"Oh, very definitely. I have heard that conditions in Berlin are horrible, and I will remain here for possibly as long as a year."

"I would guess that you would be very wise to do that."

"I'm just happy that I have the opportunity to be here."

"Will you be working further with us?"

She glanced quickly at Barksdale, and he spoke.

"She might be. We certainly want to keep that option open."

The next morning I had my gear ready and was in the lobby at eight-thirty. I had paid my bill and had said goodbye to Frau Verner. It was time to meet Barksdale and take the ride to Salzburg where we would board the plane that was assigned to him.

While waiting, I was in a reflective mood. The little town of Berchtesgaden was peaceful and relaxing. Tucked away deeply in the mountains, the horrors of war had been far removed, and life could get back to normal more easily. And it was good. Everybody had seen enough of war. Now would be a time for giving thanks for the things that were left, resume a life where former enemies could live side by side in peace. For some, it would be difficult. Many horrible acts of hatred and violence had been committed, and wounds were deep. But what had we been taught, even as children, in the church? To forgive. It was just that simple.

Barksdale arrived five minutes late. He was in a jeep with a driver. He got out and helped me with my two bags, and soon we were headed up the hill on the street leading out of Berchtesgaden which would link us to the road to Salzburg. I wondered if it would be my last visit to the small city.

We didn't try to talk much during the ride. The distance to Salzburg was not great and the time passed quickly. It took about an hour to reach the landing strip where the plane was located.

The plane was a five-seat passenger model, which I was glad to see, remembering the cramped position I had occupied in the artillery observer plane as I had flown to Berchtesgaden a few days earlier. The pilot told me that the twin-engine plane had been confiscated from the Germans.

We loaded up and were in the air quickly, moving in a westward direction. Barksdale said the next stop would be Bad Welmsburg where the plane would land on the Wegner air strip.

We didn't talk too much during the flight. I did ask Barksdale if he had been able to determine who had actually killed Leni and Gertrude. He said he had not, although both Stelling and Heuber were there, as was LeTourneau the night Leni was killed. He said the investigation was continuing, and with Hueber dead it would eventually be settled by statements from Stelling and LeTrouneau.

Barksdale told me that he would continue on to Division Headquarters after dropping me off. He said that he would need a complete report from me, and I promised to have it for him within forty-eight hours.

At one-fifty we were in the vicinity of Bad Welmsburg. Barksdale, who had been on the radio, said a jeep would be waiting for me after we were on the ground. He added a remark with a slight smile on his face.

"Colonel Margolies suggests that you might want to take the rest of the day off, sir. He says he will see you in the office in the morning."

After we disembarked from the plane there were some "goodbyes" and "good lucks" exchanged. I walked to the jeep that was there for me, loaded up my gear, started the engine and drove away. I was planning to go straight to see Heidi.

When I arrived at her home I pulled into the drive, shut off the motor, and sat temporarily in the driver's seat. Moments later she appeared at the door. She came out onto the porch and paused. I got out of the jeep and walked toward her, and at the same time, she moved forward in my direction. We were not rushing; it was, instead, more of a relaxed pace. When we were near, we both stopped. She had a pleasant expression on her face while speaking.

"Your office called to tell me you were on the way back and I kept watching from the window. And finally, you were there."

We reached for each other and held on tightly. Then we kissed, and after that, we held on again. And, I realized, I was at peace.

We pulled apart after a few moments. We held hands as we walked toward the entrance to her house. She had a mischievous grin on her face.

"Did you think for one moment that I did not know that you were coming? Come inside and you will see. I have already started your favorite soup."

I had a good feeling. It was like a homecoming. Now, I could rest easy for a while.

EPILOGUE

THIS BOOK is intended to honor all people who have lived during periods of war; those who fought, those who waited, all whose lives were disrupted, all who did not survive. Past and present.

To write about a war, or the circumstances brought about by war, it is necessary to describe some of the realities that are involved. Even so, the theme of *ARIANE* is not about war as such, it is, instead, a story about people who lived during the period of a war.

A time will come when there will be peace on earth. Until then, hatred and revenge should not dominate our lives, nor should fear and anxiety. We are safe in the hands of the one who created us.